THE
LAST
AMERICAN
PRESIDENT

WITHDRAWN
Lakewood Memorial Library
12 W. Summit Street
Lakewood, NY 14750

RICHARD ENGLE

Published by The Book About Us 2015

Copyright © 2014 Richard Engle

All rights reserved. Except as permitted under the U.S. Copyright Act of 1976, no part
of this publication may be reproduced, distributed, or transmitted in any form or by any
means, or stored in a database or retrieval system, without the prior written permission
of the publisher.

The characters and events in this book are fictional, and any likeness to any individual
is purely coincidental and not intended by the author, except for some verifiable
references to historical figures.

First edition January 2015
ISBN: 978-0-9862212-1-7

Library of Congress Control Number 2014919899

This book may be available in an e-book format.
For more information go to
www.TheBookAbout.us
Box 699
Bethany, OK 73008

The Book About Us is a division of BellWest America LLC. The Book About Us,
BellWest America and The Book About Us logo are trademarks of BellWest America
LLC

Printed in the United States of America – while it lasts!
10 9 8 7 6 5 4 3 2 1

3201300331981

CONTENTS

Acknowledgements

Prologue *1*

Chapter 1   •   Kansas *9*

Chapter 2   •   Keoki *27*

Chapter 3   •   The Wedding *43*

Chapter 4   •   Alaska *57*

Chapter 5   •   Coffee Grounds *61*

Chapter 6   •   Borinquen *74*

Chapter 7   •   Cedar Crest *78*

Chapter 8   •   Katie *83*

Chapter 9   •   The Incident *92*

Chapter 10   •   The Speech *100*

Chapter 11   •   Cassell for America *113*

Chapter 12   •   The Campaign *133*

Chapter 13   •   The Luau *159*

Chapter 14   •   Debates *175*

Chapter 15   •   Cassell's America *184*

Chapter 16   •   Roi-faineant *198*

Chapter 17   •   Betrayal *220*

Chapter 18   •   Morning in America *237*

Epilogue *248*

Afterword 251

ACKNOWLEDGEMENTS

To Tim Pope. You were the best friend I ever had.

To Destiny, my precious daughter. Thank you for giving me the inspired idea that formed the plot of this book.

To Denise, my loving wife. Thank you for your patience and support through the process of my writing and publishing this book. Yes, you are the inspiration behind the beautiful Kate – except that you are far more intelligent and not nearly as tall.

To my great friends Brady Wright and Andrew Winningham. Our conversations over breakfast week after week were of such value. Your late night editing session sharpened my writing into something acceptable. Your ongoing friendship after Tim's death means the world to me.

To Jim Marshall, Charles Key, John and Richard Allison, Randy Brogdon, Craig Dawkins, John Michener, Mark Costello, Nathan Dahm and anyone else that ever attended our morning breakfast meetings – Tim's "G" group.

Thanks to Grover Norquist and Bill Federer for your encouragement.

To Carl Denning. In case you didn't notice, you are my inspiration behind the character Michael.

To Charlie Meadows and all my friends at OCPAC.

To Jack and Stephanie West and Emoly West Walters. Emoly, I still say you should have won! You are Miss America to most everyone who knows you.

To the Republican Assemblies throughout the nation. Thanks for the opportunity to lead, serve and to learn.

To Pat Greaves, Joleen Neighbors, Josh Cossey, Ryan Wells and the 'Reader's Group'. Thanks for the advice and encouragement.

PROLOGUE

"Democracy never lasts long. It soon wastes, exhausts and murders itself. There was never a democracy that did not commit suicide."

—John Adams, *Letters*, April 15, 1814

W ATER FROM THE PREVIOUS night's rain collected in a low spot in the less-than-perfectly pitched gutters of the old house in south Chicago. Hearing the birds sing as they took turns bathing was a sweet enough way to waken, but their scratching and pecking on the aluminum diminished the charm.

Jennifer Purcell was awake now. Looking at her alarm clock, Jennifer saw the time was approaching 7:00 a.m. This would be late for other days, but far earlier than this new high school graduate had hoped. She had been up late the previous night, partying with family. Jennifer stayed home, although her classmates continued the night without her.

Her grandfather had come to see her graduate. She loved her grandpa but seldom saw him. A couple of times a year, she and her parents would go see him but this was the first time he was able to come to her. The night was a joyous event that kept her awake long after everyone else had gone to bed.

There was no reason for Jennifer to stay in bed any longer. From a quick glance out the window, she determined that the day looked promising. Since no sound was coming from downstairs, she presumed herself to be the first to wake. A quick run would be nice.

Slipping out the back door, she quietly closed the gate and, after her customary stretching, began to jog down the street toward the park. Jennifer grew up in this neighborhood. Every house, every hedge was so familiar, yet somehow it all looked different. *Is this what it means to be an adult?* she thought to herself. *If things look different, then maybe they are.*

"I want to know the truth," she said aloud to herself.

Over the years, she had heard all of her grandfather's quips and anecdotes about his life and remembered each one because of her affection for him. She also read the history books and knew the terrible things they said about him. Historians described her grandfather as having a significant role in events that shaped the world in which she currently lived; they described his actions in a manner that bemoaned the lost American empire.

Jennifer loved him but never had the courage to let anyone know that the name in those history books, her mother's maiden name being "Adams," was referring to her grandfather. She felt ashamed; silence on the subject could be excused with the idea that she was protecting her family's anonymity. When her mother told his story, she insisted her father was an innocent bystander, a scapegoat. Contradictions abounded among the three versions.

Jennifer was determined to get to the bottom of it all. She would find time with Gramps, her nickname for him when she was a bit annoyed, and encourage him to go past the jovial one-liners to the real truth. She wanted to *hear* what he was saying this time, rather than merely listen politely and ask questions. If her grandfather was as bad as the historians claimed him to be, "Then damn it, I'll get him to admit it," she said aloud as she ran.

The idea that her sweet grandpa, her pen pal, the family Santa, a man she only knew as "good," the man who prayed with her and paid attention when she needed someone to listen, was a "traitor" was too much for her to bear. *He just can't be. There must be an explanation,* she told herself.

Folks in Louisiana seem to like him. They don't think poorly of him, at least not his neighbors in St. Louis. But then, one man's traitor is another man's hero. Oh, why did everything have to happen so long ago? Everyone older than I am has some memory of these events, but it all happened before I was born. The events are too fresh for them, too distant for me.

Turning the corner, she could see Carroll Park and the community center. The center was originally built as an elementary school, a purpose abandoned long ago. Carroll Park was the mid-way point in her run. In the distance, she spotted a man sitting in a baseball dugout waving his hands over a tablet on his lap. The dugout was the only place in the area that could serve as a place both to sit and to provide some shelter from the ever-rising morning sun.

A few generations back, the motions the man exhibited would have made him look insane but Jennifer knew exactly what was happening. He was writing in sign language using a program on his tablet. This concept was developed decades earlier as an extension of gesture recognition software. With sign writing, one can write, or sign, as fast as the writer can think. There is no need for translation since the language is universal. Sign writing was invented for the hearing-impaired, but because of its ease of use it was adapted for general use.

The man using sign language in the dugout was not just any man. At first, Jennifer thought she recognized him by his wisp of a beard. With each step, now walking rather than running, she was more certain that he was indeed her grandfather.

"Grandpa! What are you doing here?" she exclaimed.

The answer was obvious; she didn't even know why she asked. He was writing a letter to her Aunt Lenore, his sister-in-law. She knew because Grandpa was not very discreet about his sign writing. As she approached, she was able to read him sign "AA" for his initials.

"Jen!" he replied. "How are you this fine morning?"

"I've been thinking about you all morning! Are you feeling all right? It's awfully early to be out here by yourself ..."

"Hold on, honey; I'm old, but not decrepit. I woke up and came out here about an hour ago. Haven't you heard that old folks don't need as much sleep as you youngsters?"

"Well, it has been a long time since you've been here. I wouldn't want you to get lost or anything."

"There you go again!" he exclaimed. "I've been all over the world, and I don't get lost walking a few blocks from where I'm staying. I know that your house is right down *that* street," he said as he pointed in the wrong direction.

"Gramps! You are not going any—"

"Settle down, sweetheart," he interrupted. "I was just joshing you. I know where you live!" Grandpa chuckled, pointing toward the correct direction this time.

"You scared me!" Jennifer said sternly, disturbed by his joke regarding where she lived.

Then he asked, "So, you're out running this morning? Are your folks up yet?"

She took a deep breath and answered his questions. "Yeah, I woke up early and figured I would run. Everyone's still asleep. I thought you would be, too."

"Maybe everyone got up and thought the same. We all could have been creeping about to keep from waking the others; each of us quietly letting ourselves out of the house," Grandpa said with a smile.

Jennifer's tone was suddenly serious, as she decided now was the time to get her answers. "Grandpa, I'm tired of relying on second-hand stories. I want to know everything."

"Everything? I can't tell you *everything*! I would suggest you are coming to the wrong source." Grandpa paused for a moment as he pointed upward and gave a slight smile. He continued, "Although, it has been said I'm not far off."

Jennifer ignored his effort to joke as her line of inquiry persisted. "I mean everything about what happened, with you and the president, when America was still one country."

"Jen, it's a beautiful morning, and you want to know about the past? We haven't even had a chance to visit, just you and me. So let's see if I remember what you said last night; my hearing is not always that great. You're planning to go to ... was it OU or ORU? I just don't remember for sure," he said with a conniving smile.

"No, I said I'm going to Illinois State. I'm sorry, but I'm not going to either of your schools, Grandpa. ISU has a great program for teachers, and you know I want to teach."

"Yes, but you can't blame an old man for trying. How do your parents feel about you going all the way down to Norman?"

"It's *Normal*, Grandpa, in Illinois. Not Norman, in Oklahoma. I'm not going to your school!" she stated, now perturbed. "But I won't be going there except to test."

He looked off thoughtfully. "I guess I'll have to get used to the idea of you going to school, but not actually *going* there. You know the campus experience is worthwhile. I could buy a house there, and you could stay with me in Oklahoma, if that's what's keeping you from my alma mater."

"No, Grandpa, but thank you. I'm staying here and working. I'll take classes just like I did in high school, online at home. I'm taking the distance teaching courses as well so I can eventually teach online."

"Hmm ... in my day we went to school at schools, wrote letters on paper, and read books that were printed and bound. It's hard to accustom oneself to the current process of education. And that nice looking boy last night, is he doing the same?"

"He hasn't decided. Gramps, you're avoiding the subject that I really want to talk about."

"Your great aunt said to say 'hi.' I think she fell asleep as she was signing. I wonder ... if she signs in her sleep, will we know what she's dreaming?"

"Gramps, I really *do* want to know what happened." Jennifer added with a level of sincerity that she hoped would finally reach her grandfather. "Did you do the terrible things they say you did?"

Finally acknowledging her concerns, he asked, "Did they say I *did* certain things and *called* them terrible or did they say I *did terrible things*?"

Jennifer paused to consider the distinction. "A little of both. My history books say you betrayed the country and your friend, the president. They say you knew of the plans to destroy the nation, and you helped them do it. The sources also say you could have prevented all the problems, but you made them worse instead." With each word she expressed more emotion, hesitant to continue. She finally burst into tears and sobbed, "They say you should have gone to jail!"

He could say nothing as tears welled up in his eyes as well. He wrapped his arms around his granddaughter and cried with her for a few minutes.

Breaking the silence, he said, "Jen, Jen, Jen ..."

"You know Grandpa, nobody calls me 'Jen' any more, just you," she said, smiling up at him. "Everyone calls me 'Jenny' now."

"That's not true, that boy who couldn't keep his hands off yours last night—Craig, I think his name was—he called you 'Jen.' I heard him."

"He only did that because he heard you call me 'Jen.'"

"Well, I knew there was a reason to like that boy and to remember his name."

"Grandpa! Are you saying that Craig and I will ...?"

"Jen!" He stopped her short. "Your obvious fondness for him is reason enough to remember his name. Please don't read anything more into it."

Grandpa was an odd sort; every so often, he would tell you something that would end up coming true. When he was a young man, people would talk about his "powers," but he never made any claims. He had been a minister, what was called a "charismatic" back then. People would sometimes faint when he prayed for them. Even miracles were reported. Yet, it was usually a simple little thing similar to what he almost said about her boyfriend. The history books in Illinois schools called him a "mystic," comparing him to Rasputin.

"I knew during this visit I'd need to tell you what happened in my younger days." Realizing the time had come for a serious discussion with his granddaughter, he began, "Yes, I've been avoiding the subject. I wanted to keep you innocent in my mind, as the cute baby granddaughter that brought life back to me when it seemed my world had crumbled around me. You are the best thing that has happened to me in the past two decades."

As he began to speak, he carefully orchestrated his words so Jennifer would understand his point of view. "The first thing I need you to know is that I was only a bit player in the proceedings. Your school books may have suggested otherwise. My perspective is a bit different from all those who worked in the administration, including your aunt.

"By the time the significant events really came to a head, I was even more isolated from what was going on. But, over the years, I've been able to visit with most of the serious players, including the former First Lady, and doing so filled in most of the holes for me. One thing is certain: the events didn't happen the way the political junkies and Washington insiders reported.

"As with most events, big or small, you'll find history is filled with stories of real people acting and adjusting to situations that are outside their control. When such events are viewed as historically significant, the faults and virtues of the individual people involved become exaggerated. Oftentimes, the same person may become both the hero and the villain."

Grandpa looked up to the sky for a moment, pausing to gather his thoughts. "Well, let's see. No need to cover the things you already know. When it all started, I was still living in Oklahoma and ministering mostly on college campuses. However, it was in Tuscaloosa, at the University of Alabama, where a large student group came together and began their own church. I began to put out books and DVDs. Do you know what those are?" She nodded affirmatively and he continued. "I was building campus groups, including one in Lawrence, Kansas. That one was growing pretty big; about five hundred were in regular attendance by the time the governor was invited ..."

Jennifer interrupted, "That's right! He was a governor before becoming president. Is that when you first met him?"

"No, I met him when he was campaigning for governor. It took me a few years to put all the pieces together. Most of it he told me directly; he shared everything with me back then. Other parts, I didn't learn until recently. I thought about writing another book, but much of what he told me was in confidence. I can't publish those things while he's alive. I'm a good bit older than he is, so I probably won't have that opportunity. But I suppose I can tell you; his story is where I really should begin."

"The best instituted governments carry in them the seeds of their destruction: and, though they grow and improve for a time, they will soon tend visibly to their dissolution. Every hour they live is an hour the less that they have to live."

—Henry St. John, First Viscount Bolingbroke

A LAN MARTIN CASSELL GREW up in a lower class family in Pittsburg, Kansas. A small city in the southeast region of the state, initially named "Hopefield," Pittsburg was originally built on the coal mining industry. In 1876 the town was renamed "Pittsburg" with dreams of recreating an empire comparable to Pennsylvania's second city with its immense production of coal. The countryside was full of rolling hills, suggestive of the nearby Ozark Mountains found a short distance away in Missouri.

No one in the community, not even members of his family, thought Alan would have much success in life. Yet, ambition and attentiveness worked together to reveal his destiny. The fact that he was an attractive, articulate man who typically found himself in the right places at the right times didn't hurt either.

He worked constantly from the age of twelve: delivering newspapers, working for a caterer at weddings through the summers, and serving as a lifeguard at the local YMCA. He enjoyed teaching kids to swim and was always polite to the elderly who attended "Senior Swim."

Alan was one of those kids who didn't have a lot of close friends his age, but managed to stay out of trouble and get along with just about everyone. What else could he do but become a "gorilla" and attend Pittsburg State University? He worked full time at a variety of fast food restaurants to pay for school. He got his degree in Business Administration and was well on his way to permanent anonymity.

While in college, he became fascinated by politics. His interest was initiated because of a girl, of course. She invited him to visit the College Republican group. He went to the meeting, she didn't, and he never saw her on campus again. However, since he lived at home, he didn't spend as much time on campus as the resident students.

The guys in the CR group challenged his ideas about everything. Alan was always a Republican but that was the popular choice for political party in Kansas. Pittsburg historically leaned Democrat, unlike the rest of the state, but that affiliation changed over the years. The common comment on Kansas political parties was that the state had three political parties: the Republican, the Democratic, and the other Republican Party. At the time of his involvement, the long-term divisions in the GOP had closed, and the Republicans were in a period of state domination.

Alan became a faithful voter upon turning eighteen. Every school board, state legislature, county or municipal election would find Alan at the polls. Despite his hunger for politics, he had not developed any particular political philosophy. He called himself a conservative because the word matched his personality, and thus he lived to prove the label true. Alan was pro-environment and the destruction of the land by the strip mines disturbed him. The environmentalists favored making the land public and used the pitted areas as park land, often stocking the ponds with fish for the local anglers. His new CR friends convinced him the best use of the property was to keep the land private. They showed him how the mined lands were now the most prized land in the area. What had previously been an eyesore, and even dangerous, was now "gentrifying" much of the region. Since the federal government had done such a poor job with its Superfund clean-up efforts just across the border in Pitcher, Oklahoma, he was convinced government should only be the solution of last resort; Alan spent his public and professional life committed to this philosophy.

Yet, Alan also deeply believed in local government. For him, localities and states needed the right to make their own decisions on issues of concern. He resented when federal, continental and international policies meddled in local matters. He commonly quoted Woodrow Wilson on the subject of self-determination; one of his favorite quotes was Wilson's words to Congress in 1918: "Self-determination is not a mere phrase. It is an imperative principle of action which statesmen will henceforth ignore at their peril." Alan found special pleasure in using a liberal Democrat's words to molest liberal Democrat policies.

Once Alan had developed his ideas, he became adept at communicating these thoughts persuasively. More importantly, he improved efficiency through his ability to bypass legal and bureaucratic nonsense. Before long, he actively helped candidates develop white papers and created innovative solutions to problems which plagued local and state governments.

When Alan finished college, the Crawford County GOP Chairman, Jim Cherry, recruited him to be a candidate for County Commissioner. Perhaps Alan was not the best man for the job—he certainly had his doubts—but he won anyway. His victory was not really a surprise since elections at that level were basically little more than popularity contests, and he already had a firm foundation in the area. The kids he taught to swim, the guys from the CR club, and just about everyone he had ever worked with helped him in his cause. Alan was someone everyone liked, but no one really knew or got close to.

Alan always worked and never spent much on personal items, so he was quickly able to set aside money to buy an old farmhouse with sixteen acres west of town. Most of the original farm had been sold long before for strip mining. The land was now owned by a retiree who built a fine home out of view. The original farm was one hundred sixty acres, a quarter section of railroad land grant property. Alan's house was dilapidated since it had been rented to farm hands for the previous fifty years; however, the house was a good start for him and was closer to the county courthouse in Girard. The property also allowed him to become a neighbor to his political mentor, Jim Cherry.

He purchased some cattle to put on the land. He would buy calves at auction in the spring and used the livestock through the growing season to keep the grass on his land manageable. He then sold the cattle in the fall for a small profit. The location also provided him significant privacy and pleasant views.

Alan enjoyed looking out past his few acres of pasture to the rough lands of the old strip mine beyond; the scene gave him a sense of security.

By the age of twenty-five, Alan was a politician, a home owner, and a rancher, if sixteen acres can be considered a ranch. He was a success, but unsatisfied with his personal accomplishments. Of course, by this age, most men look to get married, but Alan always seemed too busy to do anything about his situation. Dates came and went; he just never seemed to meet "the right one."

Politicians are expected to ceaselessly attend events and activities which have nothing to do with the job. Alan was always polite and fulfilled every request he could, but he really preferred to work on road construction sites or at the courthouse. He disliked attending what he considered to be trivial extracurricular social events. One invitation was accepted eagerly; Miss Kansas was in Pittsburg and the commissioners were invited to meet her. *Why not a beauty queen?*, he wondered.

Perhaps his youth made him optimistic about his chances. Maybe he was just hopeful for anything to interrupt the script his life seemed to follow. *This time will be different; I'll take chances and break loose,* he told himself. The event was a Chamber breakfast on Friday morning. Jim Cherry would be emceeing since the Chamber president was out of town. Jim was the first vice president of the chamber. He also owned a local insurance agency and served as the county GOP chair. Jim arranged the seating to secure Alan's proximity to Kansas' Irish beauty. Alan hadn't even seen a picture of her, but she had to be gorgeous, right? Who ever heard of an unattractive beauty queen?

His presumption was not in error. In fact, he had never seen a woman so beautiful. If he had been asked to conjure up his personal vision of female perfection, he could only have struggled to describe the image before him. His heart pounded as he looked at her. He really didn't think a woman could look so stunning, so *right*. He had dated pretty girls in the past, but she was beyond his dreams. She was also well out of his league.

As the meeting participants assembled, Jim presented Katherine Fogarty, the beautiful Miss Kansas, to his friend and neighbor, Alan Cassell. Alan's brain was foggy as he proceeded to introduce himself to her: "Commissioner Alan Cassell, very good to meet you Katherine."

"Kate, just call me Kate," she said with a smile. Her response was gracious, as beauty queens are trained to be. She warmly took his hand and looked him in the eye. "I'm very pleased to meet you. I am excited to be here for breakfast with so many community leaders!"

Alan didn't even know what he had said in response; he was mesmerized. Later, Jim pulled him aside during the "meet and greet" portion of the event.

"Hey, buddy. Pulling rank isn't exactly the way to a lady's heart," Jim grinned. "Give 'being yourself' a try."

Alan nodded in acknowledgment of his ridiculous attempt at making an impression—as if being a county commissioner was a big deal. Alan's attraction was obvious to all in the room and most of the crowd of middle-aged and older folks were endeared by his crush.

Jim called the event to order, and after the invocation and flag salute everyone started to eat. Usually, Chamber breakfast events were not this large or formal. Quite often, they would be comfortable gatherings around a coffee pot at a bank or new retailer with eight to ten people present. This event was different because of the honored guest. There were nearly one hundred people in attendance in the large banquet hall at Pittsburg State.

Jim made the introduction of the guest, Miss Kansas, who would speak and provide a bit of entertainment for the event. He explained to the audience that Katherine "Kate" Fogarty was from Wichita and attended college in Lawrence. She was taking the rest of the school year off to fulfill her duties and would be representing Kansas in the Miss America pageant in a few months.

When Jim sat, she began to speak. There was nothing formal about the speech; she smiled so brightly that no one thought she needed to speak at all. Her tone was pleasant and personal. Alan took in the whole speech as if she had told him exactly what he needed to know to overcome his feeble attempt at self-introduction and perhaps have a chance with her after all.

Of course, she hadn't even given him a thought when making her comments. Maybe she presumed that a "commissioner" was already married. Alan had the bad habit of wearing clothes he thought made him look older. He tried to look more mature so people would accept him in his position. In reality, his youth was a large part of why the voters chose him in the first place.

She started by explaining to the crowd why she was in town. The good news for Alan was that she was staying in town that night since she was to present the crown to the incoming Miss Southeast Kansas on Saturday evening. Perhaps he could work in a date.

Kate mentioned she used to ride in rodeos as a very young girl. He thought he might invite her to go horseback riding. Then she said something that nearly made him swallow his tongue and lose his breakfast at the same time:

"I have so enjoyed these last few months representing Kansas and I do hope that I have done a good job. Of course, I would love to continue to represent you all as Miss America, but if I don't win it will be good to return to ordinary life. I would like nothing more than to just be a girl on campus again with a schedule that doesn't take two full-time people to keep me on track." she said with a giggle as the audience gave a strong laugh. She continued before the room quieted and only those very close or paying close attention heard the next words, "Perhaps, even have a boyfriend. I would welcome a chance to have some normalcy in my life."

"No boyfriend!" Alan thought he said to himself. When he noticed people at the front of the crowd begin again to giggle, the young politician on the dais realized that he must have, at the very least, mouthed the statement so that his inner thoughts were revealed. Jim knew he would need to give Alan a moment to try to ask Kate out at the end of the event before the crowd dominated her time.

At that point, Alan stopped listening and gazed at Kate. He memorized everything about the moment. She wore form-fitting black slacks with a boot flare. Her shirt was white with a tall collar, loose sleeves, and just enough buttons not buttoned to be exceptionally alluring. She wore a simple gold necklace with a small diamond and simple but elegant diamond earrings, all of which served as a precursor to the sparkle that came with her smile and deep blue eyes. Her simple attire and remarkable beauty was, for Alan, the fulfillment of the morning program.

She had a perfect body: tall, but not gangly; slender, but healthy; too well-endowed to be a "super model," but not so much as to keep her from some modeling. Her skin was fair with a ruddy tone.

However, her hair was her most striking feature of all. The base color was certainly red, perhaps an auburn, lightened by the sun. The color was not a color that could be easily recreated by a beautician. The depth of the color was, to Alan, by far her sexiest feature. Her hair was long and flowing. It moved with her, rather than with plastic permanence as one often sees in beauty pageant girls. The body of her hair was wavy and it caught the light with every turn of her head. It gently framed her face, but the bulk of her hair was behind her in the shape of an upside down flame. He was fascinated by her hair; his fascination for her had only just begun.

After Kate finished her speech, the entertainment section of the event started. Celtic music began to play and Kate Fogarty began to dance. She performed Irish clog dancing, her arms held straight to her side as her feet moved about magically. Alan, who sat directly to her right, was mesmerized as he watched her hair bounce as she danced rhythmically to the music. He thought again about the horseback riding idea and pictured her, with that hair, riding across the prairie with him beside her.

At the end of her performance, her arms moved out with a flourish and the crowd roared their approval. Her dancing was, for most of them, the least impressive part of the morning. People usually attended these events to make connections and curry favors, rather than for the entertainment.

Jim made up an excuse to keep Alan and Kate on the platform for a few moments while the group began to break up. It was doubtful that anyone thought his reason genuine, but they all agreed this was Alan's chance.

Alan turned to Kate and said, "Katherine, do you get to ride your horse often?"

"It's Kate, remember. And I don't even have her anymore since starting at KU."

He confidently asked, "Would you like to take a ride while you are in town? That could be arranged, if you have an hour or so free."

"Wow, nothing would make me happier," she replied. When she spoke, she had a genuine smile and an even greater sparkle in her eyes. "I do have a couple hours later today. Is there a stable nearby?"

Not believing his ears, Alan continued, "More than one, actually. I'll make the arrangements and call you ... somewhere here on campus?"

"Oh, just call my cell," Kate answered as she wrote the number on a napkin. "I have an interview at eleven, then nothing until this evening at five, but I have to be back here by 3:30 or so to get ready. That'll give me more than enough time. Just let me know where to go; I have my car here." Pausing for a moment, she realized she might be taking advantage of him. "I can't expect you to do that! I'm sorry! You must have more important things to do."

Sensing the potential loss of a once-in-a-lifetime moment, he insisted, "No, no, not any trouble. Please allow me to show you our hospitality. Anyway, I was instrumental in the county's adopting a four-day, ten-hour work week, so we don't work on Fridays unless there's an emergency …"

Then he started to ramble on about the increased efficiency, lower fuel costs, and improved employee morale, as well as his emergency response team and the road repair efficiencies he instituted in the past year. Kate finally interrupted by saying, "Just buzz me on my cell and let me know the address."

With that she was gone, mixing with the patient crowd.

Jim Cherry came back to Alan with a grin. "You got a phone number on that napkin, did you?"

"You saw that?" Alan asked with an ever-broadening grin.

"Everyone did, and we couldn't be happier. So what happened?"

"Horseback riding this afternoon. Are there any stables in the area?"

Jim looked astonished. "Do you even ride?"

"Out in the Ozarks. I've gone on those trail rides, you know."

"I'm quite sure that's not what she'll be expecting. You chose poorly, son, very poorly."

"What?" Alan responded, "It worked! What's wrong?"

"I was the guy with her resume. I didn't read the whole thing out loud. Kate Fogarty was the state pre-teen barrel racing champion! For her, riding means full out galloping, with hairpin turns and the wind in her hair. Not a peaceful trot along some boring path."

"Sounds good," said Alan eagerly.

"You're talking about sitting on an old hag of a mare and wandering through the woods. If you want to impress her, you need to find a way to let her do what she expects and keep up with her at the same time."

"Oh God, what do I do now?" mumbled Alan, afraid he might lose this one shot after all.

"Let me think …" Jim paused. "I know! My son Bill's horses would be perfect. Bill did team roping until last year when he went off to Baylor. His horses are trained to stay together. I can bring them to your place …"

Alan interrupted, "Why my place?"

"Because they'll have less room to roam so you won't have to ride as long," Jim assured him. "I have a full section fenced in. Are you ready to ride four miles around the place?" Without giving a moment to respond he continued, "No, I didn't think so. I'll bring them to your place and have them tacked up for you. I presume you don't know how to do that."

Alan nodded; he was sure he didn't know how because he didn't know what Jim was talking about.

"By the time she gets there, you'll be ready for her and I'll be long gone. All you have to do is hang on. Put her on Dandy-boy and Gemstone will go where he goes. If you can stay in the saddle, she might not ever know the difference."

All went according to plan. The horses were tacked up and tied to an old hitching post at Alan's place. He was sure which horse was which and, when Kate arrived, he pointed her to the right one. He had a bit of explaining to do: why the address he had given over the phone was his home, that he was indeed single, and that he intended this meeting to be some kind of date. She had not been looking for a date but, ever-gracious and still eager for a ride, she jumped on. Following suit, he jumped on his horse. The situation seemed pretty good, except Gemstone was still tied to the post and, try as he might, Alan could not reach the knot in the reins from the mount.

"Are these your horses?" she asked.

Honesty took hold first, followed closely by a bit of disinformation: "No, my neighbor has them here. I have room, and he's trying to fully utilize his place so he can pay for his kid's college. He said I could ride them but this is the first time I have had a partner. I didn't want to take them out separately and make one jealous." Alan had no idea if what he just said made any sense but her quizzical look suggested that it didn't. "I haven't been riding for a while either. The horses could use the workout." The words tumbled out as he tried to act the part of a country boy.

Alan then felt confident, since he had explained the situation to some degree and, at the same time, alluded to his limited skills. Of course, he then had to climb down and untie the horse. Dismounting was not as refined as mounting had been. When he tried to remount the unrestrained horse, he was particularly clumsy. She suggested they walk the horses a bit to warm them up; it was a kindness on her part.

While they rode, he was struck again by her looks. Kate wore a western-styled shirt, which was unbuttoned half-way down, revealed a white halter top beneath. She had on jeans that somehow gave her room to ride and, at the same time, hugged her quite appealing curves. And, of course, she had on bejeweled cowgirl boots. Alan couldn't help but wonder how full her car had to be coming down from Lawrence if she even brought boots with her.

He was wearing a brand new western-style shirt, because until late that morning he didn't own any. His shirt was similarly open, with about three buttons undone with a jet black t-shirt beneath. He had on old jeans and a worn pair of boots. Alan would have done better to leave the western shirt off and just wear the tee.

They talked for a while as they walked the horses. He described the region and its history. He talked about his plans for the house, which already looked much better since he had made several improvements.

"If you toured the area, you would see how the privately owned land is much better preserved than any of the public lands," Alan observed, "not to mention the negative long-term impact of mining on the ground water and wildlife." A few of his cattle wandered about as the horses walked the grounds.

Kate felt there was something refreshing about Alan when he spoke of the mined lands. She saw a glimpse of his passion for something good; passion for something *other* than pursuing her. She did not mind the attention; girls don't enter pageants if they don't want to be noticed. Yet, it always seemed as if men only had one thing in mind.

Alan had gotten off-track earlier in the day when he talked about his efforts to protect taxpayer money and his opinions told her he took the interests of the people seriously. At the time it was a "What a dork" moment, but now his focus was oddly appealing. His attitude toward better stewardship of the land was an inspiration. He seemed more comfortable now than earlier, and she wanted to be relaxed as well. *Maybe after the ride we'll have a little heart-to-heart,* she said to herself. *It won't hurt. Not like I'm going to ever see him again.*

Kate blurted, "Shall we?", and Dandy-boy and Kate were off. In a similar manner, Gemstone and Alan followed, working hard to catch up to the leading horse. If Alan had just acted like all was fine, Gemstone would have matched Dandy-boy's every move, and Alan would have looked like quite the horseman. For a few moments, the plan worked.

Then he tried to control Gemstone. This was an exceptionally bad idea because Alan didn't know what to do when he was given control. First, he pulled back on the reins, just a bit, to slow the beast down. He then tried to make a turn that would cross Dandy-boy's path. Gemstone figured out immediately his rider was clueless. Well, if the rider doesn't control the horse, then the horse will control the rider. So Gemstone took off, as he was trained, to catch up with Dandy-boy and slip back into position.

Fear took hold and Alan's left hand moved to a death grip on the horn of the saddle, leaving only a couple of fingers of his hand on the reins. One quick turn by Gemstone and Alan—most of him anyway—flew off to the left. Thankfully, his boots slipped easily out of the stirrups. Sadly, his left hand did not know how to let go of the horn. With a squeal that would have made a very young girl proud, Alan fell to the ground in a heap. His momentary weightless experience ended, mid-flight, with a painful shock to his arm.

Alan knew immediately that he had pulled his arm out of its socket. He had never experienced pain like this, although he was no stranger to pain. He was shot by a BB gun one time in his eye. The eye survived and the pain subsided. Another time, he was hit in the head by a baseball bat while serving as an umpire. The pain went away not long after he regained consciousness. This pain, however, was different. He couldn't talk. He didn't think he could breathe, although part of him noticed his chest moved rapidly up and down. He lay on the ground writhing; in a futile attempt, he tried to get up. He actually forgot that Kate was there.

The forgetfulness didn't last. In a flash, she was back. Kate was alerted something was wrong with the banshee-like ear-splitting cry emitted by Alan. She quickly leapt off her horse and assessed the situation with precision, pushing him to the ground. She placed one foot on his chest near his shoulder, both hands around his wrist, and pulled with all her might.

The little girl who had been there a moment before made an encore performance, another effeminate squeal. *Is she going to kill me?* he wondered. In later years, he told the story as if he had said the question aloud. Truth is, he didn't know and she never said. His arm was back in the shoulder socket and the pain diminished to a manageable level. She moved on to see if there were other injuries.

"You tore your new shirt," she said. "Take it off; let's see if you're injured anywhere else."

She didn't know he was already embarrassed and that acknowledging that his shirt was new would add insult to his injured ego. Kate was more concerned about his physical injuries than his damaged pride.

He tried to obey her directions, but his arm would not cooperate. When she helped him take his shirt off, she noticed for the first time how pleasant his upper torso looked in the black shirt. She was checking for cuts or broken bones, but simultaneously admired his build. His collarbone and rib bones appeared unbroken, but she carefully inspected by feeling about his body, mostly for her own satisfaction. Alan did have a couple of scrapes, but nothing serious. After a couple of minutes, he stood and began to walk. Kate offered her shoulder and helped him as he slowed his steps; his attention was momentarily consumed at the thought of her hands on his body.

After walking just a few feet and collecting his thoughts, he suggested they sit down under a cottonwood tree. She found a spot clear of any cow patties and tried to help him sit down but fell instead, landing on top of him. To Alan, the experience would have been very pleasant if it had not impacted his left shoulder.

"Oh God, I am so sorry! Are you okay?" Kate exclaimed.

"My shoulder hurt while you were on it, but now it hurts, well … about the same." Alan replied, forcing a smile. "But, please let me rest here a moment. I'm not much of a rider, and I don't know the horse all that well …"

"Hey, we all fall sometimes, even from a horse we know." Kate interrupted. "Don't worry! If I had fallen you would have been here to help me. You were wise not to ride alone."

"You're not kidding!"

"Other than the shoulder, are you all right? I think I checked you out pretty good. How do your legs feel?"

"I may have a bruise or two, but I'm sure I'll be fine. A couple of scrapes, nothing to worry …"

"When I get you back to the house let me put something on those …"

"You don't have to do that; they'll heal up. Say, are the horses okay?"

Kate looked in the direction of the animals and said, "Let me get them." After she gathered the horses she tied them to a close tree by their reins on a couple of sturdy, low branches in the shade. Then, she sat next to Alan.

"They're fine," she said. "Under the tree, I am sure they will find some grass to occupy their time for a few minutes while we rest. "Now, take these. They'll help you feel better."

Alan was taken aback by the idea that she had some kind of pills. "What are they? Why did you have pills with you?"

"Don't worry; it's over-the-counter pain medicine. That's all."

"Oh, like ibuprofen?" he asked as he prepared to pop the pills in his mouth.

"Well, like it, but not exactly. Just take them. They won't hurt, I promise."

He stopped himself short, asking, "What are they, exactly?"

"If you must know, Midol," Kate replied with a slight grin.

"Yeah, I shouldn't ask questions sometimes. Thanks." Alan responded as he finally swallowed the pills. "I really feel bad about how I ruined your day. You came for a nice ride and here you are taking care of me. I'm so sorry."

"That's fine; I had a moment of fun, which is more than I've had in quite some time. You were doing fine for a little while, and it is really beautiful out here," observed Kate.

Alan couldn't help but agree. "Tell me about your barrel racing. Why did you give it up? You seem to love the horses."

Kate nodded. "I really do, but I was interested in the pageants. I can't very well take a horse on stage and do barrel racing for the talent portion."

"No, I suppose that could be messy." Alan chuckled. "Is that why you took up dancing?"

"You have to have a talent. I'm Irish and *look* Irish, so we figured people would approve. I can't play any instruments, can't sing, can't juggle, so …"

"Oh, I could teach you to juggle!" Alan joked. Then you can take up a serious talent."

"Do you think I'm that bad? Oh, I have no chance at Miss America. The competition is being held in Kansas City of all places this year …" continued Kate with a hint of sorrow in her voice.

Alan instinctively reached forward to comfort her while saying, "Hey, I really was joking, you know … Ouch!" The pain lanced through him as he reached out to put his arms around her shoulders.

"Silly," retorted Kate, "I was kidding you. I am sorry you were hurt trying to comfort me … which may have been a cheap way to get a little hug."

"Well, what exactly was that landing-on-my-lap thing where you missed and hit my shoulder?" asked Alan.

"You are not blaming me for the pain caused by your deception to get me out here, are you?" objected Kate with a smile.

"Oh, and if you had fallen you would want me to check you for broken bones the same way you checked me?" Alan brazenly retorted.

"Like you weren't checking me out all morning …" countered Kate.

"And I'm supposed to believe that you brought rhinestone-studded boots on an overnight visit where you didn't expect to do any riding?"

"Hey, I needed a new pair of boots. And, by the way, there's only one place in town to buy western wear. They have a whole rack filled with that god-awful shirt you were wearing, so you can go buy another!"

Alan was dumbstruck for a moment. "You *knew* as soon as you saw me when you got here, and you said nothing! You knew I just bought the shirt? You just played along? Why?"

Kate shyly looked down and said, "You were nice to me, and I wanted to get to know you."

He considered her comment for a moment. Gazing at her, Alan replied, "I've told you all about me. I even did that stupid formal introduction after Jim made such a friendly one. Tell me what's on your mind."

"I'm not worried about my talent. Irish dancing works for me and nobody else has a similar performance. I'm more worried about my platform." Kate answered.

"Platform?" he asked.

"You know, the subject you want to focus on for the judges. How everyone used to say, 'world peace' and the joke became 'whirled peas,'" she said with an open giggle. "My focus is literacy. My goal has been to help children to read for years, and I love it. The program I'm involved in is called 'Whiz Kidz.' It's an afterschool program where we help kids read and do homework. The kids are really wonderful; I love kids."

"Sounds great. So, what's the problem?" Alan asked.

"Literacy is becoming the new 'whirled peas.' Everyone's trying to focus on it. I've been working on reading programs since I can remember, even before I entered my first pageant. My directors suggested I change my platform, but it feels like they're trying to change me ... who I am. What do you think?" Kate's sincerity was obvious, and Alan wanted to help.

He started out, "Loaded question ... now don't take ... as if I think this ... 'cause I don't ... but are they thinking that you're ... shallow? In the 'whirled peas' kind of way? I mean, there can't be any reason to want kids *not* to read. Is there?"

"No, they just want something different," she replied.

"Changing your 'platform' won't change you. You ride horses, you dance, you're a lot of fun, you make a pretty good nurse, and you seem to care for the environment, like I do, though I bet that's been done to death too." He paused to consider how politically correct environmental concerns had been and how he could respond, "I have a feeling that you could have a dozen platforms and not scratch the surface," Alan concluded.

"Now that might just be the sweetest thing you've said today," Kate said with another one of her intoxicating smiles.

Alan was caught off-guard when she called him "sweet." "I'm sorry. I mean, I didn't intend, I mean when I say something to be nice to a girl, I mean ... I was just talking. I wasn't trying to be sweet. I just meant it."

"Now I could kiss you for that!" she blurted.

"Well, um, fine but watch the shoulder. I'm not into the whole 'love hurts' thing."

She kissed him on the cheek. They talked of their families, college, career goals, and anything else that popped into their minds.

After a long conversation, Kate realized that her free hour had certainly passed. "Let me help you into the house, and I'll get bandages on those cuts."

"Scrapes, but far be it from me to stop you," Alan replied.

He could have easily walked back to the house by himself, but he allowed her to help. When they entered the spartanly-furnished living room, she lowered him onto the couch. Kate left him in the old farmhouse while she took care of the horses; she removed the horses' tack and gave them a quick brushing.

"Not much of a ride for you boys today," she told them, "but perhaps a better one for me. Ah, you two don't know him any better than I do."

Back inside, she found the bathroom, the bandages, and nothing that warned her to stay away from him. What she didn't know was that her patient made a mad dash through the house while she was outside. He scurried around the farmhouse and picked up dirty underwear, newspapers, commission agendas, and interoffice memos, shoving them anywhere he could so she wouldn't find them when she returned. He was barely back on the couch when Kate came back inside. She bandaged his wounds, which he insisted were "scrapes" rather than "cuts." With the memory of his feminine shriek of pain still fresh, the fact of a wound being called a "scrape" over a "cut" was not what defined his manliness. As she finished, she asked, "Is there anything safe to do around here?"

At first, he was confused by the question. Then he realized: *She's asking me on a second date!* Alan was both surprised and pleased. He replied, "The Ozarks of Missouri are close; there are a lot of …"

"Oh!" she interrupted. "Carthage! Isn't Precious Moments in Carthage? It's close, right? Have you been there?"

"Yes," he replied hesitantly, "a long time ago. Do you really want to go there?" He was thinking that he might not enjoy a return visit to the world capitol of sentimentality.

"Is there something wrong with that?" Kate sheepishly responded.

"No," answered Alan, thinking quickly, "I've wanted to go back, but it's not a place you go, well a guy goes, alone. I'd love to take you there, but it isn't something we can do today. I'm not up for the drive, and you have some business tonight."

"But you will take me? Maybe next week, during the week, we could go? I can't ever get free time on weekends."

"I could come up to Lawrence and get you. They have a hotel on the property and lots to see. I could bring you back the next day."

"It's a date!" Kate cheerily replied. She then gathered her things and said goodbye. She spun around to leave only to continue around in a full circle, which ended with her giving Alan a proper kiss. Alan later said that must have been the precise moment the Midol finally kicked in because he was feeling no pain.

By the time his friend came by to pick up the horses, Alan was bouncing off the clouds. Jim came into the house and asked about the date. He promised to never tell the story, but the whole county knew in a matter of days. Alan also told Jim of the upcoming overnight date. His friend often brought reality to a situation. He mentioned that the hotel at Precious Moments was likely a very profitable one. After all, single people who visited as couples were highly inclined to take two rooms, rather than just one, since the park was considered a "religious" place. Alan knew instantly if the hotel didn't insist on two rooms, Kate would be expecting them.

Alan felt as if he owed Jim a huge debt for all he had done. Jim helped him get his job, and then—hopefully, at least—a girlfriend. When called upon, Alan could be counted on to repay the favor. Alan continued to be groomed for his future career, and the political "powers that be" saw an attractive young man, both talented and malleable, who could go far in politics.

Alan wondered if he had broken free from the constraints of fate because of Kate. That's the idea behind destiny. If something is your destiny, it won't seem unnatural or unappealing. Was Alan facing a benevolent destiny, or was he being formed into something by human forces? He never questioned why the overbooked Chamber breakfast seemed to only consist of married older folks, except him and Kate, when the community had a number of youthful and single entrepreneurs.

Even with the concept of political favor, or pay-back, he was committed to do only what he believed was right. He told his ailing mother when they first recruited him for commissioner: "They had better be recruiting me for what I believe in because I won't change my ideals for a job." He meant every word, as every young politician does. He added the logic, "It's easier to recruit someone who really believes in what you want than to change them later."

Alan understood people were often cynical about politicians. Stories abounded about corruption. Corruption is common, but not universal. Most elected officials, especially those in local offices, are honest. They might be unwise, but generally they act in accordance with what they think is right.

25

Lakewood Memorial Library
12 W. Summit Street
Lakewood, NY 14750

If Alan was on a ride with fate, he enjoyed every moment so long as Kate was part of it. The date at Precious Moments was one meeting of many over the subsequent weeks and months. Gradually, they built their relationship into something truly special. While Alan fell in love with Kate the first day, she was a little more objective. She came to love him over the next few weeks; the combination of Alan's youthful, geeky awkwardness and her tightly-controlled lifestyle provided both of them many opportunities to have a love that challenged both of their worlds. Kate grew past the pageants to become a woman of tremendous grace and dignity. She didn't become Miss America, but instead got something else she wanted—a normal life. She had told the crowd at the Chamber breakfast on the day they met that a normal life meant having a boyfriend. A normal life now meant she was the fiancée of Alan Cassell. Alan, whom many had labeled the "golden boy of the GOP," was considered far more golden with her on his arm. He still spoke across the state on political matters, and he loved his job as a commissioner. For a while, his ambition appeared to be tamed, but she expected more from his career. She was patient; she didn't have to be patient for long.

"Imperial collapse may come much more suddenly than many historians imagine. A combination of fiscal deficits and military overstretch suggests that the United States may be the next empire on the precipice."

—Niall Ferguson, *Complexity and Collapse*, "Foreign Affairs", March/April 2010

KATE FINISHED HER DEGREE in Library Science and went home to Wichita to prepare for her wedding to Alan. Her father had been very kind and her mother highly controlling, but they both liked Alan. He visited their home several times and was with her parents at her graduation ceremony. Michael Fogarty saw much of himself in Alan. Kate's mother Barbara, or "Babs" as everyone was expected to call her, was excited to have her final opportunity to create an event with her youngest child. Planning the wedding was Babs' dream. Kate was somewhat concerned her mother's dream could become her own nightmare.

Kate graduated from college in May, and the wedding was planned for August. The budding bride thought she would have plenty of time for wedding planning. However, Babs felt behind schedule and made many of the decisions before Kate returned home. The invitations were printed, even though the date had only been a suggestion. Kate hadn't even considered where to have the special event. The Fogarty's didn't attend church; therefore, Babs decided to have the wedding at the family home in Wichita.

Alan had given his blessing to Kate to make all the decisions, as if the groom ever really matters in wedding plans. Very few guests would come to Wichita for Alan. The Cherry family already said they would be in attendance, along with a few friendly faces from the county courthouse. Alan's mother Peggy would come with his younger sister Deena. Alan hoped Deena would get along with the other wedding guests, cringing at the thought that she would attempt to bring a boyfriend.

The pastor of the Beulah Community Church was asked to preside over the ceremony. Alan attended the Beulah church with the Cherry family. The setting was comfortable and the church was growing in influence; therefore attending his friend's church seemed like the right thing to do. Beulah was not affiliated with any denomination, but the previous several pastors were Baptists. The church had a Baptist flavor, which Alan favored as much as he had the Young Republican group in college.

Kate, on the other hand, had scores of friends to invite; friends from childhood, from her rodeo days, to sponsors and competitors from the pageant days now drawn to a close. Kate's friends from college all responded that they wouldn't dream of missing the wedding of the century. Of course, there was also the Fogarty family, with distant relatives flying in from various corners of the country. Kate figured on a head count of three hundred people for the wedding, but Babs aimed much higher. Michael was on Kate's side, yet he got pushed out of the conversation and only his checkbook remained. Colors, flowers, music, food, attendees, and many other details still had to be determined.

Upon her arrival home, a bombshell was revealed that had not been previously mentioned. A business associate of her father's insisted the family come out for a week to Hawaii. Babs argued that in this modern age all the planning needed in the first week could be done easily enough in Hawaii.

Michael had inherited his father's machine shop. His small business was a respected establishment, employing a half-dozen or so. Over the years, Michael improved upon the shop significantly. He built the business into a manufacturer of parts for a variety of small aircraft companies, which included Cessna, Hawker Beechcraft, and Piper.

The family was not nearly as well off as the "Hawaiian," as Michael called him. George Keoki, the "Hawaiian," was a billionaire several times over. Michael had never conducted business with him; they were both vendors to aircraft companies. Keoki's company developed computer software for all of the aeronautical companies, which incorporated the very best GPS navigation software. Keoki also invented sign writing, the system that revolutionized written communication.

For Michael, a positive trip to Hawaii was an opportunity to have an advocate in front of companies with which he had never done business. He had no idea what Keoki wanted from him. For Babs and Kate, Hawaii would be a vacation. Michael expected his trip would be a working vacation.

The Fogarty family planned to stay at Keoki's guest house. The Keoki's guest house was not really a guest house in the typical fashion; the residence was Keoki's previous home in Honolulu before he made his fortune, and he kept it for old time's sake. Built in the 1980s, the estate was a large modern-style Hawaiian home with enormous sliding glass windows that, when open, made it look like the house had almost no walls at all. In every direction were wonderful views, only partially obscured by the other homes lower on the mountain and closer to the sea.

Keoki's new personal home was elsewhere on Oahu. There were a lot of rumors about his home, but no press or business associates ever visited. The property was rumored to be magnificent, enormous, and secluded under the canopy of Hawaiian rainforest. However, the general consensus was that no one knew for sure.

Keoki was himself an enigma. Even his name was hard to get a handle on because he had so many. His given name was "Keoki Nawahiokalaniopu'u" of the long-famed family of Hawaii's royal days. "Keoki" is the Hawaiian equivalent of "George." He went by "George" with his non-Hawaiian associates, but by "Keoki" among Hawaiians. Many of his family members, on the other hand, used a shortened version of the original surname, "Nawahi." Over time, people presumed his name to be "George Keoki," which is a redundancy, but that was fine with him. His Hawaiian roots were not pure. His mother was Japanese, as was his paternal grandmother. Therefore, he was only one- quarter ethnic Hawaiian.

Keoki spoke fluent Japanese, Hawaiian, French, and English. He used American Sign Language effortlessly. He was not afraid to take risks and was known to most as a man devoted to a life of pleasure. Supremely intelligent and creative, he was a man who never seemed to work. A few minutes of inspired thoughtfulness on his part was inclined to result in some revolutionary product. Creativity seemed to run in his blood. Musicians and famed artists were common in his ancestry, but none had achieved his level of financial success.

Excited to embark on the trip, the Fogarty family was quickly off to the airport before Kate's car had even fully cooled off. She packed in such a hurry she wasn't even sure if she had swimwear. Luckily, her mother had also packed some items for her.

At Mid-Continent Airport, the Fogarty's were met by a private jet with *Keoki* emblazoned across the fuselage. The family was accustomed to flying in private planes since the Fogarty business dealt with clients in the aeronautical business; however, this plane was absolutely luxurious. Despite the comfortable surroundings, Babs did not do well with the flight. Kate could not even begin to discuss the wedding until they arrived in Honolulu.

Although flying toward the sun, they arrived very late at night, which felt even later because of the time change. When they exited the plane, Michael was presented with keys to a car and a house. He was informed that the GPS was preprogrammed with the address of their vacation destination. The advice of the navigation system worked easily enough, and upon arrival the three travelers found a note from Keoki that encouraged them to have a good night. The note also reflected he would see them the next day.

The Fogarty's were exhausted. Michael and Babs fell asleep as their heads hit the pillows. However, fatigue affected Kate differently. Kate had difficulties falling asleep after flying across time zones. On top of that, she felt guilty for being so far away from Alan so close to the wedding. She was thousands of miles away from him in, what most would say is, a very romantic place. Kate, on the other hand, was unimpressed by Hawaii. She had been there a few times before with the family. She enjoyed traveling to places with more action and fun. There is plenty of activity in Hawaii that is fun and active, but the times she had been there in the past involved doing nothing but baking under the tropical sun.

Alan would have been uncomfortable in such an environment. He was always polite and appreciative of wealthy political supporters; he never showed any envy or incredulity at shows of wealth. This attitude and approach to wealth was part of the job for him. He expressed appreciation and acted as if wealth and privilege was all a matter of course. Kate, however, often heard about his struggle with the upper class. Alan was clearly not as at ease around people of means as he was around what he saw as "normal" people.

Kate didn't fall asleep until early in the morning. While she slept in, her parents woke up and departed the house. They left a note about some breakfast and hot coffee in the kitchen. By the time she did get up, the coffee was stale. She dumped the old coffee and made a new pot.

While the coffee brewed, she wandered about the house alone for a few minutes and then decided to take a swim. She had remembered to pack her favorite suit; it was not a pageant bikini, but a more practical two-piece. She pulled her hair back into a ponytail and went on a quest for sunscreen when she heard a sound back by the pool.

There, through the window, she saw a man. He took his shirt off in preparation for a swim. As he undressed, Kate noticed that the dark, tall, and barrel-chested man seemed at least ten years her senior. He didn't have Alan's youthful build. Instead, he had a bit of rounding beyond what his bone structure required, but the weight did not seem to limit his athleticism. With a two-step run to the pool's edge, he leapt up and dove head-first into the pool with hardly a splash; not a drop of water appeared on the sun-bleached concrete edge.

Subsequently, he began to swim laps. Kate watched with interest and could not help speculating about this stranger. Her presumption was that it was the elusive "Keoki." *Is this what a billionaire looks like?* she asked herself. Somehow, she pictured an old man or even a computer geek. She never expected he would be anything like what he was. She tried to stop herself from thinking about him, which never worked in the past. She loved Alan and needed to stop herself from thinking about "other men." Her attempt to *not* think about him only made her think of him as the "other man."

Then the internal comparisons began. *Alan is fit and trim, thin and attractive,* she assured herself. *This guy is a little heavy, but still very athletic. He's dark and has very thick, but short, wavy black hair.* She saw his hair before he jumped in and thought she had seen an ever-so-slight grey streak by his ear. Now wet, his hair looked completely black but still full, not weighed down or disheveled by the water. *Alan's hair, a sandy brown, becomes a mess when wet until he slicks it back at which it seems much darker than it does when dry. This man swims around in a playful manner, almost like a dolphin, born live in the water.* Alan always seemed happy, but the only time he seemed to have fun was when he worked. Her father was the same way, but her dad smiled less often than Alan. Finally, she went out to meet the stranger.

As Kate stepped out into the warmth of the day for the first time, she realized she never found the sunscreen. On the lanai, she discovered a full outdoor kitchen with stainless steel appliances, granite counters, and a full sized sink. The area also had a plethora of cabinets, as well as some open shelves with pool towels. Walking near the edge of the pool, she addressed the stranger. "Mr. Keoki, I presume?"

His reaction indicated he hadn't noticed her until he heard her voice. He swam to the edge of the pool near her, placed his fingertips on the side, and pushed himself up to a standing position in one movement. He replied, "Just Keoki, if you don't mind."

"I'm sor—" she attempted to apologize, but he stopped her with barely a word out.

"No worries. You must be Mike's daughter. Hope your trip went well. I suppose Mike is back?" No one called her dad "Mike," but Kate was not going to be the one to correct their host.

"Mom and Dad are still out; they left before I woke up. I don't know where they went or when they'll be back," she replied.

"Oh! You were here all along. I saw the car was gone and thought you were all ..." Keoki began. "Oh well, this is your pool, for the week anyway, so I'll get out of your way. Looks like you were about to take a swim," Keoki concluded. "Mind if I wait inside?"

"Feel free to finish your swim," Kate insisted. "I haven't even put on sunscreen yet. I'll have to find some ..." she trailed off, almost embarrassed by his offer to remove himself from his own property. "Or, you may do as you like, since this is your house."

"I keep some sunscreen in here," Keoki pointed out as he walked to the lanai and opened one of the cabinets. He seemed to ignore her comments. He took out a tube of lotion, tossed it to her and said, "See you inside." Keoki turned, grabbing a towel from the cabinets for himself. He then bent to pick up the shirt he tossed aside a few minutes prior and went inside.

Kate was uncertain how to feel about him from this initial meeting. He was courteous and generous, but cold. He made no effort at all to look her over. Kate realized that it had been several years since any male had seemed so utterly unconcerned with her looks. She found the situation creepy when some very old man, or very young boy, ogled her; yet even the most discreet guy would still size her up.

She knew the whole "not my type" stuff was a fairy tale; for the male of the species, there was no such thing. They liked how a pretty girl looked, and they liked looking. Nice guys avoided making her feel uncomfortable, but that did not change the reality of their infatuation. Keoki acted as if she was just another person, fully-dressed in business clothes. She felt irritated that he didn't even care to stay and swim because of her presence.

Kate sat on one of the poolside chairs and applied the sunscreen as she contemplated, *Was he embarrassed by his looks?* However, he seemed very comfortable with himself so she immediately dismissed the idea.

Inside, Keoki patted himself dry and threw on his shirt. He went to the kitchen, poured himself some orange juice, and walked into the main parlor, opening the bar to augment his juice. Looking past the bar, through the lightly tinted glass, he gazed on Kate as she applied lotion to her long, well-toned legs. They were tan by Kansas standards, but appeared to Keoki as pure ivory. She stood, unaware she was being observed, and applied the lotion to the upper portions of her legs, taking the cream all the way into the edge of her suit. Keoki recalled Michael telling him that his daughter was getting married later in the summer. As Keoki considered the situation, he also thought about the man who would be marrying her. In a disgusted tone, he blurted out, "Lucky Bastard!" As he pushed his frustration aside, he turned and went into the music room near the main entrance to the home.

Is he really that private? she continued in her thought process. Then the worry kicked in. *Have I lost it?* She didn't want to attract him, or anyone else for that matter. She was used to male attraction happening naturally and the prospect of a man *not* being interested in her was abnormal, even worrisome.

Perhaps he gets so many girls that he doesn't care, she suggested to herself. She quickly dismissed this thought because she had met the playboy type before and they were typically aggressive in their pursuits. As she finished with the lotion, Kate began to critique herself and found no visible change to her features. *Could it be that being engaged allows me to secrete some kind of pheromone that says, "Leave me alone; I'm taken,"* she asked herself. Even if this thought was true, she assured herself, she would be fine.

Yet, she wasn't fine. Kate liked attention from the opposite sex and never had any difficulties with refusing advances from men. She had perfected the art of making men feel good about themselves, while she simultaneously turned them down.

Keoki played a piece by Chopin on his piano as his driver opened the door for Michael and Babs. When they pulled up in the borrowed car, they noticed the large, dark car and presumed Keoki had arrived. They were about to ring the bell when the chauffer approached the door. Cautiously, they entered the home with the beautiful melancholy tones of Keoki's piano drawing them forward.

As soon as he realized his friends had arrived, Keoki jumped up and acted as the guest rather than the host. He grabbed his glass from atop the piano and wiped the accumulated moisture from the wood as he greeted the Fogarty's.

Michael and Keoki began to converse in a rapid fire fashion and seemed to cover a dozen subjects at once. To the annoyance of both men, Babs asserted herself into the conversation repeatedly. When Babs finally realized she was an interloper in the conversation, she inquired, "Where's Kate?"

From his seat, Keoki used his thumb to point behind himself. "She's in the pool," he answered. Babs then left to find her daughter.

Still in deep contemplation, Kate realized her emotions were scattered, and she would have to deal with her feelings of insecurity. Her desire to swim had dwindled, but she felt the need to continue with her original plan. As she began to walk down the steps into the sun-warmed water, she was saved from the activity by the voice of her mother.

Babs told Kate that her father and Keoki were in a separate room talking about plans for the week. She wanted Kate to dress up for a charity event in the evening which the "Hawaiian," as Babs also called him, was hosting. Babs wasn't sure what Keoki's role was in the upcoming event, but she knew this was an excellent opportunity to exhibit her "beauty queen" daughter.

"But Mom, I didn't bring any of my stuff!" Kate objected.

"I did; now come inside and get dressed. We'll have plenty of time to plan the evening." her mother instructed. The concept of "we" left something to be desired when it came time for Babs to work with someone else on planning an event. Kate obeyed begrudgingly, for she knew this game of dress-up would at least keep her from having to swim.

When Kate came back out of her room after changing out of the swimwear, she was dressed in the most casual and baggy clothes had she brought to Hawaii. She then found out what her mother had done. Keoki made the mistake of mentioning a charity luau he sponsored, which was to be held that evening. Babs immediately presumed they would want Kate to prance about as "Miss Kansas," a position she had relinquished months earlier. Nonetheless, Babs expected Kate to work the crowd and pose for pictures to "help" the fundraiser. Keoki simply invited his guests to enjoy the party; Babs interpreted his invitation as an obligation, and opportunity, to express her pride in Kate's accomplishments.

Keoki was backed into a corner and accepted Kate's assistance on behalf of the organization. He was put in an uncomfortable position, since he seemed to always be in control of every situation. This particular time, however, Babs found a way to run right over him.

When Babs went to look for Kate, Keoki sarcastically mentioned something to Michael about how he admired his ability to pick out his own clothes with a wife like her in attendance. After the remark, Michael felt a kinship with "the Hawaiian" and called him by name thereafter.

Michael was further surprised by Keoki when he discovered the trip was to be all vacation; Keoki wanted nothing more than to see Michael have fun. This tempered his freshly-gained appreciation for his friend, since Michael Fogarty enjoyed working. He told the managers at the plant he would be working for the entire week. Now, he was forced into a full week of not doing what he loved. The situation aggravated him, but he knew he could not afford to offend his gracious host. The fact Keoki had the power to ruin him was enough "work" and appeasing him at least gave the trip purpose. Enjoying himself, however, would take a bit more effort. In this case, Michael found his happiness in alcohol.

At the charity event, Babs and Michael went straight to the open bar and hardly moved from the stools until late in the evening. Kate was the gracious, albeit reluctant, hostess-assistant. The beachfront event went better with Kate in the role of hostess than anyone thought possible. The representatives of the charity repeatedly thanked Keoki for bringing Kate.

Everyone in attendance seemed to know Keoki. The children treated him as if he were a beloved uncle. They expressed pure joy at his presence, and he reciprocated their joyfulness with boisterous laughter. Japanese Americans bowed respectfully to him and spoke to him in the Japanese language. Polynesians and native Hawaiians acted familiar with Keoki; they treated him as a person with great wisdom. None of the guests seemed apprehensive to approach him. Most Americans would have been awkward with a very wealthy person, yet his wealth played no any part in their attitudes toward him.

The children, hearing-impaired Hawaiian children for whom the event was created, were very warm and loving to Kate. She responded to the little ones with her genuine care and attention. She knew no sign language, though by this time the practice of signing was a required subject in high schools all over the country. Her lack of ability to sign caused her some difficulty in graduating from college. She had taken time off of KU to serve as Miss Kansas and returned to complete just one semester. By the time of her return, standards changed and basic sign writing was required for her major. Kate requested and received a special exemption from the university in time to graduate.

Kate was able to comprehend their belabored efforts to speak and they were, for the most part, able to read her lips. She enjoyed doing this kind of work, especially with the children. While she attended the event out of deference to her mother who had put her in an uncomfortable position, she ended the evening secretly appreciative to her mother that she was pressured into the activity. The event, and at least one person in attendance, had an impact on the rest of her life.

Throughout her childhood, Kate was pushed into activities by her mother, and then found herself enjoying the dreaded activities afterward. She would have regretted not going along with her mother's plans. Once she was married to Alan, she knew her mother would no longer be on hand to push her into new surroundings and activities. Kate had a conscious expectation such direction from her mother would go away when her days in the pageants ended, but this event was a final reprise. She was already so nostalgic for the "show," she dedicated herself at that moment to throwing herself headlong into even the slightest shadow of these types of opportunities. *After all, I am marrying a politician, she said to herself.*

When the event ended, Keoki sat with the Fogarty's around a fire pit and shared casual conversation. Kate was finally able to take off the four pointed crown her mother insisted she wear for the night. Babs put the headpiece in her over-sized purse. Michael was drunk, but he was not a sloppy drunk. He was what people often refer to as a "happy drunk." He didn't drink heavily very often, but when he was intoxicated he was likely to smile, laugh and tell jokes. His jokes, unfortunately, tended to be very poor puns.

Babs, like her husband, was also inebriated. When Babs was drunk, she often became inquisitive. She would also abandon her usual habit of trying to control everyone and everything.

"Keoki seems like a very generous man," she volunteered to one of the men serving drinks.

"Yes," the man replied. "He is not only generous, but he is a very great man who truly cares about … the people."

"Maybe he should run for governor of Hawaii," Babs suggested.

The man's expression suddenly changed for reasons unknown to Babs. "That is something he would *never* do," the man retorted with clear defiance. After his remark, he quickly walked away.

Kate, on the other hand, had not had a drink all night. Earlier, she asked for a White Zinfandel; however, the bartender was not confident she was of legal drinking age and asked for identification. She intended to go to the car to get her ID but by the time she approached her mother to get the keys, Kate realized she would need to be the designated driver and decided to stick to club soda for the evening.

Keoki had been drinking, but he showed no visible signs of inebriation. He had a driver waiting anyway, if needed.

Michael began to query Keoki's gift of a vacation. Keoki simply stated, "I like you, Mike! I just thought you would enjoy the trip." The situation was really that simple. Extravagant expense, such as an impromptu trip thousands of miles from home, was a minimal consideration for Keoki. To him, this vacation was like offering an acquaintance a cold drink on a hot day. Michael accepted the trip graciously, and they didn't speak of Keoki's gift again.

Keoki's kindness was overwhelming, but he acted as if this trip was a simple afternoon excursion. His down-to-earth attitude gave other people the impression he could enjoy most anything. For Keoki, the trip was about having fun with people he thought would be good company.

The Forgarty family noticed that people not associated with the event were milling about on the beach. Babs inquired, "Why are people on your beach?"

Keoki explained, "It is not 'my' beach; there are no private beaches in Hawaii. We were able to close the beach for a short time during the event because the charity was a benefit for native Hawaiians. Otherwise, all beaches are open to the public. It's one of the few edicts the American conquerors retained from when our islands were a sovereign kingdom." Keoki's matter-of-fact expression at the impropriety of American rule over Hawaii shocked his guests. Perhaps his blunt statement was a reflection of his own inebriation; regardless, no one was willing to challenge the statement.

Babs hurried to change the subject. "So, do you live near a beach?"

"I suppose I'm too private for a beach house," Keoki confided. "I live on a mountainside, but I can see the ocean. The setting is much like your home this week." Of course, he was speaking of the house the Fogarty's were staying in for the vacation. For some reason, he could not keep from addressing the property as if the house was their possession.

"I've heard your home is spectacular!" Babs expressed.

"The press makes many assumptions, but they don't have a clue. No pictures, no public events, not even a dinner party has ever been held there."

"Sounds lonely," Kate commented.

Keoki looked at her with his large, warm eyes and responded, "I've had visitors, just nothing public."

Kate's curiosity was now getting the best of her. "Will you ever use the property for something public?" she inquired. "For something you believe in, like those wonderful children?"

"A party of that nature at my home would be a success but I'd have to be very committed to the project." Keoki contemplated the concept for a moment, and then said with a smirk, "I would need some time to clean things up before I did anything like that!"

Kate remembered how Alan's house had looked when she first visited, and how he must have picked up the mess while she took care of the horses. She imagined most single men must not be too concerned about keeping things neat until they have company. For the moment, she presumed he was speaking of cleaning up in a literal manner. She hadn't considered that Keoki had a large personal staff to keep his home in perfect condition; even though she knew he had two full-time people to take care of the home he had loaned to Kate and her parents.

Michael released a yawn and, to cover his embarrassment, told another of his puns: "Why can't a bicycle stand up on its own? Because it's two tired!" Keoki laughed heartily. Kate had heard this particular joke and all of her father's puns repeatedly, but found a new appreciation for his humor when someone actually laughed.

As the evening came to an end, Keoki told Kate how much he appreciated her efforts at the event. "If I can ever do anything to help you out, let me know." Their eye contact was momentarily intense, at least from his perspective. He pulled away from her gaze and quickly changed the subject. "I understand you're getting married soon. I'll send something … nice."

Without giving her the opportunity to respond, Keoki turned away. He spotted an elderly Hawaiian woman he must have known. Practically jumping from his chair to leave Kate, he cautiously and respectfully approached the woman. When he was noticed, she addressed him in what must have been the Hawaiian language. Keoki replied with dramatic respect; to Kate it seemed unnatural for him to show obeisance to anyone.

While Keoki conversed with others on the beach, Kate suggested to her parents that she should drive them home for the night. Kate decided her poolside concerns from earlier in the day were unfounded when she considered the deep gaze he gave into her eyes a few moments ago. She convinced herself the anxiety stemmed from a case of commitment jitters.

The rest of the week was quite pleasant. Kate and her mother planned much of the wedding during their stay in Hawaii. She had several conversations with Alan, who was surprisingly understanding about her trip to Hawaii.

Michael and Keoki went all over the island together but, as far as Michael knew, avoided seeing Keoki's home. One day, they went by helicopter to another one of the islands where life was still very primitive. The place was some kind of Hawaiian "reservation." The people on the island lived a lifestyle that was a re-creation of Hawaii before the Americans deposed their monarch and illegally took control of the islands. Michael was reminded of the Amish people who live in the countryside near Wichita. Living a simple lifestyle was not his preference, but the idea had an overwhelming appeal.

Every place they went, people would come to Keoki and speak with him in languages other than English. Ordinarily, they spoke in Hawaiian or Japanese but, in one case, the person spoke French. Michael had taken French in high school many years prior and had forgotten most of the language. Yet he understood enough to be unsettled by what he thought he heard from the one man who seemed not to understand Hawaiian or Japanese. Michael decided that he must not have correctly interpreted the man. *Surely they aren't serious about having a kingdom in Hawaii?* he wondered.

Michael was sure these people could speak English, but chose deliberately not to in his presence. Years later, Michael questioned how much of the trip was designed to be "fun," and how much was cover for Keoki's secretive activities.

What Michael also did not realize at the time was that he actually *did* visit Keoki's estate on the vacation. The area didn't look like a typical billionaire's home, if typical exists. They were on the property, but Keoki never said so, and Michael was just along for the ride.

Keoki's home was not a single building; it was more like a village. The estate looked like an exaggerated version of a Polynesian village. Similar to the way national parks used to build hotels and lodges to look rustic yet were dramatically oversized with all conveniences integrated, Keoki's home was deceptively primitive.

His property was made up of over two dozen structures. One would, on first look, presume this to be an old village. A closer look, however, revealed the estate lacked nothing. Structures, which appeared small from a distance with a rustic "hut" look, were actually quite large and thoroughly modern.

One such building looked to be a simple shelter from afar, but the door and windows were so large that the perspective of the whole building was altered. That particular building housed an Olympic-sized swimming pool, a full-sized basketball court, and a bowling alley.

Keoki also had a building that housed his main kitchens and dining area. The room could easily seat two to three hundred people, but ordinarily accommodated only Keoki, his staff, and a date.

His private quarters were further up the mountain, hidden from view by the rainforest. Here he could survey the property from the lanai outside his massive bedroom suite. A beautiful waterfall cascaded into the room; the stream of the fall poured into a series of pools. The natural pools were only steps from Keoki's bed and could be seen from his bedside beneath the jungle canopy. A stream eventually meandered through the "village" and then into a lava tube where it, presumably, found its way to the sea.

Keoki had created a complex set of entities to purchase separate properties and never consolidated the lands. Nothing was put into his name. A great effort was made to prevent the property from being public record. The construction was completed at the edge of legality. In some cases, they were well beyond that edge. To protect his anonymity, he paid excess prices to complete some of the construction without permits anytime the permitting would become public. In most cases, only owners of neighboring properties were required to be notified, and effectively, Keoki was notifying himself. Several of the original property owners continued to live on the estate in Keoki's employ.

Michael was not privy to such information. He was only taken as far as the areas of the "village" near the main road. From that vantage point, one could not tell this was anything more than a simple village inhabited by poor Hawaiians. There were so many people in the area, Michael was given the impression Keoki was just visiting friends or distant relatives rather than his employees.

While they visited the property, Keoki was clearly not giving direction to anyone. Every conversation was filled with hugs, slaps on the back, and rambunctious laughter. Keoki was having fun the whole time. There were enough events between conversations that the trip was even fun for Michael the workaholic.

The rest of the vacation, the two businessmen went snorkeling and rode on zip lines through the rainforests. Keoki surfed while Michael watched him slice the waves. One evening, Keoki took Michael to a party at a typically extravagant home of a wealthy friend where young ladies hung all over them. Michael did all he could to avoid their blatant advances. Keoki, however, accepted graciously since he departed to private quarters on more than one occasion.

When all was said and done, the week in Hawaii for Babs and Kate was a productive occasion where they were able to plan the wedding and spend needed quality time together. For Michael, on the other hand, the week was entirely recreational.

Keoki was an ongoing enigma to Michael. He never seemed to work, but he was phenomenally successful. He was private, yet personable, and constantly in public places. He was a member of the exclusive club of billionaires and allowed himself to spend generously on an acquaintance like Michael, yet didn't eat or dress in a lavish manner. Michael observed that Keoki had the opportunity to have tremendous influence on the events around him, but appeared at all times aloof.

What Michael didn't perceive was that for Keoki, or any person of extraordinary wealth, the world does not revolve around the rich, but it might as well. Whatever happened in Hawaii, the Pacific Rim, or the US at large would be influenced, if not manipulated, by him. Comprehension on the subject was not easy; it was hard to tell if such events were actually caused by the likes of Keoki, or if he merely had a ringside seat to the events. Either way, Keoki Nawahiokalaniopu'u didn't have to strive to influence events. In fact, he would have to exert himself strenuously to avoid such influence, if avoidance were his goal.

It wasn't.

CHAPTER 3 • **THE WEDDING**

Mr. and Mrs. Michael Fogarty
request the honour of your presence
at the marriage of their daughter
Katherine Anne

to

Alan Martin Cassell
on the eighteenth of August
at two o'clock in the afternoon
at the Fogarty home in Wichita, KS

ALAN STAYED WITH THE Fogartys in Wichita for a few days prior to the wedding after the planning was completed. Babs had a white pergola built out from the back of the Fogarty home to the pool. She had always wanted one, and this was the occasion that made the construction "necessary." The pergola would serve as the aisle for the bride to walk up during the ceremony. Babs planned for the minister to stand at pool's edge. At the far end of the pool were tall, narrow coniferous trees which created a classic backdrop. Two white tents adjoined the pergola on each side and were set to protect the nearly five hundred guests from the searing August sun.

Alan had visited Wichita before, but had not stayed overnight on previous visits. This was his opportunity to become a member of the family, with its joys and quirks. When he visited, Alan was never alone with any of Kate's family members without her at hand. He still found himself to be more a part of Kate's family than he did his own.

Alan's attentiveness to Kate was disrupted the evening before the wedding for practical reasons.

Kate told Alan, "Honey, sometimes I have a hard time falling asleep when I'm a bit anxious about the next day ... you understand?"

"Of course," he replied. "Is there anything I can do to help you relax? Perhaps a bit of physical exertion would help."

"Alan!" she exclaimed with a startled and high-pitched, yet low volume, voice. "My parents could have heard you!"

Alan had a sincerely quizzical look and merely said, "What?" Even as the word came out, he understood what she was suggesting; he held the look to maintain the façade.

"Darling, I'm going to shower and change into my pajamas so I can begin to wind down. I know the time is early for getting ready for bed, but I need to start now. If I don't, I might not fall asleep tonight. You'll be fine for a few minutes by yourself," Kate assured him. "If you want, you can visit with my mom in my sis's old room. She uses the space for scrapbooking now."

"I don't think so," Alan quickly replied.

Kate half-giggled at Alan's retort and whispered, "Well, if you want to avoid a conversation with her, you can just pop in on my dad. He's across the hall in his study."

"Maybe I will. You don't have to worry about leaving me alone with your parents for a few minutes. I think I'll survive whatever they have planned," Alan jested.

Kate then ran up the stairs and into her room. The massive dwelling had become eerily silent as night fell on the home. The Fogarty's house was built for a very large family which, at the current time, had only Michael, Babs, Kate and Alan in residence.

Sitting alone, Alan contemplated the distinctions between Kate's family and his own. His father and mother were long separated, and he never knew for sure where his father was located at any given moment. His mother struggled with her health and complained about one thing or another whenever he contacted her. His only sister, Deena, was much younger than him; they didn't really have much of a common connection. She was regularly in and out of relationships, which seemed designed more to bandage her problems associated with her father rather than to actually find love.

Even with its quirks and flaws, Kate's family was still traditional and functional. Kate was the youngest of six children, with three sisters and two brothers. The sibling closest to her age was five years older than her. Since her early teens, Kate was a de-facto "only child," since her brothers and sisters had all moved on to married lives. She was an aunt by the age of seven.

Her parents were both protective and fond of Kate. Her siblings felt Kate was the favorite, but they seemed to hold a grudge against their parents rather than against her. Kate had nothing but the strongest affection for her brothers and sisters.

After only moments alone, Alan decided to take Kate's advice and visit with Michael. He could hear Babs through the wall as she made a racket in her "scrapbook" room. Alan expected she might pounce upon him for confirmation that she had made the proper decision on some last-minute detail of the wedding. Babs was fully in "control mode" since she was in charge of the wedding at hand. As he stepped lightly toward the closed door of Michael's study, he noticed two dogs as they walked up to Babs from behind; her back was to the door as she worked at her craft table. He was not aware the Fogartys had dogs since he had not seen them on his prior visits.

Against his better judgment, he blurted out, "A Lassie-dog like the old TV shows!" The other dog appeared to be some kind of mongrel; he had a blue-grey speckled coat.

Babs took note of the opportunity and rhetorically asked, "Isn't he a perfect example of a sable and white?"

She glanced at the bewildered look on his face and told him, "'Sable' refers to the tan-brown color, which is typically found on the coats of collies."

Alan nodded and asked Babs, "Interesting ... Is the other dog a mixed breed? Or some other—"

Aghast, Babs interrupted, "God no! He's a purebred collie called a 'blue merle.' There are four color types of collies, and blue merle is not even the rarest type ..." She continued to blather about the details of collie breeding and awards in the dogs' ancestry. Alan deeply regretted he had spoken at all. He desperately wished he had just snuck into Michael's study. While Babs rambled, Alan wondered if maybe Michael hid in his room to avoid his wife.

Kate appeared, after what seemed to be an eternity, wearing red satin pajamas Alan didn't know she owned. The torture of Babs' incessant prattle about her prize dogs was suddenly made pleasant as he contemplated the virtues of his fiancé's evening attire. Though conservative in style, loose-fitting and fully modest, the outfit still gave Alan a pleasant perspective of Kate's physical virtues. Most notable was the fact that Kate did not have a bra on under the top; her breasts stood firm and elevated against the satin. Her nipples were clearly visible through the glossy material. Alan was surprised Babs took no notice of them since he could hardly look elsewhere.

Kate took pleasure as she teased him, inserting herself into the mundane conversation. "Mother was quite successful at breeding and showing collies for several years."

Somehow the quip broke Alan from the spellbinding effect of the new garb on Kate. "So why did you quit?" he inquired.

Kate wished to retain his attention and answered for her mother, declaring in a most ill-humored manner, "She gave up on showing them and began showing me instead."

Alan didn't miss a beat. "Makes sense … upgrading from dogs to a real fox!" he boldly pronounced, showering praise on his fiancée, while simultaneously defusing a comment that could have led to problems with his future mother-in-law. After the comment, his smile was so intense that she just put her hand on his cheek and gave him a quick, firm kiss followed by a couple of pats on his cheek.

Together, they stepped out of the room to the hallway where he softly voiced, "I like the pajamas but they look hot for August."

Kate looked around, and when she was confident her mother was otherwise occupied, she purred, "I'm glad you like them. You look pretty hot yourself today."

Alan wore nothing but a simple pair of jeans, a black t-shirt, and a pair of deck shoes with no socks. He had no idea how Kate found such simple attire attractive.

He responded, even softer and in her ear, "We could always explore the subject upstairs."

Kate smiled and pulled Alan close, "Yes, we could. Don't go up at the same time I do. Okay?"

Alan held her close and nodded. He moved to give her a kiss when Michael's study door suddenly flew open.

"Alan, my boy! Come on in here. Have a cigar and some brandy with me."

Alan was taken aback by the phrase "my boy." This was the first time Michael had referred to him in that manner; he took the nickname as a form of adoption. Eager to be accepted by Michael, he nodded, "Okay … Dad?"

Kate, out of view, silently mouthed to Alan, "Don't be long."

Alan stepped into the dark-paneled study. The broad leather chairs and walls filled with books seemed almost stereotypical of a wealthy man's study. The very idea of cigars was offensive to the non-smoking Alan, but Michael's high quality cigar wafted a very pleasant aroma. "How about just the brandy?"

Michael gave a generous pour to his son-in-law-to-be and directed himself to the task at hand. "I believe you love Kate, and I trust you want to be a good husband to her."

"Yes, sir."

"As you might presume, I love my daughter. She is my last child and I don't ever want her hurt."

"Of course not."

"Alan, son, you need to know her better than you do. Only years of living together will give you a true perspective of what she needs from you."

"Any advice would be appreciated."

"I don't know if I'm the best person to give relationship advice. You can tell that my relationship with my wife is a little strained at times. But Kate and her mother are very different. Kate has an immaturity, a result of her childhood with too much sheltering by me and too much control by her mother, her riding coaches, and her pageant directors. Maybe it's not a result of any of those; maybe it's just who she grew to be. I don't know for sure."

To challenge the premise, Alan asserted, "I don't see immaturity. She's sharp as a tack and a far better scholar than me. She makes decisions in life without any fear."

"Yeah, and she looks grown up too! That isn't what I'm talking about. She has an ongoing childishness that exposes itself from time to time. She never expressed the immaturity of a rebellious teenager like her oldest brother. No, Kate has the unquestioning obedience of a child of single digit age. Kate is good, in my opinion, but not because of moral sense.

"I think I was kind and pleasant in her youth, but I'm sure I wasn't as affectionate as fathers are expected to be for a healthy relationship. I think she was sensitive about my … distance. Oh, I don't know. All the psychobabble we hear these days. Maybe I did things right; maybe I didn't. She'll have to cope and anything that goes wrong will be your problem soon, not mine."

Alan took in each word with silence. Michael's uncertainty seemed out of character for the normally hyper-confident businessman. Alan was pleased Michael was confiding his feelings to him. He also had sympathy for Michael, since he struggled with the very concept of being a good father. Alan imagined himself in the same shoes and expected he would fashion himself to be the same kind of father as Michael had been, especially if he and Kate ever had a daughter. *Kate wants lots of kids, just like her parents,* he thought to himself.

After a short pause, Michael continued, "I'll tell you this, Alan. I was very strict with the other kids, but I weakened in my resolve by the time Kate came along. I ended up regretting my strict standards with the older children, considering Kate's character qualities. She was a problem-free child for the most part. But, as a child, she was particularly swift to emotional outbursts, even beyond the norm.

"When Kate was little, her mother raised dogs—bred dogs—as a hobby. I heard her prattle on about her precious dogs a few minutes ago."

"Yes, sir," Alan confirmed with a grin and a nod.

Michael continued, "The collies were basically a family project, and they were good show dogs. Babs even achieved a profit for a couple years. Kate always participated with Babs' dogs, but she wanted a dog of her own. She decided to pick a dog that wasn't a collie. She chose a Dalmatian and named him 'Speck.'"

"That sounds like Kate," replied Alan. "She would want to pick out a dog that was different."

"That's right, different from what her mother would want, possibly to gain control over the situation." Michael agreed. He then quickly continued: "Speck ran off one day never to be seen alive again. After we looked for him for several days, we finally gave up our search. Then, nearly a week later, we received a call telling us that Speck had been found; he'd been hit by a car earlier that day. She insisted on going with her mother and brother, who drove our pick-up truck to retrieve Speck. I was at the plant, of course.

"Once they arrived, Kate leapt out of the car and grabbed the dead dog on the sidewalk. The incident happened near downtown, here in Wichita. Even though she had been warned he was dead, it was like she didn't realize the finality until that moment. It was her first experience with death."

"Those moments happen to every kid, but I can't imagine what she must have been feeling when she held him in her arms," Alan reflected, shaking his head in empathy as he tried to picture the scene.

Michael nodded in agreement then retold the event with greater detail: "Her mother told me Kate yelled out 'Speck!' at the top of her lungs as she ran to him. She dropped to her knees when she reached her dog and pulled his head up into her lap. She wept uncontrollably for as long as her mother and brother dared allow. After they came home, I created a coffin and burial plot for Speck at the back of our property. I suppose Kate showed you the bronze marker I put out there?"

"Yes, she did, and she told me much of this story but I appreciate your perspective. It's a terribly sad thing for a little girl to have to experience." Alan responded, although he thought Michael was being overly sensitive about Kate's reaction to the death of her dog.

"But that's not the entire story, Alan," Michael continued. "You see, this was not an abnormal outburst for a child of her age. I expect any little girl would act just as she did, if not with even more emotion. Once Speck was buried, Kate seemed to have coped with the loss.

"However, a few months later we took a family vacation to Mexico. Road trips were becoming popular at the time, and riding in a car with your family was a nice departure from flying everywhere. Long gone were the days of bribing police for safe passage. Street beggars and criminals targeted tourists in Mexico when I was a kid, but that had changed as the country prospered. My plan was to drive home as the vacation time was nearing an end. I never really liked vacations, but families need the togetherness once in a while," Michael advised.

"The trip included driving one of the nation's most scenic drives in Texas, and then into the national park, before returning home. We stopped in a small town on the Rio Grande not far from Big Bend. In that little border town, we needed to find a place to eat. Only one restaurant was open, which was located inside a fine-looking hotel." Michael stopped the storytelling and said, "This part is funny, you'll like it!"

Alan leaned forward with expectation and listened.

"Most of the family ordered Mexican food from the menu, knowing they'd soon be across the border where the next meal would most likely be American cuisine. Kate, being a precocious little girl, was not shy about the fact that she was tired of Mexican food. When the waiter came to take our order, she pronounced loudly, 'I want a HAM-BURGER!' The waiter expressed something that we mistook as understanding and went away.

"When everyone's order came, all looked fine and we began to eat. Her brother, Christopher, mentioned that his mother's *Chile Relleno* looked like a fried rat. Kate's eyes grew large as big as dinner plates, with concern. Babs scolded him for the comment, and he didn't say another word during the meal." Alan gave a grin, lightly amused at the comment by Christopher.

"Kate then began to mention that her hamburger didn't taste very good. At first, I discounted her concerns. Then, I noticed her food didn't look right either. I asked Kate to let me examine the hamburger up close and, after she gave me her plate, I pronounced that she had gotten exactly what she ordered—a burger made of ham! All of us began to laugh uncontrollably, except Kate of course."

"Really? Ground ham on a bun!" Alan chuckled. "Sounds terrible."

"Well, Kate's sister, Jill, then made the unfortunate comment, 'It's a good thing that you didn't order a HOT DOG!'

"Kate just screamed in disgust at the thought, and her mourning for Speck was revived in a surprising way. She ran from the table and out the door before anyone could get themselves up. I rushed to catch up, and finally did about half of a block away. Not only running and crying, she was screaming in absolute agony.

"I swept her up when I reached her. At first, she kicked and struggled, but then she quickly grabbed hold of me with a death grip. Kate continued screaming, so I found a bench and sat with her outside the hotel until she calmed down. Babs came out, but I sent her back in to finish dinner with the other children as I consoled Kate.

"After some time had passed, she finally asked me a question in nearly indecipherable words mixed with crying and all the fluids that a five-year-old emits when crying: 'Why did Speck hate me so much that he would rather die than stay with me?'" Michael paused, his face tight with emotion.

"It broke my heart to hear such a thing from her, and even more so that she had held that thought in for so long. Of course, I did all I could to comfort her, but I wasn't very good at doing so. I really couldn't do anything to change the original problem of her dog's death.

"You see, Kate felt abandoned by Speck. He was just being a dog; not concerned about anything but the squirrel, rabbit, or other dog he was chasing at the moment of his disappearance. She wanted his full and undivided attention. She had wanted to be his everything."

Michael stopped his story and hoped Alan understood his point. He took a sip of his brandy and quietly smoked his cigar, lost in thought.

Alan considered the story, not sure why Michael felt the need to relive that moment in time. Alan was glad to know any story, every story, of Kate's youth. "When did she start riding horses?" he asked.

"On the return trip, while we were in Oklahoma. I'll tell you the story but, first, I want to explain the reason I told you about Speck. If you get distracted, don't pay her enough attention, get too involved in your career … she may take that as abandonment."

"She was five!" objected Alan.

"Yeah, a daughter is always five to a father." Michael paused and then continued, "Anyway, we visited a stable and decided to rent horses for a family ride. I expected Kate would ride with me, but she insisted on having her own mount. Her talent for horse riding was discovered that day. She took to the horse as Mozart did to music. Babs and I knew we needed to help Kate develop her horsemanship abilities."

Michael paused then returned after a moment to his intended purpose. "You just have to find the balance. She'll depend on you for some things and expect you to let her do other things for herself. Give her your full attention, Alan, but always respect her."

Alan could not imagine anything less. *Attentiveness to someone as beautiful and joyous as Kate will be easy*, thought Alan.

They sat for a few minutes in silence as they quietly contemplated their conversation. Alan had finally bonded with Michael and was glad to have a father he felt he could respect. Michael had misgivings, but was pleased Alan had listened to the story.

Alan knew the conversation lasted more than forty-five minutes, and he was eager to take Kate up on her invitation. He excused himself for bed and feigned sleepiness with an exaggerated yawn. He went to Kate's room instead of his own. He heard a sound from down the hall and presumed she was in the bathroom.

Earlier, Kate had let herself into the guest room—Alan's room—instead of her own. She slipped into his bed and waited patiently. She had erred in her analysis of her own energy level and fell asleep as soon as she snuggled in against his pillow.

The wedding morning came earlier than either person expected. Both bride and groom were sleeping very well until Babs barged into Kate's room and screeched at the unexpected sight of a very male posterior in her daughter's bed. Alan was instantly alerted and jumped in the bed as he began to turn toward the door. Babs sounded an even greater alarm at the prospect of an even more revealing vision of her son-in-law-to-be. Fortunately, Alan instinctively pulled covers with him. "Babs! You could've knocked!" he exclaimed.

"Well!" Babs began cautiously, "I presumed you two had … but not in my house … and not today! … before … I … I … Just don't …"

Kate, wearing the pajamas she had put on the previous evening, was now visible to Alan behind her mother. She was outside the bedroom door making hand signs to him. True to his talent, Alan didn't miss a beat.

"Babs … Kate isn't here. She slept in my room, and I slept here. We wanted to fall asleep where the other had slept; we thought it might be nice to get accustomed to the scent of each other at night." The statement was the biggest white lie he had ever told. Actually, it may have been the biggest lie he ever told of any hue.

After his comment to her mother, Kate disappeared back into Alan's room without Babs knowing he had even seen Kate. He continued, "I'm sorry, Babs, we should have told you. I don't think either of us expected you to come in here with such intentions."

Babs apologized, but didn't believe her ears. She went to Alan's room and knocked on the door. Kate called for her to come in with the groggiest voice she could muster. When Babs asked why Kate was in the guest room, she gave the same story as Alan. Babs not only believed the tale, but wondered whether or not they had actually saved themselves throughout their courtship.

The day went into full swing with a whirlwind of activity. Neither bride nor groom ate a full meal all day. They, somehow, managed to resume their appointed rooms without seeing each other again before the ceremony.

Jim Cherry, as Alan's best man, spent every moment after he arrived with Alan. "Alan, I figured I would have to steady you, but you seem so calm."

With a confident smile Alan replied, "I guess I just know I have the right one. Why be nervous?"

At that very moment, Alan nicked himself with his razor.

"Oops, spoke too soon! Guess you are just a bit nervous, huh?" said Jim.

Kate's room, on the other hand, was the busy one with no less than five women in there at any given time. Ever present was her college roommate and maid of honor, Joanna Stevens.

When the minister arrived, Babs took him aside for a chat. "I'm worried about Kate and Alan." she began. "They haven't ever … you know. Do you believe that it is healthy for a couple to have not ever slept together before they get married?"

"Of course it's healthy! The reverse could cause long-term problems for them," the reverend responded.

"Oh, you're the old fashioned type. Well, I believe a couple should make sure they're compatible before they make such a commitment." Babs' lack of church experience became quite obvious to the pastor through her comments.

"I'm sure they will be just fine," the pastor insisted. He took their apparent chastity as a positive sign, believing them to be more devout than reality suggested. "We did have a few counseling sessions but I'll have another brief word with them before the ceremony."

The moment finally arrived.

A string quartet played. On one side of the congregation stood tables and the serving line for food; on the other side of the yard, closer to the home, were the tables for gifts. Kate was strikingly beautiful in a very traditional dress. Alan was confident, cool, and as sharp as any groom has ever looked on his wedding day. He had no jitters and except for a slight red line on his neck, he seemed the picture of confidence.

Thankfully the event was recorded, since neither the bride nor the groom remembered anything around them. Once their eyes met, everything else was a blur. He could not keep his eyes off her, and she actually blushed at his intense gaze. Kate was amazed by the love he showed he had for her. He asked so little and paid complete attention to her.

The formal part of the wedding was complete after a long while, and then the festivities began. Her father gave them a central heating and air system for their home. The gift went without fanfare as a courtesy to Alan. The old farmhouse never had a central system, just gas floor furnaces for the winter and window screens for the summer.

Michael also provided the honeymoon, along with the cost of the wedding. He was quite generous, or perhaps he was just accommodating his wife who was about to become an empty nester with him.

Alan stood to toast his wife. The speech came out awkwardly, but he had sweet intentions. The moment was not his finest since he was a bit overwhelmed.

"To Kate, my wife ..." Alan said with an unexpected pause. The emotion hit him when he verbalized of the word "wife." He brushed moisture from the corner of his eye and continued, "Wow! I didn't expect to get myself choked up on that wonderful word."

The assembled guests laughed lightly as he continued: "I am the most fortunate and, in a way, the most pitiable man alive. Any other husband can express his appreciation for his ... beloved," he said, changing his intended word from "wife" to "beloved" as to avoid the previous emotional response, "by telling her she is beautiful. Doing so proves his love as he overlooks some imperfection. In my case, I can tell you Kate that you are the most beautiful woman in the world, and few, perhaps none present, will consider my statement as any kind of exaggeration. If there are words to express your beauty, I do not know them. Perhaps there are ways to tell you of the depths of my love, but I wouldn't know where to start. Perhaps there is a language to articulate your virtues, but if there is I am not fluent. In my frailty of speech I can only say 'I love you.'"

She rose to toast him. "Alan, my love, my husband ... I don't find myself surprised to say the word 'husband,' since you are the man I knew I would love long before we met when I was just a little girl. It was as if you were written on my heart. You spoke of some perfection in me that everyone here knows not to be true. Yet I know you have that blinding love I need you to have for me. I see a man who is not perfect, yet perfectly matched to me. I believe that providence brought us together. I don't expect any better words, just a better understanding of the words 'I love you.'"

The party continued as the couple dashed into the house to change and leave for the honeymoon. Kate chose to honeymoon in a place she had been three times, but was new to Alan. The newlyweds went to Disney World in Florida.

She spent the week acting as the child she had never ceased to be, and he as the child he was never permitted to be.

While a less than typical choice, and less luxurious than her family wanted for her, Disney World was the best choice by far for them than any other destination. In the mornings, they rose as little kids eager to get to the park. They played on rides, and they danced when they heard any music. After lunch, they found the sun too warm and returned to their suite across the lake to rest. Those afternoon rest times were found to be both playful and exhausting. They returned to the parks in the evening, where they spent their time in calm appreciation for each other. They ate in international restaurants and sipped wine by the waterside as the festivities and fireworks called another perfect day to an end.

After they returned from Florida, the honeymoon ended, yet continued at the same time. The return flight to Wichita, the drive to Crawford County, the new air conditioning system, basically all proceedings seemed a natural extension of the trip. Kate found work at a library in Joplin, which gave her a forty mile plus commute each way. Alan was ordinarily home upon her return with dinner prepared and a smile on his face.

His work was not exactly full-time since he no longer needed to be as studious; perhaps he was not putting as much energy into his job as he had in the past because he now had another priority—Kate. After a few months, he was determined to increase his income and took on some substitute teaching opportunities in the Pittsburg Public School System.

Kate also found the chance to go up to Kansas City from time to time to model for local newspaper ads and early morning television. She was also flown to the coast a few times for modeling jobs, but the agency stopped calling to offer placement after she didn't take to the shoots well.

Alan also purchased a self-serve laundry and an automatic car wash, both near the college campus. Every day, he went to the businesses and worked on routine maintenance and collected the money. Both businesses were old and worn when he bought them, but he worked hard to bring back some of their lost luster.

These times were going to be remembered as the best days of their lives. Neither knew why they were drawn to do more; their needs were met, and they lived a satisfied life. Yet, as time passed, they both followed the natural course of life. Each of them striving for more of everything. After nearly a year, Kate was offered a job on campus in the media center at the university in Pittsburg. She joyfully accepted what would be the last job of her life.

Alan faced re-election that year as well. His only opponent was a student at PSU who didn't even campaign. The opponent was a Democrat in a Republican-leaning district from a neighboring town in Missouri; he had only moved into the district a few months prior to the election. Alan took the race seriously because he knew no other way. He won with nearly eighty percent of the vote, but his popularity would be tested.

CHAPTER 4 • ALASKA

"America is fast approaching the mark in which every major world power in history has either collapsed or, at a minimum, lost its world leadership and power."

—Chuck Baldwin

E VEN AS LIFE MOVED FORWARD for Alan, Kate, and most Americans, a lawsuit was filed in US District Court by an Alaska citizen against the United States of America. *Jones v. USA* was developed by a group called "Sovereignty Watch." Sovereignty Watch worked hard to expose what it believed were "anti-American" activities by the state department. In this case, they opposed activities by the department to transfer some uninhabited islands near the Bering Straight from the USA to Russia. The islands in question were closer to Russia than to mainland Alaska. The property, claimed by Russia since the Czarist days, was the legal property of the United States Government.

The state department argued the islands would be convenient to transfer to Russia because they were an expense to defend with no significant resources or population.

Sovereignty Watch, on the other hand, opposed similar transfers in the past, but took a unique approach this time. The organization held that the islands had strategic value to American security and had great natural resources, which were currently untapped. They argued the US Government had no power to sign away property within the jurisdiction of any member state.

The government of Alaska took no action on the subject of the proposed transfer of land. The governor was in favor of the transfer because of the cost to the state for policing not only the islands, but the waters that surrounded them. Fishermen worked in American waters near the islands, but under the proposed deal the waters would be made international. Other leaders in Alaska publicly agreed on the issue at hand.

Sovereignty Watch built the case on two points. First, the Constitution stated that the US Government cannot transfer any geographic part of one state to another without the agreement of the legislature of the first state. The long-accepted understanding of this provision was that such transfer could not be done to politically divide a member state against the wishes of the first state. The organization claimed Alaska had not given explicit permission and the transfer was to another "state," the state of Russia. They argued the constitutional provision was not limited only to member states of the USA.

The other half of the challenge was founded on the accepted principle of the union being perpetual and indivisible. They had no specific constitutional support on the matter, but expected the court would accept the premise and rule on the implications. In reality, they did not expect to win since the legal strength and persuasiveness of the state department is historically significant in the courtroom. Sovereignty Watch raised public awareness of the action to stall the transfer until the public had the opportunity to contact members of the Senate who might block the treaty by refusing ratification; unfortunately, the legal challenge was filed after the president had signed off on the document.

Sovereignty Watch did not file the suit in their own name since they lacked legal standing. The organization found an Alaska citizen, Randolph Jones, who volunteered to have the matter filed in his name. The case alleged the federal government was abusing Jones' rights by reducing the jurisdiction of his state without due process. Jones was a fisherman who possessed his own boat he used to navigate the cold, rich waters of the area in question. He believed the transfer ultimately endangered him and his livelihood by removing the waters he regularly inhabited from the US to Russia. The fear centered on Russia, who had no specific obligation to declare the waters to be international and, therefore, gave them the opportunity to restrict access at will. Additionally, if something happened to Jones' boat while in the area, and he needed to beach it to save the lives of his crew, he would be in violation of foreign soil with all

Alaska

the legal implications having entered onto foreign land without permission.

Problems arose in Sovereignty Watch's efforts as they attempted to create positive publicity. Jones was known as a member of the Alaska Independence Party, or AIP. The AIP was certainly a minority party since the Republicans held a clear majority of voter registrations in the state. However, Walter Hickel had won the governorship of the state as a member of the AIP many years prior. Todd Palin, husband of one-time Governor Sarah Palin, had also been a member of the AIP for seven years, which partially overlapped his wife's political career.

Not all members of the AIP supported secession for the state; however, state secession was the primary factor for the founding of AIP, which had always been a states' rights oriented party.

In 2006, adequate signatures were collected to force a public vote on secession, but the state supreme court blocked the vote. This action of the court to prohibit Alaskans from expressing their opinion on the matter encouraged many voters to change their affiliation to the AIP. Polling at the time suggested secession would have failed in 2006, but a backlash was created by the heavy-handedness of the court. That backlash grew through the following decades.

The national press dismissed the *Jones v. USA* case as an effort of a "fringe racist group trying to secede from the Union." The presumption was secessionists were racist, or segregationists, and that the AIP was made of secessionists, which Jones was not. That presumption was not overcome by Mr. Jones' heredity of mixed race. His father was black with ancestry which included Americans of slave heritage and American Indians; his mother was American of British descent.

Sovereignty Watch did not obtain the public favor they desired from the case. The organization was openly opposed to any secessionist movement, but Sovereignty Watch was forevermore associated with the AIP and similar movements. The federal court decision on *Jones v. USA* did not take long. The verdict was a surprise to observers and caused dramatic implications for the future. The court determined the argument the US could not give part of Alaska to Russia without explicit approval was moot. Therefore, the Alaskan legislature approved the transfer and the governor signed the bill.

The second issue assumed the current American union as perpetual. The

59

court, like the state department, could have affirmed the transfer of uninhabited islands was not a violation of the union. Instead, the court declared the union's permanency could not be inferred from the Constitution. After about two hundred years, a federal court finally spoke on the issue widely considered to have been decided by the Civil War; the decision opposed what all observers expected.

Although *Jones v. USA* was not framed as a legal precedent, nonetheless, those who favored its result used the case as precedent in the realm of public opinion.

CHAPTER 5 • COFFEE GROUNDS

"Democracies have ever been spectacles of turbulence and contention; have ever been found incompatible with personal security or the rights of property, and have in general been as short in their lives as they have been violent in their deaths."

—James Madison

ALAN WAS CHOSEN AS President of the Kansas Association of Counties in the last year of his first term. Since the position brought significant opportunities for Alan to help his constituents, this was expected to guarantee his re-election. The position also offered him a powerful platform for local government within the state legislature. The association handled legislative affairs with a full-time staff, but Alan's youthful looks and articulate speech made him quite the asset. This opportunity therefore provided him the experience he needed to work with state government.

Alan was elected as chairman of the county commission when he was sworn in for his second term. Early in his first term, he had aggravated the other two commissioners with his single-minded approach to county business. However, after he was married, Alan settled his political pace down and the other commissioners became more accepting. In actuality, he was a distracted newlywed. Now in his second term, with his wife working locally and his businesses in a stable state, he was ready to dig his heels in again.

In the spring, two years into his second term, there was more rainfall than usual throughout the region. In late March, a particular storm cell stalled between Parsons and Pittsburg. The county's Emergency Response Team, Alan's pet project, was activated under the direction of the sheriff. All the streams in the county were close to or above flood levels. Several parts of the county were put under evacuation orders. After calls by the governor, and a subsequent proclamation by the President of the United States, the university opened up space for emergency lodging and the Federal Emergency Management Agency (FEMA) set up shop in the county.

Although the rain was ongoing, there were no lives lost, or at continuing risk, due in part to the efficient efforts of FEMA. Three creeks, which converged in the western portion of the county, overran their banks and flooded nearby farms, causing most roads outside the cities to become closed. When first evacuated, the farmers from the area were informed this was a temporary situation.

By the second week in April, the residents in the western portion of the county, Alan's constituents, were eager to have access to their property; their homes needed protection, and livestock needed to be saved. The "experts" claimed the area was not safe to be inhabited by the general public. Alan accepted the logic human lives should not be risked for animals or property. Yet, some of the farmers merely wanted to move their livestock from lower lying pastures to higher land.

Once the rains stopped, Alan lobbied for access to the land for property owners. Despite the cessation of the rain, floodwaters still rose on the farmlands. Alan, as a government official, was allowed on site for inspection purposes. He discovered some basic construction to shore up washed out roadways would create a situation that could permit safe access. He spoke with the emergency experts who agreed with his assessment. The other commissioners, however, hesitated to do the work without secured funding from FEMA.

Alan contended, "It makes no sense to wait for federal money to arrive before we do the work; the people are hurting *now*. These repairs are something we can do ourselves, so why wait? This is the type of situation local government excels in. Therefore, we should not delay and start rebuilding the roads immediately."

He argued at length with the other commissioners, but to no avail. Finally, Alan decided to take his case to the people. He went on a second inspection visit to the property, this time accompanied by a camera crew from the local television station.

As the camera recorded, he asserted, "Just a small expenditure by the county can prevent massive financial losses by the residents of our county. How do we justify just sitting back and allowing our neighbors' property to be further damaged when those losses can be prevented in the first place? What's being suggested is that it's fine to waste a federal dollar to save a county dime and property rights don't really matter! Well, I can't and I won't."

His fellow commissioners did not like what they had viewed; they figured Alan was using the event as a publicity tactic. The citizens eventually pressured the county to yield the finances. The video deceived the public into thinking the road work would be less significant than the reality. When Alan's message was posted on the Internet, the situation was quickly publicized by television stations in Missouri, Oklahoma and Kansas; Alan Cassell became a household name across the state overnight. As a hero for the average Joe, Alan was even interviewed by national conservative radio.

The roads received the minimal repair required, without any promise of federal money, and the residents returned their homes. In the weeks that followed, the tension between the commissioners tempered largely because Alan spoke in a conciliatory manner to the local press about their concerns. He acknowledged, "We must recognize the other commissioners for their efforts in trying to protect the taxpayers of the county." His diplomatic demeanor showed others in the Republican Party he had true potential. The situation concluded when FEMA finally reimbursed the county for their expenditure.

Eventually, life went back to normal in the county and the hot, typically dry, time of summer arrived in Pittsburg. Then, someone vandalized Alan's car wash. He spent the better part of the day and made basic repairs; unfortunately, this was a day he didn't have a moment to spare because of an appointment he had in the evening near Kansas City. The café was a two hour drive away, or so he thought.

Alan called Kate at work that afternoon. "Honey," he asked. "Are you busy? Can you talk for a minute?"

"Alan!" Kate exclaimed, answering the phone with a tone of fondness in her voice. "Yes, for a minute."

"Someone vandalized the car wash. I'll be here making repairs until it's time for us to leave for Kansas City."

"Oh darling, how bad is the damage?"

"I can take care of it, but I need time to get the equipment up and running. Could you come straight here when you get off of work so we can leave from the car wash? I have another shirt in the truck with my jacket; I'll need every moment I can get to finish the repairs."

Kate paused and considered the options. "OK, we can park my car there and pick it up on the way back. We need to talk on the way up, all right?"

Alan responded, less than enthusiastically, "Yeah, I'd love to hear how your day went on the drive up. I better get busy; see you soon."

Alan went back to work, wrestling with his damaged machines to first empty and then to pound the metal parts back into shape so they could once again accept payment. He then repaired the several cut hoses with spares he kept in the adjoining maintenance building. Alan finished his work, cleaned himself up, and changed his shirt as Kate pulled up to the car wash.

As he worked to finish tucking the shirt into his pants Kate told him, "Oh Alan, you can't go like that," Kate saw her husband's khaki pants were slightly dirty with a couple of spots on the legs.

"It'll have to do. Let's go," Alan replied as he opened the door to his truck and started the engine. She dutifully jumped in, and they were off to Kansas City.

As they drove through Pittsburg and headed north, Alan spoke about the vandalism and his efforts to get the car wash back in order. He then diverted conversation to his surprise at the upcoming appointment in Kansas City. He repeatedly asked Kate why Jim Cherry was so insistent they both come to the meeting. Alan had never been disappointed by Jim; he was careful not to disappoint him in return.

As Alan pulled into a gas station to fill up and grab a snack for the road, he inquired, "Are you *sure* you know nothing about this meeting?"

"No, honey," she answered with irritation her voice. "No clue at all. Please just get me some of those peanut butter crackers I like, okay?" She was perturbed Alan asked again as if she was hiding something. She did have information she needed to share with him, but Alan had not given her the opportunity.

Jim Cherry, still the county chair of the GOP, had been secretive about his request for them to attend this meeting. "I need both you and Kate to meet me at 'The Coffee Grounds.'" Jim had told him. "I'll send the address directly to your GPS."

While neither Alan nor Kate was familiar with a place called "The Coffee Grounds" in Kansas City, Alan figured the place was just another coffee shop.

After nearly an hour of driving, Alan realized that he had not allowed Kate to say much at all.

He asked her, "How's your sign writing class going?" Kate recently started a class to learn sign writing, which was quickly becoming a necessity in her work. She showed him some of the signs she had learned, which took a little over a half-hour because he could only look over when the traffic and road conditions permitted.

Alan then changed the subject to recent county business and left Kate to hold the rest of her information to herself. When he realized he had cut her off, he was approaching the Kansas City area. He apologized and asked, "Did anything else happen today?"

"Well," she began, "you know I went to the doctor today ..."

"Whoa!" Alan exclaimed, avoiding a collision with a car. "Are you wearing your seatbelt?"

"Yes, dear," she responded with a sigh, certain she would not be able to talk since they were already in the city area. Alan was a small town boy, and driving in the Kansas City area always made him nervous.

Now, Alan attempted to pay attention to the directions being given him by the GPS. He found himself turning away from commercial areas and into the suburb of Mission Hills.

"I sure hope Jim gave me the right address," Alan commented with concern. He noticed the large, beautiful mansions on both sides of the street. His next comment was intended to lighten the mood: "I don't think we're in Kansas anymore."

"Oh yes, we are. The state border is still to our east," Kate responded seriously.

"You really need to watch some classic old movies, Hun," Alan joked.

When she realized what he meant, she answered, "Yeah, the Wizard of—"

"You are arriving at your destination, on right." Kate was interrupted by the computerized voice of the navigation system.

65

Before them sat a magnificent home set on about twenty acres of perfectly manicured lawn. The wrought iron gate was wide open; a discreet sign declared the name of the estate as "The Coffee Grounds."

"Oh God!" Alan blurted. "Bill and Sue Coffee … Coffee Grounds, shit! Jim should have told me. My pants … are the spots still there, or was it just water?"

"You'll be just fine," Kate replied without a glance. She was distracted, fussing with her hair as she looked into the mirror on the visor.

When Kate finished her primping, she looked up and was stunned by her surroundings. "Alan, I've been here before!" she squeaked with shock.

"Are you saying you *do* know what this is all about?" he asked.

"No! I told you I have no idea," she continued, "but I think you should know that we have a picture of me, by their pool, on the wall, in our hallway, at home." Each short phrase was separated from the next by her hesitant revelation.

"The only picture of you by a pool was taken when you were one of the Miss America contestants," Alan stated. His eyes grew large as he realized the import. "You've got to be kidding! I thought that picture was taken at some resort pool somewhere. They took the photo *here*?"

"We came in buses, but now that I'm here I recognize the estate. I didn't even know that they brought us into Kansas that day. You'd think they would have told me!"

"Well, I've met them, knew they were rich … just didn't know they were *this* rich." Alan stated, motioning toward the mansion. "They're old fashioned too, so let me get the door, okay?"

Alan parked the truck, jumped out, and ran around to open the door for her. The Coffee's were quite possibly the wealthiest people in the state. Bill Coffee owned commercial real estate throughout the Kansas City area, most of which was in the state of Missouri. Most notably, he owned one of the skyscrapers downtown. He had modeled himself after the former real estate mogul Donald Trump, but without the publicity stunts. Sue Coffee was the Johnson County Republican Chair and an eccentric, but devout, Christian.

As they approached the mansion, Sue opened the door for the Cassells, stating, "You must be Alan Cassell, and you must be his lovely wife, Kate, is it?"

With a broad and polite smile Alan responded, "Yes, Mrs. Coffee. It is a pleasure to see you again. Thank you for inviting us to your beautiful home."

Kate said basically the same thing, but commented more specifically on details of the home and her appreciation of the invitation.

Sue took them to a large, but distant room; she never acknowledged the fact she had met both of them on previous occasions. Bill Coffee was at the room's entrance. He greeted Alan by saying, "Alan, I'll leave you to the wolves, but you can count on me to help any way I can." He then left without another word.

Alan felt he was being led to the slaughter. The room was filled with important people: Jim Cherry, Chuck Nguyen of Wyandotte County, Mary Ruth of Shawnee County, Keith Moran of Douglas County, Steven Lis of Leavenworth County, and Ryan Methe, who was a childhood friend of Kate. Alan first met Ryan on his wedding day. All of the assembled participants were Republican County Chairs for their respective counties.

Kate spotted Ryan and nearly shrieked with joy. She ran to hug the diminutive man and carefully leaned to avoid any embarrassment from the front-on hug. "Ryan, I had no idea you would be here! What is this all about? Did you drive or fly in?"

Ryan gleefully responded, "Hey, it's great to see you! I haven't seen you since the wedding. I was glad to come when I heard, and I'm honored to be a part of this meeting. I actually flew in yesterday. The Coffees put me up in fine style."

Alan was in complete shock at what seemed to be some conspiracy. "Jim, what is this …" he stammered. "What are you do–"

Jim interrupted Alan and pulled him aside. He whispered in his friend's ear, "Don't worry, trust me, this is a great opportunity for us." Alan didn't know how to take Jim's comment, especially the word *us*.

Then, Jim smiled and openly instructed, "Just have a seat, Alan, and let's see how things proceed."

Jim directed his attention to the entire group. "Now everyone, I told you some things about Alan, er, Commissioner Cassell, and I believe you have all met him at one time or another. I was explaining earlier how he handled himself on TV when we were having the floods and his incredible polling numbers. I also want to point out that he works very hard at whatever he does. He's the only person I know who can read a budget like it's a novel. He can see right through the nonsense and explain on first look exactly what's being done that eludes most of us. He has a talent for sniffing out bureaucratic red tape and for getting things done.

"Now, Alan, you're wondering why I asked you to come. These folks didn't think you would come all the way up here without a hint, but it is clear to them now that you did. Thank you for coming. As you know, the current governor is not running again. We've made our choice and the only question, as far as we're concerned, is who will be lieutenant governor."

"Lite guv!" Alan choked, "You've got to be kidding! I'm only a county commissioner of a small county."

"I'm sorry Alan, we're not asking you to run for lieutenant governor." The others present began to hide their giggles as Jim continued, "We want you for governor."

The room went silent for a moment as Alan was dumbstruck. Then, a chime struck. Sue jumped up and said, "That must be Mary Ann; she lives two doors down and she's always running behind." She left the room to answer the door.

Jim continued, "Mary Ann Force thought you would be a perfect candidate, and she called me to organize this meeting."

Mary Ann Force was one of those people who married someone with a name that matched her ambitions. She was indeed a "force" in the party. She was Sue's predecessor as county chair and was terribly wealthy in her own right. Mary Ann Force was now the Kansas Republican National Committeewoman. She always insisted people call her by her entire name and referred to herself in third person. She began her political career as a volunteer for one of Bob Dole's Presidential campaigns decades before. She often arrived last to any meeting so it was clear her presence was all that was needed to conclude a matter.

"Mary Ann Force," Alan stood, greeting the grey-haired party leader. "I understand you instigated this plot." He chuckled lightly, his head swimming as he struggled to speak properly.

"Alan, I have friends in Crawford County." Mary Ann asserted. "You did pretty well for them when those storms hit. We could not do any better than you. Now just say 'yes' and we can get down to the real business."

"Folks, I can't just say 'yes,' I can't … surely you don't … I can't be expected to say anything at this moment!" Alan stammered. "I'm not completely sure there's not a hidden camera around here somewhere …. Are you sure this is not some elaborate prank?" he asked, pretending to look around for a camera. Continuing again, he added, "I have no idea what Kate thinks."

Ryan asked, "Well, Kate, what do you think?" Alan and Mary Ann sat down to hear her reply.

After a pause, she calmly responded, "I think that it's about time."

"Hun," Alan jumped in, "I'm just a county commissioner, and I don't think a commissioner has ever successfully run for governor. There are hundreds of us across the state; I'm just one in the crowd."

"And you know every one of them." Jim chided, "Don't sell yourself short. You're the President of the Association of Counties, and you're very electable. We know we can get you the nomination, the fundraising, and the Republican will win in November!"

"You all represent ... what ... about half the Republicans in the state," Alan started, then he was interrupted by Mrs. Force clearing her throat, so he corrected himself, "and now that you're here, Mary Ann Force, you represent the entire Republican Party of Kansas. I must say, I'm stunned. I'm young; I guess I'd be the youngest governor in the country. This would really be a leap."

Sue offered, "Alan, my boy, 'By humility and the fear of the Lord are riches and honor and life. Thorns and snares are in the way of the perverse; He who guards his soul will be far from them.' I believe this statement is important for you."

Everyone in the room looked intently at their hostess, wondering what she could mean by that quote. Alan, showing his customary quick wits, responded, "Sue, thank you, you just reached right into my heart." Giving a motion with his hand moving to over his heart he continued, "That's in ... Proverbs, is it? Do you have the reference? I would really appreciate it."

"Oh bless you, I'll go find it," Sue said as she got up to find her Bible in another room.

When she left, Alan raised his hands and shoulders with a shrug that indicated to the others present he had no better idea of what she meant than they did. To them, his response illustrated his political charisma. When Sue returned, she had the verse on a piece of paper and handed it to Alan without a word as the others spoke amongst themselves. Alan glanced at the paper for a moment, smiled, and folded it into his shirt pocket. He patted his hand over his pocket as he looked at Sue with a positive nod. The conversation turned again to securing a response from the commissioner regarding a gubernatorial race.

Alan asked, "Do I have to answer ... today ... I don't think I can make a commitment right now, though it seems my wife is on board." Turning to Kate, he inquired "You *sure* you didn't know about this?"

"I didn't, but I do think you should listen to them and find out what would be expected of us if you were to accept," Kate advised.

"I know we can bring the Republican-leaning PAC's your way," said Mary Ruth, whose county included the capital, Topeka.

Jim asked the others if they had anything to add. Lis, Moran, and Nguyen all pledged their support.

Alan asked, "Who else is running?"

"At this point, no other Republicans," said Force. "I've spoken to all the congressmen and the senators, the state legislative leaders and the attorney general. The state chair has no candidates either. The only name I did hear was Bill Coffee, who would make a very good Governor, but his business interests out of state would get in the way of electability."

Everyone agreed Bill would be very good "if," but it was an obvious effort to be polite to their host.

Jim added, "There will be other candidates, but you are our candidate. You're from a small, and relatively rural, county; you have connections to Wichita, which is essential; your wife ... wow! And I know that no other candidate will outwork you. Alan, face it, you will be governor. But, if there are no objections, I say we allow you to reflect on what we have proposed while we move on to some details on the assumption that you will say 'yes.' After all, you must admit, it's not easy to get this many of us together from all across the state. Okay? All right, we agree. Does anyone have any questions?"

Ryan started, "Alan, just let us know you don't have any skeletons in the closet, or any wacko political views, okay?"

"No literal skeletons, but my dad is long gone and I don't know where he is now." Alan offered. "My mom is not well, so she won't be any help. My kid sister ... changes boyfriends fairly often. I don't have much other family, just a few cousins I don't know well. My family was poor, my degree is in business, I never served in the military, and … Oh, I don't know … Oh yeah, you wanted to know about my politics.

"I've spoken to groups and I think each of you was in attendance at one point or another, but my philosophy is simple and conservative. Government is the solution of last resort; local government is to be utilized to the fullest. I won't favor a tax increase until every other option is exhausted. On everything else, I look to hear from you. I'm eager to learn."

"I'm good with that, and if Kate's good with you, so am I," Ryan said.

Sue then piped in, looking at Kate, "Now darling, not that it would change anything for us, but you two have been married a while. Any children in the future?"

Kate seemed embarrassed, but smiled her gracious and gleaming smile, and responded, "We do want to start a family … soon."

Alan looked like he had just been informed he missed his anniversary. Excited, he chimed, "Kate! We were supposed to talk more on the way up … are you …? I'm so sorry; I forgot you went to the doc—"

Kate, gleaming, even glowing, finally had to stop him with, "Yes."

Jim asked, "You're pregnant? *Today*?"

The ladies present laughed immediately, and the men joined in quickly. Kate explained she learned for certain that day. All present were congratulatory and Alan realized he put Kate in a bad position; he would have to apologize later. Then he found himself distracted and anxious with the thoughts of being a father.

Mary Ann Force took charge by suggesting they continue by discussing running mate options.

Chuck said, "Senator John Moht, my state senator, would be a good candidate likely to accept. He's an urban legislator with a good record of experience."

"I think Representative Judy Keeps would bring a lot of experience to the table. She also comes from a larger city," Steven suggested.

The group argued for a while about which person they thought would be best for the job. Alan insisted he respected both options, and that either choice would make a good candidate for governor, let alone lieutenant governor.

All the while, Kate held her hand over her mouth, giggling. Mary Ann Force asked, "Kate darling, what could be so funny?"

"I'm not the politician, but I just was thinking of the bumper stickers. They would read as either 'castle moat' or 'castle keeps.'"

The group immediately realized they just lost two quality candidates over the sound of the combination of names.

Bill Coffee heard some laughing and came back in to observe. He asked, "Is it possible Congresswoman Sims would want to take the opportunity?" Congresswoman Denise Sims didn't like Washington. She wanted to return to Kansas to live with her family near Big Springs. Her husband never went to DC during her tenure. Instead, he chose to stay and run the family farm. Her children were teenagers now and needed a mom at home. She had announced she would not run for governor, but lieutenant governor was a less demanding job and the family farm was in proximity to Topeka.

"Perhaps when you're ready to move on," Bill continued, speaking directly to Alan, "her kids will be grown and she'll be ready to serve as governor."

The group agreed it would be a great advantage to have a member of congress who really wanted to come home to her family to be "lite guv," if they could talk her into running. Alan asked if she would be willing to campaign as well as serve.

Mary Ann Force said getting a congresswoman on the ticket could ward off other Republican candidates. "That's what we need her for!"

The meeting went on. Kate and Alan had not eaten yet that evening, just some sandwich crackers and sodas on the way up. Finally, Sue suggested that a mother-to-be needs to eat and to rest. She offered to have some food made, but Alan insisted he could get something on the road and get his wife home that much sooner. Before they left, everyone promised to help with the future campaign, congratulated Kate again, and insisted Alan let them know his decision as soon as possible.

Mary Ruth asked if she could talk to her neighbors, the Billingslys, about him. She explained they were very politically active and would be a great addition to his campaign, especially Mrs. Billingsly.

Into the dark of the night, Alan took hold of Kate and apologized for not paying attention regarding her doctor's appointment; he also expressed sincere regret for any embarrassment at telling the group of her pregnancy before she had the opportunity to tell him. She was very understanding and excused his infractions. He smiled, kissed her, hugged her, kissed her again, and then opened the door for her.

Perhaps she was too eager to forgive him for ignoring her. Perhaps Alan's inattentiveness was a precursor to actions that would be much more serious than his insensitivity that day. The night would come back to haunt them both.

CHAPTER 6 • **BORINQUEN**

The most fundamental purpose of government is defense, not empire.

—Joseph Sobran

I N THE WARM WATERS OF THE Caribbean Sea sits the island of Puerto Rico, the smallest of the Greater Antilles. Culturally and linguistically Hispanic, this enchanting island is geographically located east/southeast of Cuba and Hispaniola. Despite the distance from the mainland, every citizen of Puerto Rico was a citizen of the United States.

Puerto Rico became a part of the United States as a result of the Spanish-American War. The same war also gave Cuba, the Philippines, and other lands as territories to the United States. Cuba and the Philippines, however, were granted independence long before. In 2009, the United Nations Special Committee on Decolonization expressed the UN's desire to grant the people of Puerto Rico self-determination, or independence.

As citizens of the US, Puerto Ricans were subject to every law passed by Congress, despite not having a vote. They also paid federal taxes, but those taxes were carefully accounted for and given to the territorial government. Despite any inequity, Puerto Ricans supported retaining the semi-self-governing status known as "Commonwealth" or *Estado Libre Asociado* known by the initials "ELA," which literally means "Associated Free State." While support for ELA was stronger than the statehood or independence movements, it never achieved an outright majority in the polls. Changes elsewhere in the Americas changed opinions in Puerto Rico.

The United States Congress agreed to accept a monetary system of continental currency, a couple of decades following the UN Special Committee's discussions on Puerto Rico. Similar to the European Euro, the "Amero" had long been advocated and was extremely controversial. The United States finally agreed to a transcontinental money system, which included Canada and Mexico and most of South America. However, like Britain and the pound, America also retained the dollar. The Amero had a very positive effect on Latin American economies; the system had the opposite effect on the US. The compromise appeased most of the nationalist-leaning Americans, but had a negative fiscal impact. By accepting either the Amero or dollar for all obligations, the American economy suffered. The national debt approached three hundred percent of the Gross Domestic Product.

The US still had troops abroad, as it had since World War II. Germany, Japan, Korea, Iraq, Afghanistan, Cuba, and Namibia all had large American bases, even though the conflicts that warranted them were long over; there were nearly one thousand American military bases outside the fifty United States. Puerto Ricans were drafted in most of the previous conflicts and contributed disproportionately to the forces on the bases.

The *Movimiento de la Independencia Puertorriqueña*, which was the Puerto Rican independence movement, had new life. Puerto Ricans suffered the worst of the American economic troubles; economies that surrounded Puerto Rico prospered with the Amero, but since they were under the dual Amero/Dollar system, their economy weakened. Changes in Cuba allowed Americans to vacation on that island for far less than it cost to go to Puerto Rico. Meanwhile, Puerto Rico received an influx of prosperous Cubans and Venezuelans who vacationed in Puerto Rico; some of these visitors even created new businesses in Puerto Rico, taking full advantage of the economic crisis.

The long established, but historically minimal, political party known as *Partido Independentista Puertorriqueño*, or Puerto Rican Independence Party, finally won a majority of the votes for governor and in the legislature. The victory came, partly to the support of some English-speaking Americans who took up residence in Puerto Rico to encourage independence.

The new government declared independence immediately upon taking the reins. The new nation-state was named "Borinquen," which is a Spanish version of what the aboriginal inhabitants called the land. This was also the area Puerto Rican people had called "the islands of Puerto Rico" for many generations. Puerto Rico, meaning "Rich Port," is only the name of the largest and most populous of the islands making up the country. By adopting the Arawak/Taino name, the new government hoped to distance itself from its colonial history and to possibly attract the nearby US Virgin Islands to confederate with them. The Virgin Islands did eventually accept the overture, but after about twenty years.

A constitutional crisis hit the US when all citizens of Puerto Rico, were also declared by the courts as retaining their status as citizens of the United States. Therefore, benefits of US citizenship, such as Social Security payments, were to continue for Puerto Ricans.

Congress tried to block the dual citizenship; nevertheless, the US Supreme Court determined American citizens can't have their citizenship rights denied, despite the location of their residence at any time. The court did allow the US Government to withdraw American citizenship from Puerto Rican elected officials.

The IRS quickly announced that income taxes would continue to be owed on incomes of United States citizens earned outside the country, but this proclamation only encouraged wealthy Puerto Ricans to renounce US citizenship. Middle class and poor Puerto Ricans had no reason to renounce their US citizenship; the enforcement of the United States income tax law was limited to US territories. Puerto Ricans were told they would only have to pay US taxes on their income if, and when, they went to the US. Even in such instances, they could only be prosecuted for evading taxes if the US could prove taxes were owed. The Borinquen legislature took action that prohibited the violation of its citizens' financial privacy to prevent such prosecution.

After the Puerto Rican elections, which resulted in victory for the Independence Party, nearly a quarter million Americans visited the islands in order to establish dual citizenship before the new government took office.

Borinquen then became a banking haven like many of the small Caribbean nations had always been. The economy of the island flourished as the English language became more common than it had been prior to independence.

Few Americans recognized the long-term implications the departure of Puerto Rico would have on the nation. The most significant outcome, however, was that a dual citizenship precedent was established.

We no longer want despots,
tyranny shall fall now;
the unconquerable women also will
know how to fight.
We want liberty,
and our machetes
will give it to us.
Come, Boricuas, come now,
since freedom
awaits us anxiously,
freedom, freedom!

From the 1868 Borinquen National Anthem by Lola Rodriguez de Tió.

CHAPTER 7 • **CEDAR CREST**

The price of empire is America's soul, and that price is too high.

—J. William Fulbright

ALAN CHANGED HIS MIND about going home the evening of the meeting at the Coffee's. Just to get home, they would have had to pick up fast food and drive well into the night. He was inspired, so a different plan emerged. On the way into town, before the meeting, he had spotted a new hotel. The hotel was not a luxury hotel, but it was new and seemed romantic to him. Next door was an Applebee's restaurant. Alan and Kate enjoyed the Applebee's near their home in Pittsburg; the food was always enjoyable, and the restaurant gave them a sense of comfort and familiarity.

He checked in to the hotel and took his wife to the restaurant. She expressed concern about not having a change of clothes, but Alan had an answer for that: Wal-Mart. They picked up a few basic items for the next day and returned to the hotel.

Alan was romantic and tender to his mother-to-be wife. She was exhausted. Once they were settled at the hotel, he gave her a back massage and then gently rubbed her legs until she was fast asleep. As he rubbed her legs and feet, he reflected on the events of the day. He was trying to determine exactly which day she conceived. He had the event narrowed down to three possibilities when he blurted a query out to his sleeping wife.

Kate didn't stir. She did, however, begin to snore. To the best of Alan's knowledge, Kate had never snored before. For a few minutes, he thought the noise was endearing. He played with her nose and lips, causing her to make a variety of sounds. After just a few minutes, he grew bored and laid down to sleep, but found the sound prevented any kind of slumber. He turned on the television to generate sounds that would cancel the noise of her snoring. He sincerely hoped this was a temporary pregnancy-related affliction.

Kate awoke before Alan and decided to reward his considerate actions from the previous evening. "Alan," she whispered, leisurely caressing his chest to wake him. "The doctor told me being pregnant doesn't prevent any 'normal' activity on our part."

"You talked to him about that?" he responded in a groggy voice.

"Yes, I did. He's my doctor; I wanted to make sure," she informed him. "And, I really liked how you massaged me last night." She slowly imitated his massage from the night before, but on his chest as opposed to his back.

Now far less sleepy, Alan remarked, "Well, I'm glad you liked it."

"And I liked how you rubbed my legs ..." she purred, as she caressed his legs, instigating a morning love making session with him.

If Alan had known his actions of the previous evening would result in her loving initiative, he would have established a habit of such activities long before.

Kate told Alan she had been excused from work early the previous day when she mentioned to her department head that she was "with child." Alan's schedule was always very flexible so he proposed they consider the race for governor over lunch ... in Topeka.

Alan purchased a lunch for two at a deli after arriving in Topeka with the intention of having a quiet picnic with his wife. He proceeded to drive to a place called Cedar Crest, which boasted over two hundred forty acres of grass, ponds, and groves; on the land was the governor's mansion.

They sat on the opened tailgate of the pickup truck and ate lunch as they looked at the property.

Alan joked, "I think a few head of cattle would make better use of the land than the deer who currently roam here. Hey, we could add a corral and horse barn so 'we' could ride." Kate chided him for thinking that changing the grounds would be appropriate, while missing the joke he would be a participant in such an activity.

Upon actually viewing the governor's mansion, Kate reflected more seriously on her rash comments of the previous day. "It's so massive. The grounds are overwhelming," she began. "I love you dearly, Alan, and I really do think you have a future in state politics, and perhaps more ..." She paused, choosing her words carefully. "But surely there will be some more powerful, or more experienced, Republican that will decide to run. I'm afraid you might lose."

"I can't argue with any of that," said Alan reassuringly as he put his arm around Kate. "I have my own fears about something this big, too. But a lot of very good people, people I trust, think I have a real shot."

Upon finishing lunch, they drove around the park that encircled the mansion. Alan spotted something and screeched the truck to a halt, threw the gearshift into reverse, and backed to look at what he thought he had seen. Sure enough, between the trees and through the fencing, he spied a barn, a corral, and a young girl on horseback. The girl was the current governor's granddaughter.

Suddenly, Kate wasn't concerned about other candidates anymore; she was inspired. Kate was going to ride on these grounds, she was going to have a horse stabled in that barn, and she was going to do whatever it took to win this election for him. For them. *For the Cassell family*, she thought, remembering the new addition to their lives.

They drove further around the estate and stopped for a few minutes at a scenic outlook. "What could be more serene?" he asked rhetorically. Alan knew from this venue he could truly apply himself and commit to working for the people of Kansas. He imagined his platform would be tax reductions, education reform, and improvements in public services. Kansas was in good economic shape, by comparison to the rest of the nation, which made this a perfect time for reform. All seemed well with the Cassells; in the very middle of the nation, all seemed well for Kansas.

Alan needed to respond to those who had recruited him to run for governor. He hadn't asked why they wanted him. He should have asked the group if they agreed with him on key issues or whether he was just an attractive candidate they could manipulate in office.

Alan was just a county commissioner, but he knew quite a bit about the workings of government, having studied the subject thoroughly. He knew what being a governor would require of him. The extensive base of decisions a governor makes escaped most candidates. Other contenders campaigned on broad themes and intended to govern similarly.

In most states, the job of governor was one of inexhaustible complexity and Kansas was no different. Public policy is expressed through public statements, bills signed, appointments made, and a plethora of other means. Those same means of productivity also limited a governor. Appointees of previous administrations, current legislators, existing bureaucrats, lobbyists, local political entities, members of congress from the state, and the press all often worked to slow or minimize the policies of a governor. The system was inefficient for certain, but such checks and balances worked to protect the populace from tyranny.

While Alan was confident he could not be manipulated in office, he didn't know that public policy could, and would, be manipulated by those who surrounded him as governor.

Yes, of course he would run. He called Jim Cherry, then the others from the meeting, regarding his decision. In the true manner of a politician, in each case, he told the individual he wanted him or her to be the very first to know of his decision. He never said the person *was* the first, only that it was his desire that he or she be the first.

When Alan talked with Mary Ann Force, he discerned the true nature of her instigation.

She said to Alan, "A couple of weeks ago, at the state committee meeting, Jim Cherry and I had lunch together and began discussing potential candidates. I was quite concerned the party had no clear gubernatorial candidate. We should be able to retain the statehouse if we have a solid candidate like you on our side.

"Jim shared my concerns, asking my opinion on who we could get to run for office. Jim knows everyone better than I do, and he liked everyone I suggested. Unfortunately, there was one reason or another that each of them just could not be our candidate."

Alan could see through Mary Ann's naiveté. Jim had manipulated his conversation with her so only Alan would be seen as a viable candidate. To Mary Ann Force, he was the right candidate because he had no known negatives. Alan Cassell had no negatives as far as she knew because Jim Cherry was the person who presented him as an option.

The Coffee group sprang into action, as promised. The members collectively organized the campaign, secured Congresswoman Sims as lieutenant governor, and raised the required funds.

CHAPTER 8 • **KATIE**

"What is government itself but the greatest of all reflections on human nature? If men were angels, no government would be necessary. In framing a government which is to be administered by men over men, the great difficulty lies in this: you must first enable the government to control the governed; and in the next place oblige it to control itself."

—James Madison

ALAN WAS WELL-LIKED, AND Kate was extremely popular in Kansas. Therefore, the gubernatorial campaign was energized in no time. Alan transformed small-town meetings into great rallies. The press loved the candidate and adored the image of Kate as a potential first lady. Her favorite activity was visiting schools and she had immense credibility when she spoke of the importance of literacy. No candidate worked harder or longer than Alan Cassell.

Kate, at the time she was six months pregnant, joined Alan for a campaign stop in Leavenworth. The press was out in force, and the event was extremely successful. The bright sun of the day turned overcast as the sun began to set. Alan and Kate were supposed to drive home to prepare for the next series of events in Kansas' largest city, Wichita. The event was billed as a "Homecoming" for Kate.

Alan was glad to have her near him any time he could. She took a leave of absence at the college, with the expectation she would return only if the campaign lost. The college was certain Alan would win and hired her replacement immediately.

As they drove south on Hwy 5 toward Kansas City, the rains began.

Alan slowed his truck well below the posted speed limit because of rain and unfamiliar road. In a matter of moments, the rain obscured his view so much he found himself sitting forward on the seat, staring carefully through the windshield and the beating wipers.

Concerned, Alan stated, "Kate, we may have to stop in the city if this keeps up." His statement was the last thing she heard him say before she fell asleep.

There were no other vehicles on the road, but something else was. Around a gradual curve, Alan spotted a cow on the road. He swerved to avoid the animal, but the loud "thump," accompanied by the sound of crumpling steel indicated he had failed. The driver's side of the truck clipped the animal's back legs. The force of the impact caused the truck to spin uncontrollably on the wet surface. Alan struggled valiantly to regain control, but to no avail. Going less than forty-five miles per hour should have been safe enough, but he could not have predicted the cow in the middle of the highway.

The truck slid off the highway, into, and then out of the ditch; the channel which was not very deep, but flowed heavily with runoff. A broken-down fence of the adjoining farm finally stopped the vehicle's momentum.

Alan heard Kate scream. The passenger side of the truck had a metal fence post driven all the way through the door. The post impaled her, just below the ribcage.

"Oh my God! Kate!" shouted Alan, as she, almost without thinking, pulled herself from the fence post. He could not tell how deep the wound was, and she became liberated from the iron post before she truly understood the situation.

"I'm fine, Alan," Kate managed to whisper. "I'm sure it looks much worse than it is. Are you ..." Kate's sentence was left incomplete, as she lapsed into unconsciousness.

Alan, panic-stricken at the sight of a fissure in his wife's side, managed to call 911. "There's been an accident on Highway 5," Alan practically shouted into his cell phone. The dispatcher asked if they accurately showed their location from the cell phone. Alan impatiently confirmed the location was accurate.

"We need a medical chopper here quick," Alan continued. "My wife is unconscious; she was pierced in her side with a fence post. She's six months pregnant!" The gravity of that last sentence hit Alan hard. He was informed that a chopper had been dispatched and would be there soon.

The rain had stopped in the city at the time of the call and was down to a drizzle when the helicopter arrived at the scene of the accident. They were both flown to the nearest trauma center, Providence Medical Center.

For Alan, the delays seemed to last an eternity. They asked him questions and attended to his minor wounds. He wanted them to put all their energy into taking care of Kate. Alan resigned himself to losing the baby, but worried most about Kate.

Kate was in surgery for hours. After the first hour, a nurse came to tell Alan that the doctors had successfully delivered the baby, and Kate was alive, although she was very weak; they were working to save the life of his daughter. *We have a little girl*, Alan thought, realizing the immensity of the statement.

A nurse asked Alan if they had chosen a name. He and Kate had, of course, discussed the subject, but no decision had been made. He sat outside the surgery rooms, remembering their conversation from a couple of months earlier.

He suggested at the time, "I think I'd like to name our baby after one of us; 'Alan' if it is a boy and 'Katherine' if it is a girl."

"What do you think about a middle name?" she asked.

"How about using your father's name as a middle name? 'Alan Michael' has a good sound. And, for a girl, we could use my mom's name as the middle name."

"I don't think 'Katherine Peggy' sounds good at all." Kate answered.

"Her name is actually 'Margaret,'" Alan responded. "I think 'Katherine Margaret' has a great sound. We could call her 'Katie' as a nickname."

Kate agreed, "Sounds good, but I just don't know ... yet."

Reprieved from his reminiscences, he told the nurse, "Put 'Katie' on the bracelet, but don't file the birth certificate until my wife is conscious. We haven't made a final decision yet."

The baby he thought was lost was now alive, but he had not seen her yet. He made a quick call to his in-laws to let them know they were grandparents again. They had been informed of the accident earlier and were on their way. He tried to reach his mother, but had to leave a message.

Although no family support had arrived yet, members of the Kansas City press were at the hospital. Alan never learned who told them of the incident.

He was not ready to talk and begged the hospital to respect his privacy, keeping the press away. The incident had created great sympathy among the public.

However, Alan was preoccupied with other concerns. He sat alone slumped in a waiting room chair. His tattered sport coat was in the chair next to him and his soggy shoes beneath. He feigned interest in the sitcom on the television. He couldn't hear a word and didn't know the show, but his attention was occasionally taken when the live audience would break out in laughter. He was racked with guilt, despite having no means of preventing the accident. He wanted to take it all back, to stay on their little farm and raise their daughter at home where they would be safe.

"Who needs it?" he said aloud.

Alan hated himself upon his admission that he needed politics in his life. Inside him was a drive that would take risks and, even now, he would make the same choices again. He would risk it all to advance in politics, sacrificing everything to advance himself. His love for Kate, and for baby Katie, would always take a backseat to his ambition.

Wallowing in misery over his new-found revelations, a reprieve finally came. Soft steps from behind him came in the form of a pure white uniform. The nurse informed him, "You can see your daughter; she is out of surgery."

Alan unconsciously stood. He stepped away from the chair, but soon realized he was barefoot. His heart pounded, and his actions were erratic. Alan worked to pull his wet socks up and to force his shoes over them. He grabbed his jacket, but realized it no longer had value; he simply threw the tattered fabric toward the nearest trash can.

As Alan Cassell and the nurse walked down the long, stark hall, his footwear made that unmistakable squeaky, sloshy sound of wet shoes, which was followed closely by the strong clip of a dress shoe heel. Alan hated the attention he attracted. In deference to the onlookers, he assembled himself as he walked down the corridor. A slight tuck of his shirt was followed by fingering through his hair, and then again with the shirt. While he adjusted his appearance, he considered the idea that he was about to meet his own daughter. Tragedy be damned, he was happy.

Alan knew she was alive, but Katie didn't seem real to him until he was permitted to see and touch her. There she was, behind the glass. Bright red hair wisped about her tiny head. She was smaller than any baby he had ever seen, but she was beautiful. The smiling nurse took his hand and pulled him into the nursery. He was permitted to touch his little girl, in the brief interlude between sessions in the incubator.

Alan stood by Katie's side, beside the incubator, for as long as he was permitted. He was finally informed he could see his wife. As he walked toward Kate's room, he thought the worst might be over. His wife was stable, and they had a beautiful baby daughter.

Outside her room, he was met by a surgeon. His face was serious as he began to speak. "I'm afraid I have some bad news, Mr. Cassell," the doctor began. "Your wife is fine but, as a result of her injuries, she will not be able to have any more children."

Alan absorbed those words and realized what the information would mean to Kate. She was excited at the prospect of having several children. *But*, Alan thought, *at least we have Katie.*

"As long as little Katie is OK, I think we can live with that," Alan replied.

The doctor had more bad news for Alan. He gently said, "I want you to know that the prognosis for your daughter is not at all certain. Only time will tell."

Alan created his own meaning from those words. He was unwilling to accept their beautiful little daughter might not survive.

Stepping into the room, he viewed his nearly unrecognizable wife. Kate had a plethora of cuts and bruises he had not yet seen. She was now awake, but barely.

Alan embraced his wife as tears welled in his eyes. "I'm so sorry," he apologized, overcome with emotion.

Kate, fully aware the accident was not his fault, tried to comfort her husband. "There's nothing you could have done, Alan. Don't blame yourself; it was just an accident."

Her attempt to comfort him only made him feel worse. He composed himself quickly, explaining he had not slept since the accident. Then they discussed their daughter.

"I hope you won't think it presumptuous of me, but I told the nurse to put 'Katie' on her wristband," Alan told her.

"'Katie' is a wonderful name, Alan," replied Kate. "I can even live with 'Katherine Margaret' as her full name. Let's just say I get to pick the name of our next child though."

Alan's face turned pale. Kate, with concern in her voice, asked him what was wrong. "I'm so sorry, Kate," Alan began, barely able to hold back his own tears, "but the doctors told me that … that … you won't be able to have any more…" Alan couldn't find a way to finish the sentence. He simply continued with, "Katie will be our only…"

Kate wept as he held her tightly in his arms.

Over the next three days, Kate continued to improve and regain her strength, while little Katie did not. She lost weight she could not afford to lose and had jaundice. Kate's parents, Michael and Babs, stayed at the hospital as much as they could, taking short breaks to rest at their hotel.

Alan's mother Peggy also came to the hospital. Peggy's frailty made her presence a struggle, but she spent all the time she could at the hospital. Peggy was with baby Katie more than she was with Kate or Alan.

Alan didn't leave the hospital for a moment, borrowing the shower in Kate's room and sleeping on the floor, since he found he could not sleep on the chair. The one evening he tried the gurney they offered, he fell asleep, turned over during the night, and fell hard to the floor. Thereafter, he determined sleeping on the floor was the better option.

The hospital staff tried to get him to rest outside of the hospital, but his notoriety kept them from forcing the issue. He told them, "We came in together, and we will leave together, as a family!"

As both Kate and Alan dozed off on their third night at the hospital, they were jarred awake by Alan's sister Deena who burst into the room in tears. "Katie is slipping away," was all she could say.

Alan grabbed a wheelchair and put Kate in it without permission. He ran with her in the chair, following Deena to the neonatal-ICU. Peggy was already there, crying. They burst into the room to reach Katie in her last moments.

"I want to hold my daughter," Kate insisted. The doctor nodded, since he could do no more for Katie. Alan knelt beside his wife, with one arm around her, as he gently stroked Katie's hair.

Katie didn't know she was dying. Kate and Alan knew they were losing more than a daughter; something inside them was dying as well. They were both inconsolable when she passed. They should have been drawn together, but instead Kate turned to Babs and Alan to his mother.

The following morning, Michael spoke to the press. In the impromptu press conference, he explained the situation to the general public.

"As you all know," he clarified, "Alan Cassell and his wife, my daughter, Kate, were in a serious accident three days ago. Alan was treated for minor injuries, while Kate underwent surgery for her more serious injuries. Their daughter, Katie, had to be delivered during Kate's surgery. Tragically, last night, Katie Cassell lost her fight for life.

"Despite this tragic and extreme personal loss, Alan will remain in the race. However, to allow him and his wife time to mourn their loss, all active campaigning will cease, and any scheduled events will be cancelled. When the time comes when Alan and Kate feel able to resume the campaign, an announcement will be made by way of press conference. We want to thank everyone for their concern and prayers over these past three days; we humbly ask for Alan's and Kate's privacy to be respected through this tragic time."

The television stations throughout Kansas, as well as in adjoining states, followed the story each day. The death of baby Katie was taken as a national tragedy. Cards and gifts came to the Cassell house in uncountable numbers.

Later that day, a number of people from the campaign visited Alan for a few minutes at a time in a family visiting room the hospital arranged for him. Michael coordinated the temporary shelving of campaign activities. Mailings and events were cancelled. Fundraising was postponed, though unsolicited funds were accepted. The campaign refused to take advantage of public sympathies. The two other Republicans that filed for office would either suspend their campaign activities or risk looking crass to the voting populace.

Mrs. Billingsly was among those present at the hospital. As suggested by Mary Ruth of Topeka, Mrs. Billingsly was an invaluable asset to Alan.

"Alan," she queried, "how would you like me to address the individuals and groups who have already signed on to sponsor events? As you know, some can be rescheduled, but others will need to be cancelled. I just need to know your preferences, and I can take care of the rest."

"I'll trust you to make the right decisions in that regard," replied Alan, still too numb with the tragedy to think about the mundane details of politics.

Mrs. Billingsly was accompanied by her sister and brother-in-law; they sat quietly in the back of the room. The presence of these family members was only a convenience to her. Her brother-in-law was working temporarily in the state, and her sister was in town on vacation.

After a few minutes of visiting with his staffer, Alan was overcome for a moment at the loss of "sweet Katie." "Right after the accident, I was sure that the baby was dead," Alan recounted. "I had accepted her death as fact and could have lived with the loss. But, having her live for three days, then die ... that was like having part of my heart cut out of me ..." His words trailed off as tears welled up in his eyes.

Mrs. Billingsly's brother-in-law stepped up and squatted beside him. His gentle words helped Alan.

"You know the accident was not your fault. Kate does not hold you responsible, so you need to try to stop holding yourself accountable," he started. "You mourn your daughter because you had a little time to get to know her. While you won't get to raise her, you will always be her father, and Kate will always be her mother. You two need to turn to each other for comfort through this difficult time."

He stepped back to his seat and said no more. Alan excused himself. He had a habit of taking advice on personal matters with a grain of salt. He would typically be polite and act to the person like the advice given was vital, then do nothing about changing his situation. This time, however, he said nothing. He was grateful to hear someone still considered him a father. He didn't know how to be a father, secretly believing he was responsible for Katie's death.

At that moment, he understood the tragedy was indeed an accident. He loved his little girl as much as a father could in those three days. Somehow, those few moments of gentle strokes to Katie's face, and the memory of the tiny hand that gripped his pinky finger, were enough to give him a glimpse into life as a parent. He had been mourning Katie's loss, and he grieved over the loss of the opportunity to be a father. Now he understood he would always be a father, despite the circumstances; this realization stirred an amazing confidence in Alan. Unexpectedly, he saw Katie as a real person who was valuable in every moment she was with him. He had little opportunity to be with her, but had been a perfect success as a father for as long as he had the chance.

Alan had to see Kate immediately. He went into her room asking, "Kate darling, are you up?" Kate turned her teary head toward him and nodded. "We need to talk about Katie," he plainly said to his weary wife.

"Yes … we had a wonderful little girl," she started, "and we will miss her, but I was thinking … we were pretty good parents for the little time we had her." Where Alan needed assistance finding peace, Kate had the same epiphany without help.

Alan sat on her bedside and they talked about Katie, sharing the joy they had been given by the tiny baby. Every moment of her life was precious. They agreed to be thankful for the time they had with her and to celebrate her birthday every year. She would have a quiet funeral and be buried at the Beulah Cemetery near their home.

Those moments of mutual comfort saved their marriage. No one else understood the relationship they had with Katie. Her death created an unbreakable bond between Alan and Kate. The Cassells were no longer a couple; they were a family. Katie was a connection that would last forever.

CHAPTER 9 • THE INCIDENT

If monarchy is corrupting—and it is—wait till you see what overt empire does to us.

—Daniel Ellsberg

KATE WAS READY FOR THE campaign to resume a couple weeks after her return home from the hospital. They resumed the campaign with a press conference. Her physical injuries were healed so no one could tell she had ever had the accident; she also showed no signs of having been pregnant in the recent past. The visible change from being six months pregnant, a state that was highly obvious on the very slender Kate, and not pregnant at all only days later captured the sympathies of people throughout the state.

Alan and Kate expressed their love for each other in a way that won the hearts of the people of Kansas. Alan was seen as sincere, having his priorities right with his concern for his family. He was seen as a family man because of how he attended to his wife through the tragedy.

Alan stated, "While this campaign is ready to resume, my priority will always be my family. Whatever political ambitions I may have, politics will always take second place to family." Alan sounded calm and confident, but respectful.

To the surprise of few, Alan won the Republican nomination and the general election. The campaign never developed the harsh tone of most campaigns. His opponents forced him to tackle tough issues, but the media favored Alan and presented his opponents to the general public as if they were uncaring. Alan appreciated that he had to address issues to win. He didn't want the tragic events in his life to carry the election. Alan refused to win an election with the sympathy vote; it was critical to him that people saw him as a capable governor, rather than an object of pity.

That attitude served him well; otherwise, he would have been ineffective as governor. Most of Lieutenant Governor Sims' former congressional staff was offered positions in the administration. Jim Cherry leased out his farm, sold his insurance agency, and moved to Topeka to be Alan's chief of staff. Mrs. Billingsly accepted the job as the governor's scheduling secretary. Many other appointive positions were retained from the outgoing Republican administration.

Their house near Pittsburg was remodeled while they lived in Topeka. The home was modified to become an idealized version of a traditional Kansas farmhouse.

Governor Cassell accepted the advice of those close to him and once again found his power as a communicator. He pushed for lower taxes as a way to keep the Kansas economy strong. He succeeded in pressing for government reform, which gave more authority to counties, cities, and other local forms of government all the way down to water districts.

He did face some controversy, however. Kansas teachers and the education establishment opposed Cassell's plan to reform the state's education system. The teacher's union had endorsed Cassell, largely at Kate's urging, because of her work in the field. Once he was in office, they feared the dramatic changes he proposed, and the governor was taken aback by their opposition. He worked diligently to overcome their objections, but it did not come easily.

As governor, Alan worked hard, making sure he was constantly busy. Mrs. Billingsly's job was especially demanding because the governor accepted every speaking opportunity he could attend.

However, one particular invite required his direct input. A minister, named Archer Adams, had invited him to speak at an event. Jim Cherry was present when Mrs. Billingsly approached the governor about the invitation.

"Where's his church?" Governor Cassell asked.

"Lawrence, on campus. He's not the pastor, per se. A student-led group often invites him to speak for events. The university doesn't allow outside groups to have meetings on campus," she responded.

"How many?" he asked.

"I'm told about five hundred students will be in attendance."

"Wow! I wonder if they had a similar group when Kate attended the university. Did they say what they want me to talk about?"

"It's an interview format."

"Lenore, you know better than I. After all, you keep the schedule," he responded to Mrs. Billingsly. "So why are you asking me?"

She replied sheepishly, "Archer is my brother-in-law; I felt I should ask you first since we are related."

Jim piped in, "Do we have any recordings of his previous sermons, err ... interviews? I don't want us blindsided."

She responded, "Well, that's the thing. He sent two DVDs; one is called 'God and Gays' and the other is titled 'God and Guns.' The governor's contribution in the series is supposed to be 'God and Government.'"

"Whoa! We better check those out before we accept," Jim insisted.

Alan countered, "Accept the engagement, but I need to see the interview on 'gays' before I attend the conference. I don't care what he said about guns, but I need to be ready for any press reaction in regard to the other one."

Mrs. Billingsly gave the DVD to the governor, who put the disk in his bag for review at home that evening. As she walked to the door, he called out, "Lenore, have I met Archer before?"

"During the campaign you talked with him, but only one time. He spoke to you in the hospital. You seemed disturbed."

With pleasant surprise, he responded, "That was him? I like him. Of course I'll go."

Later in the evening, as he viewed the video, Alan was surprised. A preacher who talked about homosexuality was not usually so revealing or understanding. Generally, religious people condemned homosexuality in terms which made gays feel threatened or discriminated against. Other times, they accepted it, making the orthodox Bible believers belligerent. This was a college atmosphere, so the usual religious inhibitions would not appeal to the inquisitive young people in attendance.

The video opened with a close-up of Archer as he talked to a male student. The student identified himself as homosexual. Archer asked him serious and in-depth questions about his relationships. As he watched the recorded event on a computer in his private study in the governor's mansion, Alan felt uncomfortable as the student gave a high level of detail about the nature of his activities. Archer was careful as he questioned the young man not to make him feel awkward through his line of questioning. At one point, Alan choked on the water he was drinking upon hearing a particularly shocking revelation. The student had obviously tried to elicit some response from the preacher by revealing intimate details of his sexual activities.

However, if a negative reply from Archer was the student's intention, he was not satisfied, for Reverend Adams was consistently respectful and pleasant. He avoided the use of any stereotypical references to gays or their lifestyle. While he watched, Alan expected Archer to be a liberal preacher, saying homosexual relationships were good. However, he didn't accept the student's orientation openly, but he didn't condemn the young man either. Alan witnessed through the interview what he never thought possible: a preacher who found middle ground on a highly controversial issue. Governor Cassell wondered what Archer would have said about abortion before *Roe v. Wade* was overturned.

Archer Adams accepted the premise that gay people do have real loving connections to their partners. He also accepted that they received sexual satisfaction through their associations.

Alan was unclear what point the preacher was trying to make as the video continued. The interview portion of the DVD ended and Archer Adams began his sermon. Speaking calmly, he alleged that defining people by the type of sex they prefer is contrary to the scriptures.

Adams said, "It is not a sin to be a homosexual. I would suggest that there is no status of being homosexual, or heterosexual, in the Scriptures. Since the Bible does not address such a state of being, we cannot condemn what the scripture does not address. It is not a sin to be attracted to someone of the same sex or to want a loving, meaningful relationship. The Bible does speak of certain actions as sins. The text also addresses the idea of 'lusts,' but attraction alone does not infer lust.

"Any sex outside of what God defines as 'marriage' is a sin, but that only means that you are missing the mark of how and why God created you." When his sermon was finished, he ended the video with prayer. Alan felt less prepared for the interview than he had before he saw the video.

Even so, the governor traveled to Lawrence on the appointed Sunday morning. Deep clouds hung across the eastern half of the state, but no rain was evident. He was accustomed to the limo and the police escort by then. Alan thought the transportation and escort were both an extravagance, but he understood the necessity. The schedule called for breakfast with Reverend Adams before the interview began at noon. Alan had his Bible and reference books with him on the road to prepare for the meeting, but he couldn't concentrate. He would occasionally ask Jim a question, only to ignore the answer.

The breakfast meeting included Archer Adams, the governor, and Jim Cherry. Jim was wary about the event, so he made sure he was in attendance; he wanted to ensure the preacher didn't say anything that might be used to later to embarrass Governor Cassell.

The event was highly publicized and television crews were outside the hall. The press was not permitted into the hall, but the service was recorded. The media was informed they would have access to footage of the interview after its completion.

Outside the hall, a large number of protesters gathered which added to the newsworthiness of the event. Many professional educators from the university, as well as local public schools, were there to oppose Alan's controversial education reform plan.

Well away from the protests or the sounds of their chants, the campus minister and the governor met. "Governor Cassell," Archer began. "It's great to see you again, and congratulations on the electoral victory. I'm glad I am able to meet with you under more favorable circumstances than our first meeting. Please make yourself comfortable," he said as he motioned toward a seat. "We have coffee and I can get you pretty much anything you might want to eat."

"Thank you. I appreciated your kind words in the hospital; they were very helpful to me," Alan sincerely acknowledged.

"It was the least I could do under the circumstances," Archer replied. "I'm glad the words were able to bring you some comfort."

Then, in response to Archer's offer, Alan suggested, "How about a bowl of fruit? Is that possible?"

"And your friend?"

Realizing he had not made a proper introduction, he said, "I'm sorry; this is my Chief of Staff, Jim Cherry. He likes to travel with me now and again."

"Just coffee for me … I already ate," Jim insisted. "I'll sit over here and just be available if needed, okay?"

Jim made himself a cup of coffee, the governor poured himself a glass of water, and Archer went to the door, asking someone outside the room for two bowls of fruit.

Returning to the table, Archer inquired, "Cassell? Are you of the Cassells descended from President Chester Arthur?"

"I'm not certain, but I have heard we are," the governor replied.

"I have an interesting story regarding President Arthur. While he was still a young man, a minister approached him and predicted, 'This young man will be President of the United States of America.'" Archer continued, "Ironically, Chester Arthur never ran for any elected office until chosen to be vice president. Yet, the prediction eventually came true."

"Really? I never heard that particular story. Are those the exact words the preacher used?" Alan inquired.

"I can't say those were the *exact* words used then, but they are the exact words I'm using today!" Archer declared, looking intently at Alan.

Alan felt uncomfortable at the comments and the inference they made. Archer's intense stare made the story of a young man becoming president one of foreboding, rather than a gratuitous compliment, as Alan had become accustomed to. He decided to avoid delving further into the matter by asking his host, "What's the program for this afternoon?"

Meanwhile, a young woman entered the room. She carried in the two bowls of assorted fruit chunks, and then excused herself.

Archer willingly changed conversational course and responded, "A simple interview. We will sit on chairs with a table between us. Water will be on the table if you need it. I'll ask you about your time in office so far, about your wife and her time here at KU, and your personal experiences in general. We must avoid any current issues. You won't be allowed to campaign for your policies;

the university wouldn't allow for such politics. We'll keep the conversation light and personal. If you have any anecdotes, feel free. After about twenty minutes, I'll step away and begin my homily, which is intended to encourage young people to consider public service and to apply biblical principles to the community at large."

After snacking on the fruit and having had a few minutes of light conversation, Archer and Alan went out of the meeting room and onto the stage. The interview went smoothly, as promised. The governor was able to stay for a short time after the meeting and shake hands with the students, who received him enthusiastically.

Some years earlier, during expansion of the university facilities, a pedestrian overpass walkway had been built. The overpass was just beyond a courtyard outside the hall where Governor Cassell had just spoken. Protestors were gathered en masse on the elevated walkway; the activists had banners and signs positioned to be seen by the television cameras when the governor exited the building. As the number of protestors grew, local and state police had been called to keep the peace.

Once outside, Governor Cassell stopped to answer questions from the press. After just a few minutes of rapid-fire questions and answers, a loud cracking sound, followed closely by a great THUD!, interrupted the flurry of activities.

The sound was made by a chunk of concrete, which had broken loose from the walkway. The heavy piece of bridge fell onto the street below with a great crash. The crowd on the walkway had exceeded the capacity of the structure, and it failed under the stress.

The mob panicked, and people were pushing each other to get off the bridge before it collapsed completely. A large, gaping hole was already in the structure, and additional groaning and cracking sounds suggested impending disaster. The chaos within the crowd of escaping people likely added to the collapse.

Both ends of the walkway were obstructed by people trying to get off the crumbling structure. One woman could be seen from below as she was trapped in the large hole at the apex of the walkway, struggling to hang on.

Alan didn't think about his status as governor, or his security detail; he immediately slipped away from those around him and ran to the site. The state police barricaded the protesters away from the governor, but did not attempt to keep him from getting to them. Once he passed through their protective line, the direction of the barricade seemed to change and no one else was permitted to join him.

Alan instantly surmised that a person could climb on the outside of the still-standing portions of the walkway. Since the bridge had been built with irregular concrete shapes, he had places easily available to put his feet. The structure also had chain-link guards designed to keep prankster students from throwing anything onto the street below. He used the chain-link as hand holds. His feet slipped a couple of times since he was wearing dress shoes. Even so, he successfully climbed to the top and was able to pull the woman away from the broken concrete that had entrapped her foot; he helped her escape safely, seconds before the structure failed entirely.

The TV cameras, which had been filming the entire spectacle, finally recorded a cloud of dust as it obscured the Governor, who was clearly the last to exit with the rescued woman just ahead of him. Moments later, he emerged from the dust cloud, coughing but unharmed. The deep cloud cover, which hung in the background, made the whole scene appear even more ominous.

Once again, Alan Cassell found himself doing the right thing at the right time. Providential forces seemed to be at work in his life once again. This time, his heroic efforts were publicized in the national news. His action made him a hero in the minds of people across the country. He was not the first governor to save a life; it was the video and the apparent risks he took to save a woman who had been protesting him that made the scene so dramatic.

CHAPTER 10 • **THE SPEECH**

It is a cliché these days to observe that the United States now possesses a global empire—different from Britain's and Rome's, but an empire nonetheless.

—Robert D. Kaplan

M IDWAY THROUGH ALAN Cassell's first term as governor, a presidential election loomed. There was no doubt that Kansas would, once again, be a red state. The Republican nomination was a foregone conclusion, since Senator John Halprin of Texas was already the presumptive nominee. The incumbent president, a Democrat, was highly popular and running for re-election.

With the prospects for success in the general election dismal, the Republicans searched for anything to invigorate the nominating convention. The Republicans decided the attractive and heroic Governor Alan Cassell from Kansas could possibly bring life to what was generally presumed by party members to be a doomed convention and campaign.

The national problems of the previous years were long forgotten. Originally a topic of concern, Puerto Rico's independence had not created any long-term difficulties. The dual monetary system was now fully accepted by the public, and the economy was on the rise. Chinese manufacturing interests had purchased many non-operational factories and made consumer products in America, which previously had been made in China; America was a net exporter again.

However, the national debt was continuing to grow and Senator Halprin was convinced the administration was creating a temporary boom with borrowed money. Taxes were high on businessmen in America, but Congress approved the president's plan to give generous tax credits for foreign investors in domestic manufacturing ventures.

While employment was high, the American inclination toward entrepreneurialism was on the wane. Tax policies pushed Americans away from owning their own businesses; nationally, retirement funds were highly invested in federal debt.

Republicans were convinced the current economy was a house of cards. The party wanted the young, heroic Governor to make a keynote speech at the Republican National Convention that would expose the underlying weakness of Democratic policies.

At the same time in Hawaii, the *ke ea Hawaii*, or Hawaii sovereignty movement, underwent significant changes. In the past, the movement had been fractionalized and its advocates were antagonistic toward each other. Agreeing on points of previous conflict, the groups began to find common ground. All groups believed the monarchy should be restored, but by that time, they had called for a very limited constitutional monarchy.

None of the activists insisted on removal of American military bases, as they had in the past. They agreed persons living in the state should be granted citizenship equal to those with aboriginal Hawaiian ancestry, though most still called for a legislative body comprised exclusively of native Hawaiians. They also withdrew the claim that contracts made during the illegal occupation of the Kingdom were null and void. A final change consisted of the large Japanese American population in Hawaii adding membership numbers to the various sovereignty organizations.

Under that backdrop, the GOP convention in Dallas was held in August, just two months after the incident at KU. Alan had seen numerous drafts of a speech from Republican Party staffers, but he hoped to put his own spin on it.

The Cassells stayed at the historic Adolphus Hotel in downtown Dallas. Kate no longer appeared to be a beautiful girl, but rather a woman of overwhelming classic beauty. When they appeared at the airport, the press reported on her activities as much or more than anything else that led up to the convention. Her wardrobe was recently upgraded, thanks to a sizeable gift from her father.

Alan and Kate thought little of the commotion and one evening they took a stroll, complete with Kansas state police as escorts, from the hotel to a posh downtown department store. Upon their exit from the store, they found the sidewalk overwhelmed by paparazzi more suited to the presence of a famous rock star rather than a state governor and his wife.

The couple slipped back into the store and the store's management arranged for them to leave the building via a more discreet exit, while also providing a car to take them back to the hotel. From that point on, every move Kate made was covered by dozens of photographers. Alan adapted the approved text of his speech to address the events involving his glamorous wife.

Senator Halprin was thankful the Kansas governor and first lady were expected to improve viewership of the convention. Finally, the night of his speech arrived. The Cassells reached the convention hall early in the day. After being driven in a limousine longer and taller than any Alan had ever seen, they were taken to a service entrance where Secret Service agents were stationed. The huge overhead door rose, and the limo drove silently into Reunion Arena. The Cassells were escorted to a number of suites where the largest party donors in the nation eagerly awaited the opportunity to visit the modern Republican answer to Jackie Kennedy. The press clearly preferred Kate to the much older and less-than-fashionable Mrs. Halprin.

At each donor suite, wealthy contributors presented Kate with various newspapers and magazines for her to autograph, all featuring pictures of her. Television monitors in the rooms displayed news or convention coverage, and every broadcast featured stories about Kate. Some of these stories re-hashed her beauty pageant days.

"The Miss America organizers must surely wish the judges had picked you now," joked Alan at one point.

Other shows rehashed the accident which resulted in the passing of their daughter. Kate had difficulty dealing with such reports, but held her composure.

The moment for the speech finally arrived. The arena was filled to capacity. The crowd was overly zealous, especially in light of the expected defeat for Republicans in the upcoming election—at both the national and state levels. In reality, Alan could have said virtually anything, and whatever was said would have been a sensation with that audience.

Congresswoman Helen Benton of Oregon made the introductions. The viewing screens showed pictures of the Cassells, including the video from Lawrence and the collapsing walkway. The delegates roared approval when they saw Governor Cassell emerge from the cloud of dust with the woman he had rescued. They applauded so wildly at the pictures of Kansas's first lady hardly a word of the introduction could be heard.

The governor finally stepped out onto the stage, greeting the congresswoman for the first time. Yet, they still embraced like old friends. He then began his speech.

"Delegates and friends of the Republican Party and of America, I am the fortunate man who had the privilege of escorting Kate Cassell to Dallas, Texas." The crowd erupted with laughter and applause, which quickly changed to a standing ovation when the cameras showed Kate on the jumbo screens.

He had to wait a few moments before he could begin again. "In San Francisco next month, you will have the opportunity to hear about some very positive changes, which happened during the administration of our current president."

The partisan audience did not take well to the concept of anything good from an opposition administration.

"Now, now," Governor Cassell insisted, motioning with his palms down to quiet the groans and boos that emanated from the crowd. "We should give credit where credit is due.

"The economy appears to be very strong; it's true! More Americans are working now than ever before in history. It's a good thing too—since we all must work more to pay a tax burden that is higher than any other nation in the world."

The crowd now understood his take on events and responded with applause and laughter. From that point on, the applause, laughter, and overall positive energy from the delegates continued throughout the remainder of Alan's speech.

"Yes, employment is high, and unemployment is very low. Americans work hard and long; you collectively work nearly twice as many hours per week as your counterparts in continental Europe. Your productivity and quality make 'made in America' a symbol of excellence throughout the world.

"When I was a child, growing up in a poor working class family in Kansas, nearly everything we bought, except food, was made in China. Now, America is exporting to China. We export agricultural products, as we always have; we also export machinery, technology, and even consumer products to China. Unfortunately, we are also exporting the profits from our growing industrial base to China!

"Who do we have to thank for this success? The current administration is proud of its policies that have forced American business owners to sell or close shop, while foreign manufacturers are subsidized for making their products here! Yes, you heard me correctly. We are exporting those excessive tax dollars all Americans are currently paying as well!

"Surely, we can be proud of our healthcare system," Governor Cassell continued. "America was late to the game of nationalized healthcare, but we got it right, didn't we? The administration thinks we have. They proudly point to the dramatic decrease in patients going to doctor's offices and hospitals. Could it be they don't go because they can't get in? I'm sorry, but I just don't see the virtue of shorter lines of people who can't see a doctor, a physician's assistant, or even a nurse!

"John Halprin has proposed a plan to end the lines and let each American actually see the medical professional of our choice. It's a controversial idea, and I hope you're ready for it. It's something called '*the free market!*'

"The current administration also has seemed to solve the illegal immigration crisis. With the standard of living in Mexico, and throughout the hemisphere, rising faster than in America, people previously considering immigration would rather stay home than come here! In addition, Americans are finding ways to travel more than they used to years ago. So many Americans are traveling so often that more and more of them are choosing to make the places they enjoy visiting their permanent home. Today, there are nearly ten million people who no longer claim US citizenship! For the first time in history, immigration to the United States of America is eclipsed by migration away from it.

"Our education system is leading the world. The Department of Education is claiming credit for all of the changes. In every state in the union, schools are becoming virtual. Student test scores are on the rise, costs are down, and finally, yes finally, teachers are the highly-qualified and highly-paid respected professionals they should always have been. These reforms started in Alaska, where pragmatism required change, then Texas, Montana, Vermont, and now, in my own Kansas. The progress in education is becoming a successful movement nationwide.

"The administration now points with pride to the advantages of reform. But, keep in mind, my friends, this is the same administration that fought those reforms every step of the way. States... like mine, took the initiative to enact education reform, despite many efforts to thwart change. Kansas and the other early states that pushed for reform were financially penalized by the Department of Education. But now, following all those efforts at intimidation from the federal government, the states are encouraged to reform.

"Wow! What forward-thinking by the administration. Penalize innovation then incentivize others to utilize that same innovation. To make matters worse, they are taking credit for the improvement! Incredible!

"The administration is especially proud of all the new roads and highways, as well as an urban mass transit system the nation has built over the past few years. Indeed, we have repaired, replaced or rebuilt thousands of miles of highways and rural roadways. Do you realize that every one of those projects was completed by states, counties, and localities, *not* the Federal Transportation Department?

"Of course, the federal government did contribute funds to most of those projects. But, here is the math they don't want you to know: for every dollar they used to assist transportation projects, the federal government spent *two dollars and eighty-seven cents of taxpayer money*! The Democrats want the American people to let them carry on that kind of efficiency?

"As a state governor, I can tell you state transportation dollars spent on state projects average an eighty-eight percent efficiency rate, with just twelve percent spent on non-construction related overhead. Wouldn't it make more fiscal sense to keep your transportation tax dollars in your state rather than send them to Washington, DC? John Halprin thinks so, and so do I.

"Senator John Halprin is not promising a glut of new big government programs that are too expensive and accomplish very little. John Halprin proposes we restore the premise of limited government; a federal government doing only what we need the federal government to do, allowing the states to do everything else.

"John Halprin has a track record you can be proud of. President Halprin will be a president you can be proud of. He is a president who will restore the strength of America. A president who will not take credit for *your* efforts or even for the projects *your tax dollars* pay for."

Alan's speech built to a rousing crescendo; the entire crowd was on its feet long before it ended.

"From the Atlantic to the Pacific and from the Great Lakes to the Gulf Coast, America is a great nation! Our greatness comes not from government; our greatness is in our people! We need a president who knows that America's greatness comes from the American people! We need John Halprin as the next President of the United States of America!"

The partisan crowd approved entirely of Alan's speech, but the real work of the evening had just begun. The GOP had its "War Room" up and running, with a multitude of spin doctors to hype the qualities of the speech and how it magnified the qualifications of their nominee.

Each Republican media representative was coached to extol the genius of a preemptive strike against the Democrats. They were expected to speak in glowing terms about the governor of Kansas and his wife. What had not been predicted was their questioning Senator Halprin's choice of the governor of New Jersey as his running mate. Governor Alan Cassell, they suggested, may have been a stronger choice; he certainly would have been a younger one. Cassell was barely eligible under the Constitution's age requirement. The current choice for vice president was nearly twice his age.

Alan and Kate talked about the situation privately. "If Halprin wins, then perhaps he would want me on the ticket with him in four years," Alan confidentially suggested to his wife. He thought a "new" vice president would be needed in a second Halprin term. The whole state of affairs seemed like a pipe dream, but the extremely high ratings for his speech combined with the public's acceptance of his message as "the impressive young couple," made the idea a possibility.

In the following months, Alan and Kate both threw themselves into the campaign. The Halprin campaign utilized Alan to rally the base, while Kate looked great on television and possessed a strong crossover appeal. The Cassells traveled as much as they could to promote Senator Halprin, although there were still state matters that had to be cared for by Alan.

Alan was surprised by the other Republican office holders who promised to help, but did very little in actuality. Alan traveled throughout the Midwest and the West, making two trips to Florida and one to Oregon.

Whenever the need arose, Lieutenant Governor Sims filled in for Governor Cassell quite well. She sincerely hoped Alan would not become a member of Halprin's cabinet. *I don't want to take the governor's office yet*, she thought. *In a couple more years, perhaps.*

While on the road for Halprin, Alan was able to get to know the congresswoman who had introduced him at the convention. Helen Wisniewski-Benton was originally from Michigan. The Wisniewskis moved to Salem, Oregon, when Helen was a child. She was an unusually apt student, especially in mathematics. She received an engineering degree from Oregon State University. During college, while visiting home one weekend, she met a student from Chemeketa Community College studying viticulture and enology. The student, Bob Benton, eventually became her husband. They moved onto his family's farm near Roseburg, where he fulfilled his dream of establishing a vineyard and winery. They raised three children, two of whom stayed to help Bob build the winery. Benton Wines was highly recognized for their Pinot Noir.

Helen's family, the Wisniewskis, were of Polish heritage. Her grandparents all emigrated from Poland prior to the fall of the Berlin Wall. They had many relatives in America, including some celebrated athletes.

Later, Alan flew with Senator Halprin to Portland. The senator held a large rally in the city, while Governor Cassell traveled south for a smaller rally in Roseburg. The Bentons met the governor at the small local airport. He spent the night with the Benton family before the next day's noontime rally. After the event, he returned to Portland and on to Kansas City. Kansas State Troopers were present when he left the plane and provided transportation for the return to Topeka.

The congresswoman and her husband met Alan at the Roseburg airport. "Congresswoman Benton, it's great seeing you again," said Alan. "This must be your husband, Bob, right?"

"Yes. Welcome to Roseburg, the conservative heart of Oregon," the congress-woman replied. Alan jumped into the car which Bob stood by with the door open. The Kansas state trooper who traveled with him tossed luggage into the trunk and jumped in as well.

When all four people were in the large Mercedes, they began to discuss plans. "You'll stay with us tonight, and we'll take you to the rally where I'll introduce you, okay?" Helen inquired.

"Yeah, that's the plan. Hey, I would love to hear about your vineyard since we have a moment."

"Too little rain this year," Bob commented with a hint of irritation in his voice. "The state won't let us irrigate anymore—damn fools. I've got the water, but you politicians won't let me use it. I have no patience for politicians."

"Oh Bob, hush," his "politician" wife said. "You never had patience for anyone that *wasn't* a politician either! Your vines, you only have patience for your vines, not me, not your children, not even yourself." She said this in a playful, as opposed to perturbed, manner.

Helen was short, round, and dominant. She had a grandmotherly look and nature with an intoxicating smile. "Governor Cassell was being nice, Bob. He can't tell the state of Oregon to let you use our water." She then turned to Alan and asked, "So why are you holding a rally here, while Halprin holds one in the city?"

"The strategy is for him to be there in person; if we are to win over any votes in liberal Portland, we need the press to follow him. Meanwhile, I can get away with saying anything that will rouse the base in a Republican area like this. The liberal media will never cover what we do here while he's in Portland, so we have freedom! That's the strategy in a swing state like Oregon: energize the base on the one hand, win converts on the other, and never let the right hand know what the 'far right' hand is doing," he said with a jovial laugh.

"It seems we can never quite get over the hump here in Oregon," Helen replied. "Every four years we poll within the margin of error, but we always seem to give it up to the Democrats when the Portland numbers come in. I would love John to win, but I don't know if any Republican can win this time ..."

"Here we are," Bob Benton interrupted. "Welcome to Benton Winery, the home of the finest Pinot Noir in the Umquah. The Umquah produces the best Pinot in America, of course. They call Pinot the 'Heartbreak Grape' because it needs just the right *terroir* and weather. Further north, in the Willamette, the days are too cold. Down in California, the nights are too dry and hot. Our weather brings out the purest Pinot in the nose and on the pallet."

Alan wasn't sure how to respond to Bob's comments, but he replied, "I do hope you'll let me sample a bit of this famed wine, even buy a few bottles to take home. Your wines are not sold in Kansas."

"Sell 'em all right here and can't keep up with the demand. What isn't consumed by the locals, we sell to wine tourists working their way up I-5. I'll show you around while we wait for dinner."

Alan was taken aback by the couple and their peculiar relationship; she as a member of the United States Congress and he a gruff winemaker. *And yet, he expects her to cook dinner like she was a full-time homemaker. Kate hardly makes dinner, and she doesn't work at all anymore,* he thought. *Somehow, it must work for them.*

Bob Benton took Governor Cassell and his security detail around the vineyard, while talking about petiole analysis, veraison, brix, cordons and canopy management. Once in the winery itself, Bob instructed Alan about must, tannins, maceration and racking. Very little of the conversation made any sense to Alan, but he played along, certain Bob knew the meaning of the terms of his industry. He was also looking forward to the opportunity for a taste.

Bob Benton acted as if his tour was completely understandable to the novice. Alan did understand, however, that the bottle of Estate Reserve Bob opened for him was something inexpressibly special. The wine snob terms always seemed a bunch of nonsense to Alan. Yet, putting this glass to his nose, and then a sip of wine into his mouth, made him want to create new words to describe the sensation of wine on his palate. *All the crap the snobs talk about must have some actual meaning,* he thought to himself.

Alan could only think of chocolate, how really good chocolate fills your mouth with a rich wondrous sensation. Like chocolate, except the wine didn't have a thick creamy residue like chocolate. When he swallowed, a whole new and satisfying awareness happened. Bob saw Alan's expression change and said something about "finish." Alan knew exactly what he was talking about after the first taste, the body of the wine seeping into his senses.

Alan drank wine and beer on a regular basis, but this was as if he never had tasted wine before. Kate liked white or blush wine, which Alan thought was all right, but a little too sweet. When he would go to "rubber chicken" dinners and get served some inexpensive brand of Cabernet Sauvignon or Merlot, he considered the wines harsh and unpleasant. He found beer was refreshing on a hot day, and a little buzz was welcome, but he didn't really like beer either. Alan decided this was the best wine made by man. Really, the Estate Reserve was just the first decent wine he'd ever tried.

Bob suddenly liked *this* politician from Kansas, who bragged incessantly about his product.

At dinnertime, Alan learned that Helen cooked the same way as her grandmother did. The hearty meal consisted of kielbasa and pierogi, preceded by cold borsht with hot uszka dropped in, followed by sweet nalesniki. The names of the dishes not only sounded foreign, but they tasted unfamiliar in every way. Laid out on the table was cold red beet soup with hot dumplings bobbing about, polish sausage, some golden-brown crescent-shaped ravioli-type things with un-sour sauerkraut, mushrooms, and pieces of bacon or mashed potatoes in them, both types served with a generous portion of sour cream. The sausage seemed ordinary enough upon first glance, but hers was homemade and was full of flavor. For dessert, he was served what he thought was a pancake, but was really more of a crepe wrapped around light, sweet cream cheese with powdered sugar sprinkled on top.

To his surprise, Alan enjoyed it all immensely. Of course he enjoyed the meal; he was permitted to continue to consume the wonderful "reserve" wine he and Bob had begun earlier in the evening.

In Kansas, a fine dinner at home was most commonly a steak, potato, bread with butter, and perhaps some steamed broccoli or corn on the cob. Alan thought the "steak and potatoes" meal was the ordinary home meal nationwide. He considered foreign or unique foods to be reserved for international travel or black tie banquets. That particular evening, Alan realized different, ethnic cuisine was normal for ordinary people in other parts of the country.

Alan knew most Americans were more alike than they were different; yet subtle distinctions in families will sometimes surprise even the most culturally aware person. He had spent the day hearing the vocabulary of an unfamiliar industry and eating foods he had never seen or heard of before. Yet, Helen and Bob were as American as apple pie.

As he lay down to sleep that night, he was struck by the realization that Bob was striking back at him and Helen for the shop talk on the way in from the airport. He had hit Alan with shop talk of his own. *The ole geezer got me! Quite impressive for someone who claims to not understand politics!*, he told himself, amused.

The rally for Halprin went as well as anticipated. More than a thousand devoted Republicans cheered at his every word, working themselves into a frenzy of hopefulness. However, the near-desperation expressed by the faithful convinced Alan that the cause was lost. The realization took the wind out of his sails. Alan had never lost a political race. This election had appeared early on to be an uphill battle, but he had remained optimistic through the campaign. The polls never moved in favor of the Republican following the convention, and although Alan's speech was a rousing success, the nation knew the GOP was not going to take the White House. In effect, Alan and Kate's popularity translated into very few votes for Halprin. The whole campaign was an exercise in futility.

Surely Halprin knows it's a lost cause; how does he campaign as he does? Alan contemplated. He realized through this election that running for office is not always about winning. All candidates want to win, but some know that they won't, barring some tragedy upon their opponent or miracle for themselves. Yet they often ran just as strong and hard.

There is virtue in being a standard-bearer for your ideals and the ideals of those who support you. A great respect goes out to those who run the race with the zest of a candidate who has a serious chance. This is true even if you can read the writing on the wall, and it says, "Go home, curl up in a ball like a baby, and forget you ever tried."

Senator Halprin was running hard, but he was going to lose; it was electoral math. The solid red states of the South and the central farm states from Texas to North Dakota, as well as most of the Mountain West would still be red. The blue states of the Pacific Coast, the Northeast and the industrialized Midwest would stay blue. The swing states were Florida, New Jersey, Ohio, Missouri, Colorado, Oregon and New Mexico. The problem was that only Missouri looked promising, and the GOP was losing ground quickly in Virginia, Georgia and Indiana. The Republicans began to hemorrhage as the polls continued to show no gain. The press suggested a Democratic rout; Halprin worked hard to retain Republican members of congress rather than to actually win the White House.

Alan gained a new level of respect for John Halprin. He had considered the senator a good person, though not as consistently conservative as himself. Now he saw Halprin as a man ready to fight for the cause rather than for self; he admired his attitude and dedication. Alan pledged himself to help the campaign even more, regardless of his personal assessment of the final result, but the revelation of impending doom had a subconscious effect. Events in Kansas seemed more pressing than before, so Alan regretfully declined additional opportunities to campaign around the country for Halprin, focusing his efforts on state matters. His decision was made just in time, since the willingness of Kansas voters to loan their governor out to a presidential campaign was at its limit.

On the other hand, the first lady of Kansas continued to maintain her regular schedule of campaign events, lending her considerable popularity to the flailing campaign of Senator Halprin. While the citizens of Kansas wanted their elected leader to spend more time in state, they were willing to lend Kate to the national party for as long as she was needed. Kate's popularity with Republicans continued to grow, and she was seen as a selfless supporter of a lost cause.

CHAPTER 11 • CASSELL FOR AMERICA

"The American congress will always do the right thing, only after exhausting all other possibilities."

—Winston Churchill

N O ONE WAS SURPRISED WHEN the GOP lost the White House again, or when there was a net loss of a few seats in the US House of Representatives. However, despite their few losses in the House, the Republicans had a net gain of one in the Senate. John Halprin's valiant efforts prevented the predicted Democratic surge.

Alan left the campaign with a much better understanding of national politics. He acquired a number of national contacts, as well as a friendly relationship with most of Halprin's campaign and senatorial staff. He found new appreciation of the opportunities his job as governor provided to the general public. Kansas was a small state, approachable, and governable. While he could never know the voters statewide as well as he did in Crawford County, he did know all of the key players, major business people, and his own appointees.

Alan had realized through time that a viable presidential candidate can't shake hands with every maximum donor. In addition, a president will make appointments of people he never meets, talk with ambassadors he doesn't really know, and must sign bills he personally doesn't read. He was actually relieved the imagined scenario of becoming Halprin's second vice president was not going to become a reality.

Shortly after the general election, Alan suffered a personal loss. His mother, Peggy Cassell, passed away. Oddly, the day that he got the call about her passing, his recently-promoted administrative assistant, Lenore Billingsly, was having lunch with her sister and brother-in-law.

Ironically, Archer Adams managed to be around whenever Alan needed help with a personal matter. Alan asked him for a private meeting later that afternoon. Archer visited, listening to Alan's mixed feelings about his mother. Archer offered very few words, but Alan was persuaded he had "the balm of Gilead."

Alan insisted Archer perform his mother's funeral, which was, as it turned out, his first memorial service. College-aged church attendees seldom die, but when they do, the families ordinarily choose a minister from a church they attend near their homes.

With his mother's passing, Alan was forced to consider his extended family and their role in his life. After years of searching for focus, Alan's sister Deena was finally married. She and her husband managed the car wash and laundry back home in Kansas. Her husband also worked full-time at the local farm implement dealership. She had turned out all right after all.

Alan was, however, concerned his father might show up at the funeral. He hadn't heard from him since before his second term as commissioner; Alan didn't really know if his father was alive or dead. Archer simply asked questions, allowing Alan to reach his own conclusions about how to deal with his absentee father.

Alan and Deena's father did attend the funeral, but left before the service ended. He never said a word to Alan; he stepped up to Deena at one point and warmly embraced her shoulder as she wept. He then walked out without acknowledging his mourning son.

Hardly a soul at the funeral knew who he was and the only concern on the minds of the assembled was, *What could be so important that he had to leave before the service ended?*

The only positive thing about the funeral was Alan's opportunity to renew so many relationships with people he had lost contact with after he moved to Topeka. Each of the people he reconnected with felt their relationship was untainted because they saw Alan on television or in the papers. He realized he had a very different circle of people around him since winning the election for governor. Except for Jim Cherry, the group was entirely different now.

Alan was tangibly relieved his mother was not going to suffer any longer. Archer did a fine job commemorating Peggy Cassell's life. The service was not about the successes of her son, the previous trials of her daughter's romantic life, or about her own failed marriage. The funeral centered on the eternal nature of a well-lived life.

"I had the honor of meeting Peggy only once," Archer recounted at one point in the service, "but I believe I learned a great deal about her during that brief time. She was constantly at the side of her darling granddaughter, Katie. She unceasingly remained at Katie's bedside until the newborn baby passed.

"I had the opportunity to pray with her during those sad days. I was also able to sense her devotion to her family and the eternal nature of the relationship between a grandmother and her short-lived granddaughter. Such moments are not merely snapshots in time, only existing in one place and then gone. No, such moments are part of the very fabric of eternity."

Archer's words provided a comforting concept for the assembled mourners, which conveyed the continuity of life.

As a further indication of the progress she had made in her life, Deena was executor of Peggy's estate, which consisted of little more than a small post-war home with two bedrooms and a single small bath. Deena inherited the house, although she and her husband had a newer, larger one south of town. The most significant provision of Peggy's will, however, was that her body was to be cremated, and her ashes spread on Katie's grave.

Alan protested and tried to convince Deena to let him buy a plot and coffin to give her a traditional burial. Yet Deena was firm in her resolve to honor her mother's request. Alan didn't really care, but thought he ought to try to change her mind.

On the other hand, Kate was not happy at all with the idea and, upon learning the provision, complained to her husband the night before the funeral. "I don't want to be thinking of your mother when I visit Katie ..." She paused for a moment, then continued, "Katie's gravesite."

"Well, that's where she's going to be," Alan retorted.

Kate argued, "I don't want you visiting your mother when you go to Katie ..."

"Kate, I didn't want this either. I argued with Deena; I begged her, offering to pay for everything. She's resolute. She says this is what mother wanted, and she's determined to honor the request. If I can't reason with Deena, there is nothing I can do to stop her. She is the executor of the estate and has the legal power to follow my mother's wishes."

"Tell her the answer is 'NO!'" Kate angrily insisted. "Alan, you have to be firm. She has no right to put your mother's ashes on Katie's plot."

"A lot of good that'll do; it's not as if she was asking for permission. I'll say 'No' and she'll do it anyway, by herself, therefore destroying my relationship with my sister. Is that what you want?"

Alan and Kate's argument lasted for several minutes. They very seldom argued, in comparison to other couples, but they did strongly disagree about his mother's arrangements. No one wins a marital argument. He wished he could find a way to keep Deena from committing his mother's ashes to Katie's grave, but when neither Kate nor Alan could figure a way out of the situation, they agreed to attend the pseudo-ceremony Deena had planned for right after the service at the funeral home.

Despite being early December, the night before was still and comparatively warm. The day of the funeral started sunny and dry. However, a winter front moved in at just the right time, bringing sleet and a glazing of ice that covered the land. The weather provided Alan with an opportunity, which prevented the spreading of his mother's ashes on Katie's grave.

He and Kate pulled Deena aside, where he calmly and compassionately expressed, "Deena, we can't put the ashes out today; the ice will prevent them from settling on the ground and the wind will blow them away. We can't have that happen. You'll have to take care of the urn for the time being, okay?" Deena agreed, and Kate was relieved.

The campaign season returned to Kansas a few months later. Alan's re-election campaign was uneventful. A businessman from the Kansas City area was the Democratic nominee. He put up his own money to finance his campaign, yet Alan was able to raise nearly three times as much without significant efforts on his part. He actually felt guilty he needed to do so little to campaign, but Jim Cherry told him, "It is more important for an incumbent to govern than to campaign." The governor's supporters were more than willing to take the lead in campaigning, while his attention to the work of state business portrayed him as a man of the people yet again.

Less than a month after the gubernatorial re-election, and just over a month prior to his second inauguration, an old friend came to visit Alan at the state capitol.

Lenore walked into the Governor's office with a broad smile. "You have a surprise visitor, Governor Cassell."

"You're smiling, so the visitor must not be Archer," he replied. Archer's visits put Lenore on edge. She didn't believe in him, as Alan obviously did, and was concerned that Archer was using her position to gain access to the governor. "Lenore, you needn't worry about Archer. I like him and I trust him. Even if you weren't related, I would continue to have him here. If he's in town, I want to visit with him, okay?"

"Yes, sir," she stated with relief. From that day forward, her relationship with Archer improved. The pressure was off, regarding the governor, and she could begin to deal with him as family again. Lenore stated, "It's actually Senator Halprin."

"Well, I bet he's running again! Show the next President of the United States in."

Alan called out, "Senator, come on in here."

"Governor, congratulations are in order for your re-election," John Halprin replied. "I hear your education reform is still giving you some heartburn, huh?"

"That's true, John. I didn't exactly get the bill I wanted, and we are having exactly the problems I thought we would without the implementation of my full plan. My opponents insisted on including a phase-in schedule, and now they want to 'fix' the timetable before the system was ever fully implemented. It's still better than what we had, so I guess I shouldn't complain too much ..."

Alan paused for a moment, changing the subject. "You didn't have to come here to congratulate me or to ask me about 'ed' reform in Kansas. You certainly didn't have to come all this way to ask me to support you for the presidential nomination either. That's a given. The field is wide open and waiting for you.

You've been to Iowa recently, I hear. Regardless, you've got my support. I'll go to the mat to help you, just like last time."

Halprin smiled and responded, "Yeah, I believe you would, Alan. You did more campaigning—you and Kate, that is—did more for the Republican Party during my campaign than any other elected officials."

"Thank you! We were happy to help," Alan replied, now waiting less than patiently for the anticipated announcement.

"I have been thinking about the upcoming presidential race. You're right, I have made a couple of preliminary trips to New Hampshire and Iowa to keep the crowd out of the way, but I didn't reach a final decision until a couple days ago."

Alan was sure he was about to be one of the very first to know that Senator Halprin, or more properly, former Senator Halprin, since he hadn't run for re-election, was making a second run at the White House. He was very pleased with the notion; he knew all the work John had put in during the previous campaign would be rewarded. The current vice president was not running, causing the Democrats to react in general disarray. John Halprin would win this time, he was sure.

"Alan, I really came to ask you to do me a favor," John continued.

Alan had no idea what more he could do for his friend. So, he put out a feeler. Was John asking him to be his vice presidential candidate? "John, the nomination is most certainly yours for the taking. You ran a strong race, and you made us all proud. But isn't it a little early to be solidifying the ticket?"

John feigned shock at Alan's assumption. "What! Wow, Alan, you think I'm asking you to be my vice president? Everyone told me you were ambitious but my God man, you really are ..."

"I'm sorry John, it just sounded ..." stammered Alan, clearly embarrassed he had totally misread John's intentions.

"Well, settle down," John continued, patting Alan on the shoulder. "I'm not asking you to be vice president. I'm not running; I'm asking you to run."

Alan felt an utter feeling of déjà vu, just like when he mistakenly thought the group at the Coffee Grounds wanted him for *lieutenant* governor.

"What the hell are you talking about, John?" Alan blurted out. "You want *me* to run ... for president ... *now*?"

"That's right, Alan. You, Alan Cassell, as President of the United States;

don't pretend you haven't thought about the idea on your own. Otherwise, why would you have assumed I wanted you as my vice president?"

"OK, yes, I have," admitted Alan. "But not yet! I'd be the youngest president ever. Every governor, every senator, hell, probably every mayor thinks of running for president at some point or another. But you, coming to Kansas to ask me to run for the highest office in the country ... takes the idea out of the realm of fantasy and into the world of reality. Do you really mean it?"

"Nice compliment, Alan," John responded. "You really are a natural politician."

"Hey John, I wasn't trying to compliment you, really," Alan objected. "You could walk into any office in the country and say what you said to me ... whoever you asked would have an actual chance at the White House. You need to tell me why you won't run."

John leaned back in his chair and thought for a moment. "My decision not to run came first, without any specific reasons that I can logically itemize. Then, I had to think of what I would tell the press. I never really settled on why I'm actually not going to run for office. I'm going to use the old stand-by, 'family,' but honestly, I don't know how to put it in words. I ... I just don't think I have another campaign in me. I completely exhausted myself, my family, and everyone who helped the last time. I saw I was not going to win months before Election Day, but killed myself trying to beat the expectation game. I'm happy now. I'm actually making decent money, don't miss the Senate, and I don't want to go through the stress of another campaign. I just don't need it."

"But the country needs *you*, John. America is craving a change. This time, you would win. Winning is better than losing and a lot less stressful. Try it; you'll see," Alan practically begged Halprin.

"I'm not running, and that's final!" John retorted. "I can't believe you got me to say it again. If you know me at all, you know I don't like to repeat myself. If you don't want the nomination, then I'll book a flight to Wyoming."

"Governor Clark!?" Alan shouted. "That old crackpot! If he runs, I'd *have* to run against him ... and I'd win!"

Mark Clark was the eccentric Republican governor of Wyoming who had made a negative impression to the general public on the national news when he made his first speech to the state legislature. He called for a reduction in public surveillance cameras in the cities and on the state highways. His statement was taken out of context by the major media outlets. The offending portion of the speech was, "A safe state is a slave state, and a free state is always a dangerous place to live. We must accommodate ourselves to a bit of danger in order to secure for ourselves true liberty."

John smiled, as he saw Alan's expression and heard his response. "It's settled then. You're running. So what do you say we tell your lovely wife?"

"Okay, but tell me you were kidding about Mark Clark," implored Alan.

"You're going to need his support; you should be careful what you say about a Republican Governor," John said with a broad smile and a light chuckle.

"Bullshit! The last time Wyoming voted for a Democrat, it wasn't a state yet. Admit you were kidding, now, *please*," Alan pleaded, feigning shock at his suggestion.

"Of course I was kidding," John chuckled. "I thought your reference to him as a 'crackpot' was an understatement. Hey, if that's the worst you say about him, then he'll likely support you. On second thought, I'd avoid his endorsement; it could hurt your campaign."

With John still in the room, Alan called Kate at Cedar Crest. "Kate, honey, how about we change our plans for the evening?"

"You complain that I don't cook, and you don't come home for dinner when I do. What is it this time?" she replied in disbelief.

"No, no, I, eh, we ... need to have dinner at home, no change there ..." Alan said, fumbling for words.

"What?" demanded his wife. "I'm supposed to set another place for someone with no notice? You won ... you don't need any more contributions. Who is it this time?"

"John Halprin."

At hearing Alan's answer, she immediately acquiesced, "John's in town? We can get dinner out or I can call the chef to make something special. I can put what I was making for us in the fridge for another time."

"No, we need to visit privately. The state can't pay either; this isn't state business." Alan responded firmly.

"I didn't make enough food for three," Kate objected. "What do you want me to do? Order Chinese?" Kate sarcastically finished.

Alan put his hand on the phone and asked, "John, you good with Chinese take-out?" John nodded, so Alan replied, "That's actually a very good idea, hun. Don't worry, I'll pick it up."

Alan and John discussed some of the details of the possible presidential campaign for about an hour. Then they went to the state-provided limo for the ride to the governor's mansion. The two of them joked about what the folks across America would think about the next and previous Republican nominees for president going through a Chinese drive-through restaurant in a limousine.

Alan and John walked into the dining room at Cedar Crest with two large brown paper bags filled with white cardboard containers which contained Asian food, like a couple of blue collar guys coming in from the bowling alley.

Kate gave her husband a curious look and asked, "Wouldn't any other governor consider this a state matter and have the staff put together a real dinner?"

Senator Halprin nodded affirmatively, but Alan, the consummate believer in avoiding any improprieties, stated, "Would that matter? This is political, so it's not proper. Besides, this'll be more fun anyway."

Alan started ripping open the bags and scooted the cardboard boxes around the table. John finally spoke up saying, "It's good to see you again Kate. The place looks great decked out for Christmas. So few public places bother decorating anymore. How are your folks?"

"They're fine, and how are Michelle and the boys?" Kate said, as she pulled plates from the adjoining butler's pantry.

"Everyone's happy as clams, especially now," he replied.

Preoccupied with preparing beverages for the meal, Kate said, "So, you are running again. Is that the reason we are honored to have you here?"

"No I'm not; your husband is," John casually replied.

Kate seemed to miss the point of what John said. She offered, "Yes, Alan is honored to have you here … we both are."

Alan swiftly scooped food onto his plate and acted as if he were still a poor boy from the wrong side of the tracks in Pittsburg, eager to have a take-out meal as a treat. Alan and John both noticed Kate had let the statement about Alan running for president go unchallenged. Alan was not going to say anything, but he would make sure she heard it next time. John thought he never repeated anything; Alan and Kate seemed to have a knack of getting him to do so anyway.

"Kate, please sit down," Alan instructed. "Let's not get ahead of ourselves. Let's just sit down, start eating, and then we can talk."

They both joined him at the table. Alan's tone was resolute and neither was accustomed to that level of certainty coming toward them from him. They quietly began to fill their plates, while Alan enjoyed a few more bites of sweet and sour pork.

The trio remained quiet for a few long moments, as they started eating the impromptu feast. Alan took satisfaction in the look of bewilderment on Kate's face, as well as the respectful compliance on John's. As Alan sipped his iced tea, Kate urged, "Can we talk now?"

"Sure, how was your day?" he said with a devious smile.

Kate glared at her husband and turned to their guest. "John, what brings you to Kansas?" she asked.

"I came to ask your husband a favor," John casually replied.

The vocal delay was starting to annoy Kate. "*Annnnd?*" she encouraged with irritation in her voice.

John looked at her, like he didn't understand, and then said, "Oh, he said 'Yes.'"

"What adventure has he signed me up for this time? I imagine he has committed to work twice as hard for your presidential campaign this time around." She ignored her husband, who was eating as if this was his first meal in a week or his last ever. Alan maintained a Cheshire cat smile between bites.

John was determined to keep up the cryptic responses. "He agreed to run."

Another one word question erupted from Kate, "*For?*"

Tongue planted firmly in cheek, John said, "The marathon, Kate. I asked him to take my place in the Boston Marathon."

Finally, John switched tones. He blatantly said, "He's running for president, and I'm going to help him get elected."

Alan didn't have anything in his mouth at the moment. He wanted to observe the full effect of her reaction to the news. His smile was absolutely childlike.

Hers, however, was not; not a happy child anyway. Perhaps, her smile was that of a newborn that had had a surprising new experience. The surprise of the announcement just hung in the air, her reaction delayed by shock. After a moment of staring, she began to turn pale. She put her fork down and stood to leave the table. This was not the response Alan had expected from his wife. He got up from the table, shrugged in John's direction, and followed her out of the room. They went into his study and sat on a couch. She began to tear up. He just held her in silence. When she looked up, she whispered in disbelief, "Is this for real? You're not acting like it's real."

"Yes, darling, it's for real."

"Are you really sure you want this?"

"Yes, I'm sure. We have talked about this before."

"But not now! You're still very young. What will you do for the rest of your life after ...?"

"I don't know. What do you say we go back in there and ask John?"

"Let me fix my face first." Kate went in the bathroom and assured herself that she was presentable. They went back into the dining room together to face a bewildered John.

"Kate was a bit overwhelmed with the information," Alan began. "I need to ask, John, what do I do when I'm out of office? I'm young, and eight ... err ten ... years from now, I'll still be relatively young."

"That's your only question?"

"No, it was just the first question Kate asked that I didn't have an answer for; I have hundreds more."

"I imagine you'll do the same thing I am. Accept speaking engagements, serve on various boards of directors, and live a long, healthy, and privileged life. You will, no doubt, be able to keep busy."

Kate jumped in to derail the personal and to delve into the practical. "Are you going to openly endorse Alan?"

"Just like you two did for me, I will endorse, support and travel for Alan's campaign. I will send everyone I can your way."

"Surely there are others that'll run," asserted Kate. "What about Governor Bell?"

Alan chuckled. "You know John, Kate has a point. Out here in 'flyover country,' we have a name for a Republican governor of California."

John asked, "What's that?"

"You haven't heard that one?" quipped Alan. "We call a Republican governor of California 'Mr. President.'"

"Oh yeah, it's been a few years since I heard that one, and I walked right into it. Bell told the RNC at their spring meeting that he's too old to run for president. For some reason, the announcement didn't get any national press."

Kate reverted to the original subject, asking, "What do you get out of endorsing Alan?"

"America," John replied bluntly.

"What do you mean by that?" asked Alan.

"We have serious problems. You might not want to have to deal with these issues, but if you don't then we all will. As expected, the economy is slumping again. We're the current economic plaything of the Chinese and Europeans. They hold our debt, and they know it's not sustainable. They don't cash in our debt in order to have power over America, so they can push us to do what they want in global politics."

Alan inquired, "What do they want?"

"They want whatever they want, whenever they want it. They're as fickle as we were when we had the world at our beck and call. Right now, they want us to back off on creating more debt."

"They won't have a problem with me then. I've believed we needed to make serious cuts at the national level for a long time. I'll be more aggressive about the debt problem than anyone, even you, John. I think we need to pull our military out of foreign bases, cut foreign aid, and cut out an awful lot of needless federal programs."

"I would've opposed you on pulling out of foreign bases in the past, but we must do so now," John said. "I think you'll find that you'll have to keep most of the foreign aid going though. What programs would you cut?"

"I would start with the Department of Education; Reagan was right. There should never have been a federally funded department in the first place. That's just the beginning. We need to back off on *every* program that has a state version in each individual state. Face it John, the federal government has become the Department of Redundancy Department!"

"The federal government just funds the state programs. The states don't have the money without the federal government," John insisted.

"States can raise taxes a little and get more done with less," countered Alan. "In Kansas, we spend sixty cents to get a federal dollar. If federal taxes went down a dollar, and state taxes went up forty cents, we could do everything we're doing now without a dime of federal money. What's worse is that DC spends two dollars to give us the one. So, if we cut federal taxes two dollars and we raise fifty cents here, we'll have an extra ten cents to—I don't know—get ice cream for dessert!"

"So you would run on a platform of massive reform?" asked John, clarifying that he understood exactly where Alan was coming from.

"I would, and I believe it would work. The feds have their noses into everything because, in the past, we had some states that were significantly poorer than others. DC used federal money to level the playing field for everyone. But the nation just doesn't work the same way anymore. It's not like Louisiana will keep black people from getting an education or West Virginia will put eight-year-olds in the coal mines. The system is broken. Well, really it's not. Our current government is designed to do something we don't need done anymore. Every state is begging for the same money to do the same things for their people, and the federal government is making us jump through hoops to get the money *we* sent *them* in the first place. It's just inefficient. Do you think I can run on that premise?"

"I think you'll have to," John agreed. "That means a proposal to dispose of federal departments like Commerce, Transportation, Labor, Energy, Health, Agriculture, Human Services, Housing… Am I missing any … uh, Urban Development? Any others?" asked John.

"No, I think we should keep Defense, State, and a few choice others. I acknowledge there are vital parts of each department that would have to be retained by the federal government, like the Nuclear Regulatory Commission by Energy. Maybe move it to, well, wherever it was before we had an energy department."

"That's about two-thirds of the discretionary budget of the federal government. You would have a hell of a sales job on your hands. It's not like those departments don't have supporters and lobbyists."

Alan asserted, "I'm sure there are a number of ways to accomplish what we need; if we don't do something, something drastic, we're at risk as a nation."

125

"The alternative would be to not have states at all and do everything directly through the federal government," posited John. "I just don't think that is a viable option."

"Or desirable," added Alan. "You know me, John. I firmly believe that state and local government is better, more efficient, and more responsive."

John thought for moment and said, "I agree. Perhaps we can pitch it as something along the lines of 'new federalism,' like what was talked about in the '80s, or was it the '90s?"

"How would I know? I wasn't around!" Alan stated with surprise. "I just read about these concepts in history books."

"Hey! Alan, I was a kid back then. I'm going by what I read as well, not personal experience. How old do you think I am?" John finished with a laugh.

"Sorry about that, but I suppose we're getting ahead of ourselves," Alan added. "There's something more elemental we need to discuss: how does one go about running for president?"

Kate, who had been patiently listening to all of the policy discussion, finally interjected, "I was wondering when you two policy wonks would get around to that part."

John responded, "For you, it's simple. Just do what I tell you, every step of the way."

Alan looked sternly at John. "I can do that. Are you promising to be with me 'every step of the way'?"

"Not exactly. I won't run your campaign, but I have people who will push the process along. My associates won't lead you wrong."

"So you want me to take on your team lock, stock, and barrel?"

"I had the best team the GOP could muster. If you don't want them ..."

Alan interrupted, "No, I wasn't saying that, I ..."

Cutting him off, John said, "I was going to say that you're an idiot if you don't want them. I'll admit ... they're all still expecting me to run. I haven't told anyone yet.

"They have families to feed, and they expect to work for my campaign. They've all made sacrifices waiting this long. They're good people, but they need to work.

"When I announce that I'm not running, they will scour the countryside looking for someone to work for. They would financially prosper working for competing Republican candidates. The more active the nomination battle, the more money they make on the ad buys. The team makes more money, and the party devours itself in Iowa and New Hampshire and South Carolina and so on, until someone runs out of money. The last guy standing then hires the team from his vanquished competitors. The system is not the best, but it's the system we have, and you can't change it."

Alan took it all in. Kate was lost by the revelation of how presidential campaigns work. Alan simply asked, "What do I do first?"

John smiled and replied, "I said *you* can't change it, but I think I can. I've been talking you up for two years to the team. I let it slip that I might want you for veep. It seems the information slipped all the way to your office, right?

Alan sheepishly admitted, "Well, yes."

"Very soon, I'm going to have a meeting with every key person from my team. I'm taking them to South Carolina to a resort. I'll take each one aside and secure their loyalty to whatever I ask, before they have any suspicion of what I'm going to ask. They'll all follow my lead because without loyalty they don't get a penny. Then, I bring them together and tell the group that I want them to support you. You and Kate, I need you both, will enter the room at that moment. You don't have to go stealth or anything. They'll presume you to be my early vice president choice so your presence won't trigger any suspicions. Of course, you'll have to keep all these details completely confidential until we're ready to go public."

Kate, who was bothered by the underhanded politics of it all, suggested, "This sounds very Mario Puzo Godfather-ish. Essentially, some kind of underworld anointing."

John replied, "Sorry Kate, but they can work for you or against you." Turning back to Alan, he continued, "Some *will* work against us and the whole thing will become public. The announcement will have to be spun as just an endorsement. We will need to send a press release moments before you walk in, telling of your exploratory committee.

"Now, here's the hard part. I can only get you about a hundred thousand dollars from my sources. Until you begin to hold your own events, that is. You'll need to hit the ground running with some major fundraising. If you can't, well, to abuse Kate's analogy, 'Give them something to dip their beak in,' then you'll lose them. You will need to establish funds for the team to live on while they work for you.

"Alan, I know that you're not a wealthy man. You don't have business or inheritance ..."

"I have more business experience than Bill Clinton and Barack Obama combined! I have more private sector experience than those two, even with Hillary Clinton thrown in for good measure!" Alan quipped.

"Yes, Alan, I know. I'm not talking about public perception, although that's a pretty good start. We will be able to use your positive attention from the public to gain the nomination. I meant that you have no avenue to get a war chest started, personally."

"Wait a minute, is that possible ... Hillary worked at Rose ..." John trailed off, his thoughts working overtime.

"John, I've been in a job since I was twelve and haven't divested myself from the businesses in Pittsburg. It's true. A different scale of finances than the law firm Hillary worked for perhaps, but still true," assured Alan.

"OK, we'll save that discussion for another time. What we need, what we must have, is a serious fundraiser attended by some very wealthy supporters planned and ready to go the very moment we have everything in place. We can't let our plans go public until the team is on board, but we have to have the main elements in place."

Kate asked, "How much money will we need?"

John looked at Kate and said, "To raise at that fundraiser? You'll need to raise at least two and a half."

Alan fearfully asked, "Two and a half what?"

Kate jumped in. "Million, Alan. John says you have to start with two and a half *million* dollars." Then, turning to John, she clarified, "Dollars, right, not Ameros or Euros?"

"Yes, dollars," John affirmed.

Alan inquired, "If I can't ..."

Kate interrupted, "You can."

"What does it say if I can't ...?"

Kate insisted, "Alan ... you can!"

128

"Please, Kate, let me ask John. What does it mean if I can't?"

John sighed and replied, "I would say it means your answer is 'No.'"

"Whoa, it all rides on that!" Alan said with a sense of disbelief. "I have to be able to jump in at millions of dollars or you head off to Wyoming after all!"

Kate asked, with a puzzled look, "Wyoming? What's Wyoming all about?"

John chuckled. "It's a joke. I threatened to get Governor Clark to run if Alan said 'No.' Don't worry, I really was joking."

"I would hope so," said Kate.

Alan was still nervous. "John, you get me into this, lay out this plan to get me the nomination, get me to say 'I'll run,' and then you drop the bomb on me."

"Sorry Alan, I know I lured you in and got you emotionally invested in the idea. You bought Chinese take-out and everything. Probably should have saved that money!" John said with a grin.

Alan smiled at John's comment. He turned thoughtfully to Kate and queried, "I don't know how, Kate, I don't think Bill Coffee …"

"No, not Bill and Sue. Hopefully they'll help, but I don't think they should be the centerpiece for getting that kind of money," remarked Kate.

John reached out to Kate and held her wrist. "Kate, your father can't contribute that much; it's not allowed. He can't even loan you the money."

"I couldn't ask him to commit that kind of money, even if it was legal. Besides, I don't know that he could if he wanted to. I wasn't thinking of him …"

"What are the limits of contribution these days?" Alan inquired.

John replied, "It just went up to fifty-eight hundred dollars per person. If you accept federal money, that's all you can ever take from them. If you reject the funds, and I suppose you will, it'll help you raise more money in the long run and help you with your base at the same time. Then you can accept eleven thousand, six hundred per person, but the second half has to be set aside for the general election. The problem is if the contributors give you one check for ten grand and don't specify fifty-eight hundred is for the nomination, then you only get five grand now. It gets even more complicated with multi-signer checking accounts, and the limits seem to change more often than the seasons. You'll need a staffer who knows what they're doing to work with every major donor."

129

Alan looked toward the ceiling as he did the numbers, "Two and a half million at fifty-eight hundred dollars each, comes to just over four hundred thirty maximum donors. So … Kate, do you know four hundred people to give me fifty-eight hundred each? I think I can come up with the other thirty."

Kate looked at her husband with a dead-serious stare. "Yes."

Alan and John sat silently for a moment. Alan finally broke the silence, stating, "It seems the first lady of Kansas has been keeping a secret from her husband." Then, turning to Kate, he asked, "Kate, what do you have up your sleeve?"

Kate pulled Alan close, whispering in his ear, "Keoki."

Alan pulled back suddenly and blurted, "He's liberal!"

"Yes, but he'll put it together."

"Why would he?"

"He just will, trust me."

Alan realized that he needed to know if what his wife was suggesting was even feasible—or legal. He asked John, "If someone really rich was a supporter and wanted to hold a fundraiser at his home, would that be acceptable?"

"Yes, without any restrictions, as long as it is on his residential property."

"What if he invited—let's call them 'friends'—could he put his friends up at his home?" Alan inquired further.

"Yes, but he could only spend twenty-five hundred dollars on the event itself. But, if the guests were already there, he could be hospitable. This guy would have to have a very big home to lodge enough people to raise that much money."

Alan, ever quick with figures said, "Two per room, sounds like we need a two hundred and fifteen room house. I think that's a possibility."

"Who the hell are you talking about?" John yelled. "And why didn't you hook me up with him? Oh, and no foreign nationals. You knew that, right?"

"Let's just say he's a friend of the family." Alan replied. "He never helped my campaigns in the past, but this is different. No offense, John, but he wouldn't have supported you. I don't even know for sure he'll do this for me, but if Kate thinks so, we need to explore the option."

Kate asserted, "He will."

"Your wife seems confident."

"Well, she knows him better than I do," Alan said as he continued with his line of questioning. "Can he provide transportation to his home for his friends who are visiting him, which just happens to be during the time period of the event?"

"It sounds like you're trying too hard. Big donors will pay their own way to get to an event," John asserted.

"This guy's friends are not big donors or usual donors to the Republican party. He would need to get the people to his house; it's remote."

"Tell me it's in the US."

"It is. Can he do it?"

John responded, "I can say there's nothing technically wrong with what you're asking, but you're going to have the FEC look long and hard at something of that magnitude. If even one single donor says they gave for *any* reason other than that they wanted to give to you, then you're going to face some real problems. We want to make sure their reason for donation is not because your mystery billionaire gave them a trip in exchange. Even if you didn't know he made the deal, and could prove it, you would still face a lot of public perception problems."

"I think you know I won't cross that line. I do like knowing where the line lies though. I suppose the perception problems can be overcome with a significant war chest?"

"Likely, yes. How much is he inclined to spend to have a few friends over for a slumber party?"

"I think he has his own jet. Right honey?" Alan asked Kate.

"Yes, but it can only hold around a dozen people. I think he's looking to buy a larger one right now," Kate answered.

Alan inquired, "Really, have you spoken to him recently?"

"No, honey, not since I called and thanked him for the towels. We've emailed each other from time to time."

John was incredulous. "Towels! You two are quite a pair. You're counting on a guy who you haven't spoken to since your wedding, who gave you *towels!*"

Kate reached out to John, embraced his wrist and said, "They were very nice Egyptian cotton towels. We haven't touched half of them yet. John, if I'd asked for Egypt, I think he would have given the entire country to me and forgotten he spent the money a week later."

"Oh, I see now. He is an old boyfriend."

Alan asserted, "God, I hope not!" Then, after a short pause, he commented, "Well, actually, that would be pretty cool."

Kate screeched, "Alan!"

"If you had left someone like him for me that would be, well … it would be for no reason other than love."

Even more annoyed, she growled, "Alan, stop it. No, he was not my boyfriend. He's, he's just not! I mean … never was!"

Alan turned to John and said, "He's really not. We were engaged before they met. He's a friend of her father. Kate trusts him, and I trust her. We will make some calls and look into whether this is a viable option or not. Do you want to spend the night here? We can talk shop and the state can buy you breakfast, or we can talk politics and I'll make these wonderful apple pancakes Helen Benton showed me how to make."

John laughed. "She made those for me, too. It's something Polish that starts with an 'R.' Unfortunately, I can't pronounce the rest of the word. But they're great, from what I can remember. You'll both have more questions in the morning. I've got my bag in the rental car back at the capitol. Can we get it?"

"Yeah, maybe we can take the limo through the Dairy Queen on the way back!" Alan joked, grabbing the phone to call the state trooper on duty. He asked for the senator to be taken to the capitol to get his bag, and then be returned to the mansion afterward.

Before he left, John pulled a retractable marker from his jacket pocket and wrote something as he spoke. "Be sure to be thinking about this while you sleep, okay?" On one of the brown paper bags that came from the Chinese restaurant, he wrote "Cassell for America" and handed the bag back to Alan.

CHAPTER 12 • THE CAMPAIGN

"In the eyes of empire builders men are not men but instruments."

—Napoleon Bonaparte

JOHN HALPRIN RETIRED TO THE guest room of his choice. Once in the room, he made a quick cell phone call to a prominent business mogul he served with on one of the various corporate boards.

"This is John," he announced, pausing to hear the man on the other end. "Yes, he'll do it." After another pause, Halprin continued, "I'm bringing him in; he knows to do what I tell him."

After the statement, the other voice spoke for a longer time before Halprin had another opportunity to speak.

"Yes, he is very idealistic," he replied, "but that doesn't mean we can't control him. For him, everything's on the table, except foreign aid because I convinced him to leave that alone. He knows he has to stop building up the debt."

Again the other voice spoke, and Halprin replied in an aggravated tone, "Look, you asked me to do a job and I'm getting it done. There's no need to second guess me. He's young and impressionable; I have the inside track. You don't have anything to worry about. I'll keep it under control."

The other voice spoke again, which elicited a calmer, more humble reply, "Yes, I know what I'll have to do if it gets out of hand. Don't worry. I understand my part in all of this." He ended the call and went to bed for the evening.

The governor's mansion seemed excessive for a childless married couple, and John wondered how they coped with the quiet atmosphere. At the same time, he realized Alan and Kate likely wondered how he coped with the ruckus caused by his children and young grandchildren. Such mundane thoughts replaced the serious themes contained in the conversation just completed; the call was over, and he didn't give the conversation a second thought as he drifted off to sleep.

On the other side of the mansion, the night began as a sleepless one for the Cassells. Alan pondered all the questions he could think to ask in the morning. Kate planned how she was going to approach Keoki and get him to do the fundraising event. She had promised her husband and John Halprin she would get him to help, and she needed to be successful in the venture.

Kate thought about Keoki often. Despite her efforts to the contrary she often found herself comparing him with Alan. This evening she was facing an opportunity to have one on one visits with him and the idea excited her.

Neither Alan nor Kate knew the other was awake until they simultaneously turned in the bed, and saw each other's eyes open. "You're awake?" Alan asked.

"Yes, can't sleep. Thinking about … about things," she replied softly. Kate could not tell Alan that it was Keoki she was thinking of while in bed with him. *What kind of bed does he sleep in? Is he alone tonight?* And presuming he was not alone she asked herself, *What is she like?* Her eyes wide open looking right into Alan's yet she was blind to him and could only see Keoki in her mind's eye.

Kate was oblivious to the guilt that used to overcome her when she fantasized about Keoki. Certain that she loved Alan, yet fascinated by every consideration of the tall, dark handsome man who had everything and didn't care to want her. Or, so she presumed.

"You're face is so beautiful." Alan said stroking her cheek with the back of his hand, then running his fingers through her hair. Even he noticed that she was distant in some way. Her blue eyes seemed warmer and darker whenever she was deep in thought. Alan had no clue that his wife's thoughts were on the man she was going to speak to about funding his campaign for president.

Presuming he was wanting to make love, and knowing her own body was eager for such she told Alan, "We have a guest! We would need to be quiet."

"We? Am I the one who makes noise?" he asked jokingly.

Alan, suddenly eager to take his affections to a higher level, began to stroke his wife's leg under the sheets, she whispered, "Just be quiet tonight, please."

As the couple began to make love, they forgot the guest in residence and concentrated on each others bodies. It was one of the most intense intimate occasions in their marriage. While Kate enjoyed everything about Alan, his body, his foreplay, his ability to please her, she also found it impossible to force thoughts of Keoki from her mind. Even she could not tell if she succeeded or if the intensity of the occasion was due, at least in part, to her contemplation of a man she had not seen in years.

Alan was enthralled with every inch of Kate's body. He took time caressing, kissing, and then caressing each spot again. Alan was always amazed by the consistency of her skin tone. His own body had several areas of variance in color. Not so for Kate, from the tips of her toes, along her perfectly formed legs, across her hips, back, neck, and of course, her breasts—all of her skin was of the most beautiful, even tone. Her skin was soft, yet the firmness of her body was at every point evident as he stroked her. He was not in a hurry; he wanted to savor the pleasures of his wife's love.

All the while he observed the changes in her expression. At moments, she would seem almost in pain with her eyes closed and an intense grip. Then seconds later, she revealed a great smile accompanied by joyous groans.

While they made love, at a point that he was looking up to her face, he moved his hands to her waist. His finger tips moved lightly over her skin where his left hand found, for just a moment, the one place where her body was imperfect. It was the scar from the accident that had taken their child. He quickly moved his hand from that spot; he knew that Kate disliked any attention to 'the mark.' He was sure that she was unaware that he had even touched it, but he dare not say anything as it would ruin the moment for them.

Their final moment resulted in both of them with wide eyes looking at each other in pleased astonishment.

She then threw herself upon his chest and they both laughed as he rolled her to his side. Their love making complete, he kissed her cheeks and then her eyelids; they kissed repeatedly with her breasts pressed against him and their legs intertwined. His arms wrapped around her, his hands continually caressing her.

They fell asleep in that embrace.

Just before dawn, Alan partially awoke and lay beside his wife, thinking to himself. He had certainly enjoyed their love making, but something troubled him. He had simply commented about her face and touched her cheek lightly; her reaction to the gentle motions he had made had turned the situation into foreplay. He had been pleased to comply with her wishes, but now he was curious. He presumed she had been thinking about his prospects of becoming president. He remembered that the last time she took that kind of initiative was the morning after the Coffee Grounds meeting.

Is she into power? he asked himself, presuming she was thinking of his impending campaign. *Why is it that she seems to start things when she knows I'm running for something new?* Then, with a melancholy attitude, he thought, *I can't run for anything higher after this.*

Alan's thoughts diverted to other issues, like how he would orchestrate his activities prior to the official announcement of his presidential candidacy. He knew he was entirely responsible for how events would come together before the upcoming meeting in South Carolina. *I'll have to tell Jim and Lenore. I need staff that can keep a secret, yet work with me. I guess I'll keep the news to them alone. How do I pull all this off? That's the real question. I wonder if Archer would keep my plans concealed ... I suppose it's like a confession so he would have to keep my secret.*

After his silent contemplation of the matter, Alan got up, showered, and began breakfast for the trio.

Later that day, he asked Jim Cherry to have lunch with him at Cedar Crest. Kate was out, keeping herself busy with duties as first lady. He had the meal, which was provided by the state, with his chief of staff; they had official business to deal with, as well as his decision.

Entering the private quarters at Cedar Crest, Jim spotted Alan in the dining room with two place settings for lunch. The cleaning staff had left no sign of the previous evening's dinner with Senator Halprin. However, Alan had made it a point to retrieve the paper bag from the trash. He thought the writing by John would be worth keeping.

Jim called out, "Governor, how was Senator Halprin?"

"Great. He left for KC and the airport about an hour and a half ago."

"So, do I get the inside track? Is he running and what part are you going to play?" Jim inquired in rapid-fire fashion.

Alan responded in kind. "Yes, no, and '*the* part.'"

"Huh?"

"Well, if you recall your own questions, I answered them in order."

Jim thoughtfully responded, "Yes, he's running; no, you don't have a part? And I don't remember a third question."

"Your first question was 'If you get the inside track?' Were you assuming the answer was 'Yes'? Doesn't matter; of course you get the inside scoop. I couldn't do much without your input."

"But your second answer was 'No!'"

"That's because he's not running for president."

Jim was more confused than before. "Okay, Alan, yes I get the inside stuff; no, he's not running." Alan nodded affirmatively as Jim continued, "Wow, huge! Really, he's not gonna run again? Geez, I'm sure he would have won. But I don't remember my third question now."

"Jim, you're not on top of your game today. Do I have any staff at the capitol? Are they getting anything done today?"

"I'm sorry, Governor. I was distracted by the potential of you being vice president. If he's not running, then who will? It's gonna be murder out there with Halprin out of the race. Why did he wait to tell anyone?"

"He wanted me to know the news first. He wanted me to ... do him a favor. I need you to do me one as well, starting with not telling anyone about this conversation. Actually, I am going to need quite a few favors over the next few months, Jim. This is why we're having lunch here in the residence."

Jim still didn't understand, but Alan occasionally spoke in that manner; if a person blurted out several questions, he would answer each one in order. Somehow, his rapid-fire answers would throw them off. He had mastered the art of answering the question he wanted to answer with the press, which was advantageous for him since he often threw them off their game.

Jim was almost annoyed now, but decided he needed to be nice to his boss. "I'm sorry, sir, but I'm missing something."

"Sir!" said Alan with shock in his voice. "You've never called me 'sir'! I must have really aggravated you. I told you, Jim, I'm running!"

"You didn't tell … For what? Oh my God, *you*! You're running for president! You're shittin' me! Halprin's not running because he doesn't want to run against you!"

"John's not running because he doesn't want to run. He wants me to run. He's endorsing me and setting his team up to run the campaign," Alan finally blurted.

Jim was stunned; he didn't know how to respond. Someone else had recruited his governor to run for president. His face began to pale. He had a sick feeling Alan was being taken from him. Since his last child had left for college, Alan had come to dominate Jim's life. First, it was the county commission, and then the governorship. Jim had leased out his farm and closed down his insurance agency to work with Alan in Topeka. He had moved his wife to Topeka, a city she detested.

At the same time, Jim was concerned this was some sort of deception. *What could Halprin be doing to my friend? It can't be for real.*

"Are you serious?" Jim finally asked. "Was Halprin really recruiting you?"

"Please call him John, at least to me," Alan replied. "Yes, he was serious and this opportunity is very real. While he considered his options, John continued going through the motions of running for office. His plan is to make me the 'heir apparent.' I'm running, and I will win! With your help, I believe I can be a very good president."

Jim was relieved that Alan had included him in the statement. "You'll be a great president! We have a lot of work to do to get there though."

"Hold on, Jim." Alan asserted. "We have a lot of work to do here, before we get there! I want you to know how I treasure your counsel. I wouldn't think of doing this without you. I need you here. During the campaign, I need you to … pretty much run things here. You do that anyway; I've been the public face. Jim, you're the administrator. It's your talent. I'm not stepping down to run. The only way that will work is if you're not involved in the campaign, not much anyway. And I do hope I can convince you to come to DC in two years."

Jim was saddened, and somehow relieved, that he would not be an integral part of the 'greatest campaign' in America, a presidential campaign. He had never been able to get close to a presidential candidate. Kansas is commonly taken for granted in the general election and is not strategically placed among the primaries. Alan's suggestion for him to remain in Kansas was also a relief because he knew he was an excellent public administrator.

"I would be happy to do that, Alan." Jim answered with a smile. "My wife will take some convincing, but I would be very pleased to be involved with a national campaign, even if it means supporting you from home. Please, just promise me that you'll bring me on the inside for the re-election campaign?"

"You've got a deal!" Alan promised his friend. "Now let's eat lunch, and I'll tell you all about our plans."

Alan rehashed the dinner with John and told Jim about Kate's confidence regarding the run. He didn't talk about the exact details of South Carolina or the fundraising expectation. They then discussed a number of state issues at length.

Meanwhile, Kate used her phone to text Keoki, while she attended a luncheon. "I need to speak to you on the phone, soon. When should I call? It's important."

Keoki's reply was immediate. "Call now; I'm driving to the North Shore to watch the surfers. The pipeline's great this time of year." Of course, Keoki wasn't driving. He was being driven by his chauffer.

Kate had only a moment to reply back to Keoki. "Not now, later," she texted, "when you're inside and can hear me well. When would that be?"

"I'll be home for lunch. I suppose that's now for you. Call at noon—HI time. I look forward to talking to you again." Kate spent the intervening time before her call to Keoki with nothing else in mind. She went through the motions of her official duties, while her emotions spun wildly at the thought of renewing her acquaintance. Keoki had promised to do anything for her years prior. She didn't know why he had made the promise, though she often wondered if he was secretly as enamored with her as she was with him. Regardless, she saved the opportunity until she could make it truly worthwhile.

After his lunch with Jim Cherry, Alan went to his office at the state capitol. On his way to his office, he stopped by Lenore's desk to check on a variety of items. He also asked her to contact her brother-in-law, Archer Adams. Alan wanted him to come as soon as it was convenient.

After a few minutes, Lenore reported to Alan that Archer would be at the capitol in about four hours.

Alan chose to use the opportunity to talk to Lenore. "Talk with me a moment, and have a seat," he requested.

Lenore took a seat beside his desk with a concerned look on her face. Alan started, "Lenore, you've shown yourself to be someone I can fully trust. I really appreciate all you do. I wouldn't want to be here without someone like you to lean on."

"Thank you, sir," she responded.

"Well, thank you!" Alan returned. "Lenore, I need to confide something significant to you. You see, I'll be getting calls from people on a national level and it must be kept quiet, for a while."

She appeared more confused, as she patiently listened.

He continued, "Senator Halprin is not running for president; he wants me to run instead." Lenore's worried look changed to one of excitement. "I'm going to do it, but we have to keep this completely quiet. If you're asked, can you deny it?"

"I can, and I will, if you like," she replied with a sense of relief in her voice. "Congratulations! I suppose congratulations are in order."

"I haven't won yet, but thank you. You'll be fielding calls for me. People will wish to speak to, or see, me. We need to keep the official logs to a minimum. Keep it honest; you'll just have to decline some calls, if getting a call from that particular person would raise the curiosity of the press. Other calls will be for meetings, which will have to be set up by you without talking to me. If they say, 'Senator Halprin said I should speak with or meet with Governor Cassell,' then you'll know the call is something I'll want to pursue, okay?"

Lenore responded dutifully, "Yes sir." She sat staring at him, and then ventured to ask, "I haven't had time to think about this, but ... will I ... do you envision me being involved in some way?"

"Would that be a problem?" asked the governor.

"Oh God, no!" she immediately responded. "You'll win; you'll be a great president! It just seems that when really good men run, there is just a different level of ... the press can be so terrible ... people can be terrible. I don't know if I'm ready for that kind of publicity."

"I don't know if any of us are," he admitted, "but we intend to win! This is not a trial balloon. Kate and I are completely in accord on this election. I really need you here when the campaign's on the road."

Lenore asked, "Is this why you called for Archer?"

"Yes," answered Alan. "He has given me excellent advice in the past. He also told me something once ... Well, it seems he knew this day would come. I think he might have some words of wisdom on the situation. I do want you to think about your availability after the campaign."

"Yes, I'll think about it. But, obviously, you don't want me to talk to my family about it yet, right?" Lenore inquired.

"That's right," confirmed Alan. "For now, it is just you, Jim, Kate, and the Senator. Well, actually, Kate is adding George Keoki right about now."

"George Keoki! He's liberal!" Lenore nearly shouted. "He raised thousands, hundreds of thousands, *against* Senator Halprin during his last campaign."

"Yeah, well, we think he'll be for us this time," Alan assured her. "You know, to win, we need people who opposed us last time. He's a friend of the Fogarty... um, Kate's family. I'll let you know if I need to bring any others on board. You're my gatekeeper; I'm depending on you." His statement ended with a tone of completion, to which Lenore had become accustomed.

"You can count on me, sir." Lenore stood and made her exit. Alan returned to the pile of state papers on his desk. His staff had recently worked on his address to the legislature, and he needed to review his planned speech. Alan wondered how he could use his upcoming second inaugural address to aid his national endeavor, but decided to keep the speech focused on only Kansas issues, leaving the presidential campaign for later.

Meanwhile, on the campus of Oral Roberts University in Tulsa, Oklahoma, Archer Adams made his excuses to depart early from a para-church ministries conference. Archer had already spoken at the event earlier in the day and was scheduled to participate in a panel discussion later; he would have to miss the conclusion of the conference.

Archer needed to leave immediately in order to make it to Topeka as soon as possible. He was at a complete loss as to why Governor Cassell wanted to see him this time. In the past, when the governor wanted to see him, he was either in Topeka visiting Lenore with his wife or in Lawrence working with his campus church group. The timing of the governor's previous requests, and Archer's availability, was taken by Archer as God's providence.

This time was different, however, and the situation was peculiar to Archer.

As he drove east on 71st Street toward the Arkansas River and on to Hwy 75, Archer frantically called airlines, only to find he could drive to Topeka faster than he could fly on any commercial flights.

His navigation system told him to stay on Hwy 75 all the way, and he could indeed make the journey in exactly four hours. Archer shook his head in amazement because of his statement to Lenore that he would be there in about four hours. Archer believed in a mystical version of Christianity, but he was often as surprised as others were when something he said was found to be more on target than he had any natural reason to anticipate.

This time he was flying blind. He was drawn to Governor Cassell, and the governor had come to depend on him for counsel. Archer appreciated his growing relationship with Alan; he just had difficulty describing the relationship. *Am I a friend, spiritual counselor, or what?* he asked himself.

Sometimes, Alan would talk about very personal matters, and other times the conversation was all politics. Archer had learned he needed to listen more than to speak when he visited the governor. Alan seemed to be a vulnerable man, and a man who could be manipulated by unscrupulous people if they got close enough. The primarily reason was because Alan was so idealistic. Archer was uncertain if he would ever be able to reach the inner man, but he was committed to be available to him and to be worthy of the trust Alan had in him.

On the passenger seat next to Archer was one of his books. He had picked it up from the table where students were selling them to conference attendees. Archer had thought he would be flying to Topeka. Sometimes when he needed to make last minute flight arrangements, he would carry a copy of a book with his face on the cover. He would lay the volume on the ticket counter as he pulled out his identification. Quite often, he would be given additional help when they saw he was a published author. This time he had expected he would need the help but, as it turned out, he just drove along with his own aging face looking up at him.

Archer Adams was a large and robust man. He had looked quite youthful until his early forties because of his sandy hair and rounded face. Now older, his hair was much lighter in color and thinner. He no longer had a youthful appearance similar to the students to which he ministered. To accommodate the changes, he had attempted to grow a beard to look professorial; his intention was to have some continued appeal to the students. Sadly for him, he had little facial hair, and his beard only grew as a thin wisp from his chin. Some compared his look to Colonel Sanders, of chicken restaurant fame, but Archer kept the "beard" anyway. *At least I have a distinct look,* he justified to himself.

Archer Adams was a direct descendent of the American Presidents and patriots John Adams and John Quincy Adams. During Oklahoma's territorial years, various descendents of the two presidents moved to the territory from Massachusetts. Archer's grandfather had married a woman who was half Chickasaw Indian. Archer attributed his minimal facial hair and high cheekbones to his Chickasaw heritage. He never talked about his political heritage, since he really knew little of the details. He had grown up in Guthrie, Oklahoma in a neighborhood considered to be on the "wrong side of the tracks." Yet, he spoke more often about his American Indian heritage than his political descent; it was more comfortable for him.

While driving, he contemplated a personal experience from his youth which he had never made public, but the event was formative in his decision to go into the ministry and elucidated his affinity for his Indian heritage. Not many years after the centennial of Oklahoma statehood, Archer's high school had arranged for a field trip to the "illegitimate" capitol of Oklahoma. Every young person from Guthrie knows the "real" capitol of Oklahoma is their fair city. The Oklahoma State Seal, as well as the institution of state government, was stolen from Guthrie in the dark of night. The illegally-taken seal was brought to Oklahoma City, never to be returned to its original home.

The trip Archer took was to the State History Center in Oklahoma City. He was intrigued by the appearance of six crosses on the state flag. His curiosity stemmed from his newfound faith and his Indian heritage. The flag depicted an American Indian war shield with a calumet and an olive branch laid over it. The shield with the crosses was of particular interest to him.

His personal goal was to learn more about the shield. Upon arrival, he and the entire class were herded through the museum guided by a dark skinned man with a long ponytail. The guide was unmistakably of American Indian heritage, but he did not disclose his tribe.

The students were given an opportunity to ask questions at the end of the tour. Archer asked about the shield, which served as inspiration for the state flag. The guide told of the Osage shield and its influence on Louise Fluke, the artist who designed the flag. He then invited the students into a vault room where items of great value to the state were securely stored. He pulled open a metal drawer to reveal the ancient shield. He pointed out there were seven crosses, as opposed to the six on the flag, as well as a six pointed star, which appeared to be a Star of David. His teacher asked about the star and its juxtaposition to the crosses. In politically correct fashion, the guide said the design was "clearly due to missionizing influence."

The guide then presented Archer with a pair of white cotton gloves and invited him to lift the shield to display the design on the reverse side.

As Archer first touched the shield, he experienced a feeling that would be classified by most people as "mystical." Fully conscious of his surroundings as he lifted and turned the object, he also felt as though he had been transported to another time and place. In what felt like delirium, he saw a young Osage brave on the banks of what appeared to be the Mississippi River, praying with a French priest. Then, somehow moving forward in time, he saw the same brave turn his shield over. The brave used what had originally been the front of the shield and made it the back instead. Archer was certain he was watching the Christian warrior make the new markings on what would then become the front of a shield; in time, this was the renowned inspiration for Oklahoma's state flag.

Archer took that formative experience as evidence of his connection to other American Indians who accepted the Christian message. He began his college career at Oral Roberts University, which had been founded by a fellow American Indian with a theological bent toward the mystical. Archer's early intent was to minister to other American Indians. After he earned his BA at Oral Roberts University, he attended the University of Oklahoma to obtain his masters degree. He found his true talent was working with college students. He then returned to ORU to acquire his PhD, where he successfully entered the ministry and became well-known as a speaker and author. As he drove away from Tulsa, he wondered how much of the experience was real and how much was a youthful, zealous believer being carried away in the moment.

Continuing north toward Topeka, he wondered about the occasion of the governor's request. The further north he drove, the worse the weather grew. It had been a brisk, but sunny, day in Tulsa. The wind picked up and a dusting of snow whipped about when Archer crossed into Kansas. He knew the governor had recently won re-election and thought the meeting might be about an invitation to give an invocation, or benediction, at the inaugural. Archer was slightly aggravated at the possibility that he had left a conference at his alma mater over something as simple as a formal prayer in public. He also worried the snow would stick, which would prevent him from making his appointed time.

The snow didn't stick. In the silence, he drove and felt a tinge of guilt at his lack of faith. He had told Lenore he would arrive in four hours, and he needed to trust he would be there on time. The highway was clear, and the traffic was light; he never needed to speed, nor was he held up in any way. Even his stop for fuel went without incident.

In addition, he felt guilt over doubting the importance of the call. Every time he had met with Alan, the meeting had been important for the governor. Those "divine appointments," as Archer called them, were sure to continue. Archer was confident the fate of the nation would one day rest on the shoulders of young Governor Cassell; he was about to find out how soon that day would come.

Most of the traffic was outbound, as Archer pulled in to the Kansas state capitol building parking area. It was past normal working hours and, at that time of year, none of the legislators were present so late in the day. Archer found a convenient parking space and walked to the security checkpoint at the entrance of the building.

The guards asked about the purpose of his visit, and Archer told them he had an appointment with the governor. Archer was told Governor Cassell was not in the office. Archer could not believe Alan had left for the night. After double-checking their records, they relented and allowed him to go to the governor's office. As he walked up the hall, he realized that he had been distracted from his purpose by many obstacles that day. He was suddenly convinced that he was not in a proper spiritual state of mind. He stopped in the hall and sat on a bench, placing his head in his hands to pray for a few moments.

Moments grew to minutes as Archer cleared his mind of the day's events. He then sought peace and God's will in view of the impending meeting.

When Archer arrived at the reception area of Alan's office, Lenore greeted him. "It's been ten minutes since they told me you were here. Are you okay?"

"Yeah, I had to make a pit stop," Archer replied. He had not lied, but the type of "pit stop" he required was not the same as the one his sister-in-law assumed.

"That's fine," she responded. "The governor will see you in just a minute. He's on the phone with the first lady back at the ,mansion. How is Sis?"

"She's fine, but she's concerned your niece is getting a bit too serious about her boyfriend from Chicago. She's visiting his family over Christmas break, so it'll be just the two of us for the holidays," Archer said.

Lenore noticed the light on her phone change. She told him, "The governor will see you now." Archer's "pit stop" had not delayed his visit with the governor a single second.

She stood from her desk and walked to the door to the Governor's office, and stopped short. "I'll be heading home while you're in there," she explained. "Why don't you stay at our place tonight? I'll make you something nice to eat, and we can talk."

Lenore gave Archer a big hug, looked him in the eyes knowingly, and let him in the door. Archer was not quite sure what to make of her motions.

"Archer, please come in," said Alan. To Lenore, he called, "Have a great evening, Lenore. See you in the morning."

Archer addressed his sister-in-law. "I'll see you later for dinner." Then, after turning to address Alan, he smiled and said, "Governor, it's good to see you again. Congratulations!"

Alan was surprised to hear the word "congratulations." He wondered if Lenore had told him, or if Archer knew by some other means. "What do you mean 'congratulations?'"

"On your re-election, of course! I haven't seen you since ..." Archer started to explain.

"Oh, yes, of course," Alan interrupted, clearly relieved by the answer. "I really appreciate you coming to see me today. I hope it wasn't inconvenient to come from Lawrence on short notice." Alan had mistakenly presumed Archer was at the KU campus that day.

Archer smiled again and, without correcting the governor, was secretly pleased to be appreciated. "No problem, Alan. I'm sorry I couldn't get here earlier in the day for you."

"Your timing is actually just about perfect. Kate—I was on the phone with her when you arrived—is about to make a very important call. I need the conversation to go well."

"What's going on?" asked Archer.

"She's calling a friend, who we hope will arrange a major fundraiser. I'm going to ... I need you to keep this confidential."

"Certainly. Always," Archer replied.

"I'm going to do it, just like you told me; I'm running for president!"

Archer looked intently at Alan; a sense of foreboding suddenly overwhelmed him. Archer hadn't had the slightest hint this was the reason he had been called to Topeka but, even as he heard the pronouncement, he knew Alan would win the election. Unfortunately, he felt uncharacteristically negative about the possible outcome of Alan becoming president. He replied in the only way he could and remain positive, "Governor, I'm certain you will be the very best president you can be."

"So you think I'll win?"

"Yes, I do. I'll vote for you," he said, "but, of course, my personal vote won't mean much in my state. I mean, Oklahoma always votes Republican."

"Archer, I need to know. You say I'll win; does that mean you think God wants me to win?"

Archer thought for a moment. "No. I've felt for a long time that you would be president one day and, even as you told me, I just felt like you would win." Looking at Alan's face, he could tell that he was not being understood.

Archer attempted to clarify, "I'm just saying that I don't know if God wants one person or another to be president. I do believe, however, He already knows the outcome."

Alan responded positively without fully comprehending Archer's metaphysical rant. "I also believe I'll win. I've never run for anything and lost. I don't intend to start now!"

Archer considered his statement for a moment. "I don't think many candidates expect to lose," he commented. "You may have an opportunity to experience a political loss someday, but I'm pretty sure you'll keep your record intact with this particular race."

"You make it sound so easy," Alan countered. "I look at all I have to do to win, and how I need other people to do things to make victory possible ... the situation just seems so very difficult and completely outside my control. Right now, as we speak, Kate is talking to a billionaire about holding a fundraiser for me. I need him to agree, and for the event to be a great success. I was going to ask you to pray for the call to go well, but how do you pray for something like that ... you know, money?"

"There are a number of things we can properly pray for regarding this," Archer answered. "We can pray that Kate has favor with God and with people, for example, but perhaps it would be better to pray for other things."

Alan took it all in; he was a bit overwhelmed. He really wanted God on his side in the race. It was almost harder thinking he would win, but not knowing if winning was God's will. "What should I be praying about?" he finally asked directly.

"I've already suggested," Archer continued, "that God might not have a favorite in any political race; he might not care to involve himself in the free will of the voters. God does care for you, Alan. I suggest we pray for you. You have some serious challenges ahead, and so does Kate. These future challenges may change you and your relationships. The final result could be for the better, but it might not. You have to be prepared for either outcome."

Alan was not comfortable with the suggestion of Archer praying for him, at least not *with* him. "Please do pray for me and Kate. I'm sure you're right; things will change. When we were in Pittsburg attending my mother's funeral, I spoke with so many people I knew when I lived there only a few years ago. Although the time since leaving Pittsburg has been short, I felt like I was a very different person. I am very concerned, and aware, that I could become someone I would not be proud of."

Archer smiled at Alan's honest concerns. "I can't tell you how relieved I am to hear these concerns. Unlike many other politicians, you have a conscience."

Alan leaned back in his chair, gazing at the ceiling for a moment. "I didn't expect this meeting to be like this, but I'm so glad you're my friend; you always help me keep my priorities straight," Alan observed. "Can I ask you to be available to advise me during the campaign? Not just one on one like today, but in strategy meetings?"

"Governor, I don't know much about politics. I don't know what I would have to add to strategy meetings."

"I think your presence would help keep me in check, assuring me I am on the right track to avoid doing things I would otherwise be ashamed of. Any time you do have advice, Archer, I want to hear it."

"Even now?" Archer asked.

"Yes, even now. What do you have?"

"I'd like to ask you to read the twentieth psalm," replied Archer. "One verse tells us not to trust horses or chariots, but to trust God instead. Alan, everyone involved in your campaign will have their own agenda. I think I read something from Thomas Jefferson, 'let no more be said of confidence in man ....' You need to trust God alone. God won't give your campaign the money, and He won't vote for you, but He is trustworthy. People will have to be involved, but you can keep your trust in God. As for Kate's phone call, I'm sure she'll be very persuasive."

"Yes, she is. I'm sure you're right. I guess you're having dinner with the Billingslys, then?"

"Indeed I am." Archer recognized Alan's reference as suggesting the meeting had come to an end. "I should be going, unless you need anything else?"

"No, Archer, just keep me in your prayers. Have a great evening. We'll talk again soon."

Archer left and found his way to his sister-in-law's home. Lenore and her husband were very hospitable to Archer. Like the governor, they had lost their only child; in their particular case, the child was lost due to illness. Therefore, they were eager to hear about Archer's daughter and other family events of significance. Archer called home and Lenore spoke to her sister briefly. They sat up late watching television. After Lenore's husband excused himself for bed, Archer and Lenore discussed the upcoming campaign. They agreed Alan would need to be protected from unscrupulous persons who would use him for their own ends.

Meanwhile at the governor's mansion, as Archer and Alan were still talking, Kate made her call to Keoki.

He answered with a boisterous, "Aloha, Kate! How is the *pua* of Kansas?"

"I don't know what '*pua*' is so I don't know how to answer that question."

"*Pua* is a flower."

"It's winter; it snowed today, so the sunflowers are all dormant for the season."

Keoki blurted, "*Wahine*, I meant you, not the state flower. I read about you often. You're beloved on the mainland."

"Thank you, Keoki, you're always so kind. Did you enjoy watching the surfers?"

"The surfers are fun, but the real show is the *moana*, the ocean. Don't hold back; you called with a purpose. What can I do for you?"

Kate carefully responded, "I did call to ask for something ... something big."

"I'm a big guy, so ask away."

"First, I must insist that you keep this between us, okay?"

Keoki joked, "*A'ole pilikia*, no problem. Are you all right?"

"I remember when I was in Hawaii you said that if you ever had an event at your home it would be a success. I want you to hold an event there for Alan."

"He just won re-election. Why do you want to have something at my *hale*'?"

Kate asserted, "Please remember your promise to keep this matter quiet. Alan's running for president, and I want you to have a major fundraiser for him at your house."

Keoki grunted at the request. After a moment he said, "I don't think you know what you're asking."

"I know you're a Democrat, but I think you'll like Alan ..."

"Kate, I'm not a Democrat!" Keoki interrupted. "They're far too conservative for me. Your husband, and you, worked for that dinosaur, Halprin. But I've been following Alan and do think I'd like him. He's been railing against Washington to allow states to run education as they see fit. Does he believe the same on other issues?"

"Yes, he does. Just last night he was talking with ... another supporter about the need to release the states from nearly all the restrictions they're now under.

Alan believes the federal government shouldn't be micro-managing the states."

"If I had my way, Hawaii would be doing a lot more for my *ohana*, um, the Hawaiian people. Republicans always want to limit what's done, and Democrats never want to do enough."

Kate replied, "I'm not going to lie to you. Alan is a conservative, and Kansas is a conservative state. He's working to limit government activity in Kansas because that's what the people of Kansas want, but he also wants to limit what the US Government does, allowing the states to have the power to fix their own issues. I know you don't like Washington telling Hawaii what to do. That goes both ways, you know. With Alan, Hawaii can do the additional things you want and Kansas can do less, if that's what they want. "And you can ask him whatever you like to your satisfaction. You can have him checked out; you'll find he's an entirely sincere man."

Keoki relented. "I don't need to, Kate. Your word is enough for me. But you still don't know what you're asking. How much do you need to raise at this event?"

"We need the event to raise two and a half million dollars," replied Kate, earnestly.

"Oh, is that all? I can do that for you." Keoki scoffed. The financial resources required were so minimal by his standards.

"No, it's not that easy," Kate continued. "There are limits and restrictions. We would need you to invite your business associates and friends. Ultimately, we need to hold one big event where we can expect your guests to donate significantly. That's why I'm asking for the event to be at your home. An invite to your home will attract people from all over the country. If you ask them they'll give, pretty much all of them, will give the maximum."

"Kate, when you were here did I say something about 'cleaning things up'?"

"Yes."

"I wasn't talking about doing the dishes; I have people for such jobs. What I meant was the reason I have kept my home a secret is because it's not exactly legal. I had a number of corporations buy up property, and friends who signed their deeds over to me. I never registered those deeds. I never got the proper paperwork on the place, as far as building codes and all. The situation would be difficult to clean up."

"I didn't know about that," she responded, "but I need you to say 'Yes' to me, please."

"Say I do it. How would this work?" asked Keoki.

"Great!" Kate exclaimed, unable to contain her pleasure. "But this would be complicated. If you invite everyone you know who could give five thousand dollars or so, how many would come?"

"Everyone? Could I fly them in?"

"Only Americans, but yes."

"I would say a thousand or so. I suppose I need to buy a bigger jet, huh."

"So, you'll do it?"

"I can't figure a way to say 'No' to you, so I guess I'll have to say 'Yes,'" Keoki told her.

Kate had prepared herself to express appreciation in the Hawaiian language: "*Mahalo*, Keoki. *Mahalo*. We'll have to have someone who understands all the legal requirements work with you on the details over time. Should they contact you or Suzzie at your office?"

"Please have them work with Suzzie. Can I tell her?"

"Yes, if she'll keep the information undisclosed. We'll make an announcement early next year, and then we can make your event public. Will your place be ready by April?"

"I'll make sure it is. I don't know how you talked me into this, but it will be the best luau ever."

"Thank you again, Keoki. It'll be great to see you again. In the meantime, have a Merry Christmas."

"*Mele Kalikimaka nani*, which is Merry Christmas, to you as well." Keoki neglected to tell Kate that "*nani*" is Hawaiian for beautiful.

The call was a complete success, and it was completed without anything that endangered the platonic nature of their relationship. Kate couldn't hold back her excitement. She called Alan immediately, shouting, "Alan, he said '*Yes!*'"

Alan calmly responded, "You said he'd do it; you were right."

"Hey, I've been carrying this around all day and I was worried about it."

"Well, it's official. I'm a candidate for President of the United States of America, and I owe it all to you, my love."

The day's activities were a complete success. Alan brimmed with confidence and pleasure. A few weeks later, he was sworn in to his second term as Governor of Kansas and the inaugural ball seemed a precursor of events to come.

A few days later, Alan was in between meetings with key state legislators about his agenda for the upcoming year when he found an appointment on his schedule with Mary Ann Force, the Kansas Republican National Committeewoman.

Jim was in the office with Alan, bantering about the legislative options, when Lenore announced her arrival. Alan turned on the charm and welcomed her enthusiastically.

"Mary Ann Force! How are you, my friend?"

"Governor, I'm fine. It's good to see you as well, Jim."

"I'll head out," Jim chimed in, "but I wanted to say hello before leaving. It's always good to see the woman who recruited America's best governor!"

As Jim opened the office door to leave, she replied with jocularity, "Oh Jim, you always know the right thing to say ... the truth!"

Now alone in the office, she looked seriously at the governor and said, "Alan, I need your help on something. I believe the information could end up to your advantage, as well."

Alan, sensing her urgency, curbed his broad smile to a pleasant, more serious look. He motioned for her to sit with him. "Mary Ann Force, what can I do for you?"

"I'm sure you know our RNC Chairwoman has resigned to run in the special election in Alabama."

Alan's serious look became sincere. "Mary Ann, I can't favor you for party chair ... right now. I would if I could, but please understand ...." He didn't use her full name, as she ordinarily required, but she didn't flinch.

"Oh no, Governor, I'm not running for the chairmanship."

"Okay, I'm sorry. I have some things in the works nationally ... with the Republican Governors. I can't get involved in internal party operations right now. I really would, if I could. Actually, it would be to my advantage if you were the RNC Chairwoman. I would pick you myself, if it were in my power."

He regretted saying the words as they came out. He realized if elected president, he would be expected to hand-pick the national party chair. Choosing someone from his own state would not be prudent.

"Several men are running and I'm not choosing sides," she explained. "I don't want to be Chair. I want the Vice Chair. The Vice Chair must be the opposite sex of the Chair, and all the Chair candidates are male. So ..."

Alan understood, "You're running for Vice Chair?"

"Yes, I am! I believe I have a very good shot at the position. I would like your support."

Alan answered with an apologetic timidity, "I'm sorry. I can't try to influence any position." He watched her countenance fall.

In a flash of inspiration, he realized there was something he could do to help her, and it would be good for him as well. "I've got it! I'm allowed to give the excess from my re-election campaign to the party. I was planning to spread the funds among county organizations, but what if I write the check to the RNC and give it to you to present?"

"Sir, the donation would be seen as tantamount to an endorsement of me."

"Yes it would, and hopefully it will help you win! But it wouldn't be an actual endorsement, so I won't have any problems from ... anyone. I believe I'm now permitted to transfer about fifty grand?"

"I think that's right, but the laws seem to change on a dime. Can I check on the amount and get back to you?"

Alan smiled with relief. "Yes, you can. Just know, I'm reserving fifty grand from my gubernatorial campaign account for ... let's say, 'your recommendation.' If I can't give all of the money to the RNC, then perhaps you'll have a list of state parties available you think could use the funds. Will that help?"

"Oh yes, Governor! Thank you very much. I do understand your concerns. I've been hearing a lot about you and Senator Halprin," she announced, as she stood to leave. Alan also stood, holding out his arms to embrace her. "Call me anytime. Let me know how it goes."

In early March, Alan and Kate traveled to a seaside resort in South Carolina. Kansas press reported the trip as a vacation. John Halprin's campaign operatives were all present, as previously planned. The Cassells were seen at the resort, and the event was leaked to the press. Early reports suggested this was a planning meeting for Halprin's second campaign. Alan's presence was simply reported as a governor who had been very involved in the first campaign.

John Halprin held "one on one" meetings with each of his old associates and aides. Excitement was high and all were prepared for a winning campaign. He never told them he was running for office; they just assumed he was. He commented on ideas for an improved campaign, but refused to admit that he would run. The group was so convinced Halprin was running again that Kate became concerned John had changed his mind.

The next day John held "the meeting." Alan had gone over his press release with John earlier in the morning. As John's meeting began, Alan strategically sent a single email to a press agency, which immediately released the announcement to television, radio, and newspapers. Within minutes, reporters were at the gates of the resort.

John spoke to the assembled invitees, expressing his appreciation for all their work in his previous campaign.

"As all of you know," he began, "presidential campaigns are extremely time-consuming and very stressful. This is especially true for losing campaigns. I have been spending my time since the last campaign ended with my family. I have been reacquainting myself with them."

The crowd, obviously unaware of the stunning announcement to come, laughed along with John.

"I have enjoyed my life as a 'free man' and my family, including my children and grandchildren, seem to enjoy having me around. I am also confident that the Republican Party will win back the White House in the upcoming election."

The group cheered, fully in support of the presumed candidate.

"However," John continued, "I do not think I will be the one leading our party to that victory."

Loud groans and shouts rang out from the audience, claiming, "No, John! You're our man!"

Raising his hands to silence the crowd, John persisted in his efforts. "I know all of you have supported me through the good times and the bad, and I truly wish I still had the fire inside that it takes to run an effective campaign. But, the fact of the matter is, I simply cannot make the same level of commitment to the election that I have had in the past. Not at this stage in my life. Without a hundred percent commitment to running a lengthy and grueling campaign, I would not be true to myself, or to any of you."

The assembled group, all of whom were anticipating John Halprin to announce his candidacy, did not know how to react. Then, Kate and Alan slipped in by the side door of the room.

Understanding the questions in the minds of everyone in attendance, John continued. "The one thing we cannot allow to happen now," he stated firmly, "is to permit infighting and petty bickering to derail what can, and will, still be a successful campaign. It's imperative that we maintain a strong and united party, focusing our full attention on fighting the Democrats rather than each other. If we allow every faction within the party to fight for the nomination, it could prove disastrous for the GOP in the general election. We must not let this happen. Starting here and now, we must be determined to unite behind a single candidate. The candidate must be someone we can all support without hesitation."

John let his listeners think about his words for a moment, and then added rhetorically, "Who do you think should be our candidate in my absence?"

He did not expect an answer; he had fully anticipated offering the name of Alan Cassell, Governor of Kansas, himself. What is more, since he was convinced everyone was expecting him to run, he was sure no one would have had time to think about an alternative candidate. On this, John Halprin was wrong.

Instead Phil Stanek, the rotund campaign finance wiz from Louisiana, blurted out, "Governor Alan Cassell!" as if it was an introduction, rather than a suggestion. Phil had put two and two together and wanted to move things forward expeditiously. Everyone in the group turned to see the governor and his beautiful wife, standing near the door. Applause rang out, and John asked them to come forward.

"Does anyone object to supporting Governor Cassell?" asked John.

"No!" came the unanimous response.

"Then, we are all agreed to support the governor's candidacy for president?" John asked for confirmation.

"Yes!" the group once again shouted in accord.

"I couldn't have conceived a better choice," John responded, happy with the way the process developed. "Most of you know I strongly considered Alan for vice president. I do believe he has what it takes to win! I'm ready to tell you all that I heartily endorse Alan Cassell for president and urge you all to work with his campaign!"

Again, applause rang through the room. The pollsters and other political vendors in the room understood that they had a readymade client for their business, one which lacked the baggage of a failed national campaign. Each person in the room came up to Kate and Alan to shake their hands, pledging to help in any way needed, knowing that "help" came with a price tag. The euphoria lasted only moments past the impromptu press conference following the meeting. The campaign had officially begun.

John Halprin spoke convincingly to the press about the meeting. He explained this was just an opportunity to thank his former campaign workers and vendors, and to let them know he was not running for office. He firmly stressed to the press his endorsement for Governor Cassell. He did not reveal, however, that he had effectively hand-picked his successor and anointed him as the next president. Senator Halprin had successfully manipulated the party structure and the political business infrastructure in a manner foreseen by few after party rules changes were put into place at the Republican Convention of 2012 in Tampa.

Alan spoke eloquently of his love for America. Kate had her arm wrapped around Alan's and gazed adoringly at him as he spoke.

It was a *coup d'état*; in only one meeting, Alan Cassell became the heir apparent to the Republican nomination for President of the United States.

John Halprin made sure Alan fully understood the most important aspects of a presidential campaign. The characteristics were not, as Alan had thought, building up a strong network on the ground in the early primary states. Rather, Alan learned that being accepted by the "powers that be," meant acquiring political and financial capital. This phase was far more critical in the early stages than garnering popular support.

Once again, Alan Cassell seemed to have the world handed to him on a silver platter. In the weeks that followed, literally hundreds of endorsements poured in for Alan. All of the conservative media acclaimed his record of reform in Kansas. The small portions of unbiased media reported on his life history; a boy born in poverty, who took a meteoric ride to the top of American politics through a series of fortuitous events. The bulk of media outlets were liberal, but still struggled to find things to criticize about the presidential possibility.

Public television and radio highlighted a women's group, who claimed Cassell was not fit because he married a beauty queen. The implication centered on Kate being shallow, and Alan being an impetuous young man interested only in outward beauty. Others berated the fact he and Kate had not raised children, or that he went to a small college and had only a four year degree. Still others criticized his heroic actions at KU. The denigrations backfired as Republicans nationwide rallied to his defense.

"It is the right of the people to alter or to abolish it, and to institute new government, laying its foundation on such principles and organizing its powers in such form, as to them shall seem most likely to effect their safety and happiness."

—Thomas Jefferson, Declaration of Independence

ALAN MET INDIVIDUALLY with most of Halprin's people from the South Carolina meeting. He was particularly impressed, however, with Phil Stanek of New Orleans. Phil was a Christian, and his parents who had immigrated from Europe after World War II, had gained national attention as leaders of the religious right as advocates for traditional family values. Phil grew up in the movement and eventually went into the fundraising business, raising money for candidates and for various Christian charities.

Phil Stanek was the man who had shouted Alan's name at the meeting in South Carolina. Phil seemed to have a sixth sense about national politics. He was highly creative and knew campaign finance laws inside and out. He was also more forthright about his mercenary nature as a campaign finance consultant than others in his position might be. Alan had a difficult assignment for him. Phil informed Alan when they met of his fee structure. Phil assured Alan his percentage was fair.

Alan agreed, "Phil, that percentage sounds fine for any fundraisers you arrange in the future. However, I have an event already arranged, and I need you to coordinate it. I need you to do this event for one-quarter of your normal fee. I'm pretty sure that when you know the details, you'll agree to the terms."

"I like you, Governor Cassell, but there's no way I can ..." Phil said, his words trailing off with disbelief. "I have staff and overhead. I know what this kind of event takes, and respectfully, you don't."

"Hear me out, and then decide. Okay?"

Phil looked at Alan, observing the governor's resolute expression. "Okay; this better be good!"

"I assume you and your staff wouldn't mind a temporary relocation to Hawaii? All costs would be covered, as well as the agreed upon commission."

"Interesting ... keep talking."

"My wife has a friend in Hawaii, George Keoki. I presume you've heard of him?"

"Yes, it's getting better."

"You'll be working with Keoki and Kate to put together the greatest single campaign fundraising event ever. Keoki is bringing several hundred millionaires together for the event. You in yet?"

"Let's see if I've got the details so far. I have to schlep out to some hot, humid island in the middle of nowhere to work with the second or third richest man in America and the second prettiest woman, after my wife of course. I need to orchestrate an event that will write new records in campaign events, giving me the extraordinary opportunity to be seen as the greatest fundraising genius of all time. Expenses are paid and, although there is a diminished percentage of the take, the event is essentially ready to go, except for the announcement. Is that about it?"

"Yeah, that's about it."

"I think I'm a go for that!"

Alan leaned back in his chair, and said, "Good. You'll be getting a call from Suzzie. She works for Keoki. She'll arrange for his jet to pick you up. Okay?"

Phil got to work immediately. They had less than a month to put the whole event together. Keoki had already begun to make some of the arrangements. He replaced his small private jet with a refurbished 747, made all the necessary legal corrections to his property issues, and added to his residence by purchasing an adjoining resort property. His private home now consisted of ninety-five acres of prime Oahu real estate, and had lodging for nearly eight hundred people.

Phil and his staff contacted every one of Keoki's planned guests, ensuring they were not doing anything outside the letter of the campaign finance laws; Phil had fewer qualms about the spirit of those laws. The event was only to be a luau at Keoki's home, but the plan was to create multiple mini-events where Alan and Kate would call on smaller groups who were "visiting" Keoki.

A full week before the event, Kate went to Hawaii help coordinate last-minute details. Alan had made several trips to Iowa and a couple to New Hampshire by that time. They instituted "Cassell for America" headquarters in six states, and no other candidate was comparable in making any headway. Two days before the event, Alan joined the group in Hawaii. He and Kate stayed in what had been the Presidential suite at the former resort. Phil arranged for Alan to ride along with the donors who would be most impressed by his flying with them.

The luau was shaping up to be as impressive as they had desired. The secrecy of Keoki's home was ended, but there was still significant mystery to the estate since the press had little more than aerial photos.

Keoki persuaded industrialists and financiers from all over the country to join the party. Some agreed to attend because Keoki invited them and others because they wanted Alan to win the election. Most attendees, however, went because they saw the need to have access to, and favor from, Cassell and Keoki.

Alan and Phil invited every Republican Congress member and governor, securing the attendance of much of the Republican National Committee and two former vice presidents.

Keoki sent every invitee a piece of Hawaiian garb to wear at the event. Each shirt, or dress, was tailor-made to the recipient. No invitation or identification would be required upon entry. Keoki had each piece of attire implanted with RFID (Radio Frequency Identification) technology. As the guests came to the luau, security personnel carried hand-held devices, which recognized the specific piece of clothing, matching the clothing to the person by using facial recognition software; therefore, people were even welcomed by name. Keoki hired every available student from the Hawaiian campus of Brigham Young University to serve as greeters and security for the event. The press were kept off property altogether.

From the moment Alan arrived, he and Kate began to make their rounds. He visited multiple private homes, hotel suites, and yachts in Honolulu, speaking briefly, smiling, and shaking hands with the guests. Phil arranged to have a staffer with Alan at all times. Any time a guest tried to give Alan a check or envelope, the staffer would take the contribution. The idea was to keep Alan from even touching any donation that might not be allowable by law. The finance staff went through every financial gift carefully. Any funds from controversial persons were reviewed; some donations were returned immediately.

While Alan was raising millions for his campaign, everyone involved seemed to profit from the event. The press coverage increased advertising revenue. Phil's profit motive was satisfied. Keoki improved his already grandiose stature and influence; he also had secret GPS access to the location of the clothing he had generously given away. Most of the guests enjoyed a luxurious vacation, while making new business contacts.

The members of Congress and other politicians at the event collected donations of their own. The state of Hawaii, in turn, collected significant tax revenues from the influx of upper class visitors. All of Cassell's campaign operatives enjoyed the tropical reprieve from the cold of Iowa and New Hampshire. Everyone seemed to have their own motive for participation in this event. Alan Cassell understood the various reasons for attendance, and he found the synergy to be positive.

There were two hidden motives Alan would not have approved of, if he had known at the time. People who favored Hawaiian independence used the event to promote their cause. Prior to this occasion, few Americans understood the events that had led to Hawaii's incorporation into the United States. The independence groups protested peacefully outside the property, giving the press a story. The tight-lipped attendees were not communicating with the press, which left the news reporters with only the Hawaiian independence story to report.

Of course, Alan would also not have approved had he known of Kate's infatuation with Keoki or of his flirtations with her.

At a quiet point during the luau, Kate observed that Keoki was disturbed by the protests. She approached him about his apprehension.

"Are you bothered because there are protests going on outside your property, or because of what they are protesting for?" she asked.

He used the opportunity to ask Kate to walk with him and discuss the matter, taking a tour of the grounds.

"I asked them not to protest the event," he told her plainly. Keoki agreed with the ideals of the protestors, but he wanted them to avoid this kind of activity during "his" luau. He emphasized his feelings, while relating the history of the American takeover of the islands.

"For many generations, until the 1890s, the Kingdom of Hawaii was peaceful and independent," he began. "But, for years, Americans had been gaining positions of power in the islands. These were rich and powerful men who went to any length to make sure they did not lose their influence. So, when Queen Lili'uokalani had 'the nerve' to attempt to establish a new constitution, something that a sovereign has every right to do in her own country, these powerful Americans conspired to overthrow the rightful government of an independent nation. Powerful forces working behind the scenes, in the darkness, can never be trusted."

"I have read a little about the history of Hawaii, but most accounts seem to minimize the role of the United States," Kate commented.

"Of course," Keoki replied, "American accounts would naturally want to limit their own culpability. This situation is the same as the way the federal government acted toward American Indians of the mainland in the 1800s. Their lands were taken by force, and nations that had existed for centuries were exterminated.

"The United States sent Marine forces onto the sovereign soil of Hawaii to intimidate the Queen. Rather than allow her people to be slaughtered, as were the Indians of the prairies where you now live, the Queen relinquished control of the islands to the subversive elements. Eventually, the US Government annexed Hawaii."

"Terrible." Kate's single word reply expressed her sympathy for his cause.

"Of course," Keoki continued, "the federal government believes it settled its debts in regards to Hawaii. When President Clinton signed the "Apology Resolution" passed by Congress in '93, on the one hundredth anniversary of the overthrow of the Kingdom of Hawaii, most Americans believed the document of regret was enough to appease the people of Hawaii. Just saying, 'We're sorry,' was supposed to make up for taking from us what was rightfully ours. Taking our land."

Keoki paused briefly and turned to Kate, asking, "How would you feel if a foreign power forcibly took over your beloved state of Kansas, Kate? If this entity removed your husband as rightful governor and replaced him with people of their choosing?"

Kate could not respond; her silence was deafening. Her expression revealed all Keoki needed.

He simply nodded, looking at her as if to say, *That is exactly how I feel.* Kate finally understood the depth of his feelings for Hawaii, as well as the independence movement. Keoki then shifted the course of conversation back to his property.

Preparation for the luau obscured the natural virtues of the estate. On the guided tour, Kate was made aware of all the conveniences and technological advances built into the property.

Keoki told her, "When I was building the estate, I wanted the buildings to blend with the land. Paradise is a difficult thing to improve on!"

They continued to walk toward the natural falls and terraced pools on the hillside near his primary residence buildings. There, they found themselves alone where he could take advantage of the privacy it afforded.

"You know, Kate, I have known many beautiful women. My wealth allows it. But you are unquestionably the most beautiful I have ever seen *anywhere* in the world," Keoki said.

Kate thanked him politely, expecting that would end the conversation; it didn't.

He continued, lightly touching the small of her back. Her body tingled at the warm touch of his strong hand on her skin, which was made bare by the cut of the dress. Despite her desire, and the adoring words, she expressed astonishment at his actions. She protested, "Keoki! No! I'm married."

"But if you weren't?" he asked.

"I am, and I love Alan. I hope you aren't doing all this as some kind of way to get me to …"

"I'm attracted to you; I've always found you attractive. You're an amazing woman."

Kate pulled away, but Keoki gently caught her arm and asked, "Can you tell me that you've never been attracted to me?"

"Keoki, you've been a wonderful friend," Kate said, avoiding the question. "That's all we can ever be. Please don't push it."

Releasing her arm, he stepped back and promised, "If a friend is all I can be, then a friend I will be. I'm very sorry to have offended you." Looking into her deep blue eyes, he could see that she was not offended, but afraid. Afraid of what surrendering to her passion would mean.

He then reverted to the purpose of his agreement to hold the event. "My reason for having this event was to please you, but also to help Alan win," Keoki explained. "I did check on him, and he does seem sincere about allowing Hawaii to follow our own path."

"Do you expect him to favor independence?" Kate inquired.

"I expect him to stay true to his own principles," Keoki observed.

"Do you favor independence?"

Keoki paused, just briefly to ensure his response was properly measured. "If we could stay in the US and have our sovereignty, then that is what I would favor for Hawaii. I do strongly believe in restoring our *ali'i*, our royalty. America took them away from us, and that was wrong. Royalty in Hawaii are servants of our people, not masters; very different than your European system."

"I don't know what he would say about the subject. We've never discussed it," Kate responded.

"When the subject does come up, will you tell our side of the story?"

"Alan is always very thorough when he makes a decision. He'll hear all sides; I'm sure of that. Let me ask, what of the Americans ... people who are not of Hawaiian ancestry. What happens to them if independence ...?"

"Everyone who lives here, except those who work for the US Government and their families, would be given full citizenship. With the Puerto Rican precedent in place, we know they don't lose US citizenship. We would all have two countries: the United States on the mainland and the Kingdom of Hawaii on the islands. I'm an American, so I would never have to relinquish my American citizenship. I would not renounce my citizenship if it was required for Hawaiian citizenship."

"What about the military bases?" questioned Kate, pragmatically.

"It's in the security interest of Hawaii to allow a friendly US to keep the bases. We don't want to disrupt things. Hawaiians understand American tourism is very important for our economic stability. All land transfers that occurred during the occupation would be recognized."

Kate was startled by his statement. "Do you really see it as an occupation?"

Keoki nodded affirmatively. "Kate, look around. We are a happy people who are healthy and prosperous," Keoki replied with a broad sweep of his hand. "We have the most beautiful place in the world as our home. We are denied nothing … nothing but the right to govern ourselves. Yes, it's an occupation because we're in a gilded cage; but a cage made from gold is still a cage. We should govern ourselves, and we would be free like the *manu*, the birds. Will you please tell this to Alan when you two do speak of it?"

"Yes, I will," Kate sincerely promised.

"I couldn't ask for anything more. We should go back; our guests will be missing us."

Kate agreed, "Let's not ever speak of … us … again, all right?"

"Thank you, yes," Keoki said, as they walked back to the party.

Kate noticed Keoki was not quite the same man he had been when she met him years earlier. He certainly looked the same, but his demeanor seemed to be more serious. She had only seen him a few times this week, but he didn't seem to be having as much fun as she knew he ordinarily would have in the past; he was driven. Perhaps, his behavior was a reflection of the event he was holding at her request. She also wondered if he was just another Hawaiian who favored independence, or if he was a driving force behind the movement. She knew the topic would come up when Alan was in the White House, or even before.

When all was said and done, the event raised more than twice as much as was originally hoped. That night, Kate couldn't sleep. She lay close to Alan, holding on to him throughout the night. At several points, she found herself tearing up with guilt regarding Keoki. The exhausted Alan, who was sleeping soundly, had no idea.

With the initial funds properly raised, Alan began his favorite part of the campaign. He flew directly from Honolulu to Kansas City and, after only a day in Topeka, he went to Iowa for old fashioned retail politics.

The establishment of the Republican Party supported Alan, but he could have won the nomination with just the support he collected from the grassroots. Alan worked harder than any other politician, and he was more down to earth as well. Some wondered why he was supported by both the establishment and the grassroots; his policies and manner won him the support of the grassroots, but it was uncertain if he could have gotten his message out as professionally without the party fat cats. Those well-heeled financiers may have set him up, but they might have done so to buy access to a candidate who would have won anyway. Alan's national appeal brought the party together in a way that had not been done since Ronald Reagan, many decades earlier.

Iowa, the first caucus state, is a state of small towns. Alan relished the opportunity to walk in and out of Main Street storefronts; shaking hands, listening to voters' concerns, and having his picture taken with them. He spoke to every Chamber event, civic club, and Republican Party event he was invited to. He actually enjoyed Iowa's famous loose meat sandwiches and was at ease among the many farmers of the state.

When he went to the first primary state, New Hampshire, on the other hand, he was relaxed among the blue collar workers of its small towns. In the next state in the schedule, South Carolina, his idealism excited the voters. In the whirlwind of the presidential campaign, ultimately Alan got to the point where he didn't have any idea where he was at any given time. He fell into a pattern of doing what was expected of him and saying what he was told to say. His campaign had more workers on paid staff than he even knew. Although there were other Republicans running, Alan never had to directly address them. He was able to run a positive campaign all the way to the Republican National Convention in Orlando, Florida.

Orlando seemed a peculiar choice for the Republican nominating convention, but the selection was made long before Alan was a candidate. A city known for children's amusements hosted a convention to nominate a youthful governor, who was childless.

Mary Ann Force was party vice chair and chair of the Committee on Arrangements by that time. She had carefully planned a convention which threw a very positive light on the nominee, the governor of her home state.

One of the most memorable events at the convention, however, was Kate's speech.

"You all know Alan Cassell as an idealistic man of principle, and the heroic governor of the great state of Kansas," Kate began, interrupted by thunderous applause followed by chants of "Cassell! Cassell! Cassell!"

"But I knew him when he was simply a county commissioner, albeit a very principled and idealistic county commissioner," she continued. "I knew him when he was simply an attractive, if slightly nervous, young man trying to impress a girl on a first date. On that first date, a horseback ride with horses Alan had borrowed from his neighbor, I learned several things about my future husband.

"First, I learned he is not a natural born politician, since he doesn't know how to lie very well." Once again, the entire convention center was rocked with applause and laughter, and the "Cassell!" chants.

"He lured me out to his place for a horse riding date. I didn't know it was a date, or that where we met was actually his place. I wasn't completely sure he was even single! Don't worry; he was quick to make sure I knew that fact. He did his best to pretend to know what he was doing with the horses. I had to bite the inside of my cheeks to prevent laughter when he actually mounted the horse while it was tied to the hitching post. I don't know what he was planning on using for reins!" The crowd laughed again and the cameras turned to the slightly embarrassed governor of Kansas. Seeing the image of her husband on the screen, she said to him, "Reins, honey, reins are those leather things people use to turn a horse one way or the other."

She turned back to the delegates and jested, "He actually tried to untie the horse while sitting on it! I suppose I was the better 'politician' that day because I never let on that I knew from the moment I arrived that he was no horseman. He finally managed to begin the ride and he looked all right, well, as far as I could tell; he was so far back there I could barely see him. The distance didn't do much to protect me from the sound he made when he fell!

"Oh, I didn't mention that he was wearing a hideous western shirt? It was obvious he had bought it earlier that same day." Pulling the torn shirt out from behind the oversized lectern, she held it up for all to see. "This," she resumed, "is what the next President of the United States thought he should wear to impress Miss Kansas." She held a runway pose, as she concluded the statement.

Laughter, then applause, resumed in force, and from Kate's words, the crowd began to see a side of the young governor of Kansas they did not know before; they grew to love him even more.

When Kate was allowed to resume her introduction, she said, "From that first date, and the ones that followed, I learned a lot about Alan Cassell. Alan Cassell, the man … not Alan Cassell, the politician. I found he was kind and caring, but also driven to succeed. While he never became an extraordinary horseman, he is an extraordinary man. I learned after a very short time that he was the man I wanted to spend the rest of my life with; he is the love of my life, and the finest man I have ever known."

As the crowd rose to its feet yet again, they were especially moved by the sight of Kate brushing away tears from the corners of her eyes. Her speech continued on to address other personal experiences regarding Alan, such as his early life and humble beginnings, a quote from his toast to her on their wedding day, and how he slept on the floor when she, and Katie, were in the hospital.

The very mention of Katie was difficult for Kate. At no other time in her life did she ever mention Katie in her public speaking. Her speech did nothing to touch on political ideals. Instead, it was an entirely personal statement about the character of her husband.

Kate accomplished something political machines and campaign gurus hope they could achieve over the course of dozens of campaign stops and scores of stump speeches; Alan Cassell became the candidate of the people.

Historically, the Democrats typically managed to carry the blue collar workers' vote. Yet Alan still had his "wrong side of the tracks" roots, and Kate's recounting of that story highlighted his background even more. Alan became all things to all people. He was a guy you would want to drink a beer with like Bill Clinton, but a guy who never drank much like Jimmy Carter. He was a man who pulled himself up from nothing like Barack Obama, and a great communicator like Ronald Reagan.

The convention was a melancholy return to Orlando for Kate. She was Grand Marshal of several parades where she and Alan had enjoyed their honeymoon. Alan became all-consumed by the campaign for eighteen months. She was his greatest asset, but too often she felt like that was all she was … an asset. She wanted more at this point in her life; more intimacy and more personal time, but Alan seemed satisfied just showing her off to the world. Perhaps it was unrealistic for her to expect to take long walks in the woods at Cedar Crest with her workaholic husband, much less one running for president.

Not unlike her childhood dog, Speck, she wanted to be Alan's "everything", but she was a grown woman who knew that what she wanted could never be.

Before the convention made his nomination official, the campaign was focused on raising money for the general election and a variety of strategy meetings. Alan gravitated toward particular people. He informally formed what would become his "kitchen cabinet," which actually began meeting in the kitchen of his Crawford County home during the pre-convention days.

John Halprin was always available for the meetings, as was Jim Cherry, despite Alan's intent to have him concentrate on Kansas matters. Mary Ann Force was the party liaison, and Lenore Billingsly served as secretary for the group. Phil Stanek was there as the finance guy, at first, but quickly showed his acumen on all things political. Archer Adams was a fish out of water in the group; however, Alan was insistent he would bring a moral stability to the proceedings. Kate was almost always at hand, though seldom included herself in the discussions. The group began to call itself, initially, the "G-8," short for "group of eight." Alan suggested, after several meetings, that they add another to the group of trusted advisors. He expected John and Jim to resist, but he was surprised that even Kate was reticent at the idea.

This group had originally formed to help Alan decide on a vice presidential nominee. Alan asked that each member of the G-8, excepting himself and Kate, advocate on behalf of one possible candidate. Alan wanted to see a free-flowing debate on the subject.

John Halprin argued for a congressman from New England for geographical balance; Mary Ann suggested a candidate who could raise money. Archer suggested the former governor of New Mexico, but did so with little conviction. Lenore refused to attempt to advocate for any one candidate. Alan was disappointed with her unwillingness to get into the debate, but accepted her decision. Jim Cherry made a presentation on behalf of two candidates; he thought either of the senior senators from Ohio or Florida would be valuable assets. The senator from Florida was a female, which would both help with that sector of the vote as well as secure the large state's electoral votes. The senator

170

from Ohio would, in Jim's opinion, secure his state, which had only narrowly gone Democrat in the previous three elections.

It was Phil Stanek, however, who hit the ball out of the park, "Ladies and gentlemen," he began, "some people suggest voters do not vote for the running mate; they vote for the top of the ticket. That attitude demeans the importance of the office of vice president, and it demeans the intelligence of the electorate. I believe the choice for vice president is very important. As has been said in the past, 'Personnel is policy.' I believe the presidential nominee's choice of a running mate is his first opportunity to act presidential. A president makes appointments; the voters understand that a president doesn't directly run the entire administration. They know it's his job to appoint the very best people to a wide variety of positions, and it's those appointees who actually run the government.

"I will propose that the vice presidential choice be one made on serious criteria. The office should be held by a person who agrees with the nominee on all vital policy matters. 'Balance' can be a proper factor when it comes to levels of experience, and perhaps on geography, but not on policy." Phil paused for a moment, and then continued. "It is disingenuous to choose a vice president who holds significantly differing views on public policy. However, it might be advantageous to have a nominee with differing appeal than that of Governor Cassell.

"It's good to have a governor as our presidential nominee because the voters see the position as similar, administrative. Having a vice president with DC experience can help win votes on a larger scale, and can help the administration in general. It is also good to have a VP nominee with statewide elective experience, so we can count on winning electoral votes.

"I will also suggest the best choice be someone with a strong personal relationship with Alan. The nation will respond well to a true team ticket.

"The candidate I am proposing is a friend of Governor Cassell, a former lieutenant governor of a battleground state, who is now a member of Congress, a woman, a mother and grandmother, a vice presidential candidate who will make us all proud ... Congresswoman Helen Benton of Oregon!"

The process did not work as Alan had hoped; he had wanted a vibrant debate. The choice of Helen Benton was clearly the right one, so there was no debate. Alan was excited about having her on the ticket. Her Polish heritage was also expected to help win votes from Pennsylvania, Ohio, Wisconsin, Illinois and Michigan, where she was born; all big electoral states with a large Polish population. The only real concern was her non-political codger of a husband.

Helen was surprised to receive a call from Alan, and even more surprised to be asked to serve as vice president. She insisted on an opportunity to ask her family before she could commit. As it turned out, her husband was unusually supportive; her children and grandchildren were elated at the prospect. After the prerequisite vetting, the announcement was made in Philadelphia at Independence Hall. It was the biggest news story in the nation in the days leading up to the Republican National Convention. One major weekly news magazine featured a story titled, "Alan Cassell's Women" with photos of Kate, Helen, and his sister Deena. The story juxtaposed the three women. Other press outlets played on the story, which worked to Alan's benefit, showing he had positive relationships with women of varied backgrounds and personalities.

One week prior to the convention, the group met in Topeka at the state party headquarters. Alan asked the G-8 to begin to include a family friend to their discussions, who had raised millions for his campaign. When George Keoki was brought in, most of them were stunned. Keoki was an unrepentant liberal, and still openly supported Democrats for a number of other offices. Alan had prepared Keoki for the meeting in advance; he had foreknowledge of the existing members of the group. Alan was pleased Keoki was willing to work with John and the other conservative-leaning Republicans, especially after Kate told him about the "dinosaur" comment.

"I'm sure everyone here knows George Keoki," Alan stated, introducing the newest selection for membership into his inner circle. All in attendance nodded affirmatively, although there were more than a few puzzled expressions.

"The whole point of this group," Alan continued, "at least in my opinion, is to have my closest friends and advisors to brainstorm together. By bringing in Keoki, I intend to show my appreciation for those who have gone the 'extra mile' to support me. Despite any political differences we have had in the past, I now have complete confidence in this man, just as I do every one of you."

While a few nodded half-heartedly in agreement, Alan could see that there were still doubters.

"Listen," he implored the group, "it is nothing special to appeal to those who always agree with you. Appealing to the base alone is great for getting the nomination. But to win the general election—and more importantly, to govern following that election—we need to reach out to others outside the Republican Party. By including Keoki, we ensure that happens."

Archer was the lone member of the group who spoke up readily for Keoki's admission. "Keoki has proven himself to be loyal to you and Kate; I welcome the opportunity."

Throughout the conversation, Kate sat silently and made sure to not make eye contact with Keoki. It was apparent to all that even she was surprised by his presence. The others could sense something else as well, but it was merely written off as disapproval.

Finally, after very little discussion on the matter, everyone saw Alan was adamant about Keoki's inclusion in the inner circle. In short order, all relented and accepted Alan's request, recognizing Alan had a right to include whomever he wanted in his group.

Alan and Kate Cassell, Jim Cherry, John Halprin, Mary Ann Force, Archer Adams, Lenore Billingsly, Helen Benton, Phil Stanek and George Keoki made up the group by then known as "G-10." Potential confusion over the terminology led them to agree that the name for the members should be the "G-Group." As it became clear Alan would win the election, Phil suggested "G-Group" was better to avoid confusion with meetings of the leaders of industrialized nations, which went by the moniker of the letter "G" and the current number of members.

As the campaign proceeded the press was constantly looking for new photos, especially of Kate; only occasionally did they care if Alan was included. They especially liked photos of her on horseback, both in Topeka and at their home in Crawford County.

Their old Crawford County place was the perfect picture of an antique farmhouse. Once Alan secured the nomination, the Secret Service began to make modifications to the home and property. A large guard house and wall around the property were erected. The old barn was modified into a command center with only a small portion reserved for Kate's horse which was hauled back and forth between Cedar Crest and their small farm for her use. The cattle were gone, and the grounds were manicured to perfection. The Secret Service installed an extravagant lighting system, a fully independent electric generator, a thirty thousand gallon water tank and, of course, a helicopter landing pad.

The changes to the property made the estate nearly unrecognizable. The farmhouse had started as a building that might have been torn down. Then, with Alan's initial efforts, the house became a bachelor pad that was barely habitable. Thanks to Kate's father, it became a survivable starter home for the young couple. In his years as governor, the farmhouse was renovated throughout and transformed into a fine country home. Now, since Alan was a presidential contender, the residence appeared simple and quaint, with rustic touches just to make it seem authentic. The spacious sixteen acres, however, were now crammed with buildings and equipment, and the land always had a buzz of activity.

CHAPTER 14 • **DEBATES**

"From the streets of Athens and Rome the voices still echo to crumbling walls. Look to the past and remember no empire rises that sooner or later won't fall. Forever the changes we still have to face. Some people say that a country is more an idea than a place."

—Al Stewart, Russians and Americans, 1984

THERE WERE THREE DEBATES that led up to the election, each concentrating on a different segment of public policy. The debates could be make-or-break for the Republican candidate, who was facing Democrat Charles Simpson. Simpson, unlike Alan Cassell, had decades of experience in Washington, DC and served for the outgoing administration as Secretary of State.

The first debate emphasized domestic policy. The debate highlighted the success Alan had had as governor of Kansas as it simultaneously portrayed Simpson as cold and detached from the everyday lives of Americans.

Answering a question from the moderator regarding his view of federal versus state involvement in the lives of the average citizen, Alan stated, "I believe government should do what it does best, and leave most matters to the people and the states. How can the federal government possibly understand the needs of the farmers in Kansas? Or even the residents of our larger cities? A bureaucrat in Washington, DC can only read reports and base decisions for individual states upon some formula developed by other bureaucrats.

"On the other hand, I live in Kansas. I was born and raised in the state. The people that work with me in state government understand very well, and in considerable detail, what the problems and needs are of the citizens of our state. So, as governor of Kansas, I haven't asked anyone in the federal government what they think is best for my state. The people who elected me tell me what they want and need, and I respond to *them*—not to Washington.

"Let me illustrate my philosophy of domestic policy this way," Alan continued, "You own your own home, with a nice little piece of land it sits on, and you are raising a family in that home and on that land, does your neighbor who lives down the road from you have a right to tell you what is best for your family? Does he have the right to establish the rules for your household, telling you how to use the land that you own? Of course not. Only when your activities begin, or at least threaten, to impact him and his home negatively does he have any right to even ask you to change your ways. Why? Because he cannot possibly know or understand your family and your needs better than you do. There is little difference between the nosey neighbor and the federal government trying to dictate what is best for each state.

"As President, I will not engage in dictating that people in California, or Maine, or any other state do things like we do in Kansas no matter how well it works for us. My job will be to serve the people, the states, and most importantly, to uphold the Constitution!"

Simpson could do little to negate Alan's home spun illustration or the point it made, especially since those in the studio audience were visibly impressed. The real-time tracking data indicated the public across the country was strongly in favor of Alan's principles of states having more to say about their own governing than Washington. Sixty-eight percent of those polled, including fifty percent which were identified as Democrats, agreed with Alan.

All the pundits agreed Alan had won the first debate. However, his win didn't move his polling numbers as dramatically as he had hoped, because he was expected to do better than the Democrat on those particular issues.

The second debate focused on fiscal policy, dealing with government revenues and spending. Alan held his own, but was portrayed by the Democrats and most of the press as an alarmist who opposed nearly every popular program of the federal government.

"The difference between Alan Cassell and myself cannot be clearer," asserted Simpson at one point during the second debate. "I believe the federal government is able to accomplish much more than state governments. It's called 'efficiency of scale.' Why bother to have a national government if we don't use the system in the most efficient manner possible? Without the support of the federal government, it would be impossible for states to care for all of their individual needs.

"On the other hand, Governor Cassell proposes to gut the federal government. He doesn't want to stop with cutting programs considered by many in both parties to be unproductive. Rather, he has even stated publically that he wants to scrap popular programs, which are still financially viable. We haven't begun to discuss the massive unemployment his plans would create. Our economy can't take the stress of what the governor proposes. I oppose his fiscal policies as reckless and simplistic. I believe the American voters will likewise reject them come November."

The live tracking data clearly showed many potential voters had reservations about Cassell's policies. The moderators for the second debate seemed to allow Simpson to attack Alan's policies, while not challenging Simpson's own, rather limited, specifics on fiscal policy. Alan's polling numbers took a slight hit after the second debate, but he still showed a small lead.

Everything rode on the final debate, which emphasized foreign policy issues. The Cassell campaign had no difficulty keeping public expectations to a minimum, since Alan had no international experience; Charles Simpson, however, was a career diplomat.

Simpson showed his expertise to the American people, although he came across as somewhat patronizing. While Simpson commented on the issues, the live tracking data showed a severe drop-off in favorable opinions, since the older Simpson seemed to be lecturing the younger Cassell. His attitude did not go over well with the public. But, when he stuck to the issues, the public was impressed with Simpson's level of expertise and comprehension of many complicated issues.

Alan stumbled on a number of questions and attempted to redeem himself with explanations that he had a "high caliber team of foreign policy experts led by Senator John Halprin." Halprin had strong credentials on international issues after years as the ranking member of the Senate Foreign Relations Committee.

Alan was eager to make a strong stand against Simpson and his policies. He had always held to the principle of self-determination. Simpson, however, agreed with America's long-standing "One-China policy." John Halprin and his advisors worked to prep Cassell on the issue; they warned him that a self-determination policy would have long-term ramifications and risks. Alan was convinced this principle would give him an edge with the electorate.

The One-China policy committed America to oppose independence for Taiwan, also known as Formosa, though the policy began quite differently. The Nationalist Government of China was chased off the continent and onto the island of Taiwan by communist forces after World War II. For many years the United States failed to recognize China's new communist government. Americans believed the Nationalist Government of Taiwan was the only authentic government in all of China. While the United States refused to interfere directly and restore the nationalist government through military means, it did agree to defend Taiwan against invasion from the continent. For a number of years, the lack of recognition of the communist Chinese government kept the nationalist government on the UN Security Council. President Richard Nixon opened relations with the communist government as an opportunity to bolster America's sagging economy. His successor, Gerald Ford, permitted the communist government to have UN membership for China, and a permanent seat on the Security Council.

The changes in Chinese relations required a delicate balance. America could do business with the communist Chinese, but were expected to continue the One-China policy, even if they continued to defend Taiwan against any Chinese efforts to regain the island. Taiwan's government operated as an independent nation, but without proper recognition. Taiwan was not permitted membership in the UN, nor allowed any of the normal privileges of an independent country.

Efforts began, as China's economy continued to grow, to create an open relationship between China and Taiwan with all the economic benefits initiated by formal relations. The people of Taiwan were sharply divided on the issue. Many favored independence, but a move toward actual independence would lead to war. Taiwan had lost all of its bargaining chips and would certainly lose a war with China. Other Taiwanese favored retaining the pseudo-independence, even if doing so prevented a connection with the largest economy in the world. Still others favored a transitional re-incorporation into China.

As Secretary of State, Simpson favored the final concept. American opposition had long been the only hindrance to China "re-taking" Taiwan. Simpson's stand gave the Chinese exactly what they wanted, and they began negotiating the transition. Simpson proudly called the policy "Hong Kong-ification," suggesting that Taiwan could be re-integrated into China in the same way the former British colony of Hong Kong had been. The concept of Hong Kong-ification, and the term itself, was ridiculed by the conservative media. Therefore, Simpson's policy helped Cassell's campaign raise millions of dollars.

Alan Cassell objected to the policy because the plan moved forward without regard to the opinion of the people of Taiwan. There had been no public vote on the issue, but polls showed that re-integration into China held the approval of a small minority on the island. Alan didn't mind ridiculing the term "Hong Kong-ification" on the campaign trail, even though his opposition was on more substantive grounds.

Although the government of Japan made no public statement on the issue, Japan's waning influence in the region would be further diminished by any re-integration of Taiwan into China. Japanese-Americans favored Cassell in unheard-of proportions because of the policy distinction. Most pundits considered this to be the reason Cassell carried Hawaii and narrowed the gap to single digits in California.

Alan worked to include comments to ridicule Simpson on the "Hong Kong-ification" policy in the third debate. Simpson responded dismissively. The American people watching the debate in studio and on television disapproved of Simpson's tactics.

Defensively, Simpson recalled comments by Cassell in the previous debate. He suggested, "Governor, you don't seem to advocate for the federal government doing anything! I don't know why you're running for president; you don't seem to want the job."

Alan responded extemporaneously, "Mr. Secretary, I do want the job, as it is expressed in the Constitution. As for wanting a different job, you've spent your career in international interests. Why don't you run for Secretary General of the UN?"

Simpson sensed that he had caught Cassell in a gaff. He quipped, "Governor Cassell, your comment exemplifies why we need someone with serious foreign policy credentials as President. The UN is not a democratic institution, and you don't 'run' for secretary general!"

The studio audience roared approval of Simpson's exposure of unforgivable ignorance on the part of the young governor. According to the live tracking that was displayed by the networks carrying the debate, Simpson's approval shot up with the comment.

Cassell paused expressionless, while the crowd quieted. After a moment of silence, the moderator goaded him for a response.

Alan smiled and said, "Secretary Simpson, I *did* know that the UN is not a 'democratic' institution, but I'm pleased to hear *you* acknowledge that fact. Now you, and all of America, know what is at the core of my objection to UN governance! I don't trust, and I believe the American voters will not trust, any institution that is unresponsive and undemocratic!"

A hush hit the audience. Governor Cassell gave a slight Cheshire grin and casually picked up his water glass. He slowly took a sip as the audience grasped the reality that the Secretary of State had fallen into the Governor's rhetorical trap. Meanwhile, Cassell's favorability rating showed a steady upswing on the television screen, as voters across the country understood the simple, yet powerful, point Alan had made. The debate continued and Alan explained that he valued the opportunity for multi-national discourse, which the UN fosters; it really didn't matter by that point.

The election, for all intents and purposes, was over at that moment. Polling the day after the last debate showed Alan with an average lead of ten points. Even the hard-core liberal pundits admitted Simpson and the Democrats were in real trouble. Cassell was seen as a man of the people, and Simpson was viewed a man who saw himself as better than the people; Cassell was the person who respected the voters, while Simpson was one who trusted foreign interests. The voters seemed willing to overlook Alan's lack of experience in foreign relations and focused on his desire to help the common man.

As November approached, the election seemed to be relatively close, according to the regularly released poll results; however, no one was really surprised by the outcome. Alan Cassell won the election by a landslide, garnering fifty-three percent of the popular vote. The overall percentage may have been close, but the real landslide was in the Electoral College.

The Electoral College was a system which required the votes from the various states be weighed according to a complicated formula. Within this voting system, Cassell had the strongest Republican win since Ronald Reagan. The traditional "red" states of the South, rural Midwest and the Mountain West stayed Republican. Alan narrowly won Ohio, New Jersey and Florida. His win in Oregon was much better than expected. He came close in Illinois, New York and Pennsylvania. It was no surprise he lost California, or the entirety of New England, excepting a surprise partial win in Maine. Maine was one of only a couple of states that divided its Electoral College votes by congressional district.

Alan earned enough support in the states he lost to create a coattail effect for quite a few congressional candidates. That year, the Republicans regained control of the US House. There was no change, however, in the Senate. The defeated Democrat, who was also the outgoing secretary of state, called the president-elect to politely concede the race. The conversation was brief, but more pleasant than Alan had expected. The phone call was the first time the two had spoken since the debates.

The call from the vanquished political foe broached none of the subjects discussed during the debates, but it did bring the topics to the forefront of Alan's conscience.

After the call, in the quiet of his office, an unexpected melancholy overcame Alan. Millions of Americans expressed glee at his victory, and he publicly celebrated with them. Deep within his heart, however, he had a feeling of foreboding. Alan Cassell had campaigned on his ideals, yet he felt as though he would not be allowed to be his own man as president. He was at the apex of his career, and he would be in the history books; yet he knew his presidency would be dominated by those who put him there, and his legacy would be events outside of his control. He wondered why this thought had not entered into his mind until this moment.

Alan and Kate watched the returns from Cedar Crest and then attended a victory party in Topeka arranged by the RNC. As the pair came into the mob-filled room, one young campaign worker gripped Alan's coat sleeve, telling him, "Now you can change the world!"

181

The comment bothered Alan and threw him off for a moment as he began his speech. He quickly regained composure, giving the prepared statement. He kissed Kate, who was beside him, and exited the room after an extended period of cheering and sign waving.

Back at the governor's mansion, he closed himself in his study for a few moments to contemplate. *Who do they think I am?* he asked himself. *I am to be the presiding officer over one level of government for one nation. I campaigned on limited government. They expect me to change the world! I don't want to change the world. I don't want to run the country; it runs itself very well without any interruption. I told them what I believed in when I was running. The president is not supposed to be an elected emperor! The federal government needs to be small and uninvolved in the daily lives of Americans. Will I ever be able to get that message across?*

The time for reflection was over. A sturdy knock hit his door and, upon his inquiry, the Secret Service entered. He was expected to sign documents and submit to an eye scan and blood sample. Campaign aides followed on their heels with documents that reflected the transition.

Try as she might, Lenore could not keep people out of the room. Phone calls were coming in from family, contributors, and world leaders. Senator Halprin arrived, advising Lenore to not pass any additional calls to the president-elect. He then instructed people to leave the grounds for the evening. Even Michael Fogarty and Ryan Methe were asked by the former Senator to leave; Kate jumped in to inform him her father and her incoming chief of staff were spending the night.

Ryan had originally recruited Kate to begin her literacy work back in Wichita. The two went to junior high and high school together. Ryan was Kate's only male friend in school, since all the other guys sought a romantic relationship. Ryan was attractive, but a full eight inches shorter than Kate, so he never made such an effort. He also avoided the subject because, as a devout Catholic, he would only date another Catholic. Years later, Ryan found a Catholic girl to marry, and it was his wife who got Ryan involved in politics. He participated in the Republican Party because of his social conservative values and had risen to the chairmanship of the state's largest county when the Coffee Grounds meeting was called to order. During Alan's tenure as governor, Ryan stepped out of politics. Then, with the onset of Alan's presidential campaign, he contacted Kate to see how he could help. She told him that she had no intention of being a "political" first lady. Her goal was to emphasize literacy and she requested his assistance in the effort.

Alan worried the ideals he pushed in his election would be cast aside, becoming little more than popular rhetoric. What he eventually found was those ideals would have more impact than he expected or desired.

Thus began the last presidency of a united American nation.

CHAPTER 15 • CASSELL'S AMERICA

"In the end it may well be that Britain will be honored by historians more for the way she disposed of an empire than for the way in which she acquired it."

—Lord Harlech

IN THE YEARS PRIOR TO THE election of Alan Cassell as President of the United States, America was a different country, historically speaking; gone were the days of American exceptionalism. Americans, as a whole, were satisfied to be called "American" without any feeling of pride in the moniker.

America was one country among equals in the family of nations; the nation was not the leader it had sought to be during the Cold War, or pretended to be in its wake. "Leader of the Free World" was no longer a title American Presidents sought or accepted. Other nations took the leadership responsibility upon themselves, but none did so with the air of arrogance projected by America or the British Empire before her. Many observers bemoaned the changes, but the thought prevailed that it was better to be among equals than to have the burden of leadership.

Even so, the job of being president was inexorably complex. Alan was accustomed to having his hands in everything as governor, but the presidency was a different kind of position. John Halprin schooled Alan on the pitfalls of being a "hands on" president. He persuaded Alan to delegate maximum authority to his appointees; appointees recommended by John Halprin. Through a network of White House personnel, Halprin designed a presidential administration similar to what would have been his if he had won four years earlier.

Alan found all of the John's suggestions to be competent and cooperative; there was no doubt in his mind that John Halprin was in complete agreement with his policy agenda. He had no reason to question the loyalty of his staff, cabinet secretaries, or the thousands of other employees of the federal government. Alan's opposition to big government had not translated into a distrust of government workers. He saw them as dedicated public servants, like himself.

Alan spent his days meeting scores of people in short, scripted appointments. He signed papers that he merely scanned, rather than the usual thorough perusal he was accustomed to. Only the most important issues would be discussed at length in the Oval Office.

Throughout the Cassell administration, Alan struggled to deal with the new "superpower" of the world; the largest nation and the largest economy in the world was China.

Quietly, China manipulated matters, giving themselves a world leadership role. Most people, including the Chinese people, were unaware of their climbing political dominance. In Europe, Germany utilized its acquiescence to minor French concerns and took working control of the European Union. Germany, therefore, positioned itself as the second most powerful country in the world. America was in a waning third place by the time Alan Cassell took office.

The global changes were slow and quiet. Americans understood they were no longer the "sole superpower," but employment was good, the nation was at peace, and the country took time to focus on domestic issues. Or so they thought.

International pressure was severe. European Union and Asian Market entities held most of America's national debt; they utilized the debt to influence every policy. The action was not conspiratorial, as was thought by some; it would have been better if it was. Demands made on America by debt-holding interests were often at odds. The American government was involved in a delicate balancing act. Many members of Congress, both Democrat and Republican, were thinly veiled lobbyists for international interests.

The best course of action was to limit government spending and begin to buy down the debt. Americans craved a balanced budget. President Cassell would be supported by the debt holders in his planned efforts to reform and reduce the federal government. The new Republican House had no taste for increased taxes; therefore, reduction in spending was the only option. Economic growth could augment tax revenues but, in the opinion of most economists, growth would be stalled without fiscal restraint.

Alan had to be careful with any effort to actually reduce the debt. Debt holders jealously guarded their opportunity to influence American policy, both foreign and domestic. Keeping America indebted was "having their cake and eating it too." They would continue to be able to cash in their debt in if they needed to, or they could "dump" bonds in retaliation against disapproved legislation. The president's trick would be to balance the budget, while spurring enough growth to inadvertently reduce debt.

The existing financial and global difficulties were hidden from most Americans. For them, Alan Cassell was the most envied man in America; he was on top of the world. He was the President of the United States and married to one of the most beautiful women on the planet. He was healthy, good looking, and fabulously popular. Alan was not denied anything he ever desired.

Conversely, his view from the top seemed to be a precipice.

Alan enjoyed his early days as president. Despite the foreboding that hit him on Election Day, he threw himself headlong into the work of being president. Alan reveled in his opportunity to press the ideals of limited government, local control, and personal responsibility. The presidency also offered an opportunity to fill many positions with people he had come to know and trust. President Cassell was particularly pleased that Lenore Billingsly and Jim Cherry were both able to join him in the administration. Lenore would be his personal administrative assistant, and Jim accepted the roles of Domestic Policy Adviser and Director of the Domestic Policy Council.

During the crucial first one hundred days of President Cassell's administration, the G-Group was revealed publically through an undiscovered leak. This information gave Alan's opponents an opportunity to criticize every quirk in the lives of the individuals involved, attempting to deride them as a group.

One enterprising graphic artist created a poster of the G-Group. He found pictures of each of the members of the group and altered the appearance of their clothing; they seemed to be wearing some type of uniform, which consisted of black slacks and white tops. Most of the members also wore black jackets; the men wore solid colored ties. The pictures were organized in a chevron. Alan was at the apex with five members to his right and four to his left. The inequality appeared balanced at first glance because the exceedingly robust Phil Stanek was on the side with the fewer members.

To Alan's right were John Halprin, Helen Benton, Archer Adams, and finally Phil. The first lady, George Keoki, Lenore Billingsly, Jim Cherry, and Mary Ann Force were on Alan's left. The work was of such quality that a couple members of the group wondered if it was actually a single photograph. However, Kate recalled that the photo of her was taken when she was actually wearing navy colored slacks and a beige blouse.

The poster created quite the stir at the White House. After about a week, publicity had diminished the negative press regarding Cassell and the group. Over time, several members of the White House staff proudly hung copies of the poster in their offices.

The president was informed a few weeks later that some unfortunate comments by Phil Stanek had been dug up by a reporter. He wanted to ask the president about the remarks at a press conference. The press secretary suggested an exclusive interview with the president in lieu of a press conference ambush.

Years earlier, Phil had told a reporter, "The Nazis seem to have won World War II." He had also suggested, "Europe is united under a fascist government dominated by Germany, and most of the Jews are gone! What Hitler couldn't accomplish by war, the German state has accomplished by 'peaceful' means."

Alan was prepared for the reporter. "I don't agree with Mr. Stanek's assessment," Alan answered the first question. "I condemn the statements in the strongest of terms. Yesterday, I contacted the German Premier, who was in Brussels on European Union business, and told him that I condemned the comments. The premier asked me if I was removing Mr. Stanek from my administration, and I had to inform him that Mr. Stanek was not a member of my administration and would not ever be one. I told him that Mr. Stanek was an acquaintance who worked in my campaign, and that he had *no* influence on foreign policy. I also called Mr. Stanek, whom I had not spoken with for months, and expressed my dismay and disappointment at hearing the statements. He apologized to me."

The reporter asked, "Will he be apologizing to the German Premier?"

"His comments were not directed to the premier, and I seriously doubt he has any access to the premier's phone number. I don't think the premier has any desire to hear from him. I expressed my sorrow for the comments."

"Will you distance yourself from Mr. Stanek? Will he continue to be part of your G-Group?"

"The relationships among G-Group members, excluding the first lady and myself, have been grossly exaggerated. As I mentioned, I hadn't even spoken with Mr. Stanek for quite a while. We should be careful in condemning Mr. Stanek for his concerns in relation to the growing influence Germany is having in Europe and around the world. I believe his comments are extreme and in error, but let's all show a bit of understanding for a man who lost relatives in concentration camps."

The interview closed the book on the controversy. Alan asked Lenore to contact the G-Group members, asking them to watch their words because anything could come back to haunt them. Alan Cassell then returned to more pleasant Presidential duties.

The day he appointed Bill Coffee as ambassador to the Bahamas was Alan's favorite day at the White House. Bill Coffee was a quiet man who worked constantly. He became the richest man in Kansas by building a real estate empire in the Kansas City area. His eccentric wife, Sue, wanted Bill to retire so they could spend their sunset years together without the stress of work. However, Bill enjoyed his work and felt he would die if he quit.

Alan had the perfect answer for his old friend. He gave Bill a job that kept him busy enough to need to stay offshore, but located in a place where he would almost be forced to enjoy himself. Bill tried to turn the position down, but both Alan and Sue insisted otherwise. When the appointment was finally accepted, Alan observed a level of joyousness in Bill's countenance he hadn't previously seen. He later told Kate that Bill's face reminded him of his sister Deena's four-year-old son the previous Christmas morning.

As Alan filled other needed positions, he felt frustrated. Alan had campaigned to eliminate certain appointments and agencies, but Congress didn't permit him to leave the positions open. The Senate majority leader, a Democrat, and the Speaker of the House, a Republican, pronounced that no effort to consolidate departments or agencies would be considered if they did not have an approved leader at its head. Congress required testimony from the secretary or director to determine if consolidation was proper, and they wanted information itemizing where the various duties would be transferred. In truth, Congress obfuscated Alan's reform agenda; they even erected obstacles against selling off nationalized businesses when highly lucrative offers were made.

Alan thought the system was utter foolishness to go through all the trouble to appoint someone, have them go through the process of confirmation, and then be expected to testify to Congressional committees on why they and their thousands of employees should be dismissed or incorporated into the employ of corporate interests upon privatization.

This was an area where John Halprin was of the most assistance. His international business connections helped him find qualified appointees who were willing to jump though the hoops required for confirmation. The officials served only long enough to get their agency, bureau, or department shut down. Each of the appointees understood they would be able to use the temporary assignment as a stepping stool to a much more powerful and higher paying job in the business world when the job was done.

President Cassell's reform agenda was well on its way to success. He often communicated that his reforms were the only way to preserve the union over the long run. As agencies, bureaus, and entire federal departments began to be dismantled, state and local governments expressed increased concern. Therefore, the Republican Speaker of the House recommended a massive revenue sharing program from the federal government to the states and localities.

Alan was furious! He called the Speaker into the Oval Office for a private meeting. The "Imperial Speaker," as Time magazine called him, arrived with all the pomp to which he had quickly become accustomed; his entourage consisted of nearly three dozen people.

The White House staff was ready for him.

The task at hand was to remove the Speaker, "Skip" Ezell, from his staff. President Cassell would then be able to disarm him with all the charm he could muster.

Gerald "Skip" Ezell was born and raised in Moss Point, Mississippi. His ancestors were significant in business in the state, but his father was the black sheep of the family; a drunkard, who worked intermittently at the local paper mill or the fish plant in Escatawapa. His mother, from neighboring Pecan, pronounced "pea-can," was a less-than-devout church-attending Baptist. Skip made much of his humble origins, often speaking of the little two bedroom house where he was raised. He would tell of how they moved in after a hurricane swept over the area, but without making any of the repairs that should have been made. He relished talking about their pet cat, who ate the little lizards that found their way into the house and how those lizards ate the palmetto bugs. The cycle seemed to keep things habitable for the poor family.

The contrast between the poor Southern boy from the wrong side of the bayou and the pompous politician he had become was deliberate. He arrived at the White House in a large limousine. The luxurious vehicle was preceded by a large van, carrying those members of his staff who would not fit in the limo. The Speaker pranced into the White House, wearing a fine custom-tailored light grey suit. He wanted everyone aware of the fact that the power player of American Government had arrived. Walking into the reception area of the West Wing, the Speaker and his party were deliberately stalled well past the time he was scheduled to meet with the president. The two politicians had met many times in the past, but everyone knew this was the first time the encounter was not expected to be harmonious.

The Speaker was interfering with the president's reform plans; Cassell was intent on bringing Ezell back onto the reservation. The president's staff and security personnel knew Ezell would not sit while waiting in the lobby, and they knew none of his accompanying employees would be permitted by Ezell to do so either.

The White House was well prepared to deal with the situation at hand. President Cassell authorized for the electronic blocking equipment to be activated, so he and Ezell could not be interrupted by electronic means. The president knew Ezell would insist at least some of his staff join him in the meeting, unless an event happened which threw him off-guard. Kate was the secret weapon.

Ever since Ezell had been attorney general for the state of Mississippi, he insisted on being called by title—except for by women he found attractive; attractive women were expected to call him "Skippy." On occasion, he would be called the nickname by a woman he did not find attractive, and he would let her know not to be so "casual." He only avoided asking a beautiful woman to use the moniker twice; the exceptions were the female governor of his state and the First Lady of the United States, Kate Cassell. He acted out of respect in both cases. Ezell had first met the Cassells at some point in the campaign and was polite enough to avoid the request.

Kate was dressed casually that day, with blue jeans and a nice blouse. She carried a garden trowel and gloves as she walked into the reception area.

"Skippy!" she shouted gleefully, as she approached him. "How are you doing?" she asked, reaching out to embrace him.

"Fine, Mrs. Cassell …"

"Oh no, not you; you call me Kate," she assured him, as she worked her hand around his elbow. "You just come with me. I'm supposed to be gardening outside the Oval, but it's really a photo op for Better Homes and Gardens!" Kate walked through the reception area, and out of it, with the Speaker in tow. She spoke the whole time, not letting him get a word in edgewise.

His staff was left in the reception area, while the Speaker was arm in arm with the first lady as she walked toward the Oval Office. Kate informed him, "Alan has been very busy today, and he hasn't had lunch yet. I told the kitchen to bring him something; you won't mind visiting with him while he eats, will you?" There didn't seem to be a choice, so the Speaker just walked along with her.

Kate burst into the Oval Office like it was just another room, pulling Ezell along. "I think his lunch must have arrived by now. He told me he would eat on the portico, so let's go out and see him." She pushed open the French doors of the office onto the portico and greeted her presidential husband. "Did you get your lunch? Good! Look who I found in the reception area." She then turned to Ezell, saying, "Skippy, why don't you take off your coat and join him. There's plenty." Kate pulled out a seat for him and patted the chair until he sat down. She went to Alan and leaned over him, giving him a long kiss. Kate then slipped out into the adjoining garden and greeted a photographer, who was in easy view of the impromptu lunch.

"Gerald," President Cassell started, "I'm glad you were able to join me today. There's an extra bowl; let me give you some, it's quite delicious!" Alan had a large crock of stew on the table with a bowl half-eaten already. He had a tall, broad glass of iced tea beside him and a pan of cornbread next to his plate. Closer to Ezell's seat was a bucket of ice with three bottles of beer.

The Speaker had been swept off his feet by the first lady and was not given the chance to be awed by the Oval Office. He was then treated to a close-up of a romantic kiss between the most powerful man in the country and his gorgeous wife, while being seated in the one chair at the table where the hot sun would beat on him in business clothes. All of this activity was within clear view of a magazine photographer. When he finally got to speak, he asked, "Is that the real thing?" The Speaker pointed to the stew.

"It's a pretty good gumbo," Alan replied. "The andouille is authentic, but the White House kitchen didn't have any 'mud bugs,' so they used lobster instead. Dig in!"

Alan was comfortable in just about every setting, including eating the very spicy gumbo on the portico outside his White House office. On the other hand, Gerald Ezell had become pretentious in his political positions. His pompous attitudes were tried, as he sat in the sun eating very spicy food. As soon as Alan saw a single drop of sweat, he invited Gerald to have a beer. The first two beers were empty in no time; Alan stuck to his sweet iced tea.

Alan then explained his reform efforts to Ezell, and his belief that these changes were critical to the survival of the nation. The Speaker knew in short order that he'd been duped. The young, inexperienced president had put him in his place and had used all the accoutrements of the presidency with skill.

The Speaker, determined to call his bluff at that point, said, "Mr. President …"

"Oh no, call me Alan," interrupted the president.

"Um, no sir, Mr. President. I will say, you have choreographed all of this quite well."

"Okay, but the gumbo is quite good!" said Alan.

"Well, the gumbo is acceptable. Good for these parts, anyways. I am impressed, but must admit I seem to be missin' the point of the exercise."

"Mr. Speaker ..."

"Um, while I must insist on calling you by title, may I also expect you call me 'Jerry' or 'Skip,' if you prefer?" said Ezell.

"All right, I'll go with 'Jerry.' I wonder, Jerry, is it a Southern thing for men to have so many names that you can organize a Rolodex by what a person calls you?"

A boisterous laugh rang out in response to the question. "I never thought about it that way. My papaw was named 'Gerald,' as was his. In my family the moniker skips a generation, thus the nickname."

The photographer in the distance heard the sound of laughing and finally realized he might get better photos if he focused beyond the first lady and onto the president and his luncheon guest.

"Mr. President, you are a man in a hurry to do everything. If I may give you a suggestion: life is good, it can be long, and it is most definitely worth living. You might want to slow down a bit. Some folks might think you would even be in a hurry to get to heaven. Well, let me assure you, eternity won't get any longer for gettin' there sooner."

Alan gave a bit of a lopsided smile. "If I'm in a hurry, it's to do good. I did wait to get married, and that worked out very well. Tell me, is it even legal to be that old when you get married in your state?" Alan briefly chuckled, and then continued, "That being said, how about if I agree to take your advice ... and give some in return?"

Jerry sat up straight and responded sarcastically, "I would be honored to receive ad-vice from the President of the United States."

"You're at the top of your career, as am I," Alan began. "I don't expect you'll run for president, but either way, you're on the top of the heap; you have no need to impress anyone anymore. How about relaxing? Get comfortable with, well, everything?"

"You went through all this effort to put me in my place. You kept my staff aloof, got the first lady to carry me out here, sat me in the sun, pushed food at me; food from my country which I know you don't eat often, and all within view of a photographer. And you want *me* to relax. This is *not* a relaxing sit-chee-ation, Mr. President, and I am definitely not relaxed."

Alan took his comments in silently for a moment. "Jerry, I am truly sorry for making you uncomfortable. And the photographer, that was coincidental. Kate already had that set up, but eating out here was intended to give an opportunity for us to get along in a casual setting. I do want to … get along."

"Well, then ..." Jerry said, getting up from his chair. He continued to speak as he moved. "I'll make myself comfortable, and perhaps we can get along, and get some things done in servitude to our nation." Jerry sat beside the president in the shade.

"Servitude?" Alan said contemplatively. "Interesting choice of words."

"Why do you say so?"

"Like slavery; interesting that you would bring that up."

Jerry was a bit perturbed at the comment. "Why is it that *every* president I have a conversation with, of any length, finds a way to bring 'slavery' into it? It's like y'all hear my drawl, and all you can think of is 'slavery'! My ancestors, most of 'em carpetbaggers, came to Miss-ippi after the war and served in the Union Army. But, truth be told, slavery wasn't that big a deal."

Surprised, Alan asked, "Not that big a deal?"

"No, not that big a deal," Jerry defended. "Not big enough to kill a half million Americans. Not big enough to cause all the problems it did. Every nation had slavery, but only here did we have a war over it. I know that folks in my country say the war wasn't over slavery; and in yours, they say it was. But, just accepting the view that it was, why did we have to fight over the issue? Why couldn't we have ended our problems without war? I say we could have avoided that war, and should have concluded that peculiar institution peaceably. Besides, we are all slaves, a little bit, anyways."

"What do you mean?" asked Alan.

"Involuntary servitude; aren't we all required to do things we would not volunteer for?" Jerry replied. "The draft, when we have one, it's 'involuntary!' More importantly, when we go to a doctor; with our socialized medicine, our doctors work for the government now. They didn't want that, protested it, but they still serve, involuntarily, right? And the big one: taxes or inflation, which is taxation by printing your fiat money. Nobody pays taxes voluntarily; it's slavery. It's necessary, but it's a little bit of slavery. Now, I wouldn't say the slaves had it easy, or that slavery was good; it was not. Slavery was about as bad as anything, short of what Hitler did to the Jews, but I would rather be a slave to a man who was honest about it than to a government who called me 'free'!"

Wanting to move on, Alan looked at the Speaker and said, "Now that's a perspective I hadn't considered, but how can we best increase the level of freedom for Americans and reduce, to the greatest level possible, the 'slavery factor'?"

"Mr. President, I believe you are on the right track. The government is far too big. It's involved in folk's daily lives more than the Soviets were in the Russians lives. Or Hitler in Germany, or Mussolini with the I-tallions or, for that matter, Castro or Chavez were in Cuba and Venezuela. Nonetheless, we pretend we are freer than any people ever were. We must cut these programs, departments, agencies … every one you're callin' for."

"So, why are you working with the majority leader to block my efforts?" Alan queried.

Ezell responded loudly, "I am not working to block them!" Then quieter, "I am just suggestin' that you are moving too fast. Slow it down a bit, so that our states, counties, parishes over in Lou'siana, and towns can catch up. We are cuttin' spending somethin' fierce, but I can't get tax cuts *that* big. So, I think we need to soften the blow. We have been collectin' the money for so long, and then parceling it out to them, that they can't do without. It's just a transition, that's all."

"I was a governor, and you were the attorney general in Mississippi. We both know how much we had to spend to get 'federal' money and how much they wasted getting the funds back to us. Then, we had to expend the money exactly how they instructed. It's a waste; you know it, and we can't afford it anymore."

"Mr. President, you are right. But we must transition. It'll never fly any other way. How about we do it as a 'No Strings Attached' program?"

"What's your plan?" asked Alan.

"I did not come here with a plan nailed down to a board. I just know we can't leave local government high and dry. If we did, you would lose the House, and we would lose you after that. Your reform is very unpopular, unless we do something like revenue sharing."

Alan gave a moment of thought before saying, "You can't be pretending that you, or any member of Congress, have the level of commitment that I have for local government!"

Without a defense, the Speaker gave a simple, "No, sir."

Alan took his response and ran with it. "Surely you know the pressures that are on me to eliminate the deficit. We are at risk of having our debt dumped on us. If we fail to honor it, or if we monetize it, then we risk economic collapse … even war!"

"War? Mr. President?" Ezell asked. "Is something going on that I have not been briefed on?"

Alan reached over to Ezell's arm, reassuring him. "No, nothing imminent," Alan responded. "I'm just a student of history. We will not get to that point, I assure you. We must honor our obligations, and we must cut spending and balance the budget. It sure wouldn't hurt to reduce the debt a bit either."

"We are agreed then, that a transitional revenue sharin' program won't get in the way. We can run the program through one of the departments that you want to keep. The Treasury would stay, right? You don't want to eliminate that one, do you?"

"There was nothing about 'transition' in your public statements." Alan said, ignoring the rhetorical question.

"Mr. President, that is called compromise. I believe you have convinced me to alter my position. I would suggest that we send thirty to fifty percent of funds we had been sending to states and local government into such a program. This action would help me pass your reforms and bolster us in the midterms."

"If I go for this," Alan insisted, "if, I say, then the program must transition down to zero, and in short order."

The two politicians continued the discussion until they came to a resolution on the fine points; details they could both agree with and expected would pass in Congress. "The Gumbo Summit," as it came to be known, was a success. Both compromised, but both saved face. Ezell's idea was adopted, though amended, and on Alan's timeline.

Alan Cassell ended the day satisfied. The meeting was a role reversal for both men. Alan played the political power monger, while the Speaker loosened up his resolve. Together, they had worked out a deal.

The president felt if the nation took the responsible course, then disaster could be averted. Americans often thought government controlled the events detailed on the nightly news. Alan allowed himself the same illusion that day. The fact was that events controlled the government, more often than not.

CHAPTER 16 • ROI-FAINEANT

If California fails, they can always move to Texas. If Texas fails, they can move to Kansas. If America fails, where does the world go?

—Glenn Beck

ALAN SAT ON A LARGE, comfortable leather sofa. He and Kate had returned to the residence after a formal occasion recognizing the retirement of a large number of employees at the State Department. The room was lit only by the television screen. The television studio on the screen filled with boisterous laughter as the late night comedian performed his monologue. Presumably, the viewing audience in homes around America found his banter as humorous as the live audience did.

Except Alan didn't find it funny. Not at all.

Kate, passing through the room behind him, came over and put her hand on his shoulder, comforting him. "Don't worry, honey," she suggested. "No one takes these late night monologues serious. In a few days, it will all blow over."

Not everyone would forget, and certainly not Alan.

The jokes revolved around the policy about-face made by the Cassell administration regarding Taiwan. Cassell had opposed forcing Taiwan into re-integration with China throughout his campaign, while his opponent was the chief architect of that policy.

With Alan Cassell in office, there was a chance to reverse the policy, allowing the people of Taiwan to determine their own destiny. Unfortunately for Alan, and presumably for the Taiwanese, the matter was too far along by the time Cassell was sworn in to office. When he tried to rectify the situation, the entire National Security Council opposed his efforts.

Earlier in the day, John Halprin had tried to console the president. "Alan," he began, "I'm sure you remember the situation with the Panama Canal as Ronald Reagan was running for President."

"Yes," Alan confirmed. "He promised never to give the Canal Zone back to Panama and openly opposed the treaty that was already in the works."

"That's right," John acknowledged, "but Reagan was not just blowing smoke to get elected. He genuinely was opposed to the treaty and he did everything he could to stop it. Problem was, by the time he was elected, it was simply too late in the process for him to do anything about the treaty, even as president. Sometimes, there are processes set in motion that cannot be stopped; momentum is just too powerful. That's what happened to you with Taiwan."

"That's probably true, John," Alan reluctantly agreed.

John nodded and placed his hand on Alan's shoulder. "Sometimes, we just have to accept the reality that certain events are out of our control." Then, he suggested, "The best course of action at this point is for you to make a public statement that reiterates your original policy on Taiwan, emphasizing that you have not changed your beliefs. However, in light of events that occurred prior to your election, it is impossible for you to reverse the move toward reintegration of Taiwan."

"I know you're right, John, and that is what I will do ... what I *must* do."

When reintegration became inevitable, opinion polls in Taiwan suddenly changed toward favoring the "Hong Kong-ification" of Taiwan. A large number of nationalist politicians, and many of the business people who had supported them, departed Taiwan for Japan, Singapore, Australia, and Hawaii.

The changes created near panic in Japan. The next elections, only months later, brought in a new government, which was conciliatory toward Beijing. Japan became a virtual satellite state of China.

The Japanese expatriate community became highly critical of the United States and its President, Alan Cassell. Most Japanese-Americans quickly joined the disenchanted chorus. Japanese-Americans involved in the Hawaii sovereignty movement pumped untold millions of dollars into it, maneuvering the concept of Hawaiian independence into a strongly anti-American effort.

When the movement took on its anti-American posture Keoki made a very public break from the movement. However, it was too late. In the preceding years, Keoki had generously given to scores of foundations, charities, and organizations that favored sovereignty for Hawaii. The movement had far too much momentum to be stopped, short of military action. With the strength of the Japanese-Americans behind the advance in force, the time for Hawaiian independence was at hand.

The Hawaii National Congress (HNC) met publically for the very first time. Originally formed in Keoki's home, where they were no longer welcome, the group met in a convention center in Honolulu for the televised event. The meeting was orchestrated purely for the press. Proclamations condemning the American takeover were well-written for an American audience.

A proclamation, which was passed despite significant opposition, called for full citizenship for all residents of Hawaii. The document excluded those who were in the employ of the United States Government and their households. Federal government employees were required to resign or risk deportation. The HNC members who supported allowing the US military bases to remain on the islands were not successful in their effort to pass a resolution. They did, however, succeeded in preventing a contrary resolution. On that matter, indecisiveness reigned.

Another reign began on that day. Members of the Hawaiian Congress interrupted their business for the coronation of the new Queen of Hawaii, which was being televised on the mainland. She addressed the crowd in the Hawaiian language, and no immediate translation was offered; the act was an intentional snub. Her intent was to speak to "her people" and not to continue the propaganda activities of "her" Congress.

The most notable public relations development of the event was the absence of a declaration of independence. The Hawaiians intended to put pressure on the United States to take action. The Hawaiians wished to respond to an aggressive or oppressive United States, rather than appear as the aggressor.

Every resolution of the HNC quickly found an equal act in the state legislature, though the legislative acts were highly lawyered versions thereof.

The state legislature also funded the HNC as a "cultural organization," and it formally celebrated the coronation. Opposition members of the legislature were shut down at every turn and debate was strictly limited.

Fearful federal government employees began mass resignations. The postal service gave bonuses to mainland employees willing to take temporary duty in Hawaii to deliver the mail.

A suit was filed in federal court calling for the US Government to fulfill its constitutional obligations under Article Four, Section Four, which stated, "The United States shall guarantee to every State in this Union a republican form of government." The legal premise being that a "queen" was a violation of the requirement for a republican form of government.

The state of Hawaii responded that it was simply recognizing a cultural icon; the Queen had no formal office in the state, nor did she have any authority in its government. The court was eager to sidestep the issue and dismissed the case.

The American press got caught up in speculation regarding *when*, rather than *if*, a declaration of independence would be made by Hawaii. Members of the US Congress made long speeches alternately supporting, or opposing, independence. Considering the seriousness of the situation, President Cassell was also expected to make a statement.

Alan brought together his G-Group for advice. Prior to the meeting, Kate told Alan everything Keoki had said to her about Hawaii. Of course, nothing was said of the pass he had made toward her..

At the meeting, Keoki refused to advise the group on the situation. He attended the gathering, and expressed his disputes with the movement, as well as his views about the illegality of American rule on the islands. However, he resisted expressing any opinion on what the president should do.

John Halprin, the expert on international affairs in the group, admitted other nations were ready to recognize Hawaii as a kingdom. He told President Cassell that Hawaii was an "exceptional situation."

"Mr. President, I advise you to tell the American people that 'if' the people of Hawaii choose to become independent from the United States, your administration will not oppose them. You could refer to your longstanding support of 'self-determination.'"

"What about our bases there?" asked Alan.

"Perhaps it's time to pack up and leave, letting Hawaii fend for itself," John stated with conviction. "The move would save us a lot of money in the long run, and I believe they can afford to defend themselves."

Archer spoke of the immorality of American actions in the takeover of Hawaii. He warned the group, "Two wrongs, any number of wrongs, never make something right. Whatever you do, sir, it must be the right thing, independent of any previous action by other people in our history. It may be wrong to forcibly keep Hawaii in the union, but it would also be wrong to abandon American citizens who wish to stay American."

Phil Stanek could hold his peace no longer, and commented, "Mr. President, I'm very surprised by the counsel thus far. I think you should carefully consider the implications, both historic and electoral. A terrible civil war was fought over the secession of the southern states. Another war began, for us, in Hawaii. The corporate memory of the American voter may be short, but failure to keep the union together will be seen as a weakness when the next election comes around—a *severe* weakness! I can't help thinking there is a question which will haunt us all. That question is, 'Is Alan Cassell the last president of a fifty state union?'"

Alan calmly answered, "Perhaps I will be; that can't be the most important concern. Phil, you spoke of weakness. Well, tell me, how strong am I as a leader if I can't do what's right? Isn't the real test of strength—personal, political, and moral strength—about doing what's right despite the consequences?"

"Is it right?" Mary Ann Force questioned. "Are you convinced? Is it the right thing for Hawaii to be independent?"

"I don't think that is the right angle to focus on. I am convinced, however, that keeping them in the union by force would absolutely be wrong. I'm sure there are plenty of American families ready to send their sons and daughters to war to protect America, but how many of them are ready to see their beloved progeny die to keep those islands?" Alan paused, and then continued. "There is no doubt at all we'd win a military action, but at what cost? I don't know how many Americans would be willing to have us establish martial law over the islands, and for our armed forces to kill Hawaiians, to kill *Americans*, to retain our governance over the islands.

"It's like divorce; it's never good. When someone gets a divorce, usually one of the partners did something wrong. Divorce is bad, but often necessary. If divorce was outlawed, then what motivation would there be for couples to be faithful to their vows? If a marriage can't be held together out of affection, then perhaps a divorce is better. The same principle should be applied to our nation. If the union can't be preserved out of our affinity for each other, our common values, our heritage as one nation, then perhaps it shouldn't be preserved at all.

"I will not do to Hawaii what I could not prevent being done to Taiwan," Alan concluded with sincerity in his voice.

Jim Cherry shouted out, "That was a completely different situation!"

Alan looked warmly at his oldest friend and mentor, and responded, "I'm sorry Jim, but it only seems different from your, perhaps from our, perspective."

Vice President Benton wiped tears from her eyes. "I can't believe we're even talking about this! Isn't there anything we can do to keep Hawaii? Can't we appease them? If you won't use force, then what can we do? I just hate the idea of losing a state!"

"Helen, I know. We all understand the gravity of the situation. I just don't think that we can bribe them to stay. If we do bribe them, then will Alaska, or Utah, or Texas do the same thing? Perhaps Massachusetts will threaten secession next, or New York, or Florida, just to get money or favorable legislation. It would change the nature of the republic; the outcome would be even worse."

Lenore stated, "It seems you've made your decision, Mr. President."

"I have made some decisions, but we have the opportunity to negotiate. I'm looking for your advice on priorities. I'll be meeting with the Speaker and the Majority Leader as well."

"America won't forgive giving up all the bases," Phil pointed out. "I think we must retain Pearl Harbor. I want you reelected, and I want to keep the House. With two fewer Democrats in the Senate, that puts us pretty close."

Phil continued, "Politics aside, we should secure the property rights of American citizens, which is everyone on the islands. We should see how much of the national debt we can convince their new government to absorb." Up till that point, no one had brought up the impact of spreading the national debt over a shrinking country.

Brainstorming, John suggested, "The debt could be a thorny issue. Anything short of a proportional share based on population could be used as precedent, encouraging other states to secede. If we negotiate the matter too far, then we risk negotiating to a position we can't, or shouldn't, accept."

Pausing a moment in thought, he continued, "What if we agree to sell government properties for debt absorption? If they don't agree, then we insist on selling the property to the highest bidder or keeping it; they'll have no choice. They won't allow us to sell a national park, the medical facilities, the post offices, or other federally owned properties. I can just imagine the reaction if we threaten to sell a navy base to China; bet they would want to buy then! No, not if they can have all federal government properties for the price of accepting a portion of the national debt.

"I don't know how the numbers would come out, but the bases alone should bring us close to population proportionate debt reallocation. We might actually come out financially better. Obviously, we would make certain the numbers work that way. If they try to take the properties by force, then we have the moral right to prevent them from doing so by force. This way, we don't compel them to accept our will; we just give them a perfectly reasonable set of options."

Everyone grunted, or mumbled, their agreement as heads nodded about the room. Alan commented, "Sounds like a plan, unless anyone has a problem with that model?" None mentioned anything. Years later, some members of the group suggested they foresaw other problems with the idea, and perhaps they did, but none said a word on that day.

As a final concern, Alan posited, "I know we're in uncharted legal territory. I'm also going to meet with the attorney general and White House counsel on the matter. If any of you have any thoughts about legal implications, then I need to hear from you so I can run the issues by them. The Constitution doesn't seem to have a process to unmake a state. We have to figure out if the process can be done by treaty, or if an act of Congress can withdraw the admission. Maybe we don't take any action at all." Alan stood up, implying the meeting was adjourned.

When President Cassell met with Attorney General Richard Dake, he asked him to serve as his personal negotiator with the Hawaiian sovereignty leadership. The attorney general insisted that dissolving statehood was not a legal possibility, but he agreed to serve the president in getting the best possible settlement. Dake's antagonism against the premise of sovereignty inspired Alan to choose him for the assignment. *Always better to work from a position of strength,* Alan thought.

A few days later, Alan accepted a call in the residence from the man who had run his California campaign. Thomas Houston was a staff attorney for a state agency in Sacramento. He was not known around the state for his day job, which was working for the state government. Thomas was best known as president of the historically powerful California Republican Assembly, or CRA. The CRA was founded in the 1930s by moderate Republicans. By the 1964 presidential season, however, the group had been overrun by conservatives. The conservatives revised the structure of the organization and retained it as a conservative powerhouse in California politics thereafter. It was CRA leaders who recruited the actor Ronald Reagan to run for governor.

"Tom, did I ever get around to thanking you for all you did for me in California?" Alan asked.

"Yes, Mr. President. You did express gratitude for my work, even though we were not successful in winning the state. I have an idea that might change that next time, though."

"I'm not ready to campaign yet."

"I understand, but I wanted to run an idea by you, if I might?"

"What do you have in mind, Tom?"

"Well, this Hawaii thing got me thinking. A lot of people in California could be convinced to make sure we stay a fifty state nation. That is if … if Hawaii goes independent, and if they're really permitted to."

"I'm not going to put troops in Hawaii to prevent the secession, if that's what you're asking."

"Yes, Mr. President, it was. I'm glad to hear your answer. If we divide California into northern and southern states, then we don't change the US flag. Even better than that, we can win in Southern California, depending on how it's divided. If the division includes the Central Valley in Southern California, we can promise you a win with another twenty-five or so Presidential Electoral Votes!"

"That has been suggested before, but it didn't ever take hold. Do you have any reason to believe this time is different?"

"Yes, sir. We have some preliminary polling that suggests Californians are inclined to divide to keep the US at fifty states."

"Sounds good to me, but do you need me to do something?"

"We need to raise money to get the issue on the ballot. If you would, please, speak to the California State Party Chair and let him know you like the idea of division. Then, he'll help us raise money to get the petitions signed, and we'll get the question on the ballot."

"You're not asking for a public endorsement, are you?"

"No, Mr. President. I just need the party to know you're on board."

"You've got a deal. I'll place the call tomorrow. Keep me posted."

"Thank you, Mr. President."

Funds to pay people who gathered signatures on petitions, and the other costs related to initiatives, were raised in short order; the issue was scheduled for the ballot.

In Oklahoma, efforts to put an initiative on a public ballot had the opposite effect. In the Sooner State, signatures were being gathered to amend the state constitution, calling for secession to occur automatically "if and when such other state or states secede as are contiguous with Oklahoma and an oceanic coastline." The petition was an obvious suggestion that Oklahoma would join Texas in secession. Alan called his closest friend from Oklahoma.

Archer answered his cell, hearing, "Please hold for the president."

"Archer, what the hell are they doing down there?"

"Mr. President? Down where?"

"Oklahoma! I'm told they're trying to get Oklahoma to secede, and *encouraging* Texas to do the same?"

"Oh, that. I don't think they're encouraging Texas to secede. It's not even a sure thing it'll get on the ballot."

"I can tell you, they have the signatures, and it's gonna be on the ballot. You live there; don't you know what's going on?"

"I only know what I read in the papers." Archer's thinly-veiled reference to Will Rogers was missed by the president, who was in a poor mood. "Seriously, Mr. President, I'm not tied into politics. I'm just tied into you."

"You're not behind this, or in with the folks working on it?"

"No sir, and I expect I'll be voting against it, if it means that much to you."

"God, man! Do you think I want the whole country to fall apart? What we're doing with Hawaii is unique. I can't let the whole country go to hell in a hand basket! We could still send troops to Hawaii, if we have to. I just don't know what to do."

"Mr. President. Alan? If I may?"

"Don't worry about that, go ahead."

Archer collected his thoughts and said, "I honestly don't know what you should do either, but I know someone who does, and I suspect you do too."

Alan had forgotten that he was speaking to a minister and felt embarrassed by his language. Archer didn't act like a typical preacher and never tried to get people to alter their language in his presence.

"Archer, I'm sorry. I'm just so frustrated."

"I didn't say that to get you to apologize to me. I'm not offended. You didn't say anything I don't hear every day. I just want to actually help you."

Alan calmed himself down. "So ... you want me to pray?"

"I think *you* want to pray. I know you need to ... I also think you're a little afraid of what the results of praying might be."

"Afraid!"

"Yes, sir! You can't tell me you're not afraid of what is happening. I know you're trying to do what's right with Hawaii, but I also know you feel guilty about Taiwan. And I think you're afraid of what'll happen to you."

"Me! I can't believe you think I've given a thought for myself in this. If Texas were to secede, then we couldn't sustain the country. One small state that's out in the middle of the Pacific is one thing, but Texas! And after all we did to the islands to force them into the union. But Texas is another matter! I don't want to be remembered as the Gorbachev of America."

"Your words are very telling, sir."

"What? You're gonna work your 'magic' on me?" Alan spoke dismissively of Archer's charismatic religious beliefs.

"Alan, I know you're upset, but please think about your own words."

"Okay buddy, what did I say?"

"Well, you said 'we' when you were talking about forcing Hawaii 'in.' You didn't have anything to do with Hawaiian history, and I would suggest your feelings are stemming from residual guilt regarding Taiwan again. Then you said you hadn't given a thought for yourself, but mentioned you didn't want be like Gorbachev."

"Bullshit! That's just bullshit! When I said 'we' I meant the US, not me. You brought up my reputation, so I thought about the implications and mentioned Gorby. So there, smart ass. I've heard enough. You aren't involved and don't know anything about Oklahoma; that's good enough for me."

Alan slammed down the phone. Archer felt that his relationship with Alan was damaged, perhaps irreparably so; he was hurt. He also felt, however, that Alan was in danger of doing something he would regret. There was nothing to do but to pray for him. Archer sent out a few emails asking for prayer for the president, but gave no hint as to the cause for the request. Then, he spent some time in personal prayer.

During his personal prayer time, Archer sensed the emails soliciting prayer for the president were a mistake. He regretted taking any action prior to entering into prayer himself, but he didn't understand why asking a few friends to pray would be a problem.

A pastor of a large church in San Antonio was among those whom Archer had asked to pray. The email was sent by the pastor to a few members of his congregation, in efforts to solicit their prayerfulness as well. Among the members who received the email was a politically active Republican.

The member made a personal assumption that the prayer need was based on secession talk in Hawaii, as well as Oklahoma. He also supposed similar talk in Texas, Alaska and Wyoming was weighing on President Cassell. He made his comments regarding his assumptions, and passed the email on. With each generation the email from Archer was altered. No harm was intended, but the political activist forwarded the edited email to a large political email list. Several news organizations received the final version of the "prayer request."

Within a couple of hours, Archer received the first interview request concerning the email. Archer was often interviewed on numerous subjects and the radio show producer said nothing about an email, so he accepted. Archer was asked about requesting prayer for the president. He responded innocently and affirmatively, having only seen his own original and non-specific request.

Archer was curious about the level of interest a radio show would have in such a small issue.

The reporter, however, took his response as an admission, suggesting the president was weak and worried about secession of the several states. Archer protested, but to no avail. After the interview, he saw the final email as it had evolved and was aghast. He accepted every interview request, denying the email was his and showing his original document to reporters. Archer also created a press release with the correct information.

One reporter asked, "Are you also denying that you spoke with President Cassell about secession in Hawaii, or any other state?"

Archer seemed taken aback by the words "any other state" and responded, "My conversations with the president are always private. The request for prayer was based on the scriptural exhortation that we all pray for those in leadership over us."

The reporter, in an understanding voice, then asked, "So you're using the clergy-penitent privilege regarding your conversation with the president."

"Yes, I treat every conversation with him, and every conversation someone asks to be private, that way."

The next day the press put together an amalgamation of the interviews and made it look like Archer had admitted to the email in its final version, then backtracked under pressure from the White House. Some suggested that the Secret Service created the so-called "original" email in order to give Archer the cover story of an amended email. They then built a case that Archer had admitted that the president had confessed to him some illegality regarding Hawaii and the other states.

Talk radio made Archer the topic of the day. Some hosts were critical of him, saying he was being disloyal to the President; others pushed that he was disloyal to the nation. Even more commentators, however, stressed that he was part of a cover-up of nefarious activities by President Cassell. None accepted Archer's very truthful story about his original, and very innocent, email.

Still upset with Archer, Alan was furious when he heard of the email the next day. The effect of the story was to weaken the president, spur secession talk in numerous states, and irretrievably damage the relationship between Alan and Archer.

The story damaged Archer in every imaginable way.

The student churches, nine campus groups in six states, all cut off their relationship with Archer's ministry. They didn't pay him or his ministry; in fact, Archer's ministry gave financial support to them.

The many churches which supported Archer as a missionary dropped their support. They did this because he no longer had any campus ministries to support. Not having campus churches to work with, or local churches to fund his efforts, he found he could no longer sell his books and DVDs.

Archer was too old to find a different ministry to work in. He did not want to establish himself as a pastor at a new church at his age either. He couldn't retire, since he hadn't built up adequate savings. The negative publicity made him radioactive in any ministry. Mercifully, a social conservative group in St. Louis offered Archer a job, which he accepted. The group had a history of success in various family values issues and had been founded by a devout Catholic lady, who had passed away many years earlier.

Archer adapted and accepted his new surroundings. The job opportunity provided him with a home near a major airport where he could easily fly to anywhere in the country. The location was also a bit closer to his only daughter, who had married that Purcell boy from Chicago.

Archer's wife, however, was a small-town girl who had lived most of her life in central Oklahoma; the move was extremely difficult for her. She didn't like the comparatively cold and wet St. Louis, or the big industrial city itself. Archer found he didn't need to travel as much as he had before the story. At first, his wife welcomed his daily presence; yet, over time, the stress of the new city and caring for him became too much for her.

She suffered a stroke. The doctors said the illness had been building up for years, but Archer was sure the stroke was his fault, due to the move and newfound financial stress.

Her sister, Lenore, took a leave of absence to take care of her and Archer. Lenore's calming tone was sorely missed when the president's calls were made or received. Heads of state, ambassadors, members of Congress, corporate leaders, and many other well-known people asked about her. Upon finding out about her sister's health, many decided to send flowers, gifts, and even catered food.

As the expressions of concern and gifts came in, Archer was grateful. Only later did he learn their concern was for Lenore's sister, rather than for *his* wife. A phone call came to the hospital from Mary Ann Force, who was surprised to hear Archer's voice. "Archer! How very kind of you to be there for Lenore, and her sister, of course! You are such a darling to do that." Bewildered, Archer just set the phone on the receiver and sat down next to his wife, starring at the blank wall of the hospital room.

Mary Ann Force assumed the worst and called right back, but no one answered. She then dialed the hospital, but could get no information. Finally, in desperation, she called Jim Cherry.

"Jim! Has something happened with Lenore's sister?"

"Yes, Mary Ann, I thought you knew she had a stroke."

"Oh, I knew that; I meant just now. I called the room and talked to Archer Adams, who was there, and all of a sudden the phone went dead. I'm just worried something happened at that moment."

Jim took it in and said, "I don't know, but I'll let you know as soon as I find out anything. It sure would be a hit for Archer if things went badly."

Mary Ann was confused. "Archer? Why would it be a hit for him? He was sweet to be there for Lenore ..."

Jim was flabbergasted. "Mary Ann! His wife had a stroke. If she passes, it'll be very hard on him."

"Oh dear, her too! Could it be something environmental?"

"You're telling me you didn't know! Lenore's sister *is* Archer's wife!"

"Oh God, really? I never knew that."

"Yes! Even if you were never told, didn't you read any of the articles about the G-Group?"

"I read parts, of some of them, but ..."

Jim put the situation together at that point, "Mary Ann, did you say something to Archer? It's been a very bad year for him. His ministry was destroyed by that email/prayer story. He had to take a job in St. Louis, and now this."

"I think I did; I feel awful. I better do something about it now."

Jim tried to stop her from ending the call, but his efforts were to no avail; he was concerned she would make matters worse. She didn't. She called and called the room until someone answered. Convincing Archer to take the phone through the nurse who answered, she apologized profusely and explained that she didn't know the relationship between him and Lenore. Archer regained enough composure to accept the apology and responded graciously to her.

Meanwhile, in Washington, DC, Attorney General Richard Dake returned from his negotiating trip to Hawaii. He was ready to report to the president.

"The islands are a mess, and I don't think there's any way to retain the state without bloodshed, Mr. President," he reported. "I also had time to research, and I now feel a treaty to recognize Hawaii's independence would be constitutional. Treaties trump acts of legislation, so to speak. Admission to the union is legislative, so ..."

"Okay, very well. What kind of deal do you have?" President Cassell inquired.

"I would say you got everything you wanted. American citizens' property rights will continue to be recognized. US Government property will transfer for a share of the national debt equal to the value; the transfer gives them a line of credit. They'll let us keep Pearl Harbor open on a no cost lease option. They want to continue talks on the other matters.

"They insist that military base leases must be annually renewed. If the bases are turned over to Hawaii, then they accept more debt at the property value when they renew. If the US Government doesn't accept the appraisal, then we're free to keep the property or sell to whomever! Of course, they must be able to limit any military activities of the buyer. They're willing to take all of the bases; they want to buy ships and other military equipment on the same deal, if we're willing. They'll need to defend themselves.

"US citizens in Hawaii are to be offered citizenship without exception. Americans who refuse Hawaiian citizenship will be automatically given a twelve month visa from the date the treaty is ratified by both parties.

"They really want to move forward quickly." Dake paused for a moment, collecting his thoughts. "I must admit, I agree. The mood is chaotic over there; no one knows exactly what's going on. The governor and the state legislature are not the leaders and are beholden to the independence group, the HNC. The sooner we secure a deal, the sooner they can have elections and get things up and running again. Hawaii needs the tourist trade in order to continue with their plans and succeed.

"They want to negotiate a treaty with a date certainly established. They asked that the team who helped transition Puerto Rico, um … Borinquen would be assembled to work on this transition. They're working on their constitution to cover all of the areas the US Government previously had control over. They have questions, ranging from Hawaiians incarcerated in federal prisons on the mainland, to post offices, communications, medical, and so on. The situation is infinitely complex.

"My legal advice is for us to move forward with acceptance and retain a positive relationship with the islands. If you'll allow me, I also advise that you communicate with the American people how very unique the Hawaii situation is. I don't believe you want this to get out of hand and lose any other states."

President Cassell thoughtfully considered the information. "Thank you, Richard. You've done well. I'm curious; how is it that you changed your mind and came to believe they could go independent?"

"On the way over, and again on the way back, Senator Halprin and I had conversations. He challenged my legal premises, and after hours of talking, I had to admit he was right, and I was wrong."

Alan smiled. "He's not even a lawyer!"

"But he is persuasive, sir."

"Well, it seems I owe him one, again. I want you to lead the transition team. You have my full support. Get us a treaty as quickly as possible, and let me know of any developments that differ in spirit from what we just discussed." Alan stood and offered his hand.

Richard replied, "Thank you, sir. Have a good evening."

As negotiations moved forward on Hawaii, and the fact of the negotiations became public, so did the initiative efforts in California and Oklahoma. The Delaware legislature began to revise their statutes to create a legal framework for the state to stand alone if the union unraveled. Their laws became the model for other states as an "emergency preparedness" concept.

Tom Houston requested the opportunity to speak with the president on a political matter, and Alan placed a call to him late one evening. "Tom, how are things going with your efforts in California?"

"Sir, we have the signatures we need, and the matter is in court for ballot determination."

"So what's your prediction, right now?"

"It'll be on the ballot, but the polls are showing a weakness we didn't have before. It still looks good, but not the 'slam dunk' we were anticipating. It seems the Democrats have figured out our plan makes part of California into a GOP battleground. They are opposing our initiative."

"Do you have a campaign plan drawn up?"

"Yes, Mr. President, but we have another option. In the complex 'direct democracy' that California has become in recent years, we can amend the issue before the voters. That's why I'm calling. You see, a couple of years ago, the courts ruled that anyone challenging an initiative may request an additional option be added to the ballot. If the 'third' option is accepted by the original petitioner, then the ballot must include the 'third' option. This has happened where a state question has had as many as six options. Whichever one gets the most votes wins. A plurality, rather than a majority, is all we need."

"So you're telling me that you want to support a third option to either being one state or two? What, divide into three states?"

"No, sir. A member of La Raza has opposed our initiative, insisting his option be included on the ballots."

Alan angrily responded, "If they want California to go back to Mexico, then the answer is an unequivocal 'NO!'"

"Many members of La Raza favor that idea, but this guy wants to have California as an independent nation!"

"Tom, you've got to be kidding me! This is out of hand. Can we just stop the whole thing right now?"

Tom collected his thoughts and proceeded carefully, "Mr. President, it's in the hands of the court; we can't cancel the vote, but this could actually work to our benefit. Only two percent of Californians support independence, and a few more support La Raza. The pro-independence vote will undoubtedly come from among people who would otherwise vote for California to remain a single state. If I approve the separation option being on the ballot, then we can be fairly confident of a win. Even if their numbers grow, they'll all come from the unified state side. And, even if I don't approve, the court may grant their request giving them the additional option."

The president responded emphatically, "I need you to disapprove. If the court puts it on the ballot anyway, then we live with what we get, and hopefully you're right about the outcome. If you approve it, then the Democrats will figure out your strategy and find another way to beat you. Besides, I find the idea of permitting the third option disingenuous when you don't support it."

Tom shot back a crisp, "Yes, sir, that's what I'll do."

Tom complied with President Cassell's instructions, but the plan didn't work. The court granted the request, and the third option was placed on the ballot.

The next day was among the most momentous in the Cassell presidency. A delegation from Hawaii was presented with a draft treaty drawn up by the attorney general. The president made a statement where he commended the ongoing friendship expected between the United States and the restored Kingdom of Hawaii.

The Hawaiian Prime Minister spoke in glowing terms of "Her Royal Highness the Queen" and her government's approval of the terms of the treaty. He expected a signing ceremony would be scheduled shortly after the treaty could be translated into Hawaiian. Several nations around the world, China and the European Union included, recognized the Kingdom of Hawaii as an independent nation, and the process began for their admission to the United Nations.

Even though the treaty signing was still two months off, the United States Government began the transition immediately. The Hawaiian Government created stipulations on citizenship, which prevented tourists from being considered residents eligible for citizenship. By allowing vacation residences of more than 2000 square feet, wealthy Americans staying in luxurious accommodations qualified for dual citizenship, while excluding the ordinary middle-class vacationer.

George Keoki, dissatisfied with the changes in citizenship laws in his native Hawaii, moved to the San Francisco Bay area in order to secure his American citizenship and business connections.

Nearly unnoticed by anyone outside the immediate family, Archer Adams' wife passed away. Her funeral was not publicized, since Archer was no longer considered famous and his wife lacked his former notoriety. The larger events of the time dominated public attention.

The Oklahoma Secession Contingency Initiative passed easily. Polls began to show the idea of secession in California was growing in popularity.

Alan called a meeting of his G-Group, scheduled to occur after Lenore's return to Washington, D.C. Archer was excluded out of respect for his loss. Alan called to express his condolences on the day of Lenore's return. The conversation was warm, but it didn't completely heal the relational wounds.

Alan wanted the group to discuss the possibility that California would vote for secession, and his options on the subject. Keoki spent the previous night in the Lincoln bedroom and was invited to join the first couple for dinner.

Alan was delayed for dinner. The press of other events kept him in the Oval Office until late into the evening.

Kate and Keoki spent the evening together, eating alone and chatting. Through the course of the dinner, Kate became emotional. Perhaps she was influenced by the alcohol she consumed. She complained Alan was always proud of her and pleased to hold her hand, hug, or even kiss in public, but had been ignoring her at the residence.

Keoki gave her his undivided attention.

Her complaints transitioned to a few tears. Keoki moved to the seat beside her to wipe the tears with his napkin. His gentle touch was welcome, but the action worried her. When dinner was over, she stood and showed him into an adjoining sitting room where they could sit and talk more. She sat on the sofa at the end near a comfortable chair. Her hand motioned for him to sit on the chair. Her eyes, however, suggested he sit on the sofa.

Sitting beside her, he asked her a question about Alan. She didn't even know what he asked. The range of emotions she was experiencing overwhelmed her; tears streamed uncontrollably. Kate knew she was least attractive when she cried, but she cried anyway. Keoki put his arm around her shoulder and held her as she sobbed. She buried her head in his chest and his other arm encircled her.

She wanted to stay in his arms and allowed the tears to flow beyond the point of her need. She didn't consciously think of it at the time, but his embrace was very much like her father's when he had held her close as a child when she mourned the loss of her dog.

Kate, calmed after minutes of crying, relished his embrace. She turned her head to the side and pressed it against Keoki's chest. Looking up, she saw his dark eyes gaze into her deep blue eyes, which were encircled by red from her tears. Her makeup stained his shirt and was smeared on her face.

He didn't see a less-than-attractive aging beauty queen struggling to retain her youthful looks. He didn't see an emotionally weak woman. He didn't see the First Lady of the United States.

All he saw was the face of a woman he had secretly loved from the moment he met her; he saw her then as he had always seen her. To him, she was completely unchanged by the years. She was the same girl he had seen from the pool as she stood on the lanai of his suburban Honolulu guest house. She was the gracious, albeit reluctant, hostess of a fundraiser for deaf Hawaiian children. She was his email pen-pal. She was that indescribable beauty standing beside him at the waterfall outside his bedroom, as America's rich and famous milled about at a political fundraiser for her husband.

He wanted that moment to continue forever; it didn't.

She moved her head up and away from his embrace, then again toward his face. She let her lips reach his. His arms had fallen to his side; he could not hold her. He should not kiss her, but he did.

He was a man who had completely devoted himself to pleasure and all the finer things in life that money could buy. He had kissed so many girls that he couldn't begin to count. This kiss should not have been any different, but it was. Her lips were as sweet as anything he had ever known, and sweeter still. Keoki was immediately convinced Kate was somehow his destiny. He had never kissed a married woman before. He had never felt he had truly loved a woman before, at least as far as he knew. He wanted to make her his own. He wanted to carry her away, spending his every waking moment showering her with loving kindness.

He could take her away; he had the wealth. She could run away with him. There was sure to be someplace they could go. He didn't say a word. They just kissed. They were like teenagers, learning to make out; it was wonderful exploration. He knew at that moment he was ready to commit everything to his love for Kate.

Kate was amazed by the sensuality of his touch, his lips, his muscles, as she explored them with her hands.

His hands slowly touched her. She tingled with every movement. He gently grasped her arms as his lips moved to kiss her eyelids, her nose, her cheeks, and her lips again. She lifted her arms to hold his head intensely against her own, giving passage to his hands to touch her breasts.

He tenderly touched them, on the sides, one with each hand, and she shivered with excitement. The trembling caused him to take a more cautious tack, misinterpreting her quaking. He moved both hands down her side below her rib cage. His left hand touched a spot still sensitive on her right side; he didn't notice the scar through her clothing. The spot was small, which no one would notice by touch, but she felt him there.

Kate pulled back, putting her hands on his brawny chest and pushing away. She wanted him in every way she knew, but his touch on the scar from the accident that took sweet Katie from her told her to back off.

Kate jumped up from the couch; she desperately wanted to jump right back down onto it. Instead, she simply put her hand on the side of his face and looked at him. "I can't," was all she said.

Keoki was left in the sitting room as the love of his life walked to another room. He was confused. His love for her told him to respect her statement. Her eyes, however, had told him something else. He followed.

She had closed the door behind her. He boldly opened it, not knowing the room was her bed chamber. She exited her bathroom, having just rinsed her face, as he entered.

She was startled that he would follow her. She backed away from him, only to be stopped by her large elevated bed.

Keoki moved up to her. He reached out to her face and cradled it in his large hand. Upon his touch, she melted into his arms. Again they kissed, but being of equal height and standing this time, their bodies were pressed together. She was aroused as their bodies were pressed, although fully clothed, against each other. He began to move her dress off and she began to pull at his shirt. She felt guilt at being unfaithful to Alan, but she felt like she was getting back at him for his inattentiveness.

He lifted her to a sitting position on her bed. Her legs found their way around him, pulling him close. Again, his hand, inadvertently, touched her right side at the point of her imperceptible scar. Again, she was brought to her senses. She pushed him away and pulled her dress back into position. "I just can't, I want to, but I just can't," she apologized.

Keoki complied. He began to pull his shirt back together and noticed a button had been pulled off. He mentioned the loss and she frantically looked until she found the button on the floor. They both adjusted their disheveled hair, and she went into the bathroom to "fix her face." Moments later, they determined to find a needle and thread to repair the shirt.

Earlier in the afternoon, Jim Cherry had been told that the president would be dining with George Keoki. He went to the residence to visit with them after completing his work for the day. The guards permitted him into the private quarters. Jim walked into the sitting room just as Keoki and Kate exited her bedroom. Jim's stunned face called for an explanation. Keoki quickly explained how his shirt lost a button during dinner, and Kate was trying to find a needle and thread to "fix it."

Kate confirmed the deception. Jim didn't buy it. The explanation was reasonable enough, but the presentation lacked credibility; the stains from Kate's cosmetics were obvious on Keoki's shirt. Jim made his excuses and left without saying anything more.

CHAPTER 17 • **BETRAYAL**

"The proud American will go down into his slavery without a fight, beating his chest, and proclaiming to the world, how free he really is. The world will only snicker."

—Stanislav Mishin

I T HAD BEEN TWO AND A HALF years since Alan Cassell took office as president. The time had been a blur of activity, but his administration had accomplished much to make him proud. The federal government had been successfully reorganized, and the budget was in balance. Alan Cassell was the first Republican president to submit a balanced budget in many decades. He was also proud of how his administration, and the people of the United States, had responded to the Hawaiian situation.

Alan convened the seventh meeting of his G-Group since the inaugural. They had met in various locations, including GOP National Headquarters, John Halprin's Capital Hill townhome, and the Executive Residence of the White House. The seventh meeting was in the Oval Office itself.

As the group gathered, each member expressed his or her sympathy again for Lenore's loss and asked about Archer. Alan apologized to Keoki for missing dinner. Keoki didn't respond beyond a simple nod.

Phil asked about the absence of the first lady. Alan didn't have an explanation, since he expected her to join them. Jim volunteered that she wasn't feeling well. Alan glared at Jim with surprise, wondering how he knew Kate wasn't feeling well when he had no clue about any illness. Keoki was silent.

Alan began the meeting by expressing his appreciation for each of them. "Your support and advice over the years, from the campaign through the first half of my first term as president have been invaluable to me. We have a lot to be proud of. We also have some serious challenges ahead that must be overcome if I'm to win re-election.

"The polls show Americans support our Hawaii policy. Relations with the Kingdom are good, and controversies are minimal. However, some in California are trying to use that experience as a precedent to separate from the union. I don't need to explain how the federal government couldn't survive without California. We need to find a way to retain California. If my administration succeeds in developing a solution to this concern, then I'm well on my way to re-election."

Phil jumped in. "Since it needs only a plurality, rather than an actual majority, California independence is almost certain to pass. The campaign for independence is well-funded and supported by many of the state legislators. They see Californian independence as an opportunity to bring taxes back to Sacramento, as opposed to Washington, DC, for programs they want to institute."

Alan started again, "Whatever is done, I have to be able to garner the support of Congress. Sadly, those Members of Congress who aren't working for the Chinese or the EU are beholden to the Arab Alliance. I've been going along with foreign interests when it's also in America's interest, or when the matter is a minor inconvenience …"

John could hold his peace no longer. His voice increased in volume as he spoke. "Alan, you have to be strong. You can't allow them to think you'll tolerate California leaving the union. Make a public statement; call out the National Guard. Let them know in no uncertain terms Hawaii's situation was unique. There will be no treaty on California! The union *will* hold! You must do this, you must!"

Alan, sitting on an upholstered chair in his office, listened intently as the former senator instructed him on what he "must" do. Even though Halprin was one who had recruited him to run for president, he was still just a former senator. The room went quiet; all eyes went to the president. President Cassell had kept his relationship with the group casual; they were able to call him by his first name. The members of the group could openly express their opinions, but John had stepped over the line.

After seemingly endless moments, Alan responded loudly and aggressively, "John, you supported me on Hawaii, but you would oppose the same kind of action in California. Don't imagine that I don't know why. I do get intelligence that you and your network within *my* administration don't control. Did you think it was beyond me to find out who the real owners are of the corporations that pay you?"

John interrupted, "Those board of directors' seats are totally legitimate!"

Alan continued unabated. "China and Germany own those companies and they pull your strings. But despite everything, everything you've done for me, don't ever think that you can pull *my* strings! I know they wanted Hawaii to be independent, and they don't want California to separate from the union. Well, you can tell your handlers I want the same thing! But I'm not going to call out the National Guard. I refuse to threaten violence against American citizens to make foreign governments happy! If your 'friends' in Europe and China want the United States to stay united, then they better come up with something I'll accept.

"This is what I was talking about," Alan stated with a calmer tone of voice. "Previous administrations thought we were pulling a fast one when we sold debt to foreign nations. Those governments knew they were buying our balls, and they've put 'em in a vice. They believe they can tighten down on them anytime they want!

"Let me tell you now, I will not, *will not*, take action based on their whims! We retain California, we lose California; I stay President, I lose re-election; the nation prospers, the nation falls apart; but whatever happens, we will do what is right for America!"

"Mr. President," Helen spoke up, "surely you aren't thinking of allowing California to secede?"

Alan was worked up and misinterpreted her question, remembering Helen's tears over Hawaii. "God, woman, are you going to fall apart again? You're the Vice President of the United States! Can you pull it together already?"

Despite being vice president, she had not met with the president in the intervening time. Contrary to Alan's presumption, she was not emotional this time. His outburst against the vice president was uncalled for, and he knew it instantly.

Jim wondered if Alan knew what was going on with the first lady and Keoki; if their possible relationship had caused his outbursts. The meeting was not going well and would not get better. Jim racked his mind, trying to think of something that would relieve the tension and turn things back around.

Keoki also wondered if Alan knew. Alan had never acted so emotional in any prior meeting. He blew off steam on occasion, but not like this. Keoki did not dare say a word. All he wanted was for the meeting to end, so he could go back to San Francisco.

Helen was angry.

Mary Ann Force was mystified by it all.

Lenore perceived that Archer's absence was the setback, or at least part of the problem. Therefore, she engaged herself in a manner which was significantly outside her norm. "Mr. President," she began, "I think we all trust you. The American people trust you. I believe you're trusted because you've proven yourself trustworthy. You tell us you won't threaten violence; then I say you're right. I'm convinced you will do what's right. If other nations agree California needs to stay part of the US, then maybe they can do something to persuade California. Maybe trade policy can be used to encourage them to vote 'No.'"

Lenore succeeded in her efforts to calm things down and created an opportunity for John to redeem himself. "Mr. President?" John spoke softly, requesting the opportunity to speak. Alan was pleasantly surprised by John's respectful approach and nodded affirmatively, thus allowing John to speak. "I feel like I must clarify; my connections to 'international' interests through business are more of an opportunity to advocate *for* America than for them to influence US policy. I hope you'll agree I've helped you get around the bureaucratic obstacles of official diplomacy; I believe this is an opportunity to use those contacts to your benefit. I can, if you like, work to create the very international pressures Lenore spoke of to 'persuade' California voters."

"That may be the very best thing we can do," Alan accepted and stood, signaling the meeting was over. Helen withdrew immediately. Lenore and Jim engaged in a bit of small talk as they exited; John engaged Phil in a similar manner.

Later that evening, upon his return to the Executive Residence, Alan found Kate on a sofa with a blanket over her as she watched television. "Kate, are you feeling all right?"

"I've been out of it. I ... don't worry about it." Kate was hoping he would worry about it. When they were first married, he would badger her with incessant inquiries if she was ill. She had hated his inquisition then, but missed it since he stopped. She missed a lot of things about Alan from when they were younger.

All day she had been thinking about how they had been when they were newlyweds. It was an opportunity for her to indulge in self-pity, and to excuse her marital infraction with Keoki. Deep down she really wanted him to ask, to hold her close, and let her spill out all the frustrations of life. She also wanted to confess her indiscretion.

Alan sat beside her on the edge of the couch and looked intently into her eyes. For just a moment, she thought he might delve into her soul and discover the truth. She wanted for him to know the truth, but the idea frightened her.

"Kate, did you speak with Jim Cherry today?" Alan asked.

"No. Why?"

"How did he know that you weren't feeling well?"

Kate didn't understand Alan's question. "Maybe he spoke with Ryan. I cancelled my schedule this morning."

"That makes sense. I wish I'd been told. I felt like I was the only person who didn't know my own wife was sick!"

"I'm sorry, Alan. I should have told you; I'm sure Ryan told Lenore, and Jim ... I guess, but I should have told you." Kate began to weep as she said, "I'm sorry Alan. I'm so sorry ..."

Alan didn't know how to read his wife's confession. To him, her emotional reaction seemed excessive. "Don't worry about it, Hun. Just get feeling better, all right?" Then Alan stood and excused himself for bed.

Alan's re-election campaign continued to ramp up. Money was being raised rather easily, which was always the case for incumbents. The nomination appeared to be somewhat automatic. A couple of eccentrics were declared for the Republican nomination, but they were not serious candidates with any elective experience.

However, the Democrats were not going quietly into the night. They had
no intention to let President Cassell retain the White House, and they had a
number of candidates who sought to unseat him. The opposition of the greatest
concern was the governor of Maryland. He was charismatic and articulate,
upbeat and attractive. Governor Gene Whitaker had nearly all the virtues for
which Alan Cassell had been previously known. He was hard working and
honest, but terribly liberal. Whitaker wanted to double spending on national
healthcare and to increase taxes on environmental "hazards," like automobiles
and homes of more than 500 square feet per resident. He also wanted to enact
a national gun ban.

Early polling showed Whitaker was popular on the East Coast and in the
industrial Midwest, but lagged among Democrats west of the Mississippi.
His intention was to take on President Cassell, thus presenting himself as the
Democratic nominee long before the question was settled. His advisors felt
that strategy was vital to pick up votes in California, where his polling numbers
revealed very low levels of support.

Whitaker may have been honest, but his henchmen were vicious. One
Whitaker activist, a cartoonist, put out his own version of the G-Group
poster; the cartoon depicted each of the members in the worst possible light.
President Cassell was depicted as a child with his thumb in his mouth; strings
attached to his limbs went up to sticks held by John Halprin on a step ladder
above him. Jim propped up the marionette president. Phil was depicted as a
grotesquely obese version of Shakespeare's Shylock. Vice President Benton was
portrayed as a miserable drunk, holding a bottle of her family's wine. Archer
was shown as Elmer Gantry, suggestively laying hands on his sister-in-law
Lenore Billingsly, who was illustrated as a sexually repressed secretary. Mary
Ann Force was shown as a ditzy blonde with an elephant hat. Most damaging,
however, was the depiction of Kate Cassell, her back turned away from Alan
and in a romantic embrace with George Keoki.

Those in political opposition found the political cartoon hilarious;
Republicans found it reprehensible. They also worried the picture exposed
some level of truth.

Among the worried Republicans was the president. He worried about Jim
propping him up. He worried the American people saw him as a puppet, or

John Halprin as his puppeteer. He worried Phil was as much of a political profiteer as suggested, or that Helen was emotionally unstable. He didn't think there was any truth to the depiction of Archer or Lenore. Alan didn't really care how they depicted Mary Ann Force, especially since the presentation was somewhat accurate.

More worrisome, aggravating, even angering to Alan, was the inexcusable depiction of his wife and Keoki.

Jim, Keoki, and Kate had different thoughts upon seeing the cartoon. The first lady called Jim immediately. They met in her office. "You wanted to see me, Mrs. Cassell."

"Jim, have you seen this cartoon?"

"Yes."

"I think you can figure out why I find it distressing."

"Yes ma'am."

"Are you responsible for the information that 'inspired' it?"

"No! I would never!"

"I don't know what you think you saw that night," she said, "but nothing happened."

"Kate, it doesn't matter what I saw, or thought I saw. I did not, and I would not, tell anyone anything."

"You were quick to tell the president that I was ill the next morning. Where did you come up with that?"

"I admit I was ad libbing. I'm sorry, but I didn't breathe a word, real or imagined, about the two of you, er, you and Keoki."

"Well, it wasn't me; it wasn't Keoki. Someone must have said something … it must have been you!"

"Mrs. Cassell, nobody needs to have said anything. It could have been a pretty easy guess."

"What?" she asked with surprise.

"A billionaire playboy and a beautiful woman; it's not a stretch to imagine a connection. It's the kind of thing that sells cartoons," Jim answered, and then he realized a potential problem. "You haven't called Keoki, have you?"

"No," she answered firmly.

"You can't talk to him, about anything. No emails, nothing."

"I know."

"Does he know he can't call you either?"

"How would I know? I haven't spoken to him since that evening, in the residence."

"I'd best contact him right away."

Jim's helpful attitude made Kate curious. "Why are you helping me?" she asked.

"It's what I do, I guess."

Jim left her office, returning to his own. In transit, he contemplated his personal intentions in helping the first lady. At first, he reasoned he was doing it to help Alan. Upon further reflection, he realized he was actually helping himself. He felt as if it was high time he do what was in his own interest.

Jim's political career started out as a volunteer party leader, and the position had cost his business dearly. He had always seen the sacrifice as a worthwhile, leading to further political opportunities. Then he sold his insurance agency and moved to Topeka to work for the man he originally recruited fresh out of college to run for commissioner. Now, he was in the nation's capital and he liked his job. He had significant authority regarding domestic policy, and Alan never questioned his decisions. He had built a reputation in the District and didn't want anything to weaken his status.

Jim called Keoki on his personal cell phone, beginning his side career as go-between for the first lady and a man he assumed was her lover.

About that time, John Halprin met with his international business contacts with every intention to do exactly as he had promised. Unfortunately, the meetings didn't turn out as he expected.

Every single contact found his proposal absurd. John knew they were right, but also knew Alan could not be persuaded to use force to prevent California from seceding. John found persuading the business associates was impossible. In each meeting, they asked him if he would take the same policy as President Cassell; he had to admit that he would not.

Those different business and government officials, the lines of distinction having been thoroughly blurred decades before, seemed to be acting in concert regarding the former senator. They expected him to throw his own hat into the ring. They believed that if Alan Cassell would not do what they wanted, then they would support their original choice. That candidate, they told him, must preserve the union; it must be him. John was harshly reminded of his promises to the associates from before Alan announced his run for the White House.

Despite his pledge, John balked at the premise of turning on his own friend and running against Alan for the Republican nomination for president. However, after he considered the consequences of another Cassell term, which was currently plagued by dissatisfied states pulling out of the union or threatening to do so, he realized that he must take action.

John was confirmed in his sentiment when he considered the specter of a Whitaker presidency. He remembered a speech made by Whitaker, where he suggested the southern and western states obstructed a progressive agenda, and that the eastern states would be better off without them.

John realized either man would preside over a shrinking America. He could not stand by while the nation his own father had died for fell apart. John realized challenging Cassell was the only way to keep the country together. Therefore, John Halprin persuaded himself he was making the right decision, as opposed to betraying his young protégé and showing deference to his employers.

John Halprin put together a team within a few days. Many people in the current administration had more loyalty to Halprin than Cassell anyway. Each person was appalled by Cassell's willingness to allow the California vote to move ahead. All was kept secret for the time being; it was one of the few times in American history a secret was kept in the District of Columbia.

The California vote, which was a special election with only one question and three options on the ballot, went for independence as expected. Action was blocked by scores of lawsuits in state and federal courts. The divided state option came in third. Tom Houston, the man who had conceived the public initiative, committed suicide the night of the vote.

Within days of the California vote, Alan was hit with two emotional body blows. The first came when Helen Benton presented Alan with a letter, announcing her retirement to Oregon; she would not be available to run for a second term as vice president. Alan felt betrayed by the move, but it was the first of many such feelings.

His campaign responded to the public with excitement over the announcement, expressing how the vice president had served with distinction, and that there would be an opportunity for the second term to be invigorated by a new vice president. Behind the scenes, they leaked that Cassell had told Benton he was going to choose another and gave her the opportunity to withdraw. The story was a lie, but it was also the only way they could redeem the situation; it didn't work.

Then, Lenore, Alan's long term personal secretary and trusted confidant, resigned to spend her elder years with her husband in Kansas.

Although Alan was feeling alone and abandoned, he was never actually alone. With every departure there were always plenty of qualified people ready to jump in, bringing new enthusiasm and experience with them. Nothing seemed to have changed in the West Wing, but something was different in the residence. Alan couldn't put his finger on the problem, but he was sure the issue was with Kate. He convinced himself that he was unchanged.

The Iowa caucus came and went. President Cassell won the Republican vote without any real opposition. New Hampshire and South Carolina were also effectively uncontested victories.

One evening, when Kate was back in Wichita visiting family, Alan watched an old John Wayne movie in the residence. As the incumbent president, he was not expected to campaign for the nomination. Everything was designed for the general election, which seemed to be against Whitaker.

A phone call came in from John Halprin. Alan paused the movie on a scene that made the old cowboy look awkward in his saddle. The image of John Wayne, seemingly extricating a wedgie, was burned into his memory for life.

President Cassell picked up the receiver with an upbeat tone. "John, haven't heard much from you for a while. How the hell are you?"

In the most somber of tones, John responded, "I need to tell you something."

"What's wrong?"

"You need to be the very first to know." Hesitantly, with an audible tremor in his voice, he continued, "I can't support you for re-election. I can't stand idly by while California leaves the country. I'm making a statement advocating the use of force to prevent independence."

Alan was more than a little incredulous. Panicked, he announced, "Whitaker wants everything west of the Mississippi to secede, so he's not an option for you! How could you?" Changing gears, he continued, "You're not going public about not voting for me, are you?"

"Yes, Alan, I am. Tomorrow."

With even more volume, Alan asked, "Who the hell are you going to support?"

John slowly released the words, "I'm running."

"John! You're shitting me! This has to be some kind of insane joke. You, running as an independent, against me! We have one difference of opinion, and you're going against me?"

"No sir." John replied with hesitation.

Alan shook uncontrollably. Emotionally overcome, he was uncertain exactly which emotion tormented him at the moment. Perhaps it was fear, or rage, or general panic; perhaps all three at once. John's reply suggested his announcement was a cruel joke, but it unnerved him to the core. "God! You just about gave me a coronary! John, that was not funny!"

John didn't know how to make his point clear. He had expected to inform Alan and quickly end the conversation. The call had already lasted longer than John expected. "Mr. President, I'm not running as an independent. I intend to win the Republican nomination."

Alan held the phone for a moment, silent.

After an interminable quiet, Alan said, "Thank you for calling." It was the last time the two would ever speak.

Alan sat down on his sofa, alone, in a dimly lit room with the uncomfortable image of John Wayne on his television screen; he was in a near catatonic state. His mind raced, but his body was as still as the picture on the screen. Then, the pieces began to come together.

John had set him up to be president so he could rake in hundreds of millions from foreign industrial interests. When John could no longer make Alan do as they wanted, then he had to run. Alan wished he had never run in the first place.

What appeared, hours earlier, to be an administration filled with success, was suddenly revealed as a farce. The cartoon showing himself as a puppet in Halprin's hands was true. Alan had cut the strings from his Geppetto and was punished for doing so. He desperately wished the call had happened months earlier, so he could have gracefully exited and given his blessing to Halprin as successor. With two primaries and Iowa's caucus won, it was too late to bow out with dignity.

That cartoon suddenly seemed prophetic. Alan quizzed himself on how he could have been so gullible. He was bewildered. *We've done so much good. I've done everything I was called on to do; then to be betrayed like this, by someone pretending to befriend me.*

No relationship was unquestioned at that moment; John was the puppet master after all. Mary Ann Force was a dim-wit, no surprise there. Helen was overly emotional. He asked himself, his breath held and heart pounding hard, *What about Kate? Was Kate actually having an affair with Keoki?* The truth didn't matter; Alan was convinced. Not only that Kate was having an affair, but that she had never really loved him. He was convinced that she had used him to get the limelight, and lifestyle, she wanted.

The absurdity of the suggestion didn't hit him at the moment. Kate Fogarty was the daughter of a wealthy industrialist and a beauty queen. If she had sought a political marriage with intent on power and money, she would not have picked an obscure local official. Even so, he was certain she had moved on to someone he couldn't ever become, a multi-billionaire.

Passing thoughts about Lenore, Phil, and Archer brought him to Jim. In the cartoon, Jim was portrayed as the man who propped him up, which was exactly what Alan needed now.

After sitting absolutely still for what must have been a half an hour, Alan picked up the phone to hear, "May I help you, Mr. President?"

"I need Jim, Jim Cherry. Now!" Alan said no more; nothing more was required or expected. The president had made his expectation clear, and it would be fulfilled.

If your boss called you in the middle of the night and you didn't disregard it, you would most likely respond, complain, and then comply if absolutely necessary. If your boss was the President of the United States, you were awakened in a manner that couldn't be ignored. Jim jumped up from bed and threw a suit on faster than a fireman heading out to extinguish a three- alarm blaze. He raced to the White House like an ambulance rushing to the hospital.

Escorted into the residence, he called out, "Mr. President?"

"In here, Jim." Jim followed the voice into the president's private study, where the television was still paused on the unusual frame of a western movie.

Alan didn't take time for pleasantries or explanations. "I think Kate is having an affair with Keoki."

Jim's heart sank and his face grimaced. His body language affirmed the assertion as he asked, "How did you find out?"

Alan's eyes became visibly enlarged at the retort. He didn't expect his suspicion to be so quickly confirmed. He didn't answer the question; he sat motionless for a moment and picked up the phone, "I need José." José Carrion was in charge of Secret Service White House protection.

Putting the phone down, he turned back and opened up to Jim for a moment, saying, "It was just a feeling. She hasn't been the same, for a while. It's been a bad night. John Halprin is run ..." Alan stopped talking as a realization hit him like a brick. "You knew! You knew and didn't tell me! I thought you were the one person, the one person in the world ...!"

Alan paused again, and then declared, "You're fired; get out!"

There was nothing Jim could say. He was disappointed with himself and didn't even try to talk Alan down. He couldn't even bring himself to apologize. Jim picked up his overcoat and left the White House never to return.

José Carrion showed up in the residence shortly after Jim left. "How may I be of service, Mr. President?"

Alan looked up, then back down, and began, "The first lady is in Wichita?"

"Yes, sir."

"Yeah, well, she will not be returning to the White House."

José didn't understand. "Sir?"

Alan raised his voice, "What about that statement was difficult to understand? She will not be returning, *ever*! You are to make sure that she does not. Understood?"

Alan, by that point, was wallowing in self-pity. He was convinced that his entire life was a lie. Alan Cassell believed he was an unwitting actor in a tragic story over which he had no control. Everyone had used him, everyone pretended to love him, and everyone ultimately betrayed him—or so he thought.

He never considered that he had also used them; how he pretended to like every American, even to love them.

From that night forward, President Cassell's administration went into autopilot, as did his re-election campaign. He continued to work in the Oval Office and kept his public schedule, including campaign appearances. Yet he had lost all passion, all interest in anything professional or personal.

Kate's extended time in Wichita raised questions which had to be answered eventually. Via a team of lawyers, a statement was released expressing that the Cassells were to be divorced without stating grounds. This wasn't the first White House divorce, but it was the only one initiated by the president. Neither party ever made a public statement about the separation.

The nation excused President Cassell for seeking a divorce because the rumors, initiated by the infamous cartoon, were widely believed. Kate bore the brunt of many brutal jokes. Alan cringed at every such occurrence. Despite the discomfort at her difficulties, he didn't speak a word to her, or even see her again, until well after the divorce was final.

The prospect of a single, attractive and relatively young president attracted throngs of women to every appearance. Before long, single men joined the throngs to garner access to the women who were certain to be in the audience. This effect gave Cassell's campaign appearances a rock concert sensation and an air of enthusiasm, which was less than genuine. Alan and his staff worked hard to keep the women from any direct contact; however, there was one instance of his capitulation to a young woman's advances.

John Halprin was late to enter the field against Cassell, but he entered with a flurry.

Phil Stanek had jumped onto the Halprin campaign. In the beginning, Halprin struggled to wrest the nomination away from Cassell. Even though Alan showed minimal enthusiasm, his incumbency gave him a significant edge in the effort. Halprin's neo-conservative approach, however, won the day with the Republican Party, giving Halprin just over fifty percent of the "delegate" votes. Mary Ann Force was given the assignment of asking President Cassell to endorse the presumed nominee.

He showed her the door without comment.

Alan Cassell was a lame duck as soon as Halprin secured the nomination. From his White House vantage point, he watched a campaign he had exceedingly little interest in, and yet had exceedingly great knowledge regarding it.

Halprin was adamant; the forty-nine states were to remain as one nation at all costs. Whitaker, on the other hand, would allow California and other states to separate from the union.

The prospect of war, Americans killing Americans, was not palatable to most voters. Whitaker's liberalism was not acceptable to Americans in much of the South, or in western states, excepting the West Coast. On the West Coast, his policy regarding automobiles was soundly rejected. Voters in those states understood if they voted for independence and for Whitaker, they would not have war or Whitaker's destructive policies because he was clear that he would permit a peaceful secession. A full month before the election, the polls showed Whitaker was going to win every state except Illinois. Halprin even lost his own state of Texas, though narrowly.

So many states issued independence declarations that Congress acknowledged the United States would cease to exist. Whitaker proposed that senators not up for re-election be retained as the body governing the transition, and for the entirety of the House of Representatives and a third of the Senate to be vacated immediately. As it happened, both senators from California were up for re-election that year, one of whom was running to fill the unexpired term of a senator who had died in office.

Whitaker was not antagonistic toward the states which desired separation. Many of his supporters, including politicians from states east of the Mississippi River, considered independence leaders and Cassell associates as traitors. For Whitaker, the departure of less progressive states was an opportunity to advance his policies in the eastern part of the continent without obstruction.

Pro-union voters from the western states blamed Whitaker for the breakup. Over time, people recognized the country was just too large to govern efficiently. Americans believed they should have the opportunity to engage variations in public policy without the long hand of a continental government pressing an amalgamated agenda.

Upon confirmation of Whitaker's win, he called President Cassell and requested he make a public statement. Whitaker hoped Cassell would bring calm to the situation, thereby avoiding hostilities.

Alan agreed to make the address. He told the American people, "My fellow

Americans, you and I are Americans and will always be American. We share a deep and abiding love for America.

"Our patriotism is not to a government, but to a nation. A nation is not merely a political entity, it is a people; a people, a heritage, and the ideals that made them great. Political realities may change, but Americans will continue to be one people, one nation.

"We may not continue to find our leaders in Washington, D.C. We may look to our various state capitols, or to some other number of political capitols. No matter, America will continue.

"We are more alike than we are different. We have ancestry from throughout the world, but we have adapted ourselves to become one *ethnos*, one nation. We are no less a single people, Americans, even if governed separately.

"This is not the end of America in the sense of cessation, but perhaps it is the end, in the sense of purpose. I claim proudly that America has a purpose. It is to that 'end' that we must continue to strive. It may be that the dissolution of our union is exactly the means by which we learn to advance America's great purpose, its noble 'ends.'

"I urge all Americans to stay calm and accept the imminent political changes. There is no cause for civil unrest or commercial disruption. I was assured by President-elect Whitaker that the free flow of persons and commerce will be unimpeded through these transitions. What we see occurring around us consists of little more than an expansion of the premise that our states are forty-nine 'experiments in democracy.' The American people in each state will make decisions that are right for them. It is vital for us all to engage the virtue of tolerance, respecting the policy distinctions of our neighbor states.

"For people elsewhere in the world, who might want to take belligerent actions against America at this unsettled time, I warn nothing would bring us together faster than a military or terrorist attack. As I prepare to depart from the presidency in January, my every effort will be to protect America from any untoward exertions from outside governments. I will not hesitate to utilize the full might of our armed forces to ensure that the transition is smooth and peaceful.

"On a personal note, I want to thank the people of America for the opportunity to serve them these four years. It has been a tumultuous time with successes and failures, both official and personal. I step away from public life never to seek political position again. I will return to my beloved Kansas and my quiet country home.

"God bless and good night."

With the ending of his speech, the career of the last American president ended.

Alan Cassell communicated in his speech that the end of the United States was a natural extension of the principles he had spent his life advocating. In truth, he felt himself to be the ultimate failure.

The BBC produced a mini-series entitled "The Fall of the American Empire" in which they compared the transition, favorably, to the end of the British Empire. The program suggested that Britain had permitted, and even facilitated, the end of its empire. Changing the structure went a long way toward creating a positive relationship with its Commonwealth partners.

The series was rebroadcast in North America and was taken by Alan Cassell as a mockery of his administration. Few Americans took their presentation as critical.

There was even a movement to honor his administration, unbeknownst to Alan, which formed as result of the dissolution of the union. "Cassellions" were Americans who celebrated the Cassell principles. Cassellion groups were founded all over North America and in Eastern Europe, where efforts to separate from the EU had begun in earnest.

Over the years, people expressed a variety of opinions on dissolution. Few problems were solved by the end of the United States, and some were begun because of it. The American people allowed their country to go from the greatest nation in the world, to a number of small and comparatively insignificant countries.

At the time, historians saw the administration of Alan Cassell and the election of Gene Whitaker as the transitional time. In reality, the seeds of dissolution had been planted even as the Cold War ended in the 1980s.

CHAPTER 18 • **MORNING IN AMERICA**

"I think the true discovery of America is before us. I think the true fulfillment of our spirit, of our people, of our mighty and immortal land is yet to come..."

—Thomas Wolfe

T HE TRANSITION OCCURRED with surprisingly little anxiety. Some wealthy people secured multiple homes in various states, so they could take refuge if events took a turn for the worse. Other less wealthy people moved to states where they already had relatives in case the borders were closed.

There was also a political migration. Activists of every ideological stripe moved to states already inclined toward their philosophy. Liberal Democrats moved to the coasts, while conservative Republicans concentrated toward the center of the former United States. Libertarians moved to Alaska and the mountain states, while religious conservatives moved to the Gulf Coast states; environmentalists moved to New England and Maryland.

Most Americans, not being political activists, stayed where they had already lived, riding out the transition comfortably.

Under the Whitaker transition, each state accepted a portion of the national debt in correlation to the federal assets located within the respective states. When all was said and done, over eighty-five percent of the national debt was covered.

Members of the armed forces who continued in service were permitted to serve where they were stationed, or to return to their home states. Nearly half were discharged outright. Every foreign base was evacuated. Military equipment was sold, either to the host nation or to one of the new "nations" of America. All was done at the discretion of the Transitional Senate Armed Services Committee.

Economically, the bankruptcy of the old union and the significant debt absorption by the states revived trade and industry from coast to coast. Seemingly counter-intuitive at the time, bankruptcy meant about fifteen percent of the old debt was cancelled. Debt absorption by the various states gave them a credit line and where the debt was based on transferred assets, the debt was effectively secured. A new series of alliances developed within a year and from these associations the new nations of the American continent were born.

Hawaii had already restored its Kingdom during Cassell's term. Delaware determined to go it alone and to pursue a business friendly atmosphere, or as detractors came to call it, "Delaware Incorporated." Excepting Mississippi and Alabama, the other states east of the Mississippi River sent delegates to a "Constitutional Convention" creating the "Reorganized United States of America."

The United Nations Security Council offered the American seat to the RUSA in exchange for agreeing to absorb an additional percentage of the old debt. They had also taken on part of the debt when they acquired the District of Columbia.

Under UN negotiated terms, only ten percent of foreign-held debt was defaulted on, whereas domestically held debt was given almost eighty percent of face value. Retirees and other Americans who had put their money in savings bonds were at first pleased to discover they would receive eighty cents on the dollar when the union dissolved. However, when it was discovered that foreign countries were getting a higher percentage, there were many public protests. Those protests only proved the point that other nations could take military action to recover their funds and the retirees could not take such an action. Therefore, the controversy was short lived.

Alabama and Mississippi joined Louisiana in a proposal to name a new country after the Bayou State, or more accurately, after the large territory purchased by President Jefferson from Napoleon Bonaparte. Within months, Arkansas and Missouri had joined them.

The Republic of Texas was revived to include Oklahoma, Kansas, New Mexico and Nebraska.

Iowa and Minnesota applied to be admitted into the RUSA.

The California Republic was short lived. The governors of Arizona, Nevada, Oregon, and Washington appealed to the California legislature, and the country of Pacifica was created.

Not surprisingly, Alaska also decided to stand alone.

The other states—Colorado, Utah, Wyoming, Idaho, Montana and the Dakotas—joined together to establish the Montana Confederacy; the capital was located in Denver.

In the RUSA, state governments were dissolved and state debts and assets were folded into the new government. State names and borders were used for little more than mailing addresses. Its constitution gave absolute power to the central government, except that an Islamic semi-autonomous region was created in the Detroit area. Governor Whitaker, who had won the presidency of the forty-nine state USA, was unanimously chosen to be president by the newly formed unicameral legislature, consisting of five hundred members from districts of equal population. Many of the districts crossed the old state lines.

The Republic of Texas and the Montana Confederacy were very limited governments, retaining the state entities and empowering them to do most of what had been done by the old federal government. Pacifica and Louisiana found middle ground by successfully mixing a strong central government with efficient, responsive state and local governments.

All of the new countries maintained close relations, similar to the two century relationship formed between the old USA and Canada. They participated in mutual defense agreements and allowed citizens to travel freely, except for a small number of "undesirables." Persons associated with the Cassell administration were not permitted into the RUSA for a period of twenty years. On its twentieth anniversary, the RUSA changed its name to remove the word "Reorganized."

Dealing with former President Cassell was a particularly delicate matter. Whitaker arranged to have the state of Kansas pay for the expenses related to the former president in exchange for debt relief. The state of Kansas assigned a single highway patrolman to serve as his security detail.

The return to Kansas was depressing to Alan, as if he needed additional causes to be demoralized. On the day his term ended, Air Force One flew to Kansas City where a presidential limousine took him to the Kansas border. There he stepped across the state line, by then an international border, and into a typical limousine driven by his lone security officer. Together, they drove south to his Crawford County home.

The farmhouse was the only home he had ever owned. The home had several incarnations during his ownership, but the final change was surreal. Pulling up to the property, the land looked as it had during his presidential term. Alan smiled as he saw the large imposing walls and ornate gates. The car pulled up to a vacant guard house. His driver stepped out of the car and fished around his front pocket until he found a key to a simple padlock. Inserting the key, he unlocked the gates and swung them open manually.

Before Alan stood a silent city, abandoned when Kansas declared its independence. Snow was untouched and a drift caused the car to stop short of the farmhouse. Alan grabbed his bag and walked through snow, shuffling in the stark quiet to his old, cold home.

Alan had not been truly alone for one moment in the past four years. Now, he rattled around his old house. He busied himself for the first few minutes, working to get the furnace running. The house eventually warmed up and the blower stopped; Alan was overcome with silence. He was haunted by memories of the sounds of people working around him. He was also haunted by memories of Kate.

Kate's absence had been bearable for Alan while he was still President. The office kept him busy day and night. Now alone, back where they spent their early years together, Alan began to regret his decision to divorce her. Her affair didn't matter to him; it didn't even matter if she never sincerely loved him. He loved her, missed her, and desperately wanted those days back.

He missed the early hardscrabble years the most. Alan reminisced on the times of cooking dinner for his new bride as she drove home from her job in Joplin. He missed watching her ride her horse as he fed the stocker calves. He regretted running for governor, let alone president. The "what ifs" hit him hard; he realized that if he hadn't sought higher office, he and Kate might just still be living in that house with a pre-teen Katie to love. Perhaps they would have had other children as well.

Life brings opportunities and choices. Alan's life had brought opportunities that seemed too good to pass up, and in pursuing them he had passed up the greatest prospects … the kinds that come without deliberate choices.

Alan Cassell had gained the whole world and lost his soul in the quest. He then lost the world as well. The extent to which he found himself a failure knew no end. Worst of all, he had given his beloved Kate an excuse to accept the love of a man who could give her everything. His one consolation was that he believed she had moved on to a better life than he could offer her.

He saw himself as a pitiful shell of a man. He had aged in office, though still in his early forties. He had lost some of his hair, and the amount that remained was going grey. He no longer carried himself as he did when in office, so there was little in his appearance to suggest he was once one of the most powerful men on earth.

Winter progressed as quietly as it had begun, and Alan didn't leave the compound a single time. His security man was bored; he had a job without any real obligations, and therefore spent his time working on the property and shopping for the reclusive former president.

Spring arrived and life returned to the trees and pasture. A dog wandered onto the property one rainy day. Alan let it in the house and cleaned it up. He ended up naming the female Labrador mix "Stormie," recalling the weather the day she showed up. Alan and Stormie became inseparable. She was his reason to wake each morning and his companion at the foot of his bed at night. Together they wandered the property, fixed the unused corral, and patched the barn roof.

One day lead to another and one month to the next. Alan became accustomed to the quiet and the loneliness. He cared little for his personal appearance and allowed his beard to grow out; he was hardly recognizable. It didn't matter, for there was no one to see him.

One grey Sunday several months after his return, Alan was awakened early by Stormie jumping about the bed. One day was no different from the next for Alan but, for some inexplicable reason, he had created the habit of sleeping later on weekends.

It had rained the previous evening. The day was still grey, but strangely warm. Alan took Stormie for a walk and the dog pulled him to the front gates. Alan hadn't been back to the gates since the car rolled in the first day of his "retirement." He gazed out through the gates with wonder in his eyes. He had forgotten how beautiful he found the countryside.

Just outside the gate sat a newspaper from the previous week. The Pittsburg Morning Sun was a daily online by that time, and was in print only on Wednesdays. His security man had taken a few days off, or the paper would have been picked up days earlier. He noticed a name he recognized as he peered at the old paper. Sneaking through the gate, he picked up the paper.

Unwrapping it from the plastic cover, Alan looked at a small reference in the lower column of the front page: "Kansas industrialist dies in Wichita—page 8." The headline was accompanied by a photo and a name, "Michael Fogarty."

His father-in-law had passed away, and he hadn't even heard. Emotions overwhelmed him as he dropped other sections of the paper and turned to page eight. Alan read every detail, all of which he had known, and wept at a quote from Michael's youngest daughter; the death had to be difficult for Kate. Her father's passing was oddly proximate to the anniversary of her daughter's birth and death a few days later.

While Alan was engrossed with the article, he failed to notice that Stormie had run off. Alan searched the property high and low for her, assuming she had run back to the grounds, but to no avail. His security man reported for work and was surprised to see Alan was awake, let alone that he wanted to go looking for his pet. The man didn't know the day was also Katie Cassell's birthday.

For the first time since arriving back in Kansas, Alan left his compound. Alan's memory was nearly perfect. As they drove to find his pet, Alan directed the driver, "Pull into the Morgan place, check behind the old red barn, see if she's at the Grantham place," and so on. Few of the properties were still owned by the people Alan remembered, but little had changed about the roads or the buildings.

Alan asked that they drive in and out the lanes that made up the old town of Beulah to search for Stormie. Few homes still stood in Beulah, but the town layout remained. The most significant edifice in the town remained the Beulah

Community Church. The church parking lot was packed with worshipers from throughout the county.

Alan became sentimental at seeing the church again. The car turned east past the church and, in another minute, they were in front of the cemetery. Alan had resisted the temptation to attend the church, but he could not pass up the opportunity to visit his daughter's grave.

The old country cemetery had been augmented by high fencing and an iron gate when Alan was elected president to prevent vandalism to Katie's grave. Alan's security man unlocked the gate, allowing him in.

Alan walked amongst the gravestones to Katie's plot, which lay just beyond an old walnut tree. As he walked past the tree, he stepped on a fallen walnut. The large seed rolled under his foot, causing him to lose his balance. Alan caught himself by grabbing Katie's tombstone. He was hard-pressed to maintain his composure as he grasped the icy cold stone. In a matter of moments, he found himself on his knees talking to Katie.

"Sorry, darling, your mother and I hadn't thought about tripping on walnuts when we chose this plot. We just thought the shade of the tree would be nice for you." Continuing, he said, "Happy Birthday, my precious daughter. I don't know if you celebrate your birthday, but I wanted you to know that I remembered. I'm sorry that I haven't come to see you. Your mom and I promised to, but I haven't been faithful." Alan began to be overcome emotionally at admitting his own failure to be faithful to a familial promise.

He continued, his voice cracking, "I'm so sorry. I've thought of you every day ... I still treasure the short time we had together. I suppose I should tell you a few things have changed since last I visited. Your mother and I aren't together anymore. It's my fault really; don't blame her. I divorced her, not that you know what that is, but I wish we hadn't separated. She was a wonderful, loving woman, and I miss her dearly. I haven't even talked to her since then. She wanted to, but I didn't let her. I guess I owed it to her to listen, a little anyway.

"Your grandfather passed away, but I suppose you already know. I hope you two will be getting to know each other now. He really was a fine man, more of a father to me than my own.

"I left the house today for the first time, well, in almost a year. You see, my dog, Stormie, ran off this morning. I came out to find her. I wanted to come see you today anyway, but her running off got me out of the house early this morning. I do hope I find her soon. She has her leash attached, and I'm worried she'll get it caught on something.

"Oh, I feel so silly talking to you like this. I don't suppose there's any chance you can actually hear me. Archer would tell me I need to be praying instead of trying to talk to you. I just can't help it. I knew you, for a few days anyway. I don't even have Archer to talk to anymore."

From behind him came a familiar voice, "I'm sure he would take your call." Looking back, he saw Kate holding a cupcake with a single candle in it.

"Kate!" he said with surprise. Considering the news article that had brought him out of his compound, he commented, "I'm so sorry about your father. I didn't know until I saw the article in the paper this morning."

"Thank you, Alan. He liked you."

"I liked him. He was the closest thing I had to a father."

"That's sweet. I should have called to let you know. You deserved better, better than to read of his passing in the news. Besides, I heard you tell that to Katie."

He turned back to Katie's grave, and said with a smile, "Okay, I'm here pouring my heart out to you; the least you could have done is let me know your mother is looking over my shoulder listening to every word, huh?"

Kate giggled and interrupted, "Your security guy recognized me, and he let me in right behind you. He would have come to your aid when you almost fell if he hadn't been letting me through the gate at that very moment."

Listening, Alan was struck by his ex-wife's beauty. Then he realized he was still kneeling on the ground. He stood up and said, "How are you doing? You look really, really great!"

"I'm all right, I suppose. Dad's funeral was Friday. I came here today for Katie. I suppose this time of the year will always hurt. I'm glad you came out here today."

Alan had never expected to see Kate again. When he divorced her, he didn't want to be reminded he was ever married at all, let alone see or speak to her again. But there they were, having a warm conversation like old friends. Alan remembered his father and mother talking in a similar manner during one of his rare appearances, long after they had been divorced. As a child, he hadn't understood their interaction. Now he understood; he was comfortable visiting with a woman he had once despised, but always loved.

"Kate, I'm sorry about how I treated you. I was so hurt when I found out, that I couldn't … I just couldn't … but now I wish I had given you an opportunity to talk."

Kate smiled slightly and motioned toward Katie's marker. "Yeah, I heard you tell that to our daughter, too." Then she continued with a greater level of seriousness. "Alan, I really wanted the opportunity to apologize for, for hurting you. I wanted you to know how sorry I was, how sorry I am."

Alan responded sheepishly, "I've had a lot of regrets. I lost it all, you know. I really screwed up, ruined the whole country, but what I really regret is not trying harder to make our marriage work."

"Alan, honey, it wasn't your fault. I caused our marriage to end, and the country doesn't blame you either. In case you don't know, people around here are proud of you."

Alan gave an odd look at his ex. "Proud? I'm the ultimate failure. I'm like Gorbachev in Russia."

"You stood by your principles, and it worked out just fine. Your farewell speech was inspired. With what you said, you prevented any bloodshed; people are happy. It was all too far gone when you got to the White House, and the way things turned out was fine for everyone. Everyone, but you. You've been holed up in that house all this time, and things are fine out here in the real world."

Kate looked down at her feet for a moment. She looked back at Alan and said, "Not to excuse anything, but you need to know. I didn't … with Keoki. We didn't actually, I mean … it was just as bad, I nearly did, but we never did."

"You're denying, now, after all this time? You admitted to my lawyers …"

"Well, I admitted that I wasn't faithful, but we didn't do it. What we did was just as wrong. You were faithful. You were never with anyone else."

It was Alan's turn; he looked down at his feet and shuffled a bit. "Actually, after the divorce, I did one time. I felt just as guilty as if we hadn't been divorced. She didn't mean anything; she was just there, and I don't even know her name." Alan suddenly realized Kate had suggested that she *still* hadn't been with Keoki.

"Kate, you said you never did ... I thought you went back to Hawaii with him, when he moved back there."

"No, Alan, I haven't seen or heard from him since he was last in the White House. I never stopped loving you. And, I didn't, don't, blame you for yielding to that girl."

"You knew about her, huh?"

"Alan, secrets are not well kept in Washington. I was forever getting phone calls from those who wanted to be considered my friends, telling me every detail."

"So where have you been all this time?"

"I never left Wichita."

"Really! I didn't know you were right here in Kansas. I didn't know! I really didn't. Um, do you suppose, maybe, we could get some lunch?"

Kate asked, "What about your dog?"

"I expect I'll find her again. I don't want to lose the opportunity to visit with you, though."

Alan and Kate Cassell went to the Pittsburg Applebee's restaurant for lunch. The décor was still the same as it had been when they went as a young couple, except for a framed copy of the local paper celebrating Alan's election as president. The people in the restaurant were very hospitable and respected their privacy for a few minutes. Alan thought they had gone unrecognized, until the waitress asked if they were back together. Alan and Kate both just smiled and said nothing.

While they ate, a Crawford County Sherriff's Deputy came into the restaurant and spoke to Alan's security man. Stormie had been found, and the deputy wanted to know what to do with her. He leaned over to Alan, told him the good news, and excused himself to put the dog in the car.

Once the security man stepped away, people from the restaurant came by their table to give their best wishes, express sympathies to Kate regarding her father, and to ask for Alan's autograph.

Alan and Kate Cassell did remarry. The ceremony was presided over by a young man who had become a minister after being inspired to help people when he heard his governor speak at a student church in Lawrence.

Alan and Kate made their home in Wichita. There she could take care of her aging mother, while Alan would have access to an international airport from which he could travel all over the world for various speaking engagements.

***

The old storytelling grandfather, having completed the account of the events of his life, insisted on giving a moral to his story. "Still today, some people imagine the former USA in an idealized way. They pretend the country's greatness was as a powerful nation, winning wars and dominating the world. Most, however, recognize that America's greatness was in the application of the principles advocated by the fifty-six men who signed the Declaration of Independence.

"Those men, in quaint clothes, who lived in a pre-industrial society, believed the birthright of all men was liberty. They believed governments are established for the sole purpose of protecting people's right to life, liberty, and property. They were not patriotic to an entity, just created, which would in years ahead come to grow and encompass an empire. They were patriots to the truths expressed in the documents they wrote.

"When those ideals were symbolic of one country's independence, they were not as transcendent as they have become. Finally, nations around the world seek the liberty those eighteenth century patriots hoped for. Their heritage is not lost, as their ideas grow across the globe.

"The light of true liberty shines as never before."

EPILOGUE

From the Atlantic to the Pacific and from the Great Lakes to the Gulf Coast, America is a great nation! Our greatness comes not from government; our greatness is in our people.

—Alan Cassell

G RANDPA HAD BEGUN TELLING his story while sitting on a hard, wooden bench in the park. After a couple of hours, some neighborhood boys came to play baseball. Grandpa and Jennifer left them to their game and walked through the neighborhood past the Catholic church and its re-opened elementary school, then over to Kedzie Avenue where they found lunch. At lunch, his storytelling was interrupted by a call from her mother.

"Hi Mom," Jennifer said. After listening a moment, she said, "Grandpa and I are spending the day together. We're at Burnie's on Kedzie getting a burger." She stopped to hear her mother's concerned words again and replied, "He's fine, Mom; were talking that's all. Don't worry. I'll call if we need anything."

Jennifer hung up the phone and begged her grandfather to continue. He was able to tell stories like nobody else she knew. Some parts of the story a grandfather just wouldn't ever tell his granddaughter, but he knew how to say enough to give her imagination the right impression without creating embarrassment for either of them. They continued talking at the restaurant until they saw dinner customers coming in. Grandpa Archer paid the bill and they resumed their walk.

Jennifer was held in rapt attention as she vicariously experienced the joys, sorrows, tragedies, and triumphs of a man who was suddenly very human, and quite a bit heroic.

As his story came to the obvious end, and they approached her home, the sun found its resting place as well. They sat on the porch and just visited.

"Grandpa, could he have kept it together? Without war?"

"What didn't happen can't be known, but I don't think so. The nation was too far gone when he got to the White House. He did the best he could, and I'm not sure that anyone could have done better."

"So it was all destined to fail? God set him up!"

"Why do you say so?"

Jennifer thought for a moment. "Well, you told him he would be president and he couldn't have been any sooner. Since he was the last, God made him be president when it ended."

"Alan made choices; those choices determined his destiny. It was easy for him to move to the next level, so he did. Those early days in Pittsburg, when he and Kate were getting along so well, he didn't have to push to get more. He chose to seek the leadership among county officials statewide. He chose to go all over Kansas, speaking to Republican groups before he was asked to run for governor.

"Jen, honey, you have life choices as well. You may get to a point where you're certain that something, or someone, is right for you. You may well be right about the choice, but be patient; timing is crucial. At my age, you get to where you realize that you don't have to hurry.

"Your destiny, God's plan for your life, or even your own plans in life, will come about rather naturally."

"Life seems so short, and I want to live up to my potential," Jennifer observed.

Grandpa smiled at her and reached out to hold her hand. He said, "Just realize that you could take the really important things for granted, just like Alan Cassell did. And you could lose the important things ... the important people in your life, by moving on to the next ... whatever. Treasure your family every day. I want to get to know my great-grandchildren. Okay?"

Street lights were in full glow when the young girl and her grandfather sat on a concrete porch in front of the South Chicago home. Crickets chirped, lightning bugs intermittently showed their lights, and a cool breeze blew by. They spoke of important things on that porch.

They spoke of values and of family.

At the end of the day, the dissolution of a great empire was not so great a matter after all.

AFTERWORD

"History is a string of seemingly invincible super powers which all, eventually, fall."

—Rick Steves

WILL AMERICA, CURRENTLY the world's lone superpower, follow the example of history and fall like all other empires? Will there be a "last" American president and an end to the United States of America? Despite our strongest wishes otherwise, the answer is "Yes!"

I was raised in Illinois, with its near idolatry of Abraham Lincoln. Following his example, the people of the state believe in the premise of the American union as perpetual.

My personal heritage of patriotism and love of the United States goes very deep. In fact, my childhood home was a mansion built by an officer of the Union Army. Three generations of my family lived in that home.

However, I lived most of my adult life in the southern states, especially Oklahoma. As a student of history, I found it difficult to condemn the American Indian tribes who aligned themselves with the Confederacy. Although acceptance may seem rebellious or unpatriotic, the fact is American Indians were not citizens of the United States at the time. Therefore, they had little cause to trust their interests would be well-served by the union.

I found a need to reconcile these disparate ideas about the nature of our nation. The subject of secession comes up on occasion in every place in

America. The general consensus seems to be that the United States Government has some eternal nature; even if we did not want to continue as a single union, the Civil War answered the question of dissolution once and for all.

The common argument is that the Civil War determined that there would never be a division of the national government regardless of the cause, need, or public desire. It is a peculiar notion that any people would consider the result of war as a moral determinant. When I was a child, my parents taught me to be critical of "might makes right" ideologies.

I now find the concept of a perpetual union to be foolish. To suggest there will be a single transcontinental national government in perpetuity is to ignore history and human nature. Whether it is for a single reason, or because of many, eventually there will be an end to the entity we know as the "United States of America." In hundreds, or possibly thousands of years, there is a certainty that war, natural disasters, or politics will change the country as we currently know it. Perhaps this will occur sooner rather than later.

Some suggest that the dissolution of the federal government would be tragic. They presume the end would be caused by war or other disastrous events. They would mourn the loss of life, economy, influence, institutions, and even identity. Certainly, events such as these are possible and ought to be avoided.

The events described in this novel are intended to be realistic and plausible, illustrating how dissolution could happen. The characters are fictional, and any likeness to any individual is purely coincidental, except for a few verifiable references to historical figures.

The story is set in the not too distant future. It shows that dissolution does not necessarily mean destruction. It is possible that such a change would best restore the lost ideals of America such as the pursuit of liberty, private property, individual responsibility, personal privileges, and representative governance limited to the protection of our rights.

When this change will come we cannot know, but it *will* come. It is possible that the United States has already irretrievably departed from its founding principles and, in doing so, may have entered into a series of events that will force the dissolution of our American union.

The end of the United States of America, as a single nation, may or may not happen in my lifetime. However, I am convinced that it will eventually happen.

It is how each of us conducts ourselves in light of this eventuality that will determine whether the events are accompanied by great loss of life and lifestyle, or if they are met by relatively little consternation. We must not stick our heads in the sand and pretend this ultimate certainty is impossible, as denial is a sure road to disaster.

This does not suggest that such eventuality is my desire. I join Alan Cassell in saying, "You and I are Americans and will always be American. We share a deep and abiding love for America.

"Our patriotism is not to a government, but to a nation. A nation is not merely a political entity, it is a people; a people, a heritage, and the ideals that made them great. Political realities may change, but Americans will continue to be one people, one nation.

"We may not continue to find our leaders in Washington, DC. We may look to our various state capitols, or to some other number of political capitols. No matter, America will continue.

"We are more alike than we are different. We have ancestry from throughout the world, but we have adapted ourselves to become one *ethnos*, one nation. We are no less a single people, Americans, even if governed separately.

"This is not the end of America in the sense of cessation, but perhaps it is the end, in the sense of purpose. I claim proudly that America has a purpose. It is to that 'end' that we must continue to strive. It may be that the dissolution of our union is exactly the means by which we learn to advance America's great purpose, its noble '*ends*.'"

I would not welcome the disruption that political dissolution would bring. I will, however, suggest that we would all be better served by viewing ourselves as a nation, and by seeing our status as Americans in a way that is disassociated from our federal capitol.

Being American is a much greater concept.

Coming soon by Richard Engle

Escape to Manitoba

The last American pres
FICTION Engle   3201300331981

Engle, Richard.
LAKEWOOD MEMORIAL LIBRARY

CPSIA information can be obtained
at www.ICGtesting.com
Printed in the USA
LVOW04s1102270816
502113LV00019B/908/P